The Best from Fantasy and Science Fiction

A Special 25th Anniversary Anthology

The Best from Fantasy and Science Fiction

A Special 25th Anniversary Anthology

Edited by
EDWARD L. FERMAN

DOUBLEDAY & COMPANY, INC.
GARDEN CITY, NEW YORK
1974

ISBN 0-385-08221-5
Library of Congress Catalog Card Number 73–9024
Copyright © 1962, 1963, 1966, 1969, 1971, 1972, 1974 by Mercury Press, Inc.
Printed in the United States of America
First Edition

For my father, Joseph W. Ferman

CONTENTS

INTRODUCTION

This is a collection of F&SF's first six special one-author issues, each honoring a major writer of science fiction: Theodore Sturgeon (September 1962), Ray Bradbury (May 1963), Isaac Asimov (October 1966), Fritz Leiber (July 1969), Poul Anderson (April 1971), and James Blish (April 1972).

The special issues were the idea of Joe Ferman, then publisher of *The Magazine of Fantasy and Science Fiction,* who was (and still is, bless him) constantly thinking of ways to renew interest in the magazine and boost those always unpredictable newsstand sales. The format set for the Sturgeon issue (with little variation since) was a major new work of fiction from each writer, accompanied by a profile, critical appreciation and bibliography (the latter has been confined to books and updated for this volume).

In terms of newsstand sales, the special issues have done well enough, but more remarkable has been the continual demand for them over the years. We do a brisk business in back issues, and these are the ones that have disappeared from our shelves most quickly. Except for the most recent two, they are now out of print and hard to find.

There are probably several reasons for their success. First, we have the writers themselves: six of science fiction's most popular and respected authors, all with good followings. Second, the non-fiction material was welcomed, in the early issues by readers starved for material *about* sf and its writers (when very little of it was being written) and in more recent years by a growing audience of students, teachers, and critics who are behind the new academic and literary respectability of science fiction. Finally, and most important, we have the fact that the special issues generated some extraordinary stories.

And so here they are, collected for the first time in book form, an apt way, we felt, to celebrate the 25th anniversary year of *The Magazine of Fantasy and Science Fiction.*

—Edward L. Ferman

Theodore Sturgeon

When You Care,
When You Love

by THEODORE STURGEON

He was beautiful in her bed.

When you care, when you love, when you treasure someone, you can watch the beloved in sleep as you watch everything, anything else—laughter, lips to a cup, a look even away from you; a stride, sun a-struggle lost in a hair-lock, a jest or a gesture—even stillness, even sleep.

She leaned close, all but breathless, and watched his lashes. Now, lashes are thick sometimes, curled, russet; these were all these, and glossy besides. Look closely—there where they curve lives light in tiny serried scimitars.

All so good, so very good, she let herself deliciously doubt its reality. She would let herself believe, in a moment, that this was real, was true, was here, had at last happened. All the things her life before had ever given her, all she had ever wanted, each by each had come to her purely for wanting. Delight there might be, pride, pleasure, even glory in the new possession of gift, privilege, object, experience: her ring, hat, toy, trip to Trinidad; yet, with possession there had always been (until now) the platter called *well, of course* on which these things were served her. For had she not wanted it? But this, now—*him,* now . . . greatest of all her wants, ever; first thing in all her life to transcend want itself and knowingly become need: this she had at last, at long (how long, now) long last, this she had now for good and all, for always, forever and never a touch of *well, of course.* He was her personal miracle, he in this bed now, warm and loving her. He was the reason and the reward of it all—her family and forbears, known by so few and felt by so many, and indeed, the

whole history of mankind leading up to it, and all she herself had
been and done and felt; and loving him, and losing him, and seeing
him dead and bringing him back—it was all for this moment and because the moment had to be, he and this peak, this warmth in these
sheets, this *now* of hers. He was all life and all life's beauty, beautiful
in her bed; and now she could be sure, could believe it, believe . . .

"I do," she breathed. "I do."

"What do you do?" he asked her. He had not moved, and did not
now.

"Devil, I thought you were asleep."

"Well, I was. But I had the feeling someone was looking."

"Not looking," she said softly. "Watching." She was watching
the lashes still, and did not see them stir, but between them now lay
a shining sliver of the grey cool aluminum of his surprising eyes. In
a moment he would look at her—just that—in a moment their eyes
would meet and it would be as if nothing new had happened (for it
would be the same metal missile which had first impaled her) and
also as if everything, everything were happening again. Within her,
passion boiled up like a fusion fireball, so beautiful, so huge—

—and like the most dreaded thing on earth, without pause the
radiance changed, shifting from the hues of all the kinds of love to
all the tones of terror and the colors of a cataclysm.

She cried his name . . .

And the grey eyes opened wide in fear for her fears and in astonishment, and he bounded up laughing, and the curl of his laughing
lips turned without pause to the pale writhing of agony, and they
shrank apart, too far apart while the white teeth met and while between them he shouted his hurt. He fell on his side and doubled up,
grunting, gasping in pain . . . grunting, gasping, wrapped away from
her, even her, unreachable even by her.

She screamed. She screamed. She—

A Wyke biography is hard to come by. This has been true for four
generations, and more true with each, for the more the Wyke hold-
ings grew, the less visible have been the Wyke family, for so Cap'n
Gamaliel Wyke willed it after his conscience conquered him. This
(for he was a prudent man) did not happen until after his retirement
from what was euphemistically called the molasses trade. His ship—
later, his fleet—had carried fine New England rum, made from the

molasses, to Europe, having brought molasses from the West Indies to New England. Of course a paying cargo was needed for the westward crossing, to close with a third leg this profitable triangle; and what better cargo than Africans for the West Indies, to harvest the cane and work in the mills which made the molasses?

Ultimately affluent and retired, he seemed content for a time to live among his peers, carrying his broadcloth coat and snowy linen as to the manor born, limiting his personal adornment to a massive golden ring and small square gold buckles at his knee. Soberly shop-talking molasses often, rum seldom, slaves never, he dwelt with a frightened wife and a silent son, until she died and something—perhaps loneliness—coupled his brain again to his sharp old eyes, and made him look about him. He began to dislike the hypocrisy of man and was honest enough to dislike himself as well, and this was a new thing for the Cap'n; he could not deny it and he could not contain it, so he left the boy with the household staff and, taking only a man-servant, went into the wilderness to search his soul.

The wilderness was Martha's Vineyard, and right through a bitter winter the old man crouched by the fire when the weather closed in, and, muffled in four great grey shawls, paced the beaches when it was bright, his brass telescope under his arm and his grim canny thoughts doing mighty battle with his convictions. In the late spring he returned to Wiscassett, his blunt certainty regained, his laconic curtness increased almost to the point of speechlessness. He sold out (as a startled contemporary described it) "everything that showed," and took his son, an awed obedient eleven, back to the Vineyard where to the accompaniment of tolling breakers and creaking gulls, he gave the boy an education to which all the schooling of all the Wykes for all of four generations would be mere addenda.

For in his retreat to the storms and loneliness of the inner self and the Vineyard, Gamaliel Wyke had come to terms with nothing less than the Decalogue.

He had never questioned the Ten Commandments, nor had he knowingly disobeyed them. Like many another before him, he attributed the sad state of the world and the sin of its inhabitants to their refusal to heed those Rules. But in his ponderings, God Himself, he at last devoutly concluded, had underestimated the stupidity of mankind. So he undertook to amend the Decalogue himself, by

adding ". . . or cause . . ." to each Commandment, just to make it
easier for a man to work with:

". . . or cause the Name of the Lord to be taken in vain.

". . . or cause stealing to be done.

". . . or cause dishonor to thy father and thy mother.

". . . or cause the commission of adultery.

". . . or cause a killing to be done."

But his revelation came to him when he came to the last one. It
was suddenly clear to him that all mankind's folly—all greed, lust, war,
all dishonor, sprang from humanity's almost total disregard for this
edict and its amendment: "Thou shalt not covet . . . *nor cause covetousness!*"

It came to him then that to arouse covetousness in another is just
as deadly a sin as to kill him or to cause his murder. Yet all around
the world empires rose, great yachts and castles and hanging gardens
came into being, tombs and trusts and college grants, all for the purpose of arousing the envy or covetousness of the less endowed—or
having that effect no matter what the motive.

Now, one way for a man as rich as Gamaliel Wyke to have resolved
the matter for himself would be St. Francis' way; but (though he
could not admit this, or even recognize it) he would have discarded
the Decalogue and his amendments, all surrounding Scripture and
his gnarled right arm rather than run so counter to his inborn, in-
grained Yankee acquisitiveness. And another way might have been
to take his riches and bury them in the sand of Martha's Vineyard,
to keep them from causing covetousness; the very thought clogged
his nostrils with the feel of dune-sand and he felt suffocation; to him
money was a living thing and should not be interred.

And so he came to his ultimate answer: Make your money, enjoy
it, but *never let anyone know*. Desire, he concluded, for a neighbor's
wife, or a neighbor's ass, or for anything, presupposed knowing about
these possessions. No neighbor could desire anything of his if he
couldn't lay a name to it.

So Gamaliel brought weight like granite and force like gravity to
bear upon the mind and soul of his son Walter, and Walter begat
Jedediah, and Jedediah begat Caiaphas (who died) and Samuel,
and Samuel begat Zebulon (who died) and Sylva; so perhaps the
true beginning of the story of the boy who became his own mother

lies with Cap'n Gamaliel Wyke and his sand-scoured, sea-deep, rock-hard revelation.

—fell on his side on the bed and doubled up, grunting, gasping in pain, grunting, gasping, wrapped away from her, even her, unreachable even by her.

She screamed. She screamed. She pressed herself up and away from him and ran naked into the sitting room, pawed up the ivory telephone: "Keogh" she cried; "For the love of God, *Keogh!*"

—and back into the bedroom where he lay open-mouthing a grating horrible *uh uh!* while she wrung her hands, tried to take one of his, found it agony-tense and unaware of her. She called him, called him, and once, screamed again.

The buzzer sounded with inexcusable discretion.

"Keogh!" she shouted, and the polite buzzer *shhh'd* her again—the lock, oh the damned lock . . . she picked up her negligée and ran with it in her hand through the dressing room and the sitting room and the hall and the living room and the foyer and flung open the door. She pulled Keogh through it before he could turn away from her; she thrust one arm in a sleeve of the garment and shouted at him, "Keogh, please, please, Keogh, what's wrong with him?" and she fled to the bedroom, Keogh sprinting to keep up with her.

Then Keogh, chairman of the board of seven great corporations, board-member of a dozen more, general manager of a quiet family holding company which had, for most of a century, specialized in the ownership of corporate owners, went to the bed and fixed his cool blue gaze on the agonized figure there.

He shook his head slightly.

"You called the wrong man," he snapped, and ran back to the sitting-room, knocking the girl aside as if he had been a machine on tracks. He picked up the phone and said, "Get Rathburn up here. *Now*. Where's Weber? You don't? well, find him and get him here. . . . I don't care. Hire an airplane. *Buy* an airplane."

He slammed down the phone and ran back into the bedroom. He came up behind her and gently lifted the negligée onto her other shoulder, and speaking gently to her all the while, reached round her and tied the ribbon belt. "What happened?"

"N-nothing, he just—"

"Come on, girl—clear out of here. Rathburn's practically outside the door, and I've sent for Weber. If there's a better doctor than Rathburn, it could only be Weber, so you've got to leave it to them. Come!"

"I won't leave him."

"Come!" Keogh rapped; then murmured, looking over her shoulder at the bed, "He wants you to, can't you see? He doesn't want you to see him like this. *Right?*" he demanded, and the face, turned away and half-buried in the pillow shone sweatly; cramp mounded the muscles on the side of the mouth they could just see. Stiffly the head nodded; it was like a shudder. "And . . . shut . . . door . . . tight . . ." he said in a clanging half whisper.

"Come," said Keogh. And again, "Come." He propelled her away; she stumbled. Her face turned yearningly until Keogh, both hands on her, kicked at the door and it swung and the sight of the bed was gone. Keogh leaned back against the door as if the latch were not enough to hold it closed.

"What is it? Oh, what is it?"

"I don't know," he said.

"You do, you do . . . you always know everything . . . why won't you let me stay with him?"

"He doesn't want that."

Overcome, inarticulate, she cried out.

"Maybe," he said into her hair, "he wants to scream too."

She struggled—oh, strong, lithe and strong she was. She tried to press past him. He would not budge, so at last, at last she wept.

He held her in his arms again, as he had not done since she used to sit on his lap as a little girl. He held her in his arms and looked blindly toward the unconcerned bright morning, seen soft-focused through the cloud of her hair. And he tried to make it stop, the morning, the sun, and time, but—

—but there is one certain thing only about a human mind, and that is that it acts, moves, works ceaselessly while it lives. The action, motion, labor differ from that of a heart, say or an epithelial cell, in that the latter have functions, and in any circumstance perform their functions. Instead of a function, mind has a duty, that of making of a hairless ape a human being . . . yet as if to prove how trivial a difference there is between mind and muscle, mind must move, to some degree, always change, to some degree, always while it lives, like a stinking sweat gland . . . holding her, Keogh thought about Keogh.

The biography of Keogh is somewhat harder to come by than that of a Wyke. This is not in spite of having spent merely half a lifetime in this moneyed shadow; it is because of it. Keogh was a Wyke in all but blood and breeding: Wyke owned him and all he owned, which was a great deal.

He must have been a child once, a youth; he could remember if he wished but did not care to. Life began for him with the *summa cum laude*, the degrees in both business and law and (so young) the year and a half with Hinnegan and Bache, and then the incredible opening at the International Bank; the impossible asked of him in the Zurich-Plenum affair, and his performance of it, and the shadows which grew between him and his associates over the years, while for him the light grew and grew as to the architecture of his work, until at last he was admitted to Wyke, and was permitted to realize that Wyke *was* Zurich and Plenum, and the International Bank, and Hinnegan and Bache; was indeed his law school and his college and much, so very much more. And finally sixteen—good heavens, it was eighteen years ago, when he became General Manager, and the shadows dark to totally black between him and any other world, while the light, his own huge personal illumination, exposed almost to him alone an industrial-financial complex unprecedented in his country, and virtually unmatched in the world.

But then, the beginning, the *other* beginning, was when Old Sam Wyke called him in so abruptly that morning, when (though General Manager with many a board chairman, all unbeknownst, under him in rank) he was still the youngest man in that secluded office.

"Keogh," said old Sam, "this is my kid. Take 'er out. Give 'er anything she wants. Be back here at six." He had then kissed the girl on the crown of her dark straw hat, gone to the door, turned and barked, "You see her show off or brag, Keogh, you fetch her a good one, then and there, here? I don't care what else she does, but don't you let her wave something she's got at someone that hasn't got it. That's Rule One." He had then breezed out, leaving a silent, startled young mover of mountains locking gazes with an unmoving mouse of an eleven-year-old girl. She had luminous pale skin, blue-black silky-shining hair, and thick level black brows.

The *summa cum laude,* the acceptance at Hinnegan and Bache —all such things, they were beginnings that he knew were beginnings. This he would not know for some time that it was a beginning, any more than he could realize that he had just heard the contemporary version of Cap'n Gamaliel's "Thou shalt not . . . cause covetousness." At the moment, he could only stand nonplused for a moment, then excuse himself and go to the treasurer's office, where he scribbled a receipt and relieved the petty cash box of its by no means petty contents. He got his hat and coat and returned to the President's office. Without a word the child rose and moved with him to the door.

They lunched and spent the afternoon together, and were back at six. He bought her whatever she wanted at one of the most expensive shops in New York. He took her to just the places of amusement she asked him to.

When it was all over he returned the stack of bills to the petty cash box, less the one dollar and twenty cents he had paid out. For at the shop—the largest toy store in the world—she had carefully selected a sponge rubber ball, which they packed for her in a cubical box. This she carried carefully by its string for the rest of the afternoon.

They lunched from a pushcart—he had one hot dog with kraut, she had two with relish.

They rode uptown on the top of a Fifth Avenue double-decker, open-top bus.

They went to the zoo in Central Park and bought one bag of peanuts for the girl and the pigeons, and one bag of buns for the girl and the bears.

Then they took another double-decker back downtown, and that was it; that was the afternoon.

He remembered clearly what she looked like then: like a strawhatted wren, for all it was a well-brushed wren. He could not remember what they had talked about, if indeed they had talked much at all. He was prepared to forget the episode, or at least to put it neatly in the *Trivia: Misc.: Closed* file in his compartmented mind, when, a week later, old Sam tossed him a stack of papers and told him to read them through and come and ask questions if he thought he had to. The only question which came to mind when he had read them was,

"Are you sure you want to go through with this?" and that was not the kind of question one asked old Sam. So he thought it over very carefully and came up with "Why me?" and old Sam looked him up and down and growled, "She likes you, that's why."

And so it was that Keogh and the girl lived together in a cotton mill town in the South for a year. Keogh worked in the company store. The girl worked in the mill; twelve-year-old girls worked in cotton mills in the South in those days. She worked the morning shift and half the evening shift, and had three hours' school in the afternoons. Up until 10 o'clock on Saturday nights they watched the dancing from the sidelines. On Sundays they went to the Baptist church. Their name while they were there was Harris. Keogh used to worry frantically when she was out of his sight, but one day when she was crossing the catwalk over the water-circulating sump, a sort of oversized well beside the mill, the catwalk broke and pitched her into the water. Before she could so much as draw a breath a Negro stoker appeared out of nowhere—actually, out of the top of the coal chute— and leapt in and had her and handed her up to the sudden crowd. Keogh came galloping up from the company store as they were pulling the stoker out, and after seeing that the girl was all right, knelt beside the man, whose leg was broken.

"I'm Mr. Harris, her father. You'll get a reward for this. What's your name?"

The man beckoned him close, and as he bent down, the stoker, in spite of his pain, grinned and winked. "You don' owe me a thang, Mr. Keogh," he murmured. In later times, Keogh would be filled with rage at such a confidence, would fire the man out of hand: this first time he was filled with wonder and relief. After that, things were easier on him, as he realized that the child was surrounded by Wyke's special employees, working on Wyke land in a Wyke mill and paying rent in a Wyke row-house.

In due time the year was up. Someone else took over, and the girl, now named Kevin and with a complete new background in case anyone should ask, went off for two years to a very exclusive Swiss finishing school, where she dutifully wrote letters to a Mr. and Mrs. Kevin who held large acreage in the Pennsylvania mountains, and who just as dutifully answered her.

Keogh returned to his own work, which he found in apple-pie order, with every one of the year's transactions beautifully abstracted for him, and an extra amount, over and above his astronomical salary, tucked away in one of his accounts—an amount that startled even Keogh. He missed her at first, which he expected. But he missed her every single day for two solid years, a disturbance he could not explain, did not examine, and discussed with no one.

All the Wykes, old Sam once grunted to him, did something of the sort. He, Sam, had been a logger in Oregon and a year and a half as utility man, then ordinary seaman on a coastwise tanker.

Perhaps some deep buried part of Keogh's mind thought that when she returned from Switzerland they would go for catfish in an old flat-bottomed boat again, or that she would sit on his lap while he suffered on the hard benches of the once-a-month picture show. The instant he saw her on her return from Switzerland he knew that would never be. He knew he was entering some new phase; it troubled and distressed him and he put it away in the dark inside himself; he could do that; he was strong enough. And she—well, she flung her arms around him and kissed him; but when she talked with this new vocabulary, this deft school finish, she was strange and awesome to him, like an angel. Even a loving angel is strange and awesome . . .

They were together again then for a long while, but there were no more hugs. He became a Mr. Stark in the Cleveland office of a brokerage house and she boarded with an elderly couple, went to the local high school and had a part-time job filing in his office. This was when she learned the ins and outs of the business, the size of it. It would be hers. It became hers while they were in Cleveland: old Sam died very suddenly. They slipped away to the funeral but were back at work on Monday. They stayed there for another eight months; she had a great deal to learn. In the fall she entered a small private college and Keogh saw nothing of her for a year.

"Shhh," he breathed to her, crying, and *shhh!* said the buzzer.

"The doctor . . ."

"Go take a bath," he said. He pushed her.

She half-turned under his hand, faced him again blazing. "No!"

"You can't go in there, you know," he said, going for the door. She glared at him, but her lower lip trembled.

Keogh opened the door. "In the bedroom."

"Who—" then the doctor saw the girl, her hands knotted together, her face twisted, and had his answer. He was a tall man, grey, with quick hands, a quick step, swift words. He went straight through foyer, hall and rooms and into the bedroom. He closed the door behind him. There had been no discussion, no request and refusal; Dr. Rathburn had simply, quickly, quietly shut them out.

"Go take a bath."

"No."

"Come on." He took her wrist and led her to the bathroom. He reached into the shower stall and turned on the side jets. There were four at each corner; the second from the top was scented. Apple blossom. "Go on."

He moved toward the door. She stood where he had let go of her wrist, pulling at her hands. "Go on," he said again. "Just a quick one. Do you good." He waited. "Or do you want me to douse you myself? I bet I still can."

She flashed him a look; indignation passed instantly as she understood what he was trying to do. The rare spark of mischief appeared in her eyes and, in perfect limitation of a mill row redneck, she said, "Y'all try it an Ah'll tall th' shurff Ah ain't rightly yo' chile." But the effort cost her too much and she cried again. He stepped out and softly closed the door.

He was waiting by the bedroom when Rathburn slid out and quickly shut the door on the grunt, the gasp.

"What is it?" asked Keogh.

"Wait a minute." Rathburn strode to the phone. Keogh said, "I sent for Weber."

Rathburn came almost ludicrously to a halt. "Wow," he said. "Not bad diagnosing, for a layman. Is there anything you can't do?"

"I can't understand what you're talking about," said Keogh testily.

"Oh—I thought you knew. Yes, I'm afraid it's in Weber's field. What made you guess?"

Keogh shuddered. "I saw a mill hand take a low blow once. I know *he* wasn't hit. What exactly is it?"

Rathburn darted a look around. "Where is she?" Keogh indicated the bathroom. "I told her to take a shower."

"Good," said the doctor. He lowered his voice. "Naturally I can't tell without further examination and lab—"

"*What is it?*" Keogh demanded, not loud, but with such violence that Rathburn stepped back a pace.

"It could be choriocarcinoma."

Tiredly, Keogh wagged his head. "Me diagnose that? I can't even spell it. What is it?" He caught himself up, as if he had retrieved the word from thin air and run it past him again. "I know what the last part of it means."

"One of the—" Rathburn swallowed, and tried again. "One of the more vicious forms of cancer. And it . . ." He lowered his voice again. "It doesn't always hit this hard."

"Just how serious is it?"

Rathburn raised his hands and let them fall.

"Bad, eh? Doc—*how bad?*" . . .

"Maybe some day we can . . ." Rathburn's lowered voice at last disappeared. They hung there, each on the other's pained gaze.

"How much time?"

"Maybe six weeks."

"*Six weeks!*"

"Shh," said Rathburn nervously.

"Weber—"

"Weber knows more about internal physiology than anybody. But I don't know if that will help. It's a little like . . . your, uh, house is struck by lightning, flattened, burned to the ground. You can examine it and the weather reports and, uh, know exactly what happened. Maybe some day we can . . ." he said again, but he said it so hopelessly that Keogh, through the roiling mists of his own terror, pitied him and half-instinctively put out a hand. He touched the doctor's sleeve and stood awkwardly.

"What are you going to do?"

Rathburn looked at the closed bedroom door. "What I did." He made a gesture with a thumb and two fingers. "Morphine."

"And that's all?"

"Look, I'm a G.P. Ask Weber, will you?"

Keogh realized that he had pushed the man as far as he could in his search for a crumb of hope; if there was none, there was no point in trying to squeeze it out. He asked, "Is there anyone working on it? Anything new? Can you find out?"

"Oh, I will, I will. But Weber can tell you off the top of his head more than I could find out in six mon . . . in a long time."

A door opened. She came out, hollow-eyed, but pink and glowing in a long white terry-cloth robe. "Dr. Rathburn—"

"He's asleep."

"Thank God. Does it—"

"There's no pain."

"What is it? What happened to him?"

"Well, I wouldn't like to say for sure . . . we're waiting for Dr. Weber. He'll know."

"But—but is he—"

"He'll sleep the clock around."

"Can I . . ." The timidity, the caution, Keogh realized, was so unlike her. "Can I see him?"

"He's fast asleep!"

"I don't care. I'll be quiet. I won't—touch him or anything."

"Go ahead," said Rathburn. She opened the bedroom door and eagerly, silently slipped inside.

"You'd think she was trying to make sure he was there."

Keogh, who knew her so very well, said, "She is."

But a biography of Guy Gibbon is *really* hard to come by. For he was no exceptional executive, who for all his guarded anonymity wielded so much power that he must be traceable by those who knew where to look and what to look for, and cared enough to process detail like a mass spectroscope. Neither was Guy Gibbon born heir to countless millions, the direct successor to a procession of giants.

He came from wherever it is most of us come from, the middle or the upper-middle, or the upper-lower middle or the lower-upper middle, or some other indefinable speck in the midrange of the inter-flowing striations of society (the more they are studied, the less they mean). He belonged to the Wykes entity for only eight and a half weeks, after all. Oh, the bare details might not be too hard to come by—(birth date, school record,) and certain main facts—(father's occupation, mother's maiden name)—as well, perhaps, as a highlight or two—(divorce, perhaps, or a death in the family); but a biography, a real biography, which does more than describe, which *explains* the man—and few do—now, *this* is an undertaking.

Science, it is fair to assume, can do what all the king's horses and all the king's men could not do, and totally restore a smashed egg. Given equipment enough, and time enough . . . but isn't this a way of saying, "given money enough"? For money can be not only means, but motive. So if enough money went into the project, perhaps the last unknown, the last vestige of, anonymity could be removed from

a man's life story, even a young man from (as the snobs say) nowhere, no matter how briefly—though intimately—known.

The most important thing, obviously, that ever happened to Guy
Gibbon in his life was his first encounter with the Wyke entity, and
like many a person before and since, he had not the faintest idea he
had done so. It was when he was in his late teens, and he and Sammy
Stein went trespassing.

Sammy was a school sidekick, and this particular day he had a
secret; he had been very insistent on the day's outing, but refused to
say why. He was a burly-shouldered, good-natured, reasonably chin-
less boy whose close friendship with Guy was based almost exclusively
on the attraction of opposite poles. And since, of the many kinds of
fun they had had, the most fun was going trespassing, he wanted it
that way on this particular occasion.

"Going trespassing," as an amusement, had more or less invented
itself when they were in their early teens. They lived in a large city
surrounded (unlike many today) by old suburbs, not new ones. These
included large—some, more than large—estates and mansions, and it
was their greatest delight to slip through a fence or over a wall and,
profoundly impressed by their own bravery, slip through field and
forest, lawn and drive, like Indian scouts in settler country. Twice
they had been caught, once to have dogs set on them—three boxers
and two mastiffs, which certainly would have torn them to very small
pieces if the boys had not been more lucky than swift—and once by a
dear little old lady who swamped them sickeningly with jelly sandwiches and lonely affection. But over the saga of their adventures,
their two captures served to spice the adventure; two failures out of a
hundred successes (for many of these places were visited frequently)
was a proud record.

So they took a trolley to the end of the line, and walked a mile,
and went straight ahead where the road turned at a discreet *No Admittance* sign of expensive manufacture and a high degree of weather-
ing. They proceeded through a small wild wood, and came at last to
an apparently unscalable granite wall.

Sammy had discovered this wall the week before, roaming alone;
he had waited for Guy to accompany him before challenging it, and
Guy was touched. He was also profoundly excited by the wall itself.
Anything this size should have been found, conjectured about, cam-
paigned against, battled and conquered long since. But as well as

being a high wall, a long wall, and mysterious, it was a distant wall, a discreet wall. No road touched it but its own driveway, which was primitive, meandering, and led to ironbound, solid oak gates without a chink or crack to peek through.

They could not climb it nor breach it—but they crossed it. An ancient maple on this side held hands with a chestnut over the crown of the wall, and they went over like a couple of squirrels.

They had, in their ghost-like way, haunted many an elaborate property, but never had they seen such maintenance, such manicure, such polish of a piece of land and, as Sammy said, awed out of his usual brashness, as they stood in a solid marble pergola overlooking green plush acres of rolling lawn, copses of carven boxwood, parklike woods and streams with little Japanese bridges and, in their bends, humorful little rock-gardens: "—and there's goddam *miles* of it."

They had wandered a bit, that first time, and had learned that there were after all some people there. They saw a tractor far away, pulling a slanted gang of mowers across one of the green-plush fields. (The owners doubtless called it a lawn; it was a field.) The machines, rare in that time, cut a swath all of thirty feet wide "and that," Sammy said, convulsing them, "ain't hay." And then they had seen the house—

Well, a glimpse. Breaking out of the woods, Guy had felt himself snatched back. "House up there," said Sammy. "Someone'll see us." There was a confused impression of a white hill that was itself the house, or part of it; towers, turrets, castellations, crenellations; a fairy-tale palace set in this legendary landscape. They had not been able to see it again; it was so placed that it could be approached nowhere secretly nor even spied upon. They were struck literally speechless by the sight and for most of an hour had nothing to say, and that expressible only by wags of the head. Ultimately they referred to it as "the shack," and it was in this vein that they later called their final discovery "the ol' swimmin' hole."

It was across a creek and over a wooded hill. Two more hills rose to meet the wood, and cupped between the three was a pond, perhaps a lake. It was roughly L-shaped, and all around it were shadowed inlets, grottoes, inconspicuous stone steps leading here to a rustic pavilion set about with flowers, there to a concealed forest glade harboring a tiny formal garden.

But the lake, the ol' swimmin' hole . . .

They went swimming, splashing as little as possible and sticking to the shore. They explored two inlets to the right (a miniature water-fall and a tiny beach of obviously imported golden sand) and three to the left (a square cut one, lined with tile the color of patina, with a black glass diving tower overhanging water that must have been dredged to twenty feet; a little beach of snow-white sand; and one they dared not enter, for fear of harming the fleet of perfect sailing ships, none more than a foot long, which lay at anchor; but they trod water until they were bone-cold, gawking at the miniature model waterfront with little pushcarts in the street, and lamp-posts, and old-fashioned houses) and then, weary, hungry and awestruck, they had gone home.

And Sammy cracked the secret he had been keeping—the thing which he felt made this day an occasion: he was to go wild-hairing off the next day in an effort to join Chennault in China.

Guy Gibbon, overwhelmed, made the only gesture he could think of: he devotedly swore he would not go trespassing again until Sammy got back.

"Death from choriocarcinoma," Dr. Weber began, "is the result of—"

"But he won't die," she said. "I won't let him."

"My dear," Dr. Weber was a small man with round shoulders and a hawk's face. "I don't mean to be unkind, but I can use all the euphemisms and kindle all the false hope, or I can do as you have asked me to do—explain the condition and make a prognosis. I can't do both."

Dr. Rathburn said gently, "Why don't you go and lie down? I'll come when we've finished here and tell you all about it."

"I don't want to lie down," she said fiercely. "And I wasn't asking you to spare me anything, Dr. Weber. I simply said I would not let him die. There's nothing in that statement which keeps you from telling me the truth."

Keogh smiled, Weber caught him at it and was startled; Keogh saw his surprise. "I know her better than you do," he said, with a touch of pride. "You don't have to pull any punches."

"Thanks, Keogh," she said. She leaned forward. "Go ahead, Dr. Weber."

Weber looked at her. Snatched from his work two thousand miles away, brought to a place he had never known existed, of a magnificence which attacked his confidence in his own eyes, meeting a woman of power—every sort of power—quite beyond his experience . . . Weber had thought himself beyond astonishment. Shock, grief, fear, deprivation like hers he had seen before, of course; what doctor has not? but when Keogh had told her baldly that this disease killed in six weeks, *always,* she had flinched, closed her eyes for an interminable moment, and had then said softly, "Tell us everything you can about this—this disease, Doctor." And she had added, for the first time, "He isn't going to die. I won't let him;" and the way she held her head, the way her full voice handled the words, he almost believed her. Heaven knows, he wished he could. And so he found he could be astonished yet again.

He made an effort to detach himself, and became not a man, not this particular patient's doctor, but a sort of source-book. He began again:

"Death from choriocarcinoma is a little unlike other deaths from malignancies. Ordinarily a cancer begins locally, and sends its chains and masses of wild cells growing through the organ on which it began. Death can result from the failure of that organ; liver, kidney, brain, what have you. Or the cancer suddenly breaks up and spreads through the body, starting colonies throughout the system. This is called metastasis. Death results then from the loss of efficiency of many organs instead of just one. Of course, both these things can happen—the almost complete impairment of the originally cancerous organ, and metastatic effects at the same time.

"Chorio, on the other hand, doesn't originally involve a vital organ. Vital to the species, perhaps, but not to the individual." He permitted himself a dry smile. "This is probably a startling concept to most people in this day and age, but it's nonetheless true. However, sex cells, at their most basic and primitive, have peculiarities not shared by other body cells.

"Have you ever heard of the condition known as ectopic pregnancy?" He directed his question at Keogh, who nodded. "A fertilized ovum fails to descend to the uterus; instead it attaches itself to the side of the very fine tube between the ovaries and the womb. And at first everything proceeds well with it—and this is the point I want you to grasp—because in spite of the fact that only the uterus is truly specialized for this work, the tube wall not only supports the growing ovum but feeds it. It actually forms what we call a counter-placenta; it enfolds the early foetus and nurtures it. The foetus, of course, has a high survival value, and is able to get along quite well on the plasma which the counter-placenta supplies it with. And it grows—it grows fantastically. Since the tube is very fine—you'd have difficulty getting the smallest sewing needle up through it—it can no longer contain the growing foetus, and ruptures. Unless it is removed at that time, the tissues outside will quite as readily take on the work of a real placenta and uterus, and in six or seven months, if the mother survives that long, will create havoc in the abdomen.

"All right then: back to chorio. Since the cells involved are sex cells, and cancerous to boot, they divide and redivide wildly, without pattern or special form. They develop in an infinite variety of shapes and sizes and forms. The law of averages dictates that a certain number of these—and the number of distorted cells is astronomical—resemble fertilized ova. Some of them resemble them so closely that I personally would not enjoy the task of distinguishing between them and the real thing. However, the body as a whole is not that particular; anything which even roughly resembles a fertilized egg-cell is capable of commanding that counter-placenta.

"Now consider the source of these cells—physiologically speaking, gland tissue—a mass of capillary tubes and blood vessels. Each and every one of these does its best to accept and nurture these foetal imitations, down to the tiniest of them. The thin walls of the capillaries, however, break down easily under such an effort, and the imitations—selectively, the best of them, too, because the tissues yield most readily to them—they pass into the capillaries and then into the bloodstream.

"There is one place and only one place where they can be combed out; and it's a place rich in oxygen, lymph, blood and plasma: the lungs. The lungs enthusiastically take on the job of forming placentae for these cells, and nurturing them. But for every segment of lung given over to gestating an imitation foetus, there is one less segment occupied with the job of oxygenating blood. Ultimately the lungs fail, and death results from oxygen starvation."

Rathburn spoke up. "For years chorio was regarded as a lung disease, and the cancerous gonads as a sort of side effect."

"But lung cancer—" Keogh began to object.

"It isn't lung cancer, don't you see? Given enough time, it might be, through metastasis. But there is never enough time. Chorio doesn't have to wait for that, to kill. That's why it's so swift." He tried not to look at the girl, and failed; he said it anyway: "And certain."

"Just exactly how do you treat it?"

Weber raised his hands and let them fall. It was precisely the gesture Rathburn had made earlier, and Keogh wondered distantly whether they taught it in medical schools. "Something to kill the pain. Orchidectomy might make the patient last a little longer, by removing the supply of wild cells to the bloodstream. But it wouldn't save him. Metastasis has already taken place by the time the first symptom appears. The cancer becomes generalized . . . perhaps the lung condition is only God's mercy."

"What's 'orchidectomy'?" asked Keogh.

"Amputation of the—uh—source," said Rathburn uncomfortably.

"No!" cried the girl.

Keogh sent her a pitying look. There was that about him which was cynical, sophisticated, and perhaps coldly angry at anyone who lived as he could never live, had what he could never have. It was a stirring of the grave ancient sin which old Cap'n Gamaliel had isolated in his perspicacious thoughts. Sure, amputate, if it'll help, he thought. What do you think you're preserving—his virility? What good's it to you now? . . . but sending her the look, he encountered something different from the romantically-based horror and shock he expected. Her thick level brows were drawn together, her whole face intense with taut concentration. "Let me think," she said, oddly.

"You really should—" Rathburn began, but she shushed him with an impatient gesture. The three men exchanged a glance and settled back; it was as if someone, something had told them clearly and specifically to wait. What they were waiting for, they could not imagine.

The girl sat with her eyes closed. A minute crawled by. "Daddy used to say," she said, so quietly that she must surely be talking to herself, "that there's always a way. All you have to do is think of it."

There was another long silence, and she opened her eyes. There was a burning down in them somewhere; it made Keogh uneasy. She said, "And once he told me that I could have anything I wanted; all it had to be was . . . possible. And . . . the only way you can find out if a thing is impossible is to try it."

"That wasn't Sam Wyke," said Keogh. "That was Keogh."

She wet her lips and looked at them each in turn. She seemed not to see them at all. "I'm not going to let him die," she said. "You'll see."

Sammy Stein came back two years later, on leave, and full of plans to join the Army Air Force. He'd had, as he himself said, the hell kicked out of him in China and a lot of the hellishness as well. But there was enough of the old Sammy left to make wild wonderful plans about going trespassing; and they knew just where they were going. The new Sammy, however, demanded a binge and a broad first.

Guy, two years out of high school, working for a living, and by nature neither binger nor wencher, went along only too gladly. Sam seemed to have forgotten about the "ol' swimmin' hole" at first, and halfway through the evening, in a local bar-and-dance emporium, Guy was about to despair of his ever remembering it, when Sam himself brought it up, recalling to Guy that he had once written Sam a letter asking Sam if it had really happened. Guy had, in his turn, forgotten the letter, and after that they had a good time with "remember-when"—and they made plans to go trespassing the very next day, and bring a lunch. And start early.

Then there was a noisy involvement with some girls, and a lot more drinks, and out of the haze and movement somewhere after midnight, Guy emerged on a sidewalk looking at Sammy shovelling a girl into a taxicab. "Hey!" he called out, "what about the you know, ol' swimmin' hole?"

"Call me Abacus, you can count on me," said Sammy, and laughed immoderately. The girl with him pulled at his arm; he shook her off and weaved over to Guy. "Listen," he said, and gave a distorted wink, "if this makes—and it will—I'm starting no early starts. Tell you what, you go on out there and meet me by that sign says keep out or we'll castigate you. Say eleven o'clock. If I can't make it by then I'm dead or something." He bellowed at the cab, "You gon' kill me, honey?" and the girl called back, "I will if you don't get into this taxi." "See what I mean?" said Sammy in a grand drunken non-sequitor, "I got to go get killed." He zigged away, needing no zag because even walking sidewise he reached the cab in a straight line, and Guy saw no more of him that leave.

That was hard to take, mostly because there was no special moment at which he knew Sammy wasn't coming. He arrived ten minutes late, after making a superhuman effort to get there. His stomach was sour from the unaccustomed drinking and he was sandy-eyed and ache-jointed from lack of sleep. He knew that the greater probability was that Sammy had not arrived yet or would not at all; yet the nagging possibility existed that he had come early and gone straight in. Guy waited around for a full hour, and some more minutes until the little road was clear of traffic and sounds of traffic, and then plunged alone into the woods, past the No Trespassing sign, and in to the wall. He had trouble finding the two trees, and once over the wall, he could not get his bearings for a while; he was pleased, of course, to find the unbelievably perfect lawns still there by the flawless acre, the rigidly controlled museums of carven box, the edge-trimmed, rolled-gravel walks meandering prettily through the woods. The pleasure, however, was no more than confirmation of his memory, and went no further; the day was spoiled.

Guy reached the lake at nearly one o'clock, hot, tired, ravenously hungry and unpleasantly nervous. The combination hit him in the stomach and made it echo; he sat down on the bank and ate. He wolfed down the food he had brought for himself and Sammy's as well—odds and ends carelessly tossed into a paper sack in the bleary early hours. The cake was moldy but he ate it anyway. The orange juice was warm and had begun to ferment. And stubbornly, he determined to swim, because that was what he had come for.

He chose the beach with the golden sand. Under a thick cover of junipers he found a stone bench and table. He undressed here and scuttled across the beach and into the water.

He had meant it to be a mere dip, so he could say he'd done it. But around the little headland to the left was the rectangular cove with the diving platform; and he remembered the harbor of model ships; and then movement diagonally across the foot of the lake's L caught his eye, and he saw models—not the anchored ships this time, but racing sloops, which put out from an inlet and crossed its mouth and sailed in again; they must be mounted on some sort of underwater wheel or endless chain, and moved as the breeze took them. He all but boiled straight across to them, then decided to be wise and go round.

He swam to the left and the rocky shore, and worked his way along it. Clinging close (the water seemed bottomless here) he rounded the point and came face to face (literally; they touched) with a girl.

She was young—near his age—and his first impression was of eyes of too complex an architecture, blue-white teeth with pointed canines quite unlike the piano-key regularity considered beautiful in these times, and a wide cape of rich brown hair afloat around her shoulders. By then his gasp was completed, and in view of the fact that in gasping he had neglected to remove his mouth from the water, he was shut off from outside impressions for a strangling time, until he felt a firm grasp on his left biceps and found himself returned to the side of the rock.

"Th-thanks," he said hoarsely as she swam back a yard and trod water. "I'm not supposed to be here," he added inanely.

"I guess I'm not either. But I thought you lived here. I thought you were a faun."

"Boy am I glad to hear that. I mean about you. All I am is a trespasser. Boy."

"I'm not a boy."

"It was just a finger of speech," he said, using one of the silly expressions which come to a person as he grows, and blessedly pass. She seemed not to react to it at all, for she said gravely, "You have the most beautiful eyes I have ever seen. They are made of aluminum. And your hair is all wiggly."

He could think of nothing to say to that, but tried; all that emerged was, "Well, it's early yet," and suddenly they were laughing together. She was so strange, so different. She spoke in a grave, unaccented and utterly incautious idiom as if she thought strange thoughts and spoke them right out. "Also," she said, "you have lovely lips. They're pale blue. You ought to get out of the water."

"I can't!"

She considered that for a moment, treading away from him and then back to the yard's distance. "Where are your things?"

He pointed across the narrow neck of the lake which he had circumnavigated.

"Wait for me over there," she said, and suddenly swam close, so close she could dip her chin and look straight into his eyes. "You got to," she said fiercely.

"Oh I will," he promised, and struck out for the opposite shore. She hung to the rock, watching him.

Swimming, reaching hard, stretching for distance warmed him, and the chill and its accompanying vague ache diminished. Then he had a twinge of stomach-ache, and he drew up his knees to ease it. When he tried to extend himself again, he could, but it hurt too much. He drew up his knees again, and the pain followed inward so that to flex again was out of the question. He drew his knees up still tighter, and tighter still followed the pain. He needed air badly by then, threw up his head, tried to roll over on his back; but with his knees drawn up, everything came out all wrong. He inhaled at last because he had to, but the air was gone away somewhere; he floundered upward for it until the pressure in his ears told him he was swimming downward. Blackness came upon him and receded, and came again, he let it come for a tired instant, and was surrounded by light, and drew one lungful of air and one of water, and got the blackness again; this time it stayed with him . . .

Still beautiful in her bed, but morphine-clouded, flypapered and unstruggling in viscous sleep, he lay with monsters swarming in his veins . . .

Quietly, in a corner of the room, she spoke with Keogh:

"You don't understand me. You didn't understand me yesterday when I cried out at the idea of that—that operation. Keogh, I love him, but I'm *me*. Loving him doesn't mean I've stopped thinking. Loving him means I'm more me than ever, not less. It means I can do anything I did before, only more, only better. That's why I fell in love with him. That's why I am in love with him. Weren't you ever in love, Keogh?"

He looked at the way her hair fell, and the earnest placement of her thick soft brows, and he said, "I haven't thought much about it."

" 'There's always a way. All you have to do is think of it,' " she quoted. "Keogh, I've accepted what Dr. Rathburn said. After I left you yesterday I went to the library and tore the heart out of some books . . . they're right, Rathburn and Weber. And I've thought and I've thought . . . trying the way Daddy would, to turn everything upside down and backwards, to look for a new way of thinking. He won't die, Keogh; I'm not going to let him die."

"You said you accepted—"

"Oh, part of him. Most of him, if you like. We all die, bit by bit, all the time, and it doesn't bother us because most of the dead parts are replaced. He'll . . . he'll lose more parts, sooner, but—after it's over, he'll be himself again." She said it with superb confidence—perhaps it was childlike. If so, it was definitely not childish.

"You have an idea," said Keogh positively. As he had pointed out to the doctors, he knew her.

"All those—those things in his blood," she said quietly. "The struggle they go through . . . they're trying to survive; did you ever think of it that way, Keogh? They want to live. They want most terribly to go on living."

"I hadn't thought about it."

"His body wants them to live too. It welcomes them wherever they lodge. Dr. Weber said so."

"You've got hold of something," said Keogh flatly, "and whatever it is I don't think I like it."

"I don't want you to like it," she said in the same strange quiet voice. He looked swiftly at her and saw again the burning deep in her eyes. He had to look away. She said, "I want you to hate it. I want you to fight it. You have one of the most wonderful minds I have ever known, Keogh, and I want you to think up every argument you can think of against it. For every argument I'll find an answer, and then we'll know what to do."

"You'd better go ahead," he said reluctantly.

"I had a pretty bad quarrel with Dr. Weber this morning," she said suddenly.

"This m—when?" He looked at his watch; it was still early.

"About three, maybe four. In his room. I went there and woke him up."

"Look, you don't do things like that to Weber!"

"I do. Anyway, he's gone."

He rose to his feet, the rare bright patches of anger showing in his cheeks. He took a breath, let it out, and sat down again. "You'd better tell me about it."

"In the library," she said, "there's a book on genetics, and it mentions some experiments on Belgian hares. The does were impregnated without sperm, with some sort of saline or alkaline solution."

"I remember something about it." He was well used to her circuitous way of approaching something important. She built conversational points, not like a hired contractor, but like an architect.

Sometimes she brought in portions of her lumber and stacked them beside the structure. If she ever did that, it was material she needed and would use. He waited.

"The does gave birth to baby rabbits, all female. The interesting thing was that they were identical to each other and to the mother. Even the blood-vessel patterns in the eyeball were so similar that an expert might be fooled by photographs of them. 'Impossibly similar' is what one of the experimenters called it. They had to be identical because everything they inherited was from the mother. I woke Dr. Weber up to tell him about that."

"And he told you he'd read the book."

"He wrote it," she said gently. "And then I told him that if he could do that with a Belgian hare, he could do it with—" she nodded toward her big bed—"him."

Then she was quiet, while Keogh rejected the idea, found it stuck to his mind's hand, not to be shaken off; brought it to his mind's eye and shuddered away from it, shook again and failed, slowly brought it close and turned it over, and turned it again.

"Take one of those—those things like fertilized ova—make it grow . . ."

"You don't *make* it grow. It wants desperately to grow. And not one of them, Keogh. You have thousands. You have hundreds more every hour."

"Oh my God."

"It came to me when Dr. Rathburn suggested the operation. It came to me all at once, a miracle. If you love someone that much," she said, looking at the sleeper, "miracles happen. But you have to be willing to help them happen." She looked at him directly, with an intensity that made him move back in his chair. "I can have anything I want—all it has to be is possible. We just have to make it possible. That's why I went to Dr. Weber this morning. To ask him."

"He said it wasn't possible."

"He said that at first. After a half hour or so he said the odds against it were in the billions or trillions . . . but you see, as soon as he said that, he was saying it was possible."

"What did you do then?"

"I dared him to try."

"And that's why he left?"

"Yes."

"You're mad," he said before he could stop himself. She seemed not to resent it. She sat calmly, waiting.

"Look," said Keogh at last, "Weber said those distorted—uh,—*things* were *like* fertilized ova. He never said they were. He could have said—well, I'll say it for him—they're *not* fertilized ova."

"But he did say they were—some of them, anyway, and especially those that reached the lungs—were very much like ova. How close do you have to get before there's no real difference at all?"

"It can't be. It just can't."

"Weber said that. And I asked him if he had ever tried."

"All right, all right! It can't happen, but just to keep this silly argument going, suppose you got something that would grow. You won't, of course. But if you did, how would you keep it growing. It has to be fed, it has to be kept at a certain critical temperature, a certain amount of acid or alkali will kill it . . . you don't just plant something like that in the yard."

"Already they've taken ova from one cow, planted them in another, and gotten calves. There's a man in Australia who plans to raise blooded cattle from scrub cows that way."

"You *have* done your homework."

"Oh, that isn't all. There's a Dr. Carrel in New Jersey who has been able to keep chicken tissue alive for months—he says indefinitely—in a nutrient solution, in a temperature-controlled jar in his lab. It grows, Keogh! It grows so much he has to cut it away every once in a while."

"This is crazy. This is—it's insane," he growled. "And what do you think you'll get if you bring one of these monsters to term?"

"We'll bring thousands of them to term," she said composedly. "And one of them will be—*him*." She leaned forward abruptly, and her even tone of voice broke; a wildness grew through her face and voice, and though it was quiet, it shattered him: "It will be his flesh, the pattern of him, his own substance grown again. His hair, Keogh. His fingerprints. His—eyes. His—his *self*."

"I can't—" Keogh shook himself like a wet spaniel, but it changed nothing; he was still here, she, the bed, the sleeper, and this dreadful, this inconceivably horrible, wrong idea.

She smiled then, put out her hand and touched him; incredibly, it was a mother's smile, warm and comforting, a mother's loving protective touch; her voice was full of affection. "Keogh, if it won't work, it won't work, no matter what we do. Then you'll be right. I think it will work. It's what I want. Don't you want me to have what I want?"

He had to smile, and she smiled back. "You're a young devil," he said ardently. "Got me coming and going, haven't you? Why did you want me to fight it?"

"I didn't," she said, "but if you fight me you'll come up with problems nobody else could possibly think of, and once we've thought of them, we'll be ready, don't you see? I'll fight with you, Keogh," she said, shifting her strange bright spectrum from tenderness to a quiet, convinced, invincible certainty, "I'll fight with you, I'll lift and carry, I'll buy and sell and kill if I have to, but I am going to bring him back. You know something, Keogh?"

"What?"

She waved her hand in a gesture that included him, the room, the castle and grounds and all the other castles and grounds; the pseudonyms, the ships and trains, the factories and exchanges, the mountains and acres and mines and banks and the thousands upon thousands of people which, taken together, were Wyke: "I always knew that all this *was*," she said, "and I've come to understand that this is mine. But I used to wonder, sometimes, what it was all *for*. Now I know. Now I know."

A mouth on his mouth, a weight on his stomach. He felt boneless and nauseated, limp as grease drooling. The light around him was green, and all shapes blurred.

The mouth on his mouth, the weight on his stomach, a breath of air, welcome but too warm, too moist. He needed it desperately but did not like it, and found a power-plant full of energy to gather it up in his lungs and fling it away; but his weakness so filtered all that effort that it emerged in a faint bubbling sigh.

The mouth on his mouth again, and the weight on his stomach, and another breath. He tried to turn his head but someone held him by the nose. He blew out the needed, unsatisfactory air and replaced it by a little gust of his own inhalation. On this he coughed; it was too rich, pure, too good. He coughed as one does over a pickle-barrel; good air hurt his lungs.

He felt his head and shoulders lifted, shifted, by which he learned that he had been flat on his back on stone, or something flat and quite that hard, and was now on smooth firm softness. The good sharp air came and went, his weak coughs fewer, until he fell into a dazed peace. The face that bent over his was too close to focus, or he had lost the power to focus; either way, he didn't care. Drowsily he stared up into the blurred brightness of that face and listened uncritically to the voice—

—the voice crooning wordlessly and comfortingly, and somehow, in its wordlessness, creating new expressions for joy and delight for which words would not do. Then after all there were words, half sung, half whispered; and he couldn't catch them, and he couldn't catch them and then . . . and then he was sure he heard: "How could it be, such a magic as that: all this and the eyes as well . . ." Then, demanding, "You are the shape of the not-you: tell me, are *you* in there?"

He opened his eyes wide and saw her face clearly at last and the dark hair, and the eyes were green—true deep sea-green. Her tangled hair, drying, crowned her like vines, and the leafy roof close above seemed part of her and the green eyes, and threw green light on the unaccountably blonde transparency of her cheeks. He genuinely did not know, at the moment, what she was. She had said to him (was it years ago?) "I thought you were a faun . . ." he had not, at the moment, much consciousness, not to say whimsy, at his command; she was simply something unrelated to anything in his experience.

He was aware of griping, twisting pain rising, filling, about to explode in his upper abdomen. Some thick wire within him had kinked, and knowing well that it should be unbent, he made a furious, rebellious effort and pulled it through. The explosion came, but in nausea, not in agony. Convulsively he turned his head, surged upward, and let it go.

He saw with too much misery to be horrified the bright vomit surging on and around her knee, and running into the crevice between thigh and calf where she had her leg bent and tucked under her, and the clots left there as the fluid ran away. And she—

She sat where she was, held his head, cradled him in her arms, soothed him and crooned to him and said that was good, good; he'd feel better now. The weakness floored him and receded; then shakily he pressed away from her, sat up, bowed his head and gasped for breath. "Whooo," he said.

"Boy," she said; and she said it in exact concert with him. He clung to his shins and wiped the nausea-tears from his left eye, then his right, on his knee-cap. "Boy oh boy," he said, and she said it with him in concert.

So at last he looked at her.

He looked at her, and would never forget what he saw, and exactly the way it was. Late sunlight made into lace by the bower above clothed her; she leaned toward him, one small hand flat on the ground, one slim supporting arm straight and straight down; her weight turned up that shoulder and her head tilted toward it as if drawn down by the heavy darkness of her hair. It gave a sense of yielding, as if she were fragile, which he knew she was not. Her other hand lay open across one knee, the palm up and the fingers not quite relaxed, as if they held something; and indeed they did, for a spot of light, gold turned coral by her flesh, lay in her palm. She held it just so, just right, unconsciously, and her hand held that rare knowledge that closed, a hand may not give nor receive. For his lifetime he had it all, each tiniest part, even to the gleaming big toenail at the under-side of her other calf. And she was smiling, and her complex eyes adored.

Guy Gibbon knew his life's biggest moment during the moment itself, a rarity in itself, and of all times of life, it was time to say the unforgettable, for anything he said now would be.

He shuddered, and then smiled back at her. "Oh . . . *boy,*" he breathed.

And again they were laughing together until, puzzled, he stopped and asked, "Where am I?"

She would not answer, so he closed his eyes and puzzled it out. Pine bower . . . undress somewhere . . . swimming. Oh, swimming. And then across the lake, and he had met— He opened his eyes and looked at her and said, "you." Then swimming back, cold, his gut full of too much food and warm juice and moldy cake to boot, and, ". . . you must have saved my life."

"Well somebody had to. You were dead."

"I should've been."

"No!" she cried. "Don't you ever say that again!" And he could see she was absolutely serious.

"I only meant, for stupidity. I ate a lot of junk, and some cake I think was moldy. Too much, when I was hot and tired, and then like a bonehead I went right into the water, so anybody who does that deserves to—"

"I meant it," she said levelly, "never again. Didn't you ever hear of the old tradition of the field of battle, when one man saved another's life, that life became his to do what he wanted with?"

"What do you want to do with mine?"

"That depends," she said thoughtfully. "You have to give it. I can't just take it." She knelt then and sat back on her heels, her hands trailing pine-needles across the bower's paved stone floor. She bowed her head and her hair swung forward. He thought she was watching him through it; he could not be sure.

He said, and the thought grew so large that it quelled his voice and made him whisper. "Do you want it?"

"Oh, yes," she said, whispering too. When he moved to her and put her hair back to see if she was watching him, he found her eyes closed, and tears pressed through. He reached for her gently, but before he could touch her she sprang up and straight at the leafy wall. Her long golden body passed through it without a sound, and seemed to hang suspended outside; then it was gone. He put his head through and saw her flashing along under green water. He hesitated, then got an acrid whiff of his own vomit. The water looked clean and the golden sand just what he ached to scrub himself with. He climbed out of the bower and floundered clumsily down the bank and into the water.

After his first plunge he came up and spun about, looking for her, but she was gone.

Numbly he swam to the tiny beach and, kneeling, scoured himself with the fine sand. He dove and rinsed, and then (hoping) scrubbed himself all over again. And rinsed. But he did not see her.

He stood in the late rays of the sun to dry, and looked off across the lake. His heart leapt when he saw white movement, and sank again as he saw it was just the wheel of boats bobbing and sliding there.

He plodded up to the bower—now at last he saw it was the one behind which he had undressed—and he sank down on the bench.

This was a place where tropical fish swam in ocean water where there was no ocean, and where fleets of tiny perfect boats sailed with no one sailing them and no one watching, and where priceless statues stood hidden in clipped and barbered glades deep in the woods and—and he hadn't seen it all; what other impossibilities were possible in this impossible place?

And besides, he'd been sick. (He wrinkled his nostrils.) Damn near . . . drowned. Out of his head for sure, for a while anyway. She couldn't be real. Hadn't he noticed a greenish cast to her flesh, or was that just the light? . . . anybody who could make a place like this, run a place like this, could jimmy up some kind of machine to hypnotize you like in the science fiction stories.

He stirred uneasily. Maybe someone was watching him, even now. Hurriedly, he began to dress.

So she wasn't real. Or maybe all of it wasn't real. He'd bumped into that other trespasser across the lake there, and that was real, but then when he'd almost drowned, he'd dreamed up the rest.

Only—he touched his mouth. He'd dreamed up someone blowing the breath back into him. He'd heard about that somewhere, but it sure wasn't what they were teaching this year at the Y.

You are the shape of the not-you. Are you in there?

What did that mean?

He finished dressing dazedly. He muttered, "What'd I hafta go an' eat that goddam cake for?" He wondered what he would tell Sammy. If she wasn't real, Sammy wouldn't know what he was talking about. If she was real there's only one thing he would talk about, yes, and from then on. You mean you had her in that place and all you did was throw up on her? No—he wouldn't tell Sammy. Or anybody.

And he'd be a bachelor all his life.

Boy oh boy. What an introduction. First she has to save your life and then you don't know what to say and then oh, look what you had to go and do. But anyway—she wasn't real.

He wondered what her name was. Even if she wasn't real. Lots of people don't use their real names.

He climbed out of the bower and crossed the silent pine carpet behind it, and he shouted. It was not a word at all, and had nothing about it that tried to make it one.

She was standing there waiting for him. She wore a quiet brown dress and low heels and carried a brown leather pocketbook, and her hair was braided and tied neatly and sedately in a coronet. She looked, too, as if she had turned down some inward tone control so that her skin did not radiate. She looked ready to disappear, not into

thin air, but into a crowd—any crowd, as soon as she could get close
to one. In a crowd he would have walked right past her, certainly,
but for the shape of her eyes. She stepped up to him quickly and
laid her hand on his cheek and laughed up at him. Again he saw the
whiteness of those unusual eyeteeth, so sharp . . . "You're blush-
ing!" she said.

No blusher in history was ever stopped by that observation. He
asked, "Which way do you go?"

She looked at his eyes, one, the other, both, quickly; then folded
her long hands together around the strap of her pocketbook and
looked down at them.

"With you," she said softly.

This was only one of the many things she said to him, moment by
moment, which gained meaning for him as time went on. He took
her back to town and to dinner, and then to the West side address
she gave him and they stood outside it all night talking. In six weeks
they were married.

"How could I argue?" said Weber to Dr. Rathburn.

They stood together watching a small army of workmen swarming
over the gigantic stone barn a quarter-mile from the castle, which,
incidentally, was invisible from this point and unknown to the men.
Work had begun at three the previous afternoon, continued all night.
There was nothing, nothing at all that Dr. Weber had specified which
was not only given him, but on the site or already installed.

"I know," said Rathburn, who did.

"Not only, how could I argue," said Weber, "why should I? A
man has plans, ambitions. That Keogh, what an approach! That's
the first thing he went after—my plans for myself. That's where he
starts. And suddenly everything you ever wanted to do or be or have
is handed to you or promised to you, and no fooling about the prom-
ise either."

"*Oh* no. They don't need to fool anybody. . . . You want to pass
a prognosis?"

"You mean on the youngster there?" He looked at Rathburn.
"Oh—that's not what you mean. . . . You're asking me if I can
bring one of those surrogate foetuses to term. An opinion like that
would make a damn fool out of a man, and this is no job for a damn
fool. All I can tell you is, I tried it—and that is something I wouldn't've

dreamed of doing if it hadn't been for her and her crazy idea. I left here at four a.m. with some throat smears and by nine I had a half dozen of them isolated and in nutrient solution. Beef blood plasma —the quickest thing I could get ready. And I got mitosis. They divided, and in a few hours I could see two of 'em dimpling to form the gastrosphore. That was evidence enough to get going; that's all I think and that's all I told them on the phone. And by the time I got here," he added, waving toward the big barn, "there's a research lab four-fifths built, big enough for a city medical center. Argue?" he demanded, returning to Dr. Rathburn's original question. "How could I argue? Why should I? . . . And that *girl*. She's a force, like gravity. She can turn on so much pressure, and I mean by herself and personally, that she could probably get anything in the world she wanted even if she didn't own it, the world I mean. Put that in the northeast entrance!" he bellowed at a foreman. "I'll be down to show you just where it goes." He turned to Rathburn; he was a man on fire. "I got to go."

"Anything I can do," said Dr. Rathburn, "just say it."

"That's the wonderful part of it," said Weber. "That's what everybody around here keeps saying, and they mean it!" He trotted down toward the barn, and Rathburn turned toward the castle.

About a month after his last venture at trespassing, Guy Gibbon was coming home from work when a man at the corner put away a newspaper and, still folding it, said, "Gibbon?"

"That's right," said Guy, a little sharply.

The man looked him up and down, quickly, but giving an impression of such thoroughness, efficiency and experience that Guy would not have been surprised to learn that the man had not only catalogued his clothes and their source, their state of maintenance and a computation therefrom of his personal habits, but also his state of health and even his blood type. "My name's Keogh," said the man. "Does that mean anything to you?"

"No."

"Sylva never mentioned the name?"

"Sylva! N-no, she didn't."

"Let's go somewhere and have a drink. I'd like to talk to you." Something had pleased this man: Guy wondered what. "Well, okay," he said. "Only I don't drink much, but well, okay."

They found a bar in the neighborhood with booths in the back. Keogh had a scotch and soda and Guy, after some hesitation, ordered beer. Guy said, "You know her?"

"Most of her life. Do you?"

"What? Well, sure. We're going to get married." He looked studiously into his beer and said uncomfortably, "Who are you anyway, Mr. Keogh?"

"You might say," said Keogh, "I'm *in loco parentis.*" He waited for a response, then added, "Sort of a guardian."

"She never said anything about a guardian."

"I can understand that. What has she told you about herself?"

Guy's discomfort descended to a level of shyness, diffidence, even a touch of fear—which did not alter the firmness of his words, however they were spoken. "I don't know you, Mr. Keogh. I don't think I ought to answer any questions about Sylva. Or me. Or anything." He looked up at the man. Keogh searched deeply, then smiled. It was an unpracticed and apparently slightly painful process with him, but it was genuine for all that. "Good!" he barked, and rose. "Come on." He left the booth and Guy, more than a little startled, followed. They went to the phone booth in the corner. Keogh dropped in a nickel, dialed, and waited, his eyes fixed on Guy. Then Guy had to listen to one side of the conversation:

"I'm here with Guy Gibbon." (Guy had to notice that Keogh identified himself only with his voice.)

. . . "Of course I knew about it. That's a silly question, girl."

. . . "Because it *is* my business. *You* are my business."

. . . "Stop it? I'm not trying to stop anything. I just have to know, that's all."

. . . "All right. All right. . . . He's here. He won't talk about you or anything, which is good. Yes, very good. Will you please tell him to open up?"

And he handed the receiver to a startled Guy, who said tremulously, "Uh, hello," to it while watching Keogh's impassive face.

Her voice suffused and flooded him, changed this whole unsettling experience to something different and good. "Guy, darling."

"Sylva—"

"It's all right. I should have told you sooner, I guess. It had to come some time. Guy, you can tell Keogh anything you like. Anything he asks."

"Why, honey? Who is he, anyway?"

There was a pause, then a strange little laugh. "He can explain that better than I can. You want us to be married, Guy?"

"Oh yes!"

"Well all right then. Nobody can change that, nobody but you. And listen, Guy, I'll live anywhere, any way you want to live. That's the real truth and all of it, do you believe me?"

"I always believe you."

"All right then. So that's what we'll do. Now you go and talk to Keogh. Tell him anything he wants to know. He has to do the same. I love you, Guy."

"Me too," said Guy, watching Keogh's face. "Well okay then," he added when she said nothing further. " 'Bye." He hung up.

He and Keogh had a long talk.

"It hurts him," she whispered to Dr. Rathburn.

"I know." He shook his head sympathetically. "There's just so much morphine you can ram into a man, though."

"Just a little more?"

"Maybe a little," he said sadly. He went to his bag and got the needle. Sylva kissed the sleeping man tenderly and left the room. Keogh was waiting for her.

He said, "This has got to stop, girl."

"Why?" she responded ominously.

"Let's get out of here."

She had known Keogh so long, and so well, that she was sure he had no surprises for her. But this voice, this look, these were something new in Keogh. He held the door for her, so she preceded him through it and then went where he silently led.

They left the castle and took the path through a heavy copse and over the brow of the hill which overlooked the barn. The parking lot, which had once been a barnyard, was full of automobiles. A white ambulance approached; another was unloading at the northeast platform. A muffled generator purred somewhere behind the building, and smoke rose from the stack of the new stone boiler-room at the side. They both looked avidly at the building but did not comment. The path took them along the crest of the hill and down toward the lake. They went to a small forest clearing in which stood an eight-foot Diana, the huntress Diana, chaste and fleet-footed, so beautifully finished she seemed not like marble at all, not like anything cold or static. "I always had the idea," said Keogh, "that nobody can lie anywhere near her."

She looked up at the Diana.

"Not even to themselves," said Keogh, and plumped down on a marble bench.

"Let's have it," she said.

"You want to make Guy Gibbon happen all over again. It's a crazy idea and it's a big one too. But lots of things were crazier, and some bigger, and now they're commonplace. I won't argue on how crazy it is, or how big."

"What then?"

"I've been trying, the last day or so, to back 'way out, far off, get a look at this thing with some perspective. Sylva, you've forgotten something."

"Good," she said. "Oh, good. I knew you'd think of things like this before it was too late."

"So you can find a way out?" Slowly he shook his head. "Not this time. Tighten up the Wyke guts, girl, and make up your mind to quit."

"Go ahead."

"It's just this. I don't believe you're going to get your carbon copy, mind you, but you just might. I've been talking to Weber, and by God you just about might. But if you do, all you've got is a container, and nothing to fill it with. Look, girl, a man isn't blood and bone and body cells, and that's all."

He paused, until she said, "Go on, Keogh."

He demanded, "You love this guy?"

"Keogh!" She was amused.

"Whaddaya love?" he barked. "That skrinkly hair? The muscles, skin? His nat'ral equipment? The eyes, voice?"

"All that," she said composedly.

"All that, and that's all?" he demanded relentlessly. "Because if your answer is yes, you can have what you want, and more power to you, and good riddance. I don't know anything about love, but I will say this: that if that's all there is to it, the hell with it."

"Well of *course* there's more."

"Ah. And where are you going to get that, girl? Listen, a man is the skin and bone he stands in, plus what's in his head, plus what's in his heart. You mean to reproduce Guy Gibbon, but you're not going to do it by duplicating his carcass. You want to duplicate the whole man, you're going to have to make him live the same life again. And that you can't do."

She looked up at the Diana for a long time. Then, "Why not?" she breathed.

"I'll tell you why not," he said angrily. "Because first of all you have to find out *who he is*."

"*I* know who he is!"

He spat explosively on the green moss by the bench. It was totally uncharacteristic and truly shocking. "You don't know a particle, and I know even less. I had his back against a wall one time for better than two hours, trying to find out who he is. He's just another kid, is all. Nothing much in school, nothing much at sports, same general tastes and feelings as six zillion other ones like him. Why him, Sylva? Why him? What did you ever see in a guy like that to be worth the marrying?"

"I . . . didn't know you disliked him."

"Oh hell, girl, I don't! I never said that. I can't—I can't even find anything to dislike!"

"You don't know him the way I do."

"There, I agree. I don't and I couldn't. Because you don't know anything either—you *feel,* but you don't *know*. If you want to see Guy Gibbon again, or a reasonable facsimile, he's going to have to live by a script from the day he's born. He'll have to duplicate every experience that this kid here ever had."

"All right," she said quietly.

He looked at her, stunned. He said, "And before he can do that, we have to write the script. And before we can write it, we have to get the material somehow. What do you expect to do—set up a Foundation or something dedicated to the discovery of each and every moment this—this unnoticeable young man ever lived through? And do it secretly, because while he's growing up he can't ever know? Do you know how much that would cost, how many people it would involve?"

"That would be all right," she said.

"And suppose you had it, a biography written like a script, twenty years of a lifetime, every day, every hour you could account for; now you're going to have to arrange for a child, from birth, to be sur- rounded by people who are going to play this script out—and who will never let anything else happen to him but what's in the script, and who will never let him know."

"That's it! That's it!" she cried.

He leapt to his feet and swore at her. He said, "I'm not planning this, you love-struck lunatic, I'm objecting to it!"

"Is there any more?" she cried eagerly. "Keogh, Keogh, try—try hard. How do we start? What do we do first? Quick, Keogh."

He looked at her, thunderstruck, and at last sank down on the bench and began to laugh weakly. She sat by him, held his hand, her eyes shining. After a time he sobered, and turned to her. He drank the shine of those eyes for a while; and after, his brain began to function again . . . on Wyke business . . .

"The main source of who he is and what he's done," he said at last, "won't be with us much longer. . . . We better go tell Rathburn to get him off the morphine. He has to be able to think."

"All right," she said. "All right."

When the pain got too much to permit him to remember any more, they tried a little morphine again. For a while they found a balance between recollection and agony, but the agony gained. Then they severed his spinal cord so he couldn't feel it. They brought in people —psychiatrist, stenographers, even a professional historian.

In the rebuilt barn, Weber tried animal hosts, cows even, and primates—everything he could think of. He got some results, though no good ones. He tried humans too. He couldn't cross the bridge of body tolerance; the uterus will not support an alien foetus any more than the hand will accept the graft of another's finger.

So he tried nutrient solutions. He tried a great many. Ultimately he found one that worked. It was the blood plasma of pregnant women.

He placed the best of the quasi-ova between sheets of sterilized chamois. He designed automatic machinery to drip the plasma in at arterial tempo, drain it at a veinous rate, keep it at body temperature.

One day fifty of them died, because of choloform used in one of the adhesives. When light seemed to affect them adversely, Weber designed containers of bakelite. When ordinary photography proved impractical he designed a new kind of film sensitive to heat, the first infra-red film.

The viable foetuses he had at 60 days showed the eye-spot, the spine, the buds of arms, a beating heart. Each and every one of them consumed, or was bathed in, over a gallon of plasma a day, and at one point there were one hundred and seventy-four thousand of them. Then they began to die off—some malformed, some chemically unbalanced, many for reasons too subtle even for Weber and his staff.

When he had done all he could, when he could only wait and see, he had foetuses seven months along and growing well. There were twenty-three of them. Guy Gibbon was dead quite a while by then, and his widow came to see Weber and tiredly put down a stack of papers and reports, urged him to read, begged him to call her as soon as he had.

He read them, he called her. He refused what she asked.

She got hold of Keogh. He refused to have anything to do with such an idea. She made him change his mind. Keogh made Weber change his mind.

The stone barn hummed with construction again, and new machinery. The cold tank was four by six feet inside, surrounded by coils and sensing devices. They put her in it.

By that time the foetuses were eight and a half months along. There were four left.

One made it.

AUTHOR'S NOTE: To the reader, but especially to the reader in his early twenties, let me ask: did you ever have the feeling that you were getting pushed around? Did you ever want to do something, and have all sorts of obstacles thrown in your way until you had to give up, while on the other hand some other thing you wanted was made easy for you? Did you ever feel that certain strangers know who you are? Did you ever meet a girl who made you explode inside, who seemed to like you—and who was mysteriously plucked out of your life, as if she shouldn't be in the script?

Well, we've all had these feelings. Yet if you've read the above, you'll allow it's a little more startling than just a story. It reads like an analogy, doesn't it? I mean, it doesn't have to be a castle, or the ol' swimmin' hole, and the names have been changed to protect the innocent . . . author.

Because it could be about time for her to wake up, aged only two or three years for her twenty-year cold sleep. And when she meets you, it's going to be the biggest thing that ever happened to you since the last time.

Theodore Sturgeon

by JUDITH MERRIL

The man has *style*.

The same quality of "voice" or "presence" that makes the most un-evenly composed Sturgeon story compellingly readable, marks his personality with equally unmistakeable (if no more definable) fascination.

He is a man of varied interests and strong opinions, many skills and endless paradox. Snob-and-vulgarian, athlete-and-aesthete, mystic-and-mechanic, he is detached and merry, humble and arro-gant, over-mannered and deeply courteous—a manicured nudist, a man of elegant naturalness, thoughtful simplicity, schooled ease, and studied spontaneity.

Strangers always notice him; children respond with immediate and lasting confidence; those who know him, like or dislike him. No one is indifferent—and no two see quite the same man.

No two are presented with quite the same man. Yet there is rarely intent to deceive (I would have said *never,* but one must allow for the natural effects of, for instance, bill collectors, Internal Revenue officers, and certain publishers); nor is deception ordinarily the re-sult. The change of face or stance or style, from one audience to an-other may be anywhere from subtle to sensational; but each attitude is as genuine as the last—simply a new permutation of the internal contradictions.

Beauty is a state of mind compounded of harmony and/or con-trast with the environment of the beautiful thing, he wrote me once. *The environment does not have to be concrete, but it does have a hell of a lot to do with the reflexes of the beholder . . .*

This is one of the basic ingredients of Sturgeon's style. In his work, the choice of language, the prose (or poetic) meter, sometimes even the syntax, is generated by the situation or character: a constant variation of prose pattern is one of the elements that marks his writing style. In his person, a similar variable surface stems in the same way from the instinct for "harmony and/or contrast."

"Sturgeon is living his own biography," one close mutual friend used to say in moments of maximum frustration with the eternally sincere poseur. And though I doubt Ted has given much thought— or would care, if he did—to the figure he may someday cut in a scholar's summary, it is certainly true that he insists on revising the script constantly. He simply cannot stand idly by and see the dramatic unities destroyed by the gross, absurd hand of real happenstance: there is never a doubt which road to follow, when logic or self-interest depart from the moment's artistic necessities.

There are certain things about Ted that are (comparatively) unvarying: attributes that change, as in all of us, only with time and growth. His appearance is one.

A bit above average height (perhaps five-ten?), he is slender in build, but determinedly fit. (His first ambition was to be a circus acrobat.) He is just short of being conventionally handsome, but the trim beard he adopted years back (before they were fashionable) is the touch that turns what was almost a faun-like countenance into a faintly satanic mask.

He is a warm person, and the only formalities he practices are his own—such rituals of behavior as he has devised to suit his own purposes (or, rather, pleasures. At work—any kind of work—he is impatiently, starkly, functional). He is (almost) obsessively clean, with a passion for neatness and pleasing design. (Note the "almost," nothing is ever all-one-way with Ted. He is fond of saying: "The definition of perversion is anything done to the exclusion of everything else—including the normal position.")

He loves good food, good drink, good talk, good music, good decor, good looks, good manners. He hates dirt, sweat, too-loud voices, ill-fitting clothes, clumsy behavior. (*I feel that the nearest to a basic you can get is in living graciously. I can only know my own definition of graciousness, and it is one that precludes hating a man for his black skin, pissing on other people's rugs, going naked when it will distress others, sleeping with other men's wives, violating privacy, and any number of other delightful or uncomfortable or fun-making things . . .)*

He acquires skills with the dedication of a collector: offhand, I know him to be anywhere from competent to expert as a chauffeur, guitarist, radio (and general electronics) repairman, cook, bulldozer operator, automobile mechanic, and maker-of-whathaveyous-from-wire-hangers-toothbrushes-and-old-bottles. He also sings well, and speaks with an unusually, noticeably, clear diction—and with a wit that is, mostly, warm and friendly.

In my first list of paradoxes, I stressed the "manicured nudist."* I mentioned later that his near-obsession with cleanliness and tidiness had an exception. The exception is work. The most obvious thing about the Sturgeon style, is the *easiness* of it, but that ease is earned the hard way.

An editor, fretting about an overdue novel of Ted's, once told me: "He says he has three days' work left to do. I believe him. I know he can write a novel in three days. But which three days is it going to be?"

The editor was almost right, but also wrong. I have known Sturgeon to sit at the typewriter (in an attic or cellar or closed-off bedroom, before the garage, uncombed, paper-strewn, coffee-nerved, and sweating) for hours on end, sleepless and almost foodless, producing a steady stream of (one-draft, final-copy) words, hour after hour. (I think the record for three days, though—with catnaps and sandwiches—was not quite two-thirds of a novel.) But typing is only one part of the job.

"Nobody can do two things at the same time," Ted says lightly. "I never think while I'm writing." He doesn't. The thinking comes first, between the false starts and in the glare of the virgin white sheet on the typer roller.

(He said it a little differently in "The Perfect Host:") *You want to write a story, see, and you sit down in front of the mill, wait until that certain feeling comes to you, hold off a second longer just to be quite sure that you know exactly what you want to do, take a deep breath, and get up and make a pot of coffee.*

This sort of thing is likely to go on for days, until you are out of

---

* *Yes, if you've been wondering; those rumors are at least partly true. Ted was, for some years, an enthusiastic (nay, evangelical) nudist.*

coffee and can't get more until you can pay for same, which you can do by writing a story and selling it; or until you get tired of messing around and sit down and write a yarn purely by means of knowing how to do it and applying the knowledge.

Neither way of saying it explains why he loses weight in the process. He sweats—just like people; he does it in private. When he's done enough of it, out of the mill comes the fluent graceful prose anyone would know as Sturgeon's.

The operative phrase in that quote is "knowing how to do it and applying the knowledge." In an enormously gratifying introduction to a short story collection of mine, Ted publicly disclaimed any responsibility for me as a writer. When he learned I was writing this article, he reminded me, sternly, of his version of the matter. Having been forbidden to extend public gratitude, and with full intention of doing so, perhaps, I can take the curse off it, by taking some credit to myself first:—

It was I who taught Sturgeon how much he knew about writing; I did it by listening, and asking an occasional question, while he was teaching me everything he knew about writing. (The differences that are still evident are, I am afraid, a matter of art rather than craft.)

I am not just joking. At the time that Ted decided I should, and by-damn *would,* write science fiction, he was still recovering from the double shock of his first prolonged experience with "writer's block," and the breakup of his first marriage. He could not think ill enough of himself. (His best stories then were tragedies—or self-mockeries: "Maturity," "Thunder and Roses," "It Wasn't Syzgy," "The Sky Was Full of Ships." There was even one, less memorable, *called* "That Low.") And his sad theme, reiterated, was: "I want to be liked or admired for something I *do*—not just for what I *am*." Or, alternatively:

"I'm not a writer. You are, Phil* is. I'm not. A writer is someone who has to write. The only reason I want to write is because it's the only way I can justify all the other things I didn't do."

---

* *Phil Klass—William Tenn: at that time he was also a new writer—two stories ahead of me (he had two published). For most of a semi-starved year, just before the Big S-F Boom started, the three of us lived—or so it now seems—on one ten dollar bill loaned around in continuous rotation.*

At the same time, he was scouring his mind for what helpful odds and ends it might contain for a novice writer. (I did not mean to imply that Sturgeon formed his intent against my will; I could hardly talk or think of anything else in those days—but to me it was a hopeless hope. I knew I was literate; I could do research; I could write a tolerable article, or even a "hack" pulp story, to formula rules. But to be *A Writer,* which was something else again, one needed Talent and Imagination . . .)

The first thing he did was to give me a book.

He had seen some (sincere, young, and of course free verse) poetry of mine in a fan magazine. He liked one poem, said so, and showed up a few days later with Clement Wood's "Complete Rhyming Dictionary and Poet's Craft Book," inscribed:

> *I give it so that Judy can*
> *Become a goddam artisan.*

He suggested, gently, that I try my hand first at some of the French light verse forms. I did try one, and decided to go on to greater things. I wrote a sonnet; or so I thought. It had the right number of lines and rhymes in the right places, and it was in iambics. I sent it to Ted, and got back a five page critique, line by line. Some lines he even praised; but he began with a sort of first-grade explanation that a sonnet is *never,* not ever, in tetrameter; each line, always, has ten syllables, not eight. He wrote, in part:

Keep pure and faithful your respect for the form. Violate it nowhere, ever, not in the slightest shift of syllabic value. Our language, with all its faults, is one of the most completely expressive in history. (Joseph Conrad thought so well of it that he adopted it completely. When using it, never forget that godlike compliment.) We have a highly flexible grammar. Verbs can be placed anywhere in a sentence. Parenthetical thoughts are in the idiom. The rich sources of English have brought to it shades of meaning and choices between sounds which are unparalleled in other tongues . . .

. . . I find little fault with your punctuation, but it might help you to assume my view of it; namely, that punctuation is inflection in print. To me, "She loves me—" is heard differently from "She loves me . . ." and from "She loves me." There is a speaking difference between a colon and a semicolon and a coma . . .

. . . If you master this form, you will have such a feel for the

music of words that in your odes and your vers libre your work will be completely compelling, and in your prose your songful characters will speak, when their thoughts sing, with singing . . .

He said, apologetically, that there were only two things he could really tell me about story writing, and that one of those was not his own thought, but had been told to him by Will Jenkins. It was the basic device for generating a plot—

Start with a character, some one with certain strong, even compulsive personality traits. Put him in a situation which in some way negates a vital trait. Watch the character solve the problem.

I don't think I have ever written a successful story that emerged any other way.

The second piece of advice was his own, and this was: *see* everything you write about. Don't put a word down until you can see the whole scene for yourself—the room, or outdoors area, all the people, including the ones who do nothing; the colors and shapes; the weather; clothes, furnishings, everything. Then describe only those parts concerned in the action; or describe nothing, except what your characters do; they will be behaving in context, and the reader will be able to *rebuild* a complete scene from the pieces of the pattern you've given. It doesn't matter if this scene is different from yours; it will have the same meaning in his frame of reference that yours did for you.

This is one of the most astonishing pieces of instruction on record—simply because I have never heard it anywhere else. It seems so *obvious*—once you know it.

He wrote me the letter with the first quote I used here, about the nature of beauty; it was, in context, concerned with the ability to *create* beauty. And another letter picks up a theme he spent hours on: . . . *imagination is a thing like language skill or how to drink brandy—something which can be done well or badly, too much or not enough* . . .

It would be impossible to detail, one by one, the things he taught me, or the boosts he gave. I doubt that I remember all of them now. Most of it was so well absorbed that I no longer distinguish it as something learned from Ted. I have relayed what I recall most vividly, and will yet add an incident or two, primarily for two reasons. The first is that, in all seriousness, he learned something vital to him in the process, and I think it constituted a sort of turning point, starting up from the extreme of his depression. It was, I believe, the day I read "Bianca's Hands," in carbon (the ms. was then in England, submitted for the British *Argosy* short story contest). I did not—do not—like the story. Even more, I disliked his effort to compare it with Ray Bradbury's work. I had at that time read exactly one Bradbury story I liked. (I have since read several that were published before then, and many written afterwards, that I greatly admire. But this was 1947; most of Bradbury up till then was in the *Weird Tales* vein, and this is rarely to my taste.) In any case, I was somewhat brusque in my criticism. Ted, perhaps defensively, explained it had been written many years earlier, and that he had showed it to me for one section, just redone: several paragraphs of deliberately constructed poetry, highlighting an emotional crisis, but spelled out like prose, so that it did not appear to break into the narrative.

And it was in pointing this out (I had missed it, as he expected.) that he stopped, astonished, and said he had just realized how much he did know about how to write—that it was a skill, with him, not just a talent.

Whatever reinforcement the recognition needed came very soon afterwards, when the story won the first prize of $1000.

I never again heard the line about "something I do, not just something I am."

My other reason for leading you through my primer class as a writer is that I feel it reveals some vital aspects of Sturgeon's personality that I have not seen expounded in any of the several eulogies, prefaces, blurbs, and biographies I have read myself. Nor could I (I *tried!*) describe these facets myself, except by playback.

I might mention, here, that this article has been the most difficult piece of nonfiction I have ever done. How many false starts I made, or how many pages of unused copy will wind up in the circular file, I don't want to count. I started out to do a straightforward biographical article, with some, like, personal touches. (You know: "I was there, when . . .") And the more I tried, the more I realized I was, probably, uniquely unqualified to write anything balanced, objective, or factually informative about Ted Sturgeon. ("Probably," because there are others who know him, as person and writer, at least as well as I do; some of these have also been the beneficiaries of his astonishing capacity for advice, support, instruction, and encouragement of younger writers. But—) I believe my position is unique, because I am not only a friend, fan, colleague, and sometime protegé; I am also, in one sense, Ted's own invention.

The first Judith Merril story published was called, "That Only A Mother . . ." (I had done these pulp jobs under various by-lines.) It was on the strength of that one story, before it was published, that I got the editorial job at Bantam Books which led directly to my first anthology. Less directly, the same story had much to do with Doubleday's acceptance of my first novel, on the basis of a short and unfinished sample. It was Sturgeon who supplied the confidence, and ultimately, the challenge, to try to write the story; in between, he also supplied—by accident—the ideas for the central problem and the central character. All I did was write it; after that, it was Ted, again, who took it to his own agent; and it was in the agent's office that it was read by those people who later influenced jobs and contracts. All this was, to some extent, happenstance. But the author of the story was created by design—Sturgeon's design.

Sometime before I gathered up my courage to try the "serious story," I had already determined to be a freelance writer (of articles and "hack pulp stories"). For several reasons, irrelevant here, I wanted a pen-name. Among others, I asked Ted for ideas. He suggested my daughter, Merril's, first name. I balked; none of my reasons included the wish to change my Jewish name to anything so flamboyantly anglo-saxon-sounding.

Ted reacted with unwonted anger, and we parted in mutual irritation. Three days later, I had a letter, explaining things, with an enclosure—a sonnet called, "On The Birth of Judith Merril!"

Two lines of the poem had come to his mind, you see, while we were talking (in an ice-cream parlor!). From that point on, all my arguments were unreasonable and obstreperous. He went home to finish the story he was working on: an assigned job with a sure check at the end, which he needed badly. But the poem kept growing. Finally—

. . . *remembering something you had said about your Hebrew name, I went to the encyclopedia . . . It was right in there, reproduced also in Greek script and in Hebrew, and it means Jewess. It doesn't mean anything else but Jewess. . . .*

With this reassurance that I was bound to change my mind, he spent the next day on the sonnet. The letter goes on—

. . . *it is a Petrarchan sonnet, which means that its form is ex-*

743131

*tremely rigid and complex. The rhyme scheme is 1 2 2 1, 1 2 2 1,
3 4 5, 3 4 5. Notice that there is no rhymed couplet at the end, as
is found in Shakespearean and Wordsworthian sonnets. The idea is
presented in the octet (the first eight lines) and resolved in the sestet.
I'd rather build something like this than eat, which is demonstrable . . .*

(Well, what would *you* have done? Let a reasonable prejudice
stand in the way of a compulsive christening?) I had a name.

The man is full of self-contradictions: he is blind and perceptive;
rational and illogical; pedantic and lyrical; self-centered and warmly
outgiving. But he does each side of all the coins with *style*.

One more anecdote, about the final challenge that sent me home
to write my story:—

I was leaving the apartment he then shared with L. Jerome Stanton. It was just after the big news about "Bianca's Hands," and Ted
was effusing in all directions, including mine. He went to the door
with me, told me to go home and write a better one. I took it as mocking. He stopped himself in mid-explanation (of his sincerity) and
said, suddenly, pointing to the hall wall:

"Look!"

I did, and looked back questioningly.

"Look! Don't you see it?"

"See what?"

"The little green man, running up the wall . . . ?"

I shook my head, smiled faintly. "Nope."

"Keep looking. Look. See! Right there? He has a long green cap
sticking straight out, and he's taking tiny little steps . . ."

I didn't see any green man, and I said as much. "What's more, if
there was one, he'd be taking long draggy steps and his cap would
hang down, going up that wall . . ."

"There," he said triumphantly. "See? I write fantasy. You write
science fiction."

So I did—and came, eventually, to be asked to write about Sturgeon.
Well, as I said, I am prejudiced; and the things that seemed important to say left no room for statistics. These have, in any case, been
more than adequately compiled elsewhere. I have tried to portray
what I could of an unusual and admirable human being. But it's tough,
when you're writing about a man whose style you can't possibly match.

Bibliography of books by Theodore Sturgeon
Compiled by Sam Moskowitz

WITHOUT SORCERY, Prime Press, 355 pages, $3.00, 1948. Contains an introduction by Ray Bradbury and the following tales: The Ultimate Egoist, It, Poker Face, Shottle Bop, Artnan Process, Memorial, Ether Breather, Butyl and the Breather, Brat, Two Percent Inspiration, Cargo, Maturity and Microcosmic God.

THE DREAMING JEWELS, Greenberg: Publishers, New York, 217 pages, $2.50, 1950. A novel.

E PLURIBUS UNICORN, Abelard Press, New York, 275 pages, $2.75, 1953. Contains *Essay on Sturgeon* by Groff Conklin and the following tales: The Silken Swift, The Professor's Teddy-Bear, Bianca's Hands, Saucer of Loneliness, The World Well Lost, It Wasn't Syzgy, The Music, Scars, Fluffy, The Sex Opposite, Die, Maestro, Die!, Cellmate, and A Way of Thinking. An appendix of Science Fiction and Fantasy by Theodore Sturgeon in Anthologies (Up to 1953) is included. Original title of It Wasn't Syzgy was The Deadly Ratio.

MORE THAN HUMAN, Farrar, Straus & Young, New York, 233 pages, $2.00, 1953. Contains The Fabulous Idiot, Baby is Three and Morality as a unified whole.

A WAY HOME, selected and with an introduction by Groff Conklin, Funk and Wagnalls, 333 pages, $3.50, 1955. Contains Unite and Conquer, Special Aptitude, Mewhu's Jet, Hurricane Trio, ". . . And My Fear is Great . . .", Minority Report, The Hurkle is a Happy Beast, Thunder and Roses, Bulkhead, Tiny and the Monster, A Way Home. Bulkhead originally published as Who?; Special Aptitude as The Last Laugh.

CAVIAR, Ballantine Books, New York, $2.00, 168 pages, 1955. Contains Bright Segment, Microcosmic God, Ghost of a Chance (The Green-Eyed Monster), Prodigy, Medusa, Blabbermouth, Shadow, Shadow on the Wall and Twink.

I, LIBERTINE, published under the pen name of Frederick R. Ewing, Ballantine Books, New York, paperback edition 35¢, 151 pages, 1956.

A TOUCH OF STRANGE, Doubleday, New York, 262 pages, $2.95, 1958. Contains The Pod in the Barrier, A Crime for Llewellyn, The Touch of Your Hand, Affair with a Green Monkey, Mr. Costello, Hero; The Girl Had Guts, The Other Celia, It Opens the Sky, A Touch of Strange.

THE COSMIC RAPE, Dell, New York, 160 pages, 35¢, 1958. Short novel.

ALIENS 4, Avon Publications, New York, 224 pages, 35¢, 1959. Contains Killdozer!, Cactus Dance, The Comedian's Children and The [Widget], The [Wadget], and Boff.

BEYOND, Avon Book Division, The Hearst Corp., New York, 157 pages, 35¢, 1960. Contains Need, Abreaction, Nightmare Island, Largo, The Bones and Like Young.

VENUS PLUS X, Pyramid Books, 160 pages, 35¢, 1960. A novel.

VOYAGE TO THE BOTTOM OF THE SEA, Pyramid Books, New York, 159 pages, 35¢, 1961. An adaptation from motion picture.

SOME OF YOUR BLOOD, Ballantine Books, New York, 143 pages, 35¢, 1961. A novel.

STURGEON IN ORBIT, Pyramid Books, New York, 159 pages, 1964, 40¢. Contains, Introduction by Theodore Sturgeon and the following tales: Extrapolation, The Wages of Synergy, Make Room for Me, The Heart, and The Incubi of Parallel X.

THE JOYOUS INVASIONS, Victor Gollancz Ltd., London, 208 pages, 1965, 25s. Contains To Marry Medusa, The Comedian's Children and The [Widget], the [Wadget], and Boff.

STARSHINE, Pyramid Books, New York, 174 pages, 1966, 60¢. Contains "Derm Fool," The Haunt, Artnan Process, The World Well Lost, The Pod and the Barrier, and How to Kill Aunty.

STURGEON IS ALIVE AND WELL, G. P. Putnam's Sons, New York, 221 pages, 1971, $4.95. Contains Foreword by Theodore Sturgeon and the following tales: To Here and the Easel, Slow Sculpture, It's You!, Take Care of Joey, Crate, The Girl Who Knew What They Meant, Jorry's Gap, It Was Nothing—Really!, Brownshoes, Uncle Fremmis, The Patterns of Dorne, and Suicide.

THE WORLDS OF THEODORE STURGEON, Ace Books, New York, 286 pages, 95¢. Contains From Plynck to Planck, An editorial-introduction by Theodore Sturgeon, plus the following tales: The Skills of Xanadu, There Is No Defense, The Perfect Host, The Graveyard Reader, The Other Man, The Sky Was Full of Ships, Shottle Bop, Maturity, and Memorial.

STURGEON'S WEST (With Don Ward), Doubleday, New York, 186 pages, 1973, $5.95. Contains Ted Sturgeon's Western Adventure (introduction) by Don Ward and the following tales: Well Spiced, Scars, Cactus Dance, The Waiting Thing Inside (with Don Ward), The Man Who Figured Everything (with Don Ward), Ride in, Ride Out (with Don Ward) and The Sheriff of Chayute.

Ray Bradbury

To the Chicago Abyss

by RAY BRADBURY

Under a pale April sky in a faint wind that blew out of a memory
of winter, the old man shuffled into the almost empty park at noon.
His slow feet were bandaged with nicotine-stained swathes, his hair
was wild, long, and grey as was his beard which enclosed a mouth
which seemed always atremble with revelation.

Now he gazed back as if he had lost so many things he could not
begin to guess there in the tumbled ruin, the toothless skyline of the
city. Finding nothing he shuffled on until he found a bench where sat
a woman alone. Examining her, he nodded and sat to the far end of
the bench and did not look at her again.

He remained, eyes shut, mouth working, for three minutes, head
moving as if his nose were printing a single word on the air. Once
written, he opened his mouth to pronounce it in a clear, fine voice:

"Coffee."

The woman gasped and stiffened.

The old man's gnarled fingers tumbled in pantomime on his unseen lap.

"Twist the key! Bright red, yellow-letter can! Compressed air.
Hisss! Vacuum pack. Ssst! Like a snake!"

The woman snapped her head about as if slapped to stare in dreadful fascination at the old man's moving tongue.

"The scent, the odor, the smell. Rich, dark, wonderous Brazilian
beans, fresh ground!"

Leaping up, reeling as if gunshot, the woman tottered.

The old man flicked his eyes wide. "No! I—"

But she was running, gone.

The old man sighed and walked on through the park until he

reached a bench where sat a young man completely involved with
wrapping dried grass in a small square of thin tissue paper. His thin
fingers shaped the grass tenderly, in an almost holy ritual, trembling
as he rolled the tube, put it to his mouth, and, hypnotically, lit it. He
leant back, squinting deliciously, communing with the strange rank
air in his mouth and lungs. The old man watched the smoke blow
away on the noon wind and said:

"Chesterfields."

The young man gripped his knees, tight.

"Raleighs," said the old man. "Lucky Strikes."

The young man stared at him.

"Kent. Kools. Marlboro," said the old man, not looking at him.
"Those were the names. White, red, amber packs grass-green, sky-
blue, pure gold with the red slick small ribbon that ran around the
top that you pulled to zip away the crinkly cellophane, and the blue
government tax-stamp—"

"Shut up," said the young man.

"Buy them in drug-stores, fountains, subways—"

"Shut up!"

"Gently," said the old man. "It's just, that smoke of yours made
me think—"

"Don't think!" The young man jerked so violently his home-made
cigarette fell in chaff to his lap. "Now look what you made me do!"

"I'm sorry. It was such a nice friendly day—"

"I'm no friend!"

"We're all friends now, or why live?"

"Friends?" the young man snorted, aimlessly plucking at the
shredded grass and paper. "Maybe there were 'friends' back in 1970,
but now—"

"1970. You must have been a baby then. They still had Butter-
fingers then in bright yellow wrappers. Baby Ruths. Clark Bars in
orange paper. Milky Ways . . . swallow a universe of stars, comets,
meteors. Nice—"

"It was never nice." The young man stood suddenly. "What's
wrong with you?"

"I remember limes, and lemons, that's what's wrong with me. Do
you remember oranges?"

"Damn rights. Oranges, hell. You calling me a liar? You want me to feel bad? You nuts? Don't you know the law? You know I could turn you in, you?"

"I know, I know," said the old man, shrugging. "The weather fooled me. It made me want to compare—"

"Compare rumors, that's what they'd say, the Police, the Special Cops, they'd say it, rumors, you trouble-making bastard, you—"

He seized the old man's lapels which ripped so he had to grab another handful, yelling down into his face.

"Why don't I just blast the living Jesus out of you. I ain't hurt no one in so long, I—"

He shoved the old man. Which gave him the idea to pummel and when he pummeled he began to punch and punching made it easy to strike and soon he rained blows upon the old man who stood like one caught in thunder and down-poured storm, using only his fingers to ward off the blows that fleshed his cheeks, shoulders, his brow, his chin, as the young man shrieked cigarettes, moaned candies, yelled smokes, cried sweets until the old man fell to be kick-rolled and shivering. The young man stopped and began to cry. At the sound, the old man, cuddled, clenched into his pain, took his fingers away from his broken mouth and opened his eyes to gaze with astonishment at his assailant. The young man wept.

"Please . . ." begged the old man.

The young man wept louder, tears falling from his eyes.

"Don't cry," said the old man. "We won't be hungry forever. We'll rebuild the cities. Listen, I didn't mean for you to cry, only to think where are we going, what are we doing, what've we done? You weren't hitting me. You meant to hit something else, but I was handy. Look, I'm sitting up. I'm okay."

The young man stopped crying and blinked down at the old man who forced a bloody smile.

"You . . . you can't go around," said the young man, "making people unhappy. I'll find someone to fix you!"

"Wait!" The old man struggled to his knees. "No!"

But the young man ran wildly off out of the park, yelling.

Crouched alone, the old man felt his bones, found one of his teeth lying red amongst the strewn gravel, handled it sadly.

"Fool," said a voice.

The old man glanced over and up.

A lean man of some forty years stood leaning against a tree nearby, a look of pale weariness and curiosity on his long face.

"Fool," he said again.

The old man gasped. "You were there, all the time, and did *nothing?*"

"What, fight one fool to save another? No." The stranger helped him up and brushed him off. "I do my fighting where it pays. Come on. You're going home with me."

The old man gasped again. "Why?"

"That boy'll be back with the police any second. I don't want you stolen away, you're a very precious commodity. I've heard of you, looked for you for days now. Good Grief, and when I find you you're up to your famous tricks. What did you say to the boy made him mad?"

"I said about oranges and lemons, candy, cigarettes. I was just getting ready to recollect in detail wind-up toys, briar-pipes and back-scratchers, when he dropped the sky on me."

"I almost don't blame him. Half of me wants to hit you, itself. Come on, double-time. There's a siren, quick!"

And they went swiftly, another way, out of the park.

He drank the home-made wine because it was easiest. The food must wait until his hunger overcame the pain in his broken mouth. He sipped, nodding.

"Good, many thanks, good."

The stranger who had walked him swiftly out of the park sat across from him at the flimsy dining room table as the stranger's wife placed broken and mended plates on the worn cloth.

"The beating," said the husband, at last. "How did it happen?"

At this, the wife almost dropped a plate.

"Relax," said the husband. "No one followed us. Go ahead, old man, tell us, why do you behave like a saint panting after martyrdom? You're famous, you know. Everyone's heard about you. Many would like to meet you. Myself, first, I want to know what makes you tick. Well?"

But the old man was only entranced with the vegetables on the chipped plate before him. Twenty-six, no, twenty-eight peas! He counted the impossible sum! He bent to the incredible vegetables like a man praying over his quietest beads. Twenty-eight glorious green peas, plus a few graphs of half-raw spaghetti announcing that today business was fair. But under the line of pasta, the cracked line of the plate showed where business for years now was more than terrible. The old man hovered counting above the food like a great and inexplicable buzzard, crazily fallen and roosting in this cold apartment, watched by his samaritan hosts until at last he said:

"These twenty-eight peas remind me, of a film I saw as a child. A comedian—do you know the word?—a funny man met a lunatic in a midnight house in this film and—"

The husband and wife laughed quietly.

"No, that's not the joke yet, sorry," the old man apologized. "The lunatic sat the comedian down to an empty table, no knives, no forks, no food. 'Dinner is served!' he cried. Afraid of murder, the comedian fell in with the make believe. 'Great!' he cried, pretending to chew steak, vegetables, dessert. He bit nothings. 'Fine!' he swallowed air. 'Wonderful!' Eh . . . you may laugh now."

But the husband and wife, grown still, only looked at their sparsely strewn plates.

The old man shook his head and went on. "The comedian, thinking to impress the mad-man, exclaimed, 'And these spiced brandy peaches! Superb!' 'Peaches?' screamed the madman, drawing a gun. 'I served no peaches! You must be insane!' And shot the comedian in the behind!"

The old man, in the silence which ensued, picked up the first pea and weighed its lovely bulk upon his bent tin fork. He was about to put it in his mouth when—

There was a sharp rap on the door.

"Special police!" a voice cried.

Silent but trembling, the wife hid the extra plate.

The husband rose calmly to lead the old man to a wall where a panel hissed open and he stepped in and the panel hissed shut and he stood in darkness hidden away as, beyond, unseen, the apartment door opened. Voices murmured excitedly. The old man could imagine the Special Policeman in his midnight blue uniform, with drawn gun, entering to see only the flimsy furniture, the bare walls, the echoing linoleum floor, the glassless, cardboarded-over windows, this thin and oily film of civilization left on an empty shore when the storm tide of war went away.

"I'm looking for an old man," said the tired voice of authority beyond the wall. Strange, thought the old man, even the Law sounds tired now. "Patched clothes—" But, thought the old man, I thought everyone's clothes were patched! "Dirty. About eighty years old . . ." but isn't everyone dirty, everyone old? the old man cried out, to himself. "If you turn him in, there's a week's rations as reward," said the police voice. "Plus ten cans of vegetables, five cans of soup, bonus."

Real tin cans with bright printed labels, thought the old man. The cans flashed like meteors rushing by in the dark over his eyelids. What a fine reward! Not TEN THOUSAND DOLLARS, not TWENTY THOUSAND DOLLARS, no, no, but . . . five incredible cans of real not imitation soup, and ten, count them, ten brilliant circus-colored cans of exotic vegetables like string beans and sun-yellow corn! Think of it! *Think!*

There was a long silence in which the old man almost thought he heard faint murmurs of stomachs turning uneasily, slumbered but dreaming of dinners much finer than the hairballs of old illusion gone nightmare and politics gone sour in the long twilight since A.D., Annihilation Day.

"Soup. Vegetables," said the police voice, a final time. "Fifteen solid-pack cans!"

The door slammed.

The boots stomped away through the ramshackle tenement pounding coffin lid doors to stir other Lazarus souls alive to cry aloud of bright tins and real soups. The poundings faded. There was a last banging slam.

And at last the hidden panel whispered up. The husband and wife did not look at him as he stepped out. He knew why and wanted to touch their elbows.

"Even I," he said gently. "Even *I* was tempted to turn myself in, to claim the reward, to eat the soup . . ."

Still they would not look at him.

"Why," he asked. "Why didn't you hand me over? Why?"

The husband, as if suddenly remembering, nodded to his wife. She went to the door, hesitated, her husband nodded again, impatiently, and she went out, noiseless as a puff of cobweb. They heard her rustling along the hall, scratching softly at doors, which opened to gasps and murmurs.

"What's she up to? What are *you* up to?" asked the old man.

"You'll find out. Sit. Finish your dinner," said the husband. "Tell me why you're such a fool you make us fools who seek you out and bring you here."

"Why am I such a fool?" The old man sat. The old man munched slowly, taking peas one at a time from the plate which had been returned to him. "Yes, I am a fool. How did I start my foolishness? Years ago I looked at the ruined world, the dictatorships, the desiccated states and nations, and said, "What can I do? Me, a weak old man, what? Rebuild a devastation? Ha! But lying half asleep one night an old phonograph record played in my head. Two sisters named Duncan sang out of my childhood a song called REMEMBERING. 'Remembering, is all I do, dear, so try and remember, too.' I sang the song and it wasn't a song but a way of life. What did I have to offer a world that was forgetting? My memory! How could this help? By offering a standard of comparison. By telling the young *what once was,* by considering our losses. I found the more I remembered, the more I *could* remember! Depending on who I sat down with I remembered imitation flowers, dial telephones, refrigerators, kazoos (you ever *play* a kazoo?!), thimbles, bicycle clips, not bicycles, no, but bicycle *clips!* isn't that wild and strange? Anti-macassars. Do you know them? Never mind. Once a man asked me to remember just the dashboard dials on a Cadillac. I remembered. I told him in detail. He listened. He cried great tears down his face. Happy tears? or sad? I can't say. I only remember. Not literature, no, I never had a head for plays or poems, they slip away, they die. All I am, really, is a trashheap of the mediocre, the third-best hand-me-down useless and chromed-over slush and junk of a race-track civilization that ran 'last' over a precipice. So all I offer really is scintillant junk, the clamored-after chronometers and absurd machineries of a neverending river of robots and robot-mad owners. Yet, one way or another, civilization *must* get back on the road. Those who can offer fine butterfly poetry, let them remember, let them offer. Those who can weave and build butterfly *nets,* let them weave, let them build. My gift is smaller than both, and perhaps contemptible in the long hoist, climb, jump toward the old and amiably silly peak. But I *must* dream myself worthy. For the things, silly or not, that people remember are the things they will search for again. I will, then, ulcerate their half-dead desires with vinegar-gnat memory. Then perhaps they'll rattle bang the Big Clock together again, which is the city, the state, and then the World. Let one man want wine, another lounge chairs, a third a batwing glider to soar the March winds on and build bigger electro-pterodactyls to scour even greater winds, with even greater peoples. Someone wants moron Christmas trees and some wise man goes to cut them. Pack this all together, wheel in want, want in wheel, and I'm just there to oil them, but oil them I do. Ho, once I would have raved, 'only the best is best, only quality is true!' But roses grow from blood manure. Mediocre must be, so most-excellent can bloom. So I shall be the *best* mediocre there is and fight all who say slide under, sink back, dust-wallow, let brambles scurry over your living grave. I shall protest the roving apeman tribes, the sheep-people munching the far fields prayed on by the feudal land-baron wolves who rarefy themselves in the few skyscraper summits and horde unremembered foods. And these villains I will kill with canopener and corkscrew. I shall run them down with ghosts of Buick, Kissel-Kar, and Moon, thrash them with licorice whips until they cry for some sort of unqualified mercy. Can I *do* all this? One can only try."

The old man rummaged the last pea, with the last words, in his mouth, while his samaritan host simply looked at him with gently amazed eyes, and far off up through the house people moved, doors tapped open and shut, and there was a gathering outside the door of this apartment where now the husband said:

"And *you* asked why we didn't turn you in? Do you hear that out there?"

"It sounds like everyone in the apartment house—"

"Everyone. Old man, old fool, do you remember—motion picture houses, or better, drive-in movies?"

The old man smiled. "Do *you?*"

"Almost. Look, listen, today, now, if you're going to be a fool, if you want to run risks, do it in the aggregate, in one fell blow. Why waste your breath on one, or two, or even three if—"

The husband opened the door and nodded outside. Silently, one at a time, and in couples, the people of the house entered. Entered this room as if entering a synagogue or church or the kind of church known as a movie or the kind of movie known as a drive-in, and the hour was growing late in the day, with the sun going down the sky, and soon in the early evening hours, in the dark, the room would be dim and in the one light the voice of the old man would speak and these would listen and hold hands and it would be like the old days with the balconies and the dark, or the cars and the dark, and just the memory, the words, of popcorn, and the words for the gum and the sweet drinks and candy, but the words, anyway, the words . . .

And while the people were coming in and settling on the floor, and the old man watched them, incredulous that he had summoned them here without knowing, the husband said:

"Isn't this better than taking a chance in the open?"

"Yes. Strange. I hate pain. I hate being hit and chased. But my tongue moves. I must hear what it has to say. But this is better."

"Good." The husband pressed a red ticket into his palm. "When this is all over, an hour from now, here is a ticket from a friend of mine in Transportation. One train crosses the country each week. Each week I get a ticket for some idiot I want to help. This week, it's you."

The old man read the destination on the folded red paper:

"CHICAGO ABYSS," and added, "Is the Abyss still there?"

"This time next year Lake Michigan may break through the last crust and make a new lake in the pit where the city once was. There's life of sorts around the crater rim, and a branch train goes west once a month. Once you leave here, keep moving, forget you met or know us. I'll give you a small list of people like ourselves. A long time from now, look them up, out in the wilderness. But, for God's sake, in the open, alone, for a year, declare a moratorium. Keep your wonderful mouth shut. And here—" The husband gave him a yellow card. "A dentist I know. Tell him to make you a new set of teeth that will only open at meal times."

A few people, hearing, laughed, and the old man laughed quietly and the people were in now, dozens of them, and the day was late, and the husband and wife shut the door and stood by it and turned and waited for this last special time when the old man might open his mouth.

The old man stood up.

His audience grew very still.

The train came, rusty and loud at midnight, into a suddenly snow-filled station. Under a cruel dusting of white, the ill-washed people crowded into and through the ancient chair cars mashing the old man along the corridor and into an empty compartment that had once been a lavatory. Soon the floor was a solid mass of bed-roll on which sixteen people twisted and turned in darkness, fighting their way into sleep.

The train rushed forth to white emptiness.

The old man thinking: "quiet, shut up, no, don't speak, nothing, no, stay still, think! careful! cease!" found himself now swayed, joggled, hurled this way and that as he half-crouched against a wall. He and just one other were upright in this monster room of dreadful sleep. A few feet away, similarly shoved against the wall, sat an eight year old boy with a drawn sick paleness escaping from his cheeks. Full awake, eyes bright, he seemed to watch, he *did* watch, the old man's mouth. The boy gazed because he must. The train hooted, roared, swayed, yelled, and ran.

Half an hour passed in a thunderous grinding passage by night under the snow-hidden moon, and the old man's mouth was tight-nailed shut. Another hour, and still boned shut. Another hour, and the muscles around his cheeks began to slacken. Another, and his lips parted to whet themselves. The boy stayed awake. The boy saw. The boy waited. Immense sifts of silence came down the night air outside, tunneled by avalanche train. The travelers, very deep in invoiced terror, numbed by flight, slept each separate, but the boy did not take his eyes away and at last the old man leaned forward, softly.

"Sh. Boy. Your name?"

"Joseph."

The train swayed and groaned in its sleep, a monster floundering through timeless dark toward a morn that could not be imagined.

"Joseph . . ." The old man savored the word, bent forward, his eyes gentle and shining. His face filled with pale beauty. His eyes widened until they seemed blind. He gazed at a distant and hidden thing. He cleared his throat ever so softly. "Ah . . ."

The train roared round a curve. The people rocked in their snowing sleep.

"Well, Joseph," whispered the old man. He lifted his fingers softly in the air. "Once upon a time . . ."

Ray Bradbury

by WILLIAM F. NOLAN

I met Ray Bradbury when his reputation was being launched in July of 1950, two months after *The Martian Chronicles* had been published. He was living in Venice, California, and his first daughter, Susan, was less than nine months old. Now Susan is a married woman of 24, with three younger sisters, and Ray is one of the most famous and popular contemporary writers in America, having gained an international reputation with the *Chronicles* (which has sold more than two million copies) and the many books which followed. He currently owns a warmly-furnished, rambling upstairs-downstairs house in Cheviot Hills, large enough for his family and their two automobiles, one of which is an E Type Jaguar, prized by his wife Maggie, who drives it with élan. Bradbury still refuses to learn to handle a car, just as he steadfastly refuses to board a jet—and these are perhaps his last "holdouts" against the atomic age in which he lives. In 1955, when the Bradbury clan was beset with mumps, Ray allowed his girls to rent a TV set. Once the Monster was installed the battle was lost; the set was soon purchased. For years Ray even fought to keep telephones out of his house, and now periodically changes his phone number to offset a host of unwanted calls which cut into his writing time.

"His has consistently been the voice of the poet raised against the mechanization of mankind," a critic once declared, and this fear of engulfment has often been echoed in his stories. Bradbury has never mistrusted machines, yet he has always mistrusted the men who use them.

"The machines themselves are empty gloves," he has often stated. "And the hand that fills them is always the hand of man. This hand

can be good or evil." Bradbury elaborates: "Today we stand on the
rim of Space, and man, in his immense tidal motion, is about to flow
out toward far new worlds . . . but he must conquer the seed of his
own self-destruction. Man is half-idealist, half-destroyer, and the real
and terrible fear is that he can still destroy himself before reaching
for the stars. I see man's self-destructive half, the blind spider fiddling
in the venomous dark, dreaming mushroom-cloud dreams. Death
solves all, it whispers, shaking a handful of atoms like a necklace of
dark beads . . . We are now in the greatest age in history, and we will
soon be capable of going off into space on a tremendous voyage of
survival. Nothing must be allowed to stop this voyage, our last great
wilderness trek."

These are the words of a space age moralist, and Bradbury has
often demonstrated his deep concern for mankind's future in the
stories he has written. Aldous Huxley called him "one of the most
visionary men now writing in any field," and an English reviewer
added to this image: "He sees man standing like Faustus, god-like
power in his grasp, but aware of his own mortal frailty."

In person, Ray is anything but a sombre moralist; he is, in fact, disarmingly cheerful, with a lively sense of humor, often wild, sometimes
ribald, an ebullient fast-talking fellow whose enthusiasms tend to
overwhelm the meek. At 53, he seems much younger, even with his
heavy glasses, and his personality strikes sparks in any room. The
warmth he generates is contagious and always welcome. But he is
also very sensitive, is easily hurt, and is quick to anger if he feels that
he has been unjustly dealt with in a situation.

A prime example of Bradbury the Outraged in action was his suit
against the famed TV show, "Playhouse 90" which presented a
90-minute drama, *A Sound of Different Drummers,* dealing with a
time in the future when censorship ruled and the "Bookmen" were
called out to burn the houses of those who defied their society by
secreting books. Bradbury exploded when he saw this show, called
his lawyer and immediately sued "Playhouse 90" and the network for
plagiarism. This show, he declared, was simply a re-written version
of his own *Fahrenheit 451.* After a pitched legal battle, Ray eventually
achieved victory in the higher courts and received a handsome settlement. "Most of us would never *dream* of trying to sue that outfit,"
admitted one Hollywood writer, "but Bradbury not only sued, he
won!"

In *New Maps of Hell,* Kingsley Amis dubbed Bradbury "the Louis Armstrong of science fiction," and explained this by saying: "He is the one practitioner well known by name to those who know nothing whatever about his field." This is certainly true. No other sf writer has reached so vast an audience. His work has appeared in over a thousand anthologies.

It is Bradbury's greatest pride that his fiction is now being selected regularly for high school and college texts such as *New Horizons Through Reading and Literature* and *Modern English Readings.* To date, some textbooks have reprinted his stories, and on the contents page his name stands next to Poe, Thurber, Hemingway, Steinbeck and Saroyan.

Ray has soared far beyond the field which nurtured him, and it is no longer correct to attach the label "science fiction" to his work. Of his 300 published stories, only 100 could legitimately be counted in the sf category; another 50 are pure fantasy and the rest are "straight" stories set in Ireland or Illinois or Mexico. Of course, these include his crime yarns as well as several offbeat items which all but defy classification.

Bradbury has never claimed to be a science fiction writer in the strict sense of the term, and agrees with Isaac Asimov who stated: "In my opinion, Ray does not write science fiction; he is a writer of *social* fiction." And, as *Time* magazine put it: "Bradbury's elf of fantasy is obviously only one element in a larger talent that includes passion, irony and wisdom."

In October of 1950, in discussing *The Martian Chronicles,* Bradbury declared: "I've never really called myself a sf writer, *other* people have. In fact, I tried to get Doubleday to take the sf emblem off the book."

However, despite such honest declarations, Ray has always admired and defended the field of science fiction, and feels that it affords a writer the widest possible range in which to deliver serious social commentary. In this respect, Bradbury has utilized the field as a "sounding board," and as a kind of "stage setting" for his parables of the future.

Writing in *The Nation,* regarding science fiction, he stated: "There are few literary fields, it seems to me, that deal so strikingly with themes that vitally concern us all today. There are few more exciting genres, there are none fresher or so full of continually renewed and renewable concepts. It is the field of *ideas,* where you may set up and knock down your own political and religious states. There are no boundaries, no taboos or restrictions to hold back the science fiction writer. He can function as a moralist of the space age, and show us the dangers and the risks, and possibly help us avoid costly mistakes when we reach new worlds . . ."

Bradbury has been attacked for the improper use of science in some of his books.

Ray's reply to such criticism: "It is all too easy for an emotionalist to go astray in the eyes of the scientific, and surely my work could never serve as a handbook for mathematicians. Somehow, though, I am compensated by allowing myself to believe that while the scientific expert can tell you the exact size, location, pulse, musculature and color of the heart, we emotionalists can find and touch it quicker."

Emotion has always been the key to Bradbury's work. He writes out of the primary emotions: love, joy, hate, fear, anger. "Find out what excites and delights you, or what angers you most, then get it down on paper," he advises the neophyte writer. "After all, it is your individuality that you want to isolate. Work from the subconscious; store up images, impressions, data—then dip into this 'well of self' for your stories. The characters you choose will be parts of yourself. I am all the people in all my books. They are mirror reflections, three times or a dozen times removed and reversed from myself. So, the trick is: feed the subconscious, fill the well."

Who is the *real* Ray Bradbury? What kind of man has been formed, and from what background, in his 53 years of life?

"I was born on a Sunday afternoon in August," says Ray, "while my father and brother were attending a baseball game on the other side of town."

The town was Waukegan, Illinois; the year was 1920—and Mrs. Bradbury was having her third child. Ray's brother, Leonard, four years his senior, would grow up with him. But Leonard's twin brother, Samuel, had died at the age of two. In 1926, a sister was born—but tiny Elizabeth Bradbury was also destined to die of pneumonia in 1927, and thus Ray Douglas Bradbury was the last child Esther Moberg Bradbury would raise.

"My father, Leonard Spaulding Bradbury, was a power lineman for Public Service," says Ray. "He came from a family of newspaper editors and printers. My grandfather and great grandfather formed

Bradbury & Sons, and published two northern Illinois newspapers at the turn of the century, so you might say that publishing and writing were in my blood. However, as a boy, I felt a much closer kinship to an ancestor of mine, Mary Bradbury, who was tried as a witch in Salem during the seventeenth century."

Indeed, young Ray's hyper-active imagination was whetted by his Aunt Neva, who read to him from the wonderous books of L. Frank Baum when he was six as he mentally followed the yellow brick road to the enchanting land of Oz. His mother read Poe to him each evening by candlelight, and he was soon old enough to discover Tarzan of the Apes and John Carter of Mars as he delightedly perused his Uncle Bion's collection of Edgar Rice Burroughs at nine.

"I loved Tarzan," says Ray, "and began cutting out the Burroughs comic strips and pasting them in a huge scrapbook. I had started collecting Buck Rogers comics in 1929, continuing this through '37. I also saved Flash Gordon panels, and Prince Valiant was another favorite. I still have all these beautifully-drawn comic adventures down in the cellar carefully packed away in an old trunk. When I want to recapture that era I just tip back the lid."

Magic entered his life in 1931, when the eleven-year-old boy attended a local stage show which featured Blackstone, the famed magician. Ray was invited onstage, where he was duly presented with a live rabbit from the conjurer's tall silk hat. Overwhelmed with such wizardry, young Bradbury announced to his parents that he would soon become the world's greatest magician.

"Our house became a jumble of dice cabinets and ghost boxes," he recalls. "I sent away to Chicago for my magic kit, put on a paper moustache and made a top hat out of cardboard. Then I'd perform at Oddfellows' Halls and American Legion meetings—and, at home, I talked Dad into assisting me in a mental telepathy routine put on for captive relatives. They accepted quietly rather than have me play the violin, my *other* talent!"

"Lon Chaney was my idol," says Ray. "I tried to imitate his genius for disguise, dressing as a bat with black-velvet wings which I cut from my grandmother's opera cape, or making use of jute sacking and uncorded rope in turning myself into a gorilla." Bradbury gleefully recalls hanging in night trees "to scare hell out of my little classmates," while drawings of skeletons and cobwebbed castles filled his school notebooks.

The fear of death has been a recurrent theme in Bradbury's work, and this fear took root in Ray's childhood. He admits: "A good part of my young life was spent anticipating a merciless doom that might descend the day before some personal triumph or happiness was fulfilled." When he was seven, playing on the shore of Lake Michigan, he had seen his cousin almost drown (an experience which he later transferred into fictional terms in *The Lake*). And when his brother failed to return until very late one evening from the dark ravine near their home, Ray was sure that Death had claimed him. (This incident was vividly recreated in *The Night*.)

In 1932 the Bradburys moved to Arizona, and the boy fell under the influence of a neighbor's collection of pulp science fiction magazines. Here were *Amazing Stories* and *Wonder Stories* with their lurid covers and incredible prose. Here were giant ants, bug-eyed monsters, scaly Things from another world and daring, raygun-wielding spacemen who calmly rescued terrified maidens from alien clutches.

"Of course I was hooked," admits Ray. "I was creating my own fantasies on brown rolls of butcher paper by then, writing in pencil—until, on Christmas, 1932, I was given a toy-dial typewriter. I then switched over to this machine, which typed only capitals, and began writing sequels to the stories I'd read. It was then I determined to become a writer because I couldn't imagine a more wonderful life. In fact, I *still* can't!"

Bradbury's amateur stage appearances in Illinois as a purveyor of magic had revealed an aptitude for acting, and although he'd now given up the idea of becoming a professional magician he was fascinated by radio performers. He began to hang around the local Arizona station, KGAR, in the hope that he would be hired, bragging to school chums that they'd soon be hearing his voice on their radios.

"Eventually KGAR's resistance crumbled," says Ray, "and I was assigned the job of reading the comic section over the air to the kids each Saturday night." The boy put in four months at this job, and attempted to change his voice for each character from Tailspin Tommy to Jiggs and Maggie. ("I even assumed a thick German accent for the Katzenjammer Kids.") After the comic-reading stint had ended Bradbury became sound-effects man and bit player on other programs, frustrated only because he could not write the scripts for each show.

In 1934, when Ray was still thirteen, he left his budding radio career and moved with his family to California. Upon discovering that the girl next door owned "an honest-to-god typewriter," Ray began dictating stories to her at a furious rate.

Attending Los Angeles High, Bradbury began to see his budding literary efforts printed in the school paper, *The Blue & White Daily,* and two of his poems were published in student pamphlets. He also wrote several plays in which, as he says, "I made darn sure I got juicy lead roles. These parts were always tailor-made for a five foot, ten inch, slightly fat, bespectacled youth!"

Under Jennet Johnson, he took a class in the short story, and began to read the work of Hemingway and Thomas Wolfe, both of whom were to prove strong influences on his style. By skipping lunch twice a week for several months he managed to save enough to buy his first genuine typewriter at seventeen and began shooting off stories to *The Saturday Evening Post* and *Harper's.* They shot them right back.

In October of 1937, Bradbury attended his first meeting of the Los Angeles Science Fiction League, and this proved to be a decisive step toward his professional writing career. Here were other young men and women infected with the same fantasy virus; here was understanding and instant social acceptance. T. Bruce Yerke, who had invited Ray to the club, described him as "a wild-haired, enthusiastic individual who endeared himself to all of us, though he was often the recipient of assaults with trays and hammers by infuriated victims of his endless pranks."

Forrest Ackerman, who was one of the club's pioneer members, characterizes the teen-age Bradbury as "well-nigh impossible . . . a noisy kid with a broad sense of humor, who did endless imitations of Adolf Hitler, W. C. Fields and FDR . . . The callouses on the knees of us oldtimers in the club come from kneeling every night and saying 'Thank God we didn't drown him!' "

It was Ackerman who encouraged Ray to submit a short sf story, *Hollerbochen's Dilemma,* for the club's mimeo-magazine, *Imagination.* This appeared in the January, 1938, issue and offered no hint whatever of Bradbury's original talent. Nor did the majority of the other short pieces which Ray feverishly penned for a handful of local fanzines (those earnestly-edited amateur publications which a columnist for the *New Republic* astutely termed "a peculiar blend of *Screen Romances* and *Partisan Review*").

"During this period I began haunting the doorsteps of the local professionals, many of whom belonged to the club," says Ray. "I was desperate to learn the secrets of the pros, and would pop up with a new story nearly every week which I passed around for criticism and advice from Hank Kuttner to Leigh Brackett to Ed Hamilton to Bob Heinlein to Ross Rocklynne to Jack Williamson to Henry Hasse, all of whom were incredibly kind and patient with me and with these dreadful early efforts. In fact, the above-named authors grew lean and rangy from countless flights through the rear exits of walk-up apartments when Bradbury would suddenly appear at the front door with a new manuscript in his teeth."

Ray graduated from L.A. High in June of 1938, and immediately took a job hawking newspapers from the corner of Olympic and Norton, which netted him a bare $10 a week. Out of this meagre sum, and what he could winnow out of his parents, he rented an empty room in a local office building, installed a table and chair, and carted in his typewriter.

"I spent the hours between the morning and evening editions pounding away at that machine," he says. "I also kept my hand in acting, having joined Loraine Day's Little Theatre group. But the writing took up most of my time; I just filled the pages—with descriptions, images, bits of narrative, character sketches, impressions, dialogue and stories. I was getting rid of a lot of dead weight, learning as I went, trying to clear the deck for professional work."

By the summer of 1939 as an outlet for some of this material, Bradbury launched his own fanzine, *Futuria Fantasia*. Here, under his own name and four pseudonyms (Guy Amory, Ron Reynolds, Anthony Corvais and Doug Rogers), he filled the pages with articles, poetry, satires and half a dozen short stories. Heinlein, Kuttner, Rocklynne, Hannes Bok, Ackerman, Yerke, Hasse, and Damon Knight also contributed brief items to "FuFa," but despite editor Bradbury's plea for financial aid to continue the publication ("Contributions will be happily fondled and sewed up in a green velvet sack.") FuFa died after 4 issues.

Emerging from the protective womb of sf fandom, Bradbury achieved definite, if somewhat shaky, professional status in November of 1940 with *It's Not the Heat, It's the Hu—,* a satirical slap at cliches which appeared in *Script,* a West Coast slick which also gave other talented but unknown writers (among them William Saroyan) their first break. The fact that the magazine was unable to pay for material at that point in its uncertain existence in no way diminished Bradbury's immense joy at seeing his name at last set in professional type.

"However," says Ray, "when several more months passed with no checks in the mail I began to doubt my ability to actually crack a paying market. I told myself that if I didn't make a sale by my twenty-first birthday I'd quit beating my head against the wall."

Just a month before he turned twenty-one, in late July, a check arrived for $27.50 from *Super Science Stories* in payment for a story Ray had plucked from the pages of FuFa and re-written with Henry Hasse. This was *Pendulum,* and it appeared that November under the double by-line.

"My end of the check came to $13.75," says Ray, "and it seemed like a million to me! I walked away from the Little Theatre group for good; acting was behind me. By God, I was a *writer!* When 1941 ended I had written 52 stories in 52 weeks, and had made three sales with the help of my agent Julius Schwartz."

In 1942, on the basis of another half-dozen story sales, Ray left his newspaper job to apply himself to full-time production. He'd invaded the pages of *Weird Tales,* and it was here that his unique talent would flourish. With his second story for this magazine, *The Wind,* printed early in 1943, he began to examine his own fears and childhood memories in order to fashion emotionally-real fantasies. And by December of that year his first quality science fiction story appeared, *King of the Gray Spaces,* a warm, moving account of a boy who left friends and family behind to become a rocket pilot. Ray Bradbury was already making his mark as a highly-original creator within the sf-fantasy field, but his course was still uncertain.

Confused and directionless, Bradbury was simultaneously producing very good and very bad work. The type of non-gimmick, non-scientific sf he wanted to write met stiff resistance among editors. The only editorial encouragement and help he ever received came from the detective pulps. Science fiction editors advised him to "conform," to write a more standardized formula story if he wished to sell. Bowing to pressure, he produced three painfully-obvious imitations of Leigh Brackett for *Planet,* and plunged into the detective magazines with trite, conventional tales of crime and murder. Only in *Weird Tales* did his work prove to be fresh and original, and he was gaining an early following with stories such as *The Sea Shell, The Lake* and *The Jar*.

Unfit for military service because of eye trouble, Bradbury contributed to the war effort in the forties by writing radio plays for the Red Cross Blood Bank.

"In late 1945 I needed $500 to finance a trip into Mexico," relates Bradbury. "I knew that I would have to make some slick-paper sales, to the higher-paying markets, in order to earn the extra money. Since I had been appearing regularly in the pulps I was afraid that the slick magazine editors would be prejudiced against using my real name. So I bundled off three new stories as 'William Elliott,'—and, on three successive days, I got checks from *Collier's, Mademoiselle* and *Charm!* Which gave me more than enough for our trip. I immediately wrote each editor, telling him my real name, and it turned out none of them had ever heard of Ray Bradbury, and that they'd be delighted to restore my byline. That was my crackthrough; the wall was down. It was a tremendous week!"

That same year saw the publication of Bradbury's powerful treatment of racial conflict, set in the realistic atmosphere of a baseball park, *The Big Black and White Game*. Appearing in *The American Mercury,* the story was selected by Martha Foley for *Best American Short Stories of 1946*—fulfilling a boyhood dream and moving the young author into the exclusive ranks of America's top short storyists.

Marriage was "the next fearful step" in Bradbury's life, and his courtship of Marguerite Susan McClure, a UCLA graduate, began in a most unusual fashion.

"Maggie worked in a downtown bookstore," relates Bradbury. "Each afternoon she'd watch this fellow come in, carrying a briefcase. He'd nose around, pick up several books, discard them, then leave. When a number of volumes were reported missing Maggie was convinced she'd found the thief: the suspicious-looking guy with the briefcase—which was me! That's how we met. Luckily, the missing books were recovered, and I ended up stealing Maggie."

They were married in September of 1947, just a month before Ray's first book, *Dark Carnival,* was released by Arkham House. On the evening prior to his wedding day, Bradbury stacked up thousands of pages of manuscript, totalling some two million words, and made a giant bonfire of them. ("It was all bad writing, stuff that needed burning, and I've never regretted destroying it.")

A week after his first daughter was born Ray wrote a poetic tale, *Switch on the Night,* in order, he says "to teach her not to fear the dark as I did as a boy." (This story was published as an award-winning children's book in 1955.)

The next major step in Bradbury's rapidly-ascending career had to do with Mars, and a series of delicately-wrought, poetic tales of the Red Planet.

"I'd been reading a lot of wonderful fiction by Wolfe, Steinbeck, Hemingway, Sinclair Lewis, Sherwood Anderson, Jessamyn West, Katherine Anne Porter and Eudora Welty, and an idea came to me: Do a series of stories about Mars, about the people there, and the coming of the Earthmen, and about the loneliness and terror of space. Over the years the stories formed themselves, inspired sometimes by poetry which Mag would read aloud to me on summer evenings —such as *And the Moon Be Still as Bright*—sometimes by essays or long conversations. In 1948 the whole thing took abrupt shape for me, and by 1950 it was a published reality."

With the success of *The Martian Chronicles,* Bradbury became a major literary figure, and renowned critics such as Christopher Isherwood, Clifton Fadiman and Gilbert Highet began hailing his talent. In England, Angus Wilson declared: "For those who care about the future of fiction in the English language this book is, I believe, one of the most hopeful signs of the last twenty years . . ."

And the venerable British Journal, *Punch,* said of his work: "To take the paraphernalia of 'science fiction'—the rocket ships, the robots and galactic explorations . . . and fashion from them stories as delicate as Farre's songs or Cezanne's watercolors, is a very considerable achievement. It is hard to speak with restraint of these extraordinary tales."

In 1952 director John Huston indicated, in a letter to Bradbury, that he hoped to interest a studio in financing a film version of the *Chronicles*—and this was very exciting news to Ray, since Huston was one of his "personal gods," a director with whom he had dreamed of working. As it turned out, this deal never materialized, but Huston did contact Bradbury in the fall of 1953, offering him the chance to do the screenplay on *Moby Dick.*

"I was staggered," says Ray. "As a boy, I had attempted to read the book, but had given up. I told Huston I'd give him a yes or no in the morning—and then plunged into Melville, reading all night. By dawn I knew I could do the screenplay, and that September, with Maggie, I headed for Ireland on what was to become a pretty wild adventure."

Bradbury's only real film experience involved an original story he had worked on that year for Universal, *It Came From Outer Space,* and on which he had done a long treatment used as the basis for the Harry Essex screenplay. *Moby Dick* was a far more complex assignment, and involved transferring the essence of Melville to cinema terms. Naturally apprehensive on such a project, Bradbury was unprepared for Huston's aggressive, wild personality.

"He says he is out to corrupt me," Bradbury air-mailed from Dublin. "Huston looks forward to putting me on a horse, riding me to hounds, jetting me in a speed-plane and generally burying me in drinks and dames."

Huston met Ray in Dublin, and invited Bradbury to walk the Irish countryside with him and a fellow-writer, Peter Viertel (there to work on another film).

Vividly recalling that first afternoon with Huston, Ray says: "We were crossing an open field when John spotted a huge black bull nearby, glowering at us. Before we could stop him, he'd whipped off his coat and was waving it like a matador's cape in the brute's face, shouting 'Ho, Toro, Ho-oh!' My God, we were paralyzed. Finally the bull snorted, shook his head and walked away. John was actually disappointed that he hadn't charged!"

Huston has always been a notorious practical joker and Bradbury, of course, was fair game during the filming of *Moby*.

"We were more than halfway through the final version of the script," Bradbury relates, "when John brought in a telegram he said was from the head office at Warners. It read: 'FIND WE CANNOT PROCEED WITH FILM UNLESS SEXY FEMALE ROLE WRITTEN IN AT ONCE.' I crumpled the thing up and actually stamped on it. John couldn't keep a straight face. I saw him on the couch, doubled up and laughing like a big monkey."

Bradbury, however, managed to turn the tables neatly on a later occasion. "John had invited a group of 100% Lords and Ladies out to his Irish estate for dinner. He kept needling me to stay for the evening and I kept telling him I had nothing formal to wear. Well, he just kept needling me in front of Pete Viertel. Finally, when John had stepped out of the room, Pete hustled me upstairs. 'Let's show the bastard!' he chuckled, and dug up an old plaid skirt, some black leggings, a fringed purse, and a dinner jacket. 'Don't you see?' he asked, 'Kilts!' When the ultra-distinguished guests had arrived and John was in their midst playing the casual host, I came down the stairs. From the doorway, in a ringing voice, Pete announced me as 'Laird McBradbury.' All the Lords and Ladies turned in my direction. I saw John's jaw drop three feet! A lovely moment."

Ray spent six months in Ireland working on the screenplay, writing and re-writing some 1500 pages to arrive at a final 134. *Moby Dick,* with minor script revisions by Huston, was released in 1956, and although this saga of the Great White Whale was not the critical success Ray had hoped for, (due, in large part, to Gregory Peck's weak performance as Captain Ahab) the $5,000,000 film enhanced Bradbury's reputation, paving the way for other script work.

"I was called into one of the big studios to re-work a fantasy script," says Ray, "and the producer asked me how I liked it after I'd read the last page. 'Fine,' I said, 'I *ought* to like it, because it's *mine.*' The guy had stolen one of my short stories, given the idea to another writer, then called me in to do the final version, failing to realize that *I* was the author of the original story he'd stolen! He ended up paying for the rights, and I got the hell out of there. This anecdote, it seems to me, is typical of Hollywood."

Bradbury's experience with Huston had supplied material for a basket of Irish stories and plays, in addition to providing him with the chance to see some of the world's great cities: Venice, Rome, Florence, Milan and Paris. In the summer of 1957 London was added to this list when Sir Carol Reed, the British director, sent for Bradbury in order to have him adapt his *And the Rock Cried Out* into a full-length screenplay.

"This has yet to be filmed," says Ray, "since Reed ran into problems getting the financial go-ahead. I had the same kind of bad luck with the *Chronicles* at MGM in 1961 when I worked for several months on a 158-page screenplay based on the book. And I did another unpro-duced version in 1964. At least Francois Truffaut brought *Fahren-heit 451* to the screen but I didn't work on the screenplay."

Bradbury always has several literary irons in the fire, and even the projects which fail to materialize often pay him handsome dividends. (He got $10,000 from one TV show for an adaptation of *The Rocket,* and another $10,000 option money on *The Wonderful Ice Cream Suit* as a projected film. Neither story was produced.)

In addition to his books, poems, short stories, TV and film scripts, plays and articles Bradbury "keeps in mental trim" by lecturing several times a month. He has spoken to PTA groups, luncheon clubs, college classes and Writers' Conferences coast-to-coast. In his "spare time" he paints in oil, and serves on committees. ("If there were three of me I could keep *all* of us busy!")

As early as 1951 Ray was making 100 reprint sales each year, and his total is now in the thousands, with his work appearing in over a dozen languages in many foreign publications such as *Perspektev, Europa, Crespi, Temps Modernes, Nuovi, Vitalino,* and *Hjemmet.*

Bradbury is a strong defender of Los Angeles, and nothing annoys him more than a New Yorker who speaks darkly of the "perils" of living near Hollywood. ("I can attest that a New York writer, afraid for his virginity, can live in Los Angeles and rarely, if ever, go to a wild cocktail party, be thrown into a swimming pool with a blonde starlet or be compromised by a Salton Sea real estate promoter.")

Bradbury is a prose poet in the age of space, a man possessed by the beauty of the written word; his work reflects a passion for the shape and sound and precise rhythms of the language—and he has been able to translate this passion into imaginative literature of a very high order. Having produced over two dozen books and more than 700 shorter pieces (including television scripts and published speeches), he is as busy as ever, planning a new stage production, another book of stories, an opera based on his *Lost City of Mars,* a TV series and a sequel to *Dandelion Wine* titled *The Farewell Summer.*

"I've written every day of my life for the past forty years," he says, "and I plan to go on writing for forty more. By then I'll be 93 and I'll consider slowing down."

He's serious about his productivity. "Success is a continuing process," he says. "Failure is a stoppage. The man who keeps moving and working does not fail."

Ray Douglas Bradbury is still moving—and succeeding.

Bibliography of books by Ray Bradbury
Compiled by William F. Nolan

DARK CARNIVAL—Arkham House, 1947—313 pages. Contains 27 stories.

THE MARTIAN CHRONICLES—Doubleday, 1950—222 pages. Contains 15 stories and 11 "bridge passages" linking them.
Note: In later editions 2 other stories were added to the book, The Wilderness and The Fire Balloons.

THE ILLUSTRATED MAN—Doubleday, 1951—252 pages. Contains Prologue/Epilogue and 18 stories.

TIMELESS STORIES FOR TODAY AND TOMORROW—Bantam, 1952—306 pages. Contains Introduction and The Pedestrian by Bradbury—plus 25 other stories by various authors. Edited by Bradbury.

THE GOLDEN APPLES OF THE SUN—Doubleday, 1953—250 pages. Contains 22 stories.

FAHRENHEIT 451—Ballantine, 1953—201 pages. Original edition contains title novel plus two stories: The Playground and And the Rock Cried Out. This book was later released with these stories removed, with no title change.

THE OCTOBER COUNTRY—Ballantine, 1955—307 pages. Contains 15 stories reprinted from DARK CARNIVAL, most of them re-written, plus four stories: The Dwarf, The Watchful Poker Chip of H. Matisse, Touched With Fire and The Wonderful Death of Dudley Stone.

SWITCH ON THE NIGHT—Pantheon, 1955—49 pages. A book for children, illustrated by Madeleine Gekiere.

THE CIRCUS OF DR. LAO AND OTHER IMPROBABLE STORIES—Bantam,

1956—210 pages. Contains intro by Bradbury—plus title novella and 11 other stories by various authors. Edited by Bradbury.

DANDELION WINE—Doubleday, 1957—281 pages. Contains 20 short stories, plus new material, re-written to form a "novel."

A MEDICINE FOR MELANCHOLY—Doubleday, 1959—240 pages. Contains 22 stories.

THE DAY IT RAINED FOREVER—Rupert Hart-Davis (England), 1959—254 pages. Contains 18 stories from A MEDICINE FOR MELANCHOLY, plus Referent, Almost the End of the World, Here There Be Tygers, Perchance to Dream—along with And the Rock Cried Out.

SOMETHING WICKED THIS WAY COMES—Simon and Schuster, 1962—317 pages. A fantasy novel.

R IS FOR ROCKET (for Young Adults)—Doubleday, 1962—233 pages. Contains a selection of Bradbury stories from other books, aimed at the young adult, plus a novelet, Frost and Fire, which is the first book printing of the *Planet* story, The Creatures That Time Forgot. Also, for the first time in a Bradbury collection, is the title story, R is for Rocket (King of the Gray Spaces). Foreword by Bradbury.

THE ANTHEM SPRINTERS AND OTHER ANTICS—Dial Press, 1963—159 pages. Contains Afterword by RB, with 4 plays.

THE MACHINERIES OF JOY—Simon and Schuster, 1964—255 pages. Contains 21 stories.

THE VINTAGE BRADBURY—Vintage/Random House, 1965—330 pages. Contains Introduction by Gilbert Highet, with 25 stories from earlier collections, plus 1 other Bradbury tale, The Illustrated Man.

THE AUTUMN PEOPLE—Ballantine Books, 1965—189 pages. Note: Adapted to comic-book format by A. B. Feldstein. Contains Foreword by RB, with 8 illustrated stories.

TOMORROW MIDNIGHT—Ballantine Books, 1966—189 pages. Note: Adapted to comic-book format by A. B. Feldstein. Contains Introduction by RB, with 8 illustrated stories.

S IS FOR SPACE (for Young Adults)—Doubleday, 1966—239 pages. Contains Introduction by RB, with 13 stories from earlier collections, plus 3 other Bradbury tales, Chrysalis, Pillar of Fire and Time in Thy Flight.

TWICE 22—Doubleday, 1966—406 pages. Contains 44 stories—the complete contents of THE GOLDEN APPLES OF THE SUN and A MEDICINE FOR MELANCHOLY.

I SING THE BODY ELECTRIC!—Alfred A. Knopf, 1969—305 pages. Contains 17 stories, plus a cantata by RB.

THE WONDERFUL ICE CREAM SUIT AND OTHER PLAYS—Bantam Books, 1972—162 pages. Contains Introduction by RB, with 3 plays.

THE HALLOWEEN TREE—Alfred A. Knopf, 1972—146 pages. A story for children.

WHEN ELEPHANTS LAST IN THE DOORYARD BLOOMED—Alfred A. Knopf, 1973. Contains poems by RB. Exact contents not available at press time.

NOTE: Ten Bradbury pamphlets have also been published. For details on these and on his complete published output including stories, scripts, verse, articles, essays, stage productions, films, reviews, speeches, radio work, interviews, published letters and anthology appearances—plus a selection of previously unpublished manuscript material—see William F. Nolan's THE RAY BRADBURY COMPANION, published by Gale Research, The Book Tower, Detroit, Michigan.

Isaac Asimov

The Key

by ISAAC ASIMOV

Karl Jennings knew he was going to die. He had a matter of hours to live and much to do.

There was no reprieve from the death sentence, not here on the Moon, not with no communications in operation.

Even on Earth there were a few fugitive patches where, without radio handy, a man might die without the hand of his fellowman to help him, without the heart of his fellowman to pity him, without even the eye of his fellowman to discover the corpse.—Here on the Moon, there were few spots that were otherwise.

Earthmen knew he was on the Moon, of course. He had been part of a geological expedition—No, selenological expedition! Odd, how his Earth-centered mind insisted on the "geo-."

Wearily, he drove himself to think, even as he worked. Dying though he was, he still felt that artificially-imposed clarity of thought. Anxiously, he looked about. There was nothing to see. He was in the dark of the eternal shadow of the northern interior of the wall of the crater, a blackness relieved only by the intermittent blink of his flash. He kept that intermittent, partly because he dared not consume its power source before he was through and partly because he dared not take more than the minimum chance that it be seen.

On his left hand, toward the south along the nearby horizon of the Moon, was a crescent of bright white Sunlight. Beyond the horizon, and invisible, was the opposite lip of the crater. The Sun never peered high enough over the lip of his own edge of the crater to illuminate the floor immediately beneath his feet. He was safe from radiation—from that at least.

He dug carefully but clumsily, swathed as he was in his spacesuit. His side ached abominably.

The dust and broken rock did not take up the "fairy-castle" appearance characteristic of those portions of the Moon's surface exposed to the alternation of light and dark, heat and cold. Here, in eternal cold, the slow crumbling of the crater wall had simply piled fine rubble in a heterogeneous mass. It would not be easy to tell there had been digging going on.

He misjudged the unevenness of the dark surface for a moment and spilled a cupped handful of dusty fragments. The particles dropped with the slowness characteristic of the Moon and yet with the appearance of a blinding speed, for there was no air resistance to slow them further still and spread them out into a dusty haze.

Jennings' flash brightened for a moment, and he kicked a jagged rock out of the way.

He hadn't much time. He dug deeper into the dust.

A little deeper and he could push the Device into the depression and begin covering it. Strauss must not find it.

Strauss!

The other member of the team. Half-share in the discovery. Half-share in the renown.

If it were merely the whole share of the credit that Strauss had wanted, Jennings might have allowed it. The discovery was more important than any individual credit that might go with it. But what Strauss wanted was something far more; something Jennings would fight to prevent.

One of the few things Jennings was willing to die to prevent.

And he was dying.

They had found it together. Actually, Strauss had found the ship; or, better, the remains of the ship; or, better still, what just conceivably might have been the remains of something analogous to a ship.

"Metal," said Strauss, as he picked up something ragged and nearly amorphous. His eyes and face could just barely be seen through the thick lead-glass of the visor, but his rather harsh voice sounded clearly enough through the suit-radio.

Jennings came drifting over from his own position half a mile away. He said, "Odd! There is no free metal on the Moon."

"There shouldn't be. But you know well enough they haven't explored more than one percent of the Moon's surface. Who knows what can be found on it?"

Jennings grunted assent and reached out his gauntlet to take the object.

It was true enough that almost anything might be found on the Moon for all anyone really knew. Theirs was the first privately-financed selenographic expedition ever to land on the Moon. Till then, there had been only government-conducted shot-gun affairs, with half a dozen ends in view. It was a sign of the advancing space age that the Geological Society could afford to send two men to the Moon for selenological studies only.

Strauss said, "It looks as though it once had a polished surface."

"You're right," said Jennings. "Maybe there's more about."

They found three more pieces, two of trifling size and one a jagged object that showed traces of a seam.

"Let's take them to the ship," said Strauss.

They took the small skim-boat back to the mother ship. They shucked their suits once on board, something Jennings at least was always glad to do. He scratched vigorously at his ribs and rubbed his cheeks till his light skin reddened into welts.

Strauss eschewed such weakness and got to work. The laser beam pock-marked the metal and the vapor recorded itself on the spectrograph. Titanium-steel, essentially, with a hint of cobalt and molybdenum."

"That's artificial, all right," said Strauss. His broad-boned face was as dour and as hard as ever. He showed no elation, although Jennings could feel his own heart begin to race.

It may have been the excitement that trapped Jennings into beginning, "This is a development against which we must steel ourselves—" with a faint stress on "steel" to indicate the play on words.

Strauss, however, looked at Jennings with an icy distaste, and the attempted set of puns was choked off.

Jennings sighed. He could never swing it, somehow. Never could! He remembered at the University—Well, never mind. The discovery they had made was worth a far better pun than any he could construct for all Strauss's calmness.

Jennings wondered if Strauss could possibly miss the significance.

He knew very little about Strauss, as a matter of fact, except by selenological reputation. That is, he had read Strauss's papers and he presumed Strauss had read his. Although their ships might well have passed by night in their University days, they had never happened to meet until after both had volunteered for this expedition and been accepted.

In the week's voyage, Jennings had grown uncomfortably aware of the other's stocky figure, his sandy hair and china-blue eyes, and the way the muscles over his prominent jaw-bones worked when he ate. Jennings, himself, much slighter in build, also blue-eyed, but with darker hair, tended to withdraw automatically from the heavy exudation of the other's power and drive.

Jennings said, "There's no record of any ship ever having landed on this part of the Moon. Certainly none has crashed."

"If it were part of a ship," said Strauss, "it should be smooth and polished. This is eroded, and without an atmosphere here, that means exposure to micrometeorite bombardment over many years."

Then he *did* see the significance. Jennings said, with an almost savage jubilation, "It's a non-human artifact. Creatures not of Earth once visited the Moon. Who knows how long ago?"

"Who knows?" agreed Strauss dryly.

"In the report—"

"Wait," said Strauss imperiously. "Time enough to report when we have something to report. If it was a ship, there will be more to it than what we now have."

But there was no point in looking further just then. They had been at it for hours, and the next meal and sleep were overdue. Better to tackle the whole job fresh and spend hours at it. They seemed to agree on that without speaking.

The Earth was low on the eastern horizon almost full in phase, bright and blue-streaked. Jennings looked at it while they ate and experienced, as he always did, a sharp homesickness.

"It looks peaceful enough," he said, "but there are six billion people busy on it."

Strauss looked up from some deep inner life of his own and said, "Six billion people ruining it!"

Jennings frowned. "You're not an Ultra, are you?"

Strauss said, "What the hell are you talking about?"

Jennings felt himself flush. A flush always showed against his fair skin, turning it pink at the slightest upset of the even tenor of his emotions. He found it intensely embarrassing.

He turned back to his food, without saying anything.

For a whole generation now, the Earth's population had held steady. No further increase could be afforded, everyone admitted that. There were those, in fact, who said that "no higher" wasn't enough; the population had to drop. Jennings himself sympathized with that point of view. The globe of the Earth was being eaten alive by its heavy freight of humanity.

But *how* was the population to be made to drop; randomly, by encouraging the people to lower the birth rate still further, as and how they wished? Lately there had been the slow rise of a distant rumble which wanted not only a population drop but a selected drop—the survival of the fittest, with the self-declared fit choosing the criteria of fitness.

Jennings thought: I've insulted him, I suppose.

Later, when he was almost asleep, it suddenly occurred to him that he knew virtually nothing of Strauss's character. What if it were his intention to go out now on a foraging expedition of his own so that he might get sole credit for—

He raised himself on his elbow in alarm, but Strauss was breathing heavily, and even as Jennings listened, the breathing grew into the characteristic burr of a snore.

They spent the next three days in a single-minded search for additional pieces. They found some. They found more than that. They found an area glowing with the tiny phosphorescence of Lunar bacteria. Such bacteria were common enough, but nowhere previously had their occurrence been reported in concentration so great as to cause a visible glow.

Strauss said, "An organic being, or his remains, may have been here once. He died, but the micro-organisms within him did not. In the end they consumed him."

"And spread perhaps," added Jennings. "That may be the source of Lunar bacteria generally. They may not be native at all but may be the result of contamination instead—eons ago."

"It works the other way, too," said Strauss. "Since the bacteria are completely different in very fundamental ways from any Earthly form of micro-organism, the creatures they parasitized—assuming this was their source—must have been fundamentally different, too. Another indication of extraterrestrial origin."

The trail ended in the wall of a small crater.

"It's a major digging job," said Jennings, his heart sinking. "We had better report this and get help."

"No," said Strauss, somberly. "There may be nothing to get help for. The crater might have formed a million years after the ship had crash-landed."

"And vaporized most of it, you mean, and left only what we've found?"

Strauss nodded.

Jennings said, "Let's try anyway. We can dig a bit. If we draw a line through the finds we've made so far and just keep on—"

Strauss was reluctant and worked half-heartedly, so that it was Jennings who made the real find. Surely that counted! Even though Strauss had found the first piece of metal, Jennings had found the artifact itself.

It *was* an artifact—cradled three feet underground under the irregular shape of a boulder which had fallen in such a way that it left a hollow in its contact with the Moon's surface. In that hollow lay the artifact, protected from everything for a million years or more; protected from radiation, from micrometeors, from temperature change, so that it remained fresh and new forever.

Jennings labelled it at once the Device. It looked not remotely similar to any instrument either had ever seen, but then, as Jennings said, why should it?

"There are no rough edges that I can see," he said. "It may not be broken."

"There may be missing parts, though."

"Maybe," said Jennings, "but there seems to be nothing movable. It's all one piece and certainly oddly uneven." He noted his own play on words, then went on with a not-altogether-successful attempt at self-control. "*This* is what we need. A piece of worn metal or an area rich in bacteria is only material for deduction and dispute. But this is the real thing—a Device that is clearly of extraterrestrial manufacture."

It was on the table between them now, and both regarded it gravely. Jennings said, "Let's put through a preliminary report, now."

"No!" said Strauss, in sharp and strenuous dissent. "Hell, no!"

"Why not?"

"Because if we do, it becomes a Society project. They'll swarm all over it and we won't be as much as a footnote when all is done. No!"

Strauss looked almost sly. "Let's do all we can with it and get as much out of it as possible before the harpies descend."

Jennings thought about it. He couldn't deny that he, too, wanted to make certain that no credit was lost. But still—

He said, "I don't know that I like to take the chance, Strauss." For the first time he had an impulse to use the man's first name, but fought it off. "Look, Strauss," he said, "it's not right to wait. If this is of extraterrestrial origin, then it must be from some other planetary system. There isn't a place in the Solar system, outside the Earth, that can possibly support an advanced life-form."

"Not proven, really," grunted Strauss, "but what if you're right?"

"Then it would mean that the creatures of the ship had interstellar travel and therefore had to be far in advance, technologically, of ourselves. Who knows what the Device can tell us about their advanced technology. It might be the key to—who knows what. It might be the clue to an unimaginable scientific revolution."

"That's romantic nonsense. If this is the product of a technology far advanced over ours, we'll learn nothing from it. Bring Einstein back to life and show him a microprotowarp and what would he make of it?"

"We can't be certain that we won't learn."

"So what, even so? What if there's a small delay? What if we assure credit for ourselves? What if we make sure that we ourselves go along with this, that we don't let go of it?"

"But Strauss," Jennings felt himself moved almost to tears in his anxiety to get across his sense of the importance of the Device, "what if we crash with it? What if we don't make it back to Earth? We can't risk this thing." He tapped it then, almost as though he were in love with it. "We should report it now and have them send ships out here to get it. It's too precious to—"

At the peak of his emotional intensity, the Device seemed to grow warm under his hand. A portion of its surface, half-hidden under a flap of metal, glowed phosphorescently.

Jennings jerked his hand away in a spasmodic gesture and the Device darkened. But it was enough; the moment had been infinitely revealing.

He said, almost choking. "It was like a window opening into your skull. I could see into your mind."

"I read yours," said Strauss, "or experienced it, or entered into it, or whatever you choose." He touched the Device in his cold, with-drawn way, but nothing happened.

"You're an Ultra," said Jennings angrily. "When I touched this," and he did so— "It's happening again. I see it. Are you a madman? Can you honestly believe it is humanly decent to condemn almost all the human race to extinction and destroy the versatility and variety of the species?"

His hand dropped away from the Device again, in repugnance at the glimpses revealed, and it grew dark again. Once more, Strauss touched it gingerly and again nothing happened.

Strauss said, "Let's not start a discussion, for God's sake— This thing is an aid to communication. A telepathic amplifier. Why not? The brain cells have each their electric potentials. Thought can be viewed as a wavering electromagnetic field of micro-intensities—"

Jennings turned away. He didn't want to speak to Strauss. He said, "We'll report it now. I don't give a damn about credit. Take it all. I just want it out of our hands."

For a moment Strauss remained in a brown study. Then he said, "It's more than a communicator. It responds to emotion and it ampli-fies emotion."

"What are you talking about?"

"Twice it started at your touch just now, although you'd been han-dling it all day with no effect. It still has no effect when I touch it."

"Well?"

"It reacted to you when you were in a state of high emotional tension. That's the requirement for activation, I suppose. And when you raved about the Ultras while you were holding it just now, I felt as you did, for just a moment."

"So you should."

"But, listen to me. Are you sure *you're* so right. There isn't a think-ing man on Earth that doesn't know the planet would be better off with a population of one billion rather than six billion. If we used automation to the full—as now the hordes won't allow us to do—we could probably have a completely efficient and viable Earth with a population of no more than, say, five million. —Listen to me, Jen-nings. Don't turn away, man."

The harshness in Strauss's voice almost vanished in his effort to be reasonably winning. "But we can't reduce the population demo-cratically. You know that. It isn't the sex urge, because uterine inserts solved the birth control problem long ago; you know that. It's a matter of nationalism. Each ethnic group wants other groups to reduce themselves in population first, and I agree with them. I want my ethnic group, *our* ethnic group, to prevail. I want the Earth to be inherited by the elite, which means by men like ourselves. We're the true men, and the horde of half-apes who hold us down are destroying us all. They're doomed to death anyway; why not save ourselves?"

"No," said Jennings strenuously. "No one group has a monopoly on humanity. Your five million mirror-images, trapped in a humanity robbed of its variety and versatility, would die of boredom—and serve them right."

"Emotional nonsense, Jennings. You don't believe that. You've just been trained to believe it by our damn-fool equalitarians. Look, this Device is just what we need. Even if we can't build any others or understand how this one works, this one Device might do. If we could control or influence the minds of key men, then little by little, we can superimpose our views on the world. We already have an organization. You must know that if you've seen my mind. It's better motivated and better designed than any other organization on Earth. The brains of mankind flock to us daily. Why not you, too? This instrument is a key, as you see, but not just a key to a bit more knowledge. It is a key to the final solution of men's problems. Join us! Join us!"

He had reached an earnestness that Jennings had never heard in him.

Strauss's hand fell on the Device, which flickered a second or two and went out.

Jennings smiled humorlessly. He saw the significance of that. Strauss had been deliberately trying to work himself into an emotional state intense enough to activate the Device and had failed.

"You can't work it," said Jennings, "you're too darned supermannishly self-controlled and can't break down, can you?" He took up the Device with hands that were trembling, and it phosphoresced at once.

"Then *you* work it. Get the credit for saving humanity."

"Not in a hundred million years," said Jennings, gasping and barely able to breathe in the intensity of his emotion. "I'm going to report this now."

"No," said Strauss. He picked up one of the table knives. "It's pointed enough, sharp enough."

"You needn't work so hard to make your point," said Jennings, even under the stress of the moment conscious of the pun. "I can see your plans. With the Device you can convince anyone that I never existed. You can bring about an Ultra victory."

Strauss nodded. "You read my mind perfectly."

"But you won't," gasped Jennings. "Not while I hold this." He was willing Strauss into immobility.

Strauss moved raggedly and subsided. He held the knife out stiffly and his arm trembled, but he did not advance.

Both were perspiring freely.

Strauss said between clenched teeth. "You can't keep it—up all—day."

The sensation was clear, but Jennings wasn't sure he had the words to describe it. It was, in physical terms, like holding a slippery animal of vast strength, one that wriggled incessantly. Jennings had to concentrate on the feeling of immobility.

He wasn't familiar with the Device. He didn't know how to use it skillfully. One might as well expect someone who had never seen a sword to pick one up and wield it with the grace of a musketeer.

"Exactly," said Strauss, following Jennings' train of thought. He took a fumbling step forward.

Jennings knew himself to be no match for Strauss's mad determination. They both knew that. But there was the skim-boat. Jennings had to get away. With the Device.

But Jennings had no secrets. Strauss saw his thought and tried to step between the other and the skim-boat.

Jennings redoubled his efforts. Not immobility, but unconsciousness. Sleep, Strauss, he thought desperately. Sleep!

Strauss slipped to his knees, heavy-lidded eyes closing.

Heart pounding, Jennings rushed forward. If he could strike him with something, snatch the knife—

But his thoughts had deviated from their all-important concentration on sleep, so that Strauss's hand was on his ankle, pulling downward with raw strength.

Strauss did not hesitate. As Jennings tumbled, the hand that held the knife rose and fell. Jennings felt the sharp pain and his mind reddened with fear and despair.

It was the very access of emotion that raised the flicker of the Device to a blaze. Strauss's hold relaxed as Jennings silently and inco-

herently screamed fear and rage from his own mind to the other.
Strauss rolled over, face distorted.

Jennings rose unsteadily to his feet and backed away. He dared do
nothing but concentrate on keeping the other unconscious. Any
attempt at violent action would block out too much of his own mind-
force, whatever it was; too much of his unskilled bumbling mind-
force that could not lend itself to really effective use.

He backed toward the skim-boat. There would be a suit on board
—bandages—

The skim-boat was not really meant for long-distance runs. Nor
was Jennings, any longer. His right side was slick with blood despite
the bandages. The interior of his suit was caked with it.

There was no sign of the ship itself on his tail, but surely it would
come sooner or later. Its power was many times his own; it had detectors that would pick up the cloud of charge concentration left behind by his ion-drive reactors.

Desperately, Jennings had tried to reach Luna Station on his
radio, but there was still no answer, and he stopped in despair. His
signals would merely aid Strauss in pursuit.

He might reach Luna Station bodily, but he did not think he could
make it. He would be picked off first. He would die and crash first.
He wouldn't make it. He would have to hide the Device, put it away
in a safe place, *then* make for Luna Station.

The Device—

He was not sure he was right. It might ruin the human race, but it
was infinitely valuable. Should he destroy it altogether? It was the
only remnant of non-human intelligent life. It held the secrets of an
advanced technology; it was an instrument of an advanced science
of the mind. Whatever the danger, consider the value— The potential
value—

No, he must hide it so that it could be found again—but only by
the enlightened Moderates of the government. Never by the Ultras—

The skim-boat flickered down along the northern inner rim of the
crater. He knew which one it was, and the Device could be buried
here. If he could not reach Luna Station thereafter, either in person
or by radio, he would have to at least get away from the hiding spot;
well away, so that his own person would not give it away. And he
would have to leave *some* key to its location.

He was thinking with an unearthly clarity, it seemed to him. Was it the influence of the Device he was holding? Did it stimulate his thinking and guide him to the perfect message? Or was it the hallucination of the dying, and would none of it make any sense to anyone? He didn't know, but he had no choice. He had to try.

For Karl Jennings knew he was going to die. He had a matter of hours to live and much to do.

II

H. Seton Davenport of the American Division of the Terrestrial Bureau of Investigation rubbed the star-shaped scar on his left cheek absently. "I'm aware, sir, that the Ultras are dangerous."

The Division Head, M. T. Ashley, looked at Davenport narrowly. His gaunt cheeks were set in disapproving lines. Since he had sworn off smoking once again, he forced his groping fingers to close upon a stick of chewing gum, which he shelled, crumpled, and shoved into his mouth morosely. He was getting old, and bitter, too, and his short iron-gray mustache rasped when he rubbed his knuckles against it.

He said, "You don't know how dangerous. I wonder if anyone does. They are small in numbers, but strong among the powerful who, after all, are perfectly ready to consider themselves the elite. No one knows for certain who they are or how many."

"Not even the Bureau?"

"The Bureau is held back. We ourselves aren't free of the taint, for that matter. Are you?"

Davenport frowned. "I'm not an Ultra."

"I didn't say you were," said Ashley. "I asked if you were free of the taint? Have you considered what's been happening to the Earth in the last two centuries? Has it never occurred to you that a moderate decline in population would be a good thing? Have you never felt that it would be wonderful to get rid of the unintelligent, the incapable, the insensitive, and leave the rest. *I* have, damn it."

"I'm guilty of thinking that sometimes, yes. But considering something as a wish-fulfillment idea is one thing, but planning it as a practical scheme of action to be Hitlerized through is something else."

"The distance from wish to action isn't as great as you think. Convince yourself that the end is important enough, that the danger is great enough, and the means will grow increasingly less objectionable. Anyway, now that the Istanbul matter is taken care of, let me bring you up to date on this matter. Istanbul was of no importance in comparison. —Do you know Agent Ferrant?"

"The one who's disappeared? —Not personally."

"Well, two months ago, a stranded ship was located on the Moon's surface. It had been conducting a privately-financed selenographic survey. The Russo-American Geological Society, which had sponsored the flight, reported the ship's failure to report. A routine search located it without much trouble within a reasonable distance of the site from which it had made its last report.

"The ship was not damaged but its skim-boat was gone and with it one member of the crew. Name—Karl Jennings. The other man, James Strauss, was alive but in delirium. There was no sign of physical damage to Strauss, but he was quite insane. He still is, and that's important."

"Why?" put in Davenport.

"Because the medical team that investigated him reported neurochemical and neuroelectrical abnormalities of unprecedented nature. They'd never seen a case like it. Nothing human could have brought it about."

A flicker of a smile crossed Davenport's solemn face. "You suspect extraterrestrial invaders?"

"Maybe," said the other, with no smile at all. "But let me continue. A routine search in the neighborhood of the stranded ship revealed no signs of the skim-boat. Then Luna Station reported receipt of weak signals of uncertain origin. They had been tabbed as coming from the western rim of Mare Imbrium, but it was uncertain whether they were of human origin or not, and no vessel was believed to be in the vicinity. The signals had been ignored. With the skim-boat in mind, however, the search party headed out for Imbrium and located it. Jennings was aboard, dead. Knife-wound in one side; it's rather surprising he had lived as long as he did.

"Meanwhile the medicos were becoming increasingly disturbed at the nature of Strauss's babbling. They contacted the Bureau and our two men on the Moon—one of them happened to be Ferrant—arrived at the ship.

"Ferrant studied the tape-recordings of the babblings. There was no point in asking questions, for there was, and is, no way of reaching Strauss. There is a high wall between the universe and himself probably a permanent one. However, the talk in delirium, although heavily repetitious and disjointed, can be made to make sense. Ferrant put it together like a jigsaw puzzle.

"Apparently, Strauss and Jennings had come across an object of some sort which they took to be of ancient and non-human manufacture, an artifact of some ship wrecked eons ago. Apparently, it could somehow be made to twist the human mind."

Davenport interrupted. "And it twisted Strauss's mind? Is that it?"

"That's exactly it. Strauss was an Ultra—we can say 'was' for he's only technically alive—and Jennings did not wish to surrender the object. Quite right, too. Strauss babbled of using it to bring about the self-liquidation, as he called it, of the undesirable. He wanted a final, ideal population of five million. There was a fight in which only Jennings, apparently, could handle the mind-thing, but in which Strauss had a knife. When Jennings left, he was knifed, but Strauss's mind had been destroyed."

"And where was the mind-thing?"

"Agent Ferrant acted decisively. He searched the ship and the surroundings again. There was no sign of anything that was neither a natural Lunar formation or an obvious product of human technology. There was nothing that could be the mind-thing. He then searched the skim-boat and its surroundings. Again nothing."

"Could the first search team, the ones who suspected nothing— Could they have carried something off?"

"They swore they did not, and there is no reason to suspect them of lying. Then Ferrant's partner—"

"Who was he?"

"Gorbansky," said the District Head.

"I know him. We've worked together."

"I know you have. What do you think of him?"

"Capable and honest."

"All right. Gorbansky found something. Not an alien artifact, rather something most routinely human indeed. It was an ordinary white three-by-five card with writing on it, spindled, and in the middle finger of the right gauntlet. Presumably, Jennings had written it before his death and, also presumably, it represented the key to where he had hidden the object."

"What reason is there to think he had hidden it?"

"I said we had found it nowhere."

"I mean, what if he had destroyed it, as something too dangerous to leave intact."

"That's highly doubtful. If we accept the conversation as reconstructed from Strauss's ravings—and Ferrant built up what seems a tight word-for-word record of it—Jennings thought the mind-thing to be of key importance to humanity. He called it 'the clue to an unimaginable scientific revolution.' He wouldn't destroy something like that. He would merely hide it from the Ultras and try to report its whereabouts to the government. Else why leave a clue to its whereabouts?"

Davenport shook his head, "You're arguing in a circle, chief. You say he left clue because you think there is a hidden object, and you think there is a hidden object because he left a clue."

"I admit that. Everything is dubious. Is Strauss's delirium meaningful? Is Ferrant's reconstruction valid? Is Jennings' clue really a clue? Is there a mind-thing, or a Device, as Jennings called it, or isn't there? There's no use asking such questions. Right now, we must act on the assumption that there is such a Device and that it must be found."

"Because Ferrant disappeared?"

"Exactly."

"Kidnapped by the Ultras?"

"Not at all. The card disappeared with him."

"Oh—I see."

"Ferrant has been under suspicion for a long time as a secret Ultra. He's not the only one in the Bureau under suspicion either. The evidence didn't warrant open action; we can't simply lay about on pure suspicion, you know, or we'll gut the Bureau from top to bottom. He was under surveillance."

"By whom?"

"By Gorbansky, of course. Fortunately, Gorbansky had filmed the card and sent the reproduction to the headquarters on Earth, but he admits he considered it as nothing more than a puzzling object and included it in the information sent to Earth only out of a desire to be routinely complete. Ferrant—the better mind of the two, I suppose —did see the significance and took action. He did so at great cost for he has given himself away and has destroyed his future usefulness to the Ultras, but there is a chance that there will be no need for future usefulness. If the Ultras control the Device—"

"Perhaps Ferrant has the Device already."

"He was under surveillance, remember. Gorbansky swears the Device did not turn up anywhere."

"Gorbansky did not manage to stop Ferrant from leaving with the card. Perhaps he did not manage to stop him from obtaining the Device unnoticed, either."

Ashley tapped his fingers on the desk between them in an uneasy and uneven rhythm. He said at last, "I don't want to think that. If we find Ferrant, we may find out how much damage he's done. Till then, we must search for the Device. If Jennings hid it, he must have tried to get away from the hiding place. Else why leave a clue. It wouldn't be found in the vicinity."

"He might not have lived long enough to get away."

Again Ashley tapped, "The skim-boat showed signs of having engaged in a long, speedy flight and had all but crashed at the end. That is consistent with the view that Jennings was trying to place as much space as possible between himself and some hiding place."

"Can you tell from what direction he came?"

"Yes, but that's not likely to help. From the condition of the side vents, he had been deliberately tacking and veering."

Davenport sighed. "I suppose you have a copy of the card with you."

"I do. Here it is." He flipped a three-by-five replica toward Davenport. Davenport studied it for a few moments. It looked like this:

$$XY^2$$
$$PC/2 \quad \oplus$$
$$=$$
$$F/A \quad \uparrow$$
$$SU$$
$$C\text{–}C$$
$$H\!H$$

Davenport said, "I don't see any significance here."

"Neither did I, at first, nor did those I first consulted. But consider. Jennings must have thought that Strauss was in pursuit; he might not have known that Strauss had been put out of action, at least, not permanently. He was deadly afraid, then, that an Ultra would find him before a Moderate would. He dared not leave a clue too open. This," and the Division Head tapped the reproduction, "must represent a clue that is opaque on the surface but clear enough to anyone sufficiently ingenious."

"Can we rely on that?" asked Davenport doubtfully. "After all, he was a dying, frightened man, who might have been subjected to this mind-altering object himself. He need not have been thinking clearly, or even humanly. For instance, why didn't he make an effort to reach Lunar Station? He ended half a circumference away almost. Was he too twisted to think clearly? Too paranoid to trust even the Station?—Yet he must have tried to reach them at first since they picked up signals. What I'm saying is that this card, which looks as though it is covered with gibberish, *is* covered with gibberish."

Ashley shook his head solemnly from side to side, like a tolling bell. "He was in panic, yes. And I suppose he lacked the presence of mind to try to reach Lunar Station. Only the need to run and escape possessed him. Even so this can't be gibberish. It hangs together too well. Every notation on the card can be made to make sense, and the whole can be made to hang together."

"Where's the sense, then?" asked Davenport.

"You'll notice that there are seven items on the left side and two on the right. Consider the left-hand side first. The third one down looks like an equals sign. Does an equals sign mean anything to you, anything in particular?"

"An algebraic equation."

"That's general. Anything particular?"

"No."

"Suppose you consider it as a pair of parallel lines?"

"Euclid's fifth postulate?" suggested Davenport, groping.

"Good! There is a crater called Euclides on the Moon—the Greek name of the mathematician we call Euclid."

Davenport nodded. "I see your drift. As for F/A, that's force divided by acceleration, the definition of mass by Newton's second law of motion—"

"Yes, and there is a crater called Newton on the Moon also."

"Yes, but wait a while, the lowermost item is the astronomic symbol for the planet Uranus, and there is certainly no crater—or any other lunar object, so far as I know—that is named Uranus."

"You're right there. But Uranus was discovered by William Herschel, and the H that makes up part of the astronomic symbol is the initial of his name. As it happens there is a crater named Herschel on the Moon—three of them, in fact, since one is named for Caroline Herschel, his sister and another for John Herschel, his son."

Davenport thought a while, then said, "PC/2— Pressure times half the speed of light. I'm not familiar with that equation."

"Try craters. Try P for Ptolemaeus and C for Copernicus."

"And strike an average? Would that signify a spot exactly between Ptolemaeus and Copernicus?"

"I'm disappointed, Davenport," said Ashley sardonically. "I thought you knew your history of astronomy better than that. Ptolemy, or Ptolemaeus in Latin, presented a geocentric picture of the Solar system with the Earth at the center, while Copernicus presented a heliocentric one with the Sun at the center. One astronomer attempted a compromise, a picture halfway between that of Ptolemy and Copernicus—"

"Tycho Brahe!" said Davenport.

"Right. And the crater Tycho is the most conspicuous feature on the Moon's surface."

"All right. Let's take the rest. The C-C is a common way of writing a common type of chemical bond, and I think there is a crater named Bond."

"Yes, named for an American astronomer, W. C. Bond."

"The item on top, XY^2. Hmm. XYY. An X and two Y's. Wait! Alfonso X. He was the royal astronomer in medieval Spain who was called Alfonso the Wise. X the Wise. XYY. The crater Alphonsus."

"Very good. What's SU."

"That stumps me, chief."

"I'll tell you one theory. It stands for Soviet Union, the old name for the Russian Region. It was the Soviet Union that first mapped the other side of the Moon, and maybe it's a crater there. Tsiolkovsky, for instance. —You see, then, the symbols on the left can each be interpreted as standing for a crater: Alphonsus, Tycho, Euclides, Newton, Tsiolkovsky, Bond, Herschel."

"What about the symbols on the right-hand side?"

"That's perfectly transparent. The quartered circle is the astronomic symbol for the Earth. An arrow pointing to it indicates that the Earth must be directly overhead."

"Ah," said Davenport, "the Sinus Medii—the Middle Bay—over

which the Earth is perpetually at Zenith. That's not a crater, so it's on the right-hand side, away from the other symbols."

"All right," said Ashley. "The notations all make sense, or they can be made to make sense, so there's at least a good chance that this isn't gibberish and that it is trying to tell us something. But what. So far we've got seven craters and a non-crater mentioned, and what does that mean. Presumably, the Device can only be in one place."

"Well," said Davenport heavily, "a crater can be a huge place to search. Even if we assume he hugged the shadow to avoid Solar radiation, there can be dozens of miles to examine in each case. Suppose the arrow pointing to the symbol for the Earth defines the crater where he hid the Device, the place from which the Earth can be seen nearest the zenith."

"That's been thought of, old man. It cuts out one place and leaves us with seven pin-pointed craters, the southernmost extremity of those north of the Lunar equator and the northernmost extremity of those south. But which of the seven?"

Davenport was frowning. So far, he hadn't thought of anything that hadn't already been thought of. "Search them all," he said brusquely.

Ashley crackled into brief laughter. "In the weeks since this has all come up, we've done exactly that."

"And what have you found?"

"Nothing. We haven't found a thing. We're still looking, though."

"Obviously one of the symbols isn't interpreted correctly."

"Obviously!"

"You said yourself there were three craters named Herschel. The symbol SU, if it means the Soviet Union and therefore the other side of the Moon, can stand for any crater on the other side: Lomonosov, Jules Verne, Joliot-Curie, any of them. For that matter the symbol of the Earth might stand for the crater Atlas since he is pictured as supporting the Earth in some versions of the myth. The arrow might stand for the Straight Wall."

"There's no argument there, Davenport. But even if we get the right interpretation for the right symbol, how do we recognize it from among all the wrong interpretations, or from among the right interpretations of the wrong symbols? Somehow there's got to be something that leaps up at us from this card and gives us so clear a piece of information that we can tell it at once as the real thing from among all the red herrings. We've all failed and we need a fresh mind, Davenport. What do you see here?"

"I'll tell you one thing we could do," said Davenport reluctantly. "We can consult someone I— Oh, my God!" He half rose.

Ashley was all controlled excitement at once, "What do you see?"

Davenport could feel his hand trembling. He hoped his lips weren't. He said, "Tell me, have you checked on Jennings' past life?"

"Of course."

"Where did he go to college?"

"Eastern University."

A pang of joy shot through Davenport, but he held on. That was not enough. "Did he take a course in extraterrology?"

"Of course, he did. That's routine for a geology major."

"All right, then, don't you know who teaches extraterrology at Eastern University?"

Ashley snapped his fingers. "That oddball, What's-his-name— Wendell Urth."

"Exactly, an oddball who is a brilliant man in his way. An oddball who's acted as a consultant for the Bureau on several occasions and given perfect satisfaction every time. An oddball I was going to suggest we consult this time and then noticed that this card was *telling* us to do so. —An arrow pointing to the symbol for the Earth. A rebus that couldn't mean more clearly 'Go to Urth,' written by a man who was once a student of Urth and would know him."

Ashley stared at the card, "By God, it's possible. —But what could Urth tell us about the card that we can't see for ourselves?"

Davenport said, with polite patience, "I suggest we ask him, sir."

III

Ashley looked about curiously, half wincing as he turned from one direction to another. He felt as though he had found himself in some arcane curiosity shop, darkened and dangerous, from which at any moment some demon might hurtle forth squealing.

The lighting was poor and the shadows many. The walls seemed distant, and dismally alive with book-films from floor to ceiling. There was a Galactic lens in soft three-dimensionality in one corner and behind it were star charts that could dimly be made out. A map of the Moon in another corner might, however, possibly be a map of Mars.

Only the desk in the center of the room was brilliantly lit by a tight-beamed lamp. It was littered with papers and opened printed books. A small viewer was threaded with film, and a clock with an old-fashioned round-faced dial hummed with subdued merriment.

Ashley found himself unable to recall that it was late afternoon outside and that the sun was quite definitely in the sky. Here, within, was a place of eternal night. There was no sign of any window, and the clear presence of circulating air did not spare him a claustrophobic sensation.

He found himself moving closer to Davenport, who seemed insensible to the unpleasantness of the situation.

Davenport said in a low voice, "He'll be here in a moment, sir."

"Is it always like this?" asked Ashley.

"Always. He never leaves this place, as far as I know, except to trot across the campus and attend his classes."

"Gentlemen! Gentlemen!" came a reedy, tenor voice. "I am so glad to see you. It is good of you to come."

A round figure of a man bustled in from another room, shedding shadow and emerging into the light.

He beamed at them, adjusting round, thick-lensed glasses upward so that he might look through them. As his fingers moved away, the glasses slipped downward at once to a precarious perch upon the round nubbin of his snub nose. "I am Wendell Urth," he said.

The scraggly gray Van Dyke on his pudgy, round chin did not in the least add to the dignity which the smiling face and the stubby ellipsoidal torso so noticeably lacked.

"Gentlemen! It is good of you to come," Urth repeated, as he jerked himself backward into a chair from which his legs dangled with the toes of his shoes a full inch above the floor. "Mr. Davenport remembers, perhaps, that it is a matter of—uh—some importance to me to remain here. I do not like to travel, except to walk, of course, and a walk across the campus is quite enough for me."

Ashley looked baffled as he remained standing, and Urth stared at him with a growing bafflement of his own. He pulled a handkerchief out and wiped his glasses, then replaced them, and said, "Oh, I see the difficulty. You want chairs. Yes. Well, just take some. If there are things on them, just push them off. Push them off. Sit down, please."

Davenport removed the books from one chair and placed them carefully on the floor. He pushed it toward Ashley, then took a human skull off a second chair and placed it even more carefully on Urth's desk. Its mandible, insecurely wired, unhinged as he transferred it, and it sat there with jaw askew.

"Never mind," said Urth, affably, "it will not hurt. Now tell me what is on your mind, gentlemen?"

Davenport waited a moment for Ashley to speak, then rather gladly, took over. "Dr. Urth, do you remember a student of yours named Jennings? Karl Jennings?"

Urth's smile vanished momentarily with the effort of recall. His somewhat protuberant eyes blinked. "No," he said at last. "Not at the moment."

"A geology major. He took your extraterrology course some years ago. I have his photograph here if that will help—"

Urth studied the photograph handed him with near-sighted concentration, but still looked doubtful.

Davenport drove on. "He left a cryptic message which is the key to a matter of great importance. We have so far failed to interpret it satisfactorily, but this much we see—it indicates we are to come to you."

"Indeed? How interesting! For what purpose are you to come to me?"

"Presumably for your advice on interpreting the message."

"May I see it?"

Silently, Ashley passed the slip of paper to Wendell Urth. The extraterrologist looked at it casually, turned it over and stared for a moment at the blank back. He said, "Where does it say to ask me?"

Ashley looked startled, but Davenport forestalled him by saying, "The arrow pointing to the symbol of the Earth. It seems clear."

"It is clearly an arrow pointing to the symbol for the planet Earth. I suppose it might literally mean 'go to the Earth' if this were found on some other world."

"It was found on the Moon, Dr. Urth, and it could, I suppose, mean that. However, the reference to you seemed clear once we realized that Jennings had been a student of yours."

"He took a course in extraterrology here at the University?"

"That's right."

"In what year, Mr. Davenport?"

"In '18."

"Ah. The puzzle is solved."

"You mean the significance of the message?" said Davenport.

"No, no. The message has no meaning to me. I mean the puzzle of why it is that I did not remember him, for I remember him now. He was a very quiet fellow, anxious, shy, self-effacing—not at all the sort of person anyone would remember. Without this," and he tapped the message, "I might never have remembered him."

"Why does the card change things?" asked Davenport.

"The reference to me is a play on words. Earth—Urth. Not very subtle, of course, but that is Jennings. His unattainable delight was the pun. My only clear memory of him is his occasional attempts to perpetrate puns. I enjoy puns, I adore puns, but Jennings—yes, I remember him well now—was atrocious at it. Either that, or distressingly obvious at it, as in this case. He lacked all talent for puns, yet craved them so much."

Ashley suddenly broke in. "This message consists entirely of a kind of word-play, Dr. Urth. At least, we believe so, and that fits in with what you say."

"Ah!" Urth adjusted his glasses and peered through them once more at the card and the symbols it carried. He pursed his plump lips then said cheerfully, "I make nothing of it."

"In that case—" began Ashley, his hands balling into fists.

"But if you tell me what it's all about," Urth went on, "then perhaps it might mean something."

Davenport said quickly, "May I, sir? I am confident that this man can be relied on—and it may help."

"Go ahead," muttered Ashley, "At this point, what can it hurt?"

Davenport condensed the tale, giving it in crisp, telegraphic sentences, while Urth listened carefully, moving his stubby fingers over the shining milk-white desk top as though he were sweeping up invisible cigar ashes. Toward the end of the recital, he hitched up his legs and sat with them crossed like an amiable Buddha.

When Davenport was done, Urth thought a moment, then said, "Do you happen to have a transcript of the conversation reconstructed by Ferrant?"

"We do," said Davenport. "Would you like to see it?"

"Please."

Urth placed the strip of microfilm in a scanner and worked his way rapidly through it, his lips moving unintelligibly at some points. Then he tapped the reproduction of the cryptic message. "And this, you say, is the key to the entire matter? The crucial clue?"

"We think it is, Dr. Urth."

"But it is not the original. It is a reproduction."

"That is correct."

"The original has gone with this man, Ferrant, and you believe it to be in the hands of the Ultras."

"Quite possibly."

Urth shook his head and looked troubled. "Everyone knows my sympathies are not with the Ultras. I would fight them by all means, so I don't want to seem to be hanging back, but . . . what is there to say that this mind-affecting object exists at all? You have only the ravings of a psychotic and your dubious deductions from the reproduction of a mysterious set of marks that may mean nothing at all."

"Yes, Dr. Urth, but we can't take chances."

"How certain are you that this copy is accurate? What if the original has something on it that this lacks, something that makes the message quite clear, something without which the message must remain impenetrable."

"We are certain the copy is accurate."

"What about the reverse side? There is nothing on the back of this reproduction. What about the reverse of the original?"

"The agent who made the reproduction tells us that the back of the original was blank."

"Men can make mistakes."

"We have no reason to think he did, and we must work on the assumption that he didn't. At least until such time as the original is regained."

"Then you assure me," said Urth, "that any interpretation to be made of this message must be made on the basis of exactly what one sees here."

"We think so. We are virtually certain," said Davenport, with a sense of ebbing confidence.

Urth continued to look troubled. He said, "Why not leave the instrument where it is? If neither group finds it, so much the better. I disapprove of any tampering with minds and would not contribute to making it possible."

Davenport placed a restraining hand on Ashley's arm, sensing the other was about to speak. Davenport said, "Let me put it to you, Dr. Urth, that the mind-tampering aspect is not the whole of the Device. Suppose an Earth expedition to a distant primitive planet had dropped an old-fashioned radio there, and suppose the native population had discovered electric current but had not yet developed the vacuum tube.

"The population might discover that if the radio was hooked up to a current, certain glass objects within it would grow warm and would glow, but of course they would receive no intelligible sound, merely, at best, some buzzes and crackles. However, if they dropped the radio into a bathtub while it was plugged in, a person in that tub might be electrocuted. Should the people of this hypothetical planet therefore conclude that the device they were studying was designed solely for the purpose of killing people?"

"I see your analogy," said Urth. "You think that the mind-tampering property is merely an incidental function of the Device?"

"I'm sure of it," said Davenport earnestly. "If we can puzzle out its real purpose, earthly technology may leap ahead centuries."

"Then you agree with Jennings when he said—" Here Urth consulted the microfilm—"It might be the key to—who knows what? It might be the clue to an unimaginable scientific revolution."

"Exactly!"

"And yet the mind-tampering aspect is there and is infinitely dangerous. Whatever the radio's purpose, it *does* electrocute."

"Which is why we can't let the Ultras get it."

"Or the government either, perhaps?"

"But I must point out that there is a reasonable limit to caution. Consider that men have always held danger in their hands. The first flint knife in the old Stone Age, the first wooden club before that could kill. They could be used to bend weaker men to the will of stronger ones under threat of force and that, too, is a form of mind-tampering. What counts, Dr. Urth, is not the Device itself, however dangerous it may be in the abstract, but the intentions of the men who make use of the Device. The Ultras have the declared intention of killing off more than 99.9 percent of humanity. The government, whatever the faults of the men composing it, would have no such intention."

"What *would* the government intend?"

"A scientific study of the Device. Even the mind-tampering aspect itself could yield infinite good. Put to enlightened use, it could educate us concerning the physical basis of mental function. We might learn to correct mental disorders or cure the Ultras. Mankind might learn to develop greater intelligence generally."

"How can I believe that such idealism will be put into practice?"

"*I* believe so. Consider that you face a possible turn to evil by the government if you help us, but you risk the certain and declared evil purpose of the Ultras if you don't."

Urth nodded thoughtfully. "Perhaps you're right. And yet I have a favor to ask of you. I have a niece who is, I believe, quite fond of me. She is constantly upset over the fact that I steadfastly refuse to indulge in the lunacy of travel. She states that she will not rest content until someday I accompany her to Europe or North Carolina or some other outlandish place—"

Ashley leaned forward earnestly, brushing Davenport's restraining gesture to one side. "Dr. Urth, if you help us find the Device and if it can be made to work, then I assure you that we will be glad to help you free yourself of your phobia against travel and make it possible for you to go with your niece anywhere you wish."

Urth's bulging eyes widened and he seemed to shrink within himself. For a moment, he looked wildly about as though he were already trapped. "*No!*" he gasped. "Not at all! Never!"

His voice dropped to an earnest, hoarse whisper. "Let me explain the nature of my fee. If I help you; if you retrieve the Device and learn its use; if the fact of my help becomes public; then my niece will be on the government like a fury. She is a terribly headstrong and shrill-voiced woman who will raise public subscriptions and organize demonstrations. She will stop at nothing. And yet you must not give in to her. You must *not!* You must resist all pressures. I wish to be left alone exactly as I am now. That is my absolute and minimum fee."

Ashley flushed. "Yes, of course, since that is your wish."

"I have your word?"

"You have my word."

"Please remember. I rely on you, too, Mr. Davenport."

"It will be as you wish," soothed Davenport. "And now, I presume, you can interpret the items?"

"The items?" asked Urth, seeming to focus his attention with difficulty on the card. "You mean these markings, XY^2 and so on?"

"Yes. What do they mean?"

"I don't know. Your interpretations are as good as any I suppose."

Ashley exploded. "Do you mean that all this talk about helping us is nonsense? What was this maundering about a fee, then?"

Wendell Urth looked confused and taken aback. "I would like to help you."

"But you don't know what these items mean."

"I—I don't. But I know what this message means."

"You do?" cried Davenport.

"Of course. Its meaning is transparent. I suspected it halfway through your story. And I was sure of it once I read the reconstruction of the conversations between Strauss and Jennings. You would understand it yourself, gentlemen, if you would only stop to think."

"See here," said Ashley in exasperation. "You said you don't know what the items mean."

"I don't. I said I know what the *message* means."

"What is the message if it is not the items? Is it the paper, for Heaven's sake?"

"Yes, in a way."

"You mean invisible ink or something like that."

"No! Why is it so hard for you to understand, when you yourself stand on the brink?"

Davenport leaned toward Ashley and said in a low voice, "Sir, if you'll let me handle it, please?"

Ashley snorted, then said in a stifled manner. "Go ahead."

"Dr. Urth," said Davenport, "will you give us your analysis?"

"Ah! Well, all right." The little extraterrologist settled back in his chair and mopped his damp forehead on his sleeve. "Let's consider the message. If you accept the quartered circle and the arrow as directing you to me, that leaves seven items. If these indeed refer to seven craters, six of them, at least, must be designed merely to distract, since the Device surely cannot be in more than one place. It contained no movable or detachable parts—it was all one piece.

"Then, too, none of the items are straightforward. SU might, by your interpretation, mean any place on the other side of the Moon,

which is an area the size of South America. Again PC/2 can mean
'Tycho,' as Mr. Ashley says, or it can mean 'halfway between Ptolemaeus and Copernicus,' as Mr. Davenport thought, or for that matter 'halfway between Plato and Cassini.' To be sure, XY^2 could
mean 'Alfonsus'—very ingenious interpretation, that—but it could refer to some coordinate system in which the Y-coordinate was the
square of the X-coordinate. Similarly C-C would mean 'Bond' or it
could mean 'halfway between Cassini and Copernicus.' F/A could
mean 'Newton' or it could mean 'between Fabricius and Archimedes.'

"In short, the items have so many meanings that they are meaningless. Even if one of them had meaning, it could not be selected
from among the others so that it is only sensible to suppose that all
the items are merely red herrings.

"It is necessary, then, to determine what about the message is
completely unambiguous; what is perfectly clear. The answer to that
can only be that it *is* a message; that it *is* a clue to a hiding place.
That is the one thing we are certain about, isn't it?"

Davenport nodded, then said cautiously. "At least, we think we
are certain of it."

"Well, you have referred to this message as the key to the whole
matter. You have acted as though it were the crucial clue. Jennings
himself referred to the Device as a key or a clue. If we combine this
serious view of the matter with Jennings' penchant for puns, a penchant which may have been heightened by the mind-tampering Device he was carrying—So let me tell you a story—

"In the last half of the sixteenth century, there lived a German
Jesuit in Rome. He was a mathematician and astronomer of note
and helped Pope Gregory XIII reform the calendar in 1582, performing all the enormous calculations required. This astronomer admired Copernicus but he did not accept the heliocentric view of the
Solar system. He clung to the older belief that the Earth was the center of the Universe.

"In 1650, nearly forty years after the death of this mathematician,
the Moon was mapped by another Jesuit, the Italian astronomer,
Giovanni Battista Riccioli. He named the craters after astronomers
of the past and since he, too, rejected Copernicus, he selected the
largest and most spectacular craters for those who placed the Earth
at the center of the Universe—for Ptolemy, Hipparchus, Alfonso X,
Tycho Brahe. The biggest crater Riccioli could find he reserved for
his German Jesuit predecessor.

"This crater is actually only the second largest of the craters visible from Earth. The only larger crater is Bailly, which is right on the Moon's limb and is therefore very difficult to see from the Earth. Riccioli ignored it, and it was named for an astronomer who lived a century after his time and who was guillotined during the French Revolution."

Ashley was listening to all this restlessly. "But what has this to do with the message?"

"Why, everything," said Urth, with some surprise. "Did you not call this message the key to the whole business. Isn't it the crucial clue?"

"Yes, of course?"

"Is there any doubt that we are dealing with something that is a clue or key to something else."

"No, there isn't," said Ashley.

"Well, then—the name of the German Jesuit I have been speaking of is Christoph Klau—pronounced 'klow.' Don't you see the pun? Klau—clue?"

Ashley's entire body seemed to grow flabby with disappointment. "Far-fetched," he muttered.

Davenport said, anxiously, "Dr. Urth. There is no feature on the Moon named Klau as far as I know."

"Of course not," said Urth excitedly. "That is the whole point. At this period of history, the last half of the sixteenth century, European scholars were Latinizing their names. Klau did so. In place of the German "u," he made use of the equivalent letter, the Latin "v." He then added an "ius" ending typical of Latin names and Christoph Klau became Christopher Clavius, and I suppose you are all aware of the giant crater we call Clavius."

"But—" began Davenport.

"Don't 'but' me," said Urth. "Just let me point out that the Latin word 'clavis' means 'key.' Now do you see the double and bilingual pun? Klau—clue, Clavius—clavis—key. In his whole life, Jennings could never have made a double, bilingual pun without the Device. Now he could, and I wonder if death might not have been almost triumphant under the circumstances. And he directed you to me because he knew I would remember his penchant for puns and because he knew I loved them too."

The two men of the Bureau were looking at him wide-eyed.

Urth said solemnly, "I would suggest you search the shaded rim of Clavius, at that point where the Earth is nearest the zenith."

Ashley rose. "Where is your videophone?"

"In the next room."

Ashley dashed. Davenport lingered behind. "Are you sure, Dr. Urth?"

"Quite sure. But even if I am wrong, I suspect it doesn't matter."

"What doesn't matter?"

"Whether you find it or not. For if the Ultras find the Device, they will probably be unable to use it."

"Why do you say that?"

"You asked me if Jennings had ever been a student of mine, but you never asked me about Strauss, who was also a geologist. He was a student of mine a year or so after Jennings. I remember him well."

"Oh?"

"An unpleasant man. Very cold. It is the hallmark of the Ultras, I think. They are all very cold, very rigid, very sure of themselves. They can't empathize, or they wouldn't speak of killing off billions of human beings. What emotions they possess are icy ones, self-absorbed ones, feelings incapable of spanning the distance between two human beings."

"I think I see."

"I'm sure you do. The conversation reconstructed from Strauss's ravings showed us he could not manipulate the Device. He lacked the emotional intensity, or the type of necessary emotion. I imagine all Ultras would. Jennings, who was not an Ultra, could manipulate it. Anyone who could use the Device would, I suspect, be incapable of deliberate cold-blooded cruelty. He might strike out of panic fear as Jennings struck at Strauss, but never out of calculation, as Strauss tried to strike at Jennings. —In short, to put it tritely, I think the Device can be actuated by love, but never by hate, and the Ultras are nothing if not haters."

Davenport nodded. "I hope you're right. But then—why were you so suspicious of the government's motives, if you felt the wrong men could not manipulate the Device?"

Urth shrugged. "I wanted to make sure you could bluff and rationalize on your feet and make yourself convincingly persuasive at a moment's notice. After all, you may have to face my niece."

Isaac Asimov

by L. SPRAGUE DE CAMP

In the summer of 1939, in the office of John W. Campbell, I met a slim, good-looking stripling of medium height, with blue eyes, dark-brown hair, and a downy mustache. This, Campbell told me, was one of his newest writers, Isaac Asimov.

Since I was some years older than he and had been writing professionally for all of two years longer, it seemed like a case of old pro to eager novice. That distinction vanished in a few months, as Isaac got the writing bit in his teeth and ran away with it. He soon pulled ahead of me in total sales, and I have been panting in his wake ever since.

The next time I saw Isaac was at a fan meeting in New York. Called upon to introduce himself, he said: "I am the world's worst science-fiction writer." For a number of years he persisted in this pose of modesty. At last he became so famous, both as a science-fictioneer and as a non-fiction popularizer of science, that it sounded silly, like Sir Edmund Hilary apologizing for being such a feeble mountain climber.

Anyway, as the years passed, my wife Catherine and I came to know Isaac better, and the better we knew him the more he became one of our very favorite people. We learned that he was born in the Soviet Union, near Smolyensk, in 1920 and was brought to the United States three years later; that his parents ran a candy store in Brooklyn; that he had just graduated from Columbia University as a chemist and was working there for his master's. He financed his higher education by professional writing. Thousands of Americans list themselves as "writers" in the Census but fail to make a living even when they write full-time. And here was Isaac, writing part-time . . .

The mustache disappeared when he got married (I have always thought it a pity) and the Hitlerian War gathered us up. Robert Heinlein, Isaac Asimov, and I all went to work for what was then the Naval Aircraft Factory and is now the Naval Air Experimental Station at the Philadelphia Navy Yard. There we worked for three and a half years, fighting the Axis with slide rule and requisition forms in quintuplicate. We did test and development engineering on naval aircraft parts, accessories, and materials.

After the war, I hung up my uniform while Isaac put his on. The Army kept him for a year. Some might not pick Isaac as a natural soldier, and certainly he would not claim he was cut out for that career. But, like Edgar Allan Poe under similar circumstances, he did all right. He made corporal by the time he got out.

He went back to Columbia, got his Ph.D., and took a chair at the Boston University School of Medicine.

For some years he worked on cancer research; but then, although he is still "Professor Asimov," he tapered off his academic work to spend more and more time on writing. For the last decade, he has been turning out big, solid scientific popularizations and reference books, in addition to his stories, so fast that I have abandoned trying to keep up with them. If I read them all, I should have no time left to write anything myself. That is a terrible thing to have one of one's favorite writers do to one. Note that, while Isaac is one of the merriest of men in private life, his stories have usually been serious in tone. Writers of funny stories, on the contrary, are often pretty solemn squares in private life.

Naturally, Catherine and I have come to know Isaac pretty well. For instance, we claim the credit or blame for introducing him to the demon rum. About 1941, in our apartment in New York, we gave him his first drink. It was just a teensy drink, but he turned a funny purple color, with spots, and complained of feeling strange. After he left us, he rode the subway back and forth until he felt normal enough to go home. It wasn't inebriety but some allergy that got him. So, wise man, he swore off the sauce and has stayed off it ever since. Such an ebullient personality doesn't need liquor anyway.

Also naturally, we have formed ideas as to what makes Isaac tick. I will not fill pages with what a lovable fellow Isaac is. Of course he is, and everybody who knows him knows it. To tell you how much the de Camps love Isaac is merely to lose ourselves in a vast throng. I will, instead, tell about some of his less obvious qualities.

For one thing, he has character of a very definite kind. Some people may be described as human mollusks, with a hard shell of self-confidence and self-assertion, inside of which they are mush. Isaac is the opposite. Because he clowns and jokes, and because he is so sympathetic and generous, he gives the impression that he is a push-over for anybody who wants to sway him or to take advantage of him. Some people have indeed taken advantage of him.

Inside this soft exterior, however, is a hard core of character. When he decides that he will not be pushed further, an elephant won't budge him. When he decides that something is not for him, neither wheedling nor bribery nor threats will induce him to partake of it.

Let me give a couple of examples. In his youth, he was never one to get into fights. If he never exactly turned the other cheek, he could usually joke his way out of a confrontation. Nor was he ever much for sports, although he had powerful muscles.

But, when a schoolmate, after failing to get a rise out of Isaac by pestering him, made some derogatory remark about Isaac's mother, Isaac went for him. The tormenter hit Isaac here, there, and every-where, but he might as well have punched the statue of General Sherman in Central Park. Isaac got his hands on the other boy's windpipe and would probably have strangled him to death if adults had not pulled him off.

Again, when he and I were working for Uncle at the Philadelphia Navy Yard, we once had a commanding officer whom I shall call "Commander Fuller." If any reader saw the original stage production of *Mister Roberts,* Commander Fuller was the captain in *Mister Roberts* to the life. If you didn't, the movie gave a pretty good idea.

Well, Commander Fuller was wont to make life hard for the ci-vilian employees in his laboratories, especially those of Jewish origin. He decided to treat Isaac in what I suppose he thought was a friendly manner, loudly crying: "Hey there, Ikey!" at every encounter and then laughing like a kookaburra. Isaac did not like the nickname "Ikey." After standing it as long as he could, he burst out:

"Commander Fuller, call me 'Isaac' or call me 'Mr. Asimov,' but *don't* call me 'Ikey'!"

Fuller went away and never bothered Isaac again.

Then again, a few years ago, he decided that he had grown too heavy. So he cut down on his calories, and the next time I saw him he was thirty pounds lighter. He stuck to the new weight, too. He has a will of steel when he chooses to employ it.

Of course, this trait has its awkward points. Since everybody (except the Commander Fullers of this world) loves Isaac, everybody wants to bring him up and improve him. (For years he has been one of the leading improvees on my wife's list.) That means, they want him to do things the way they like to do them, which may or may not be the way Isaac likes.

I have long tried, for instance, to overcome his hatred of travel by describing to him the joys of being gypped by taxi drivers in Paris, being chased by a hippopotamus in Uganda, and catching Montezuma's revenge in Yucatán. Somehow I don't seem to have gotten very far. I fear that people who undertake thus to change Isaac are trying to bail out the ocean. They would get further if they put the effort in perfecting themselves.

That leaves what is, after all, Isaac's most important trait. This is sheer intelligence. You can't beat brains. When he is faced with a predicament—whether in writing or in lifesmanship—he may clown and holler and emote a bit, but in the end he sits down and *thinks* his way through. And, since his brain works twice as fast and reaches twice as far as most people's, he is twice as likely to reach the right conclusion.

Take, for example, Isaac and the Army rifle. Since Isaac grew up where law-abiding people did not own guns, he never got on familiar terms with guns. I once undertook to teach him to shoot a pistol. It was a little like trying to teach a man who dislikes snakes how to catch a live rattlesnake with the bare hand.

However, came the Army. Isaac had known little more about a rifle than the fact that the bullet comes out the small end. He was given a Garand M-1, instructed in its use, and told to go out on the range, lie down, and shoot at a target. Although it was snowing, and Isaac wears glasses, he made sharpshooter. He simply listened to what he was told and applied these instructions intelligently.

So, if I were about to be shot off to the third planet of Alpha Centauri and were given a choice of companions, I think I should pick Isaac. Not that many other people aren't better trained or more Tarzanlike to begin with. But I should know that, when things get tough, Isaac could think our way out if anybody could.

But, how shall I ever get him to Alpha Centauri when it is almost impossible to drag him from Boston to Philadelphia?

Bibliography of books by Isaac Asimov

Fiction

PEBBLE IN THE SKY, Doubleday, 1950
I, ROBOT, Gnome, 1950
THE STARS, LIKE DUST—, Doubleday, 1951
FOUNDATION, Gnome, 1951
DAVID STARR: SPACE RANGER, Doubleday, 1952
FOUNDATION AND EMPIRE, Gnome, 1952
THE CURRENTS OF SPACE, Doubleday, 1952
SECOND FOUNDATION, Gnome, 1953
LUCKY STARR AND THE PIRATES OF THE ASTEROIDS, Doubleday, 1953
THE CAVES OF STEEL, Doubleday, 1954
LUCKY STARR AND THE OCEANS OF VENUS, Doubleday, 1954
THE MARTIAN WAY AND OTHER STORIES, Doubleday, 1955
THE END OF ETERNITY, Doubleday, 1955
LUCKY STARR AND THE BIG SUN OF MERCURY, Doubleday, 1956
THE NAKED SUN, Doubleday, 1957
LUCKY STARR AND THE MOONS OF JUPITER, Doubleday, 1957
EARTH IS ROOM ENOUGH, Doubleday, 1957
LUCKY STARR AND THE RINGS OF SATURN, Doubleday, 1958
THE DEATH DEALERS, Avon, 1958
NINE TOMORROWS, Doubleday, 1959
THE HUGO WINNERS, Doubleday, 1962
FIFTY SHORT SCIENCE FICTION TALES, Collier Books, 1963
THE REST OF THE ROBOTS, Doubleday, 1964
FANTASTIC VOYAGE, Houghton-Mifflin, 1966
TOMORROW'S CHILDREN, Doubleday, 1966
THROUGH A GLASS CLEARLY, New English Library, 1966
ASIMOV'S MYSTERIES, Doubleday, 1968
NIGHTFALL AND OTHER STORIES, Doubleday, 1969
THE BEST NEW THING, World, 1971

THE HUGO WINNERS, VOLUME TWO, Doubleday, 1971
WHERE DO WE GO FROM HERE?, Doubleday, 1971
THE GODS THEMSELVES, Doubleday, 1972
THE EARLY ASIMOV, Doubleday, 1972

Non-Fiction

BIOCHEMISTRY AND HUMAN METABOLISM, (Biochemistry), Williams & Wilkins, 1952

THE CHEMICALS OF LIFE, (Biochemistry), Abelard-Schuman, 1954

RACES AND PEOPLE, (Anthropology), Abelard-Schuman, 1955

CHEMISTRY AND HUMAN HEALTH, (Chemistry), McGraw-Hill, 1956

INSIDE THE ATOM, (Physics), Abelard-Schuman, 1956

BUILDING BLOCKS OF THE UNIVERSE, (Chemistry), Abelard-Schuman, 1957

THE WORLD OF CARBON, (Chemistry), Abelard-Schuman, 1958

THE WORLD OF NITROGEN, (Chemistry), Abelard-Schuman, 1958

THE CLOCK WE LIVE ON, (Astronomy), Abelard-Schuman, 1959

WORDS OF SCIENCE, (General Science), Houghton-Mifflin, 1959

REALM OF NUMBER, (Mathematics), Houghton-Mifflin, 1959

THE LIVING RIVER, (Biology), Abelard-Schuman, 1960

THE KINGDOM OF THE SUN, (Astronomy), Abelard-Schuman, 1960

REALM OF MEASURE, (Mathematics), Houghton-Mifflin, 1960

BREAKTHROUGHS IN SCIENCE, (Science History), Houghton-Mifflin, 1960

SATELLITES IN OUTER SPACE, (Astronomy), Random House, 1960

THE WELLSPRINGS OF LIFE, (Biology), Abelard-Schuman, 1960

THE INTELLIGENT MAN'S GUIDE TO SCIENCE, (General Science), Basic Books, 1960

THE DOUBLE PLANET, (Astronomy), Abelard-Schuman, 1960

WORDS FROM THE MYTHS, (Mythology), Houghton-Mifflin, 1961

REALM OF ALGEBRA, (Mathematics), Houghton-Mifflin, 1961

LIFE AND ENERGY, (Chemistry), Doubleday, 1962

WORDS IN GENESIS, (Bible), Houghton-Mifflin, 1962

WORDS ON THE MAP, (Geography), Houghton-Mifflin, 1962

THE SEARCH FOR THE ELEMENTS, (Chemistry), Basic Books, 1962

WORDS FROM THE EXODUS, (Bible), Houghton-Mifflin, 1963

THE GENETIC CODE, (Biochemistry), Orion Press, 1963

THE HUMAN BODY, (Biology), Houghton-Mifflin, 1963

THE KITE THAT WON THE REVOLUTION, (Science History), Houghton-Mifflin, 1963

THE HUMAN BRAIN, (Biology), Houghton-Mifflin, 1964

A SHORT HISTORY OF BIOLOGY, (Science History), Doubleday, 1964

QUICK AND EASY MATH, (Mathematics), Houghton-Mifflin, 1964

PLANETS FOR MAN, (Astronomy), Random House, 1964

ASIMOV'S BIOGRAPHICAL ENCYCLOPEDIA OF SCIENCE AND TECHNOLOGY, (Science History), Doubleday, 1964

A SHORT HISTORY OF CHEMISTRY, (Science History), Doubleday, 1965

THE GREEKS, (History), Houghton-Mifflin, 1965

THE NEW INTELLIGENT MAN'S GUIDE TO SCIENCE, (General Science), Basic Books, 1965

AN EASY INTRODUCTION TO THE SLIDE RULE, (Mathematics), Houghton-Mifflin, 1965

THE ROMAN REPUBLIC, (History), Houghton-Mifflin, 1966

THE NEUTRINO, (Physics), Doubleday, 1966

ENVIRONMENTS OUT THERE, (Astronomy), Abelard-Schuman, 1966

UNDERSTANDING PHYSICS, (Physics), Walker & Co., 1966

GENETIC EFFECTS OF RADIATION, (Physics), Atomic Energy Comm., 1966

THE NOBLE GASES, (Chemistry), Basic Books, 1966

THE UNIVERSE, (Astronomy), Walker & Co., 1966

THE MOON, (Astronomy), Follett, 1966

ENVIRONMENTS OUT THERE, (Astronomy), Abelard-Schuman, 1967

THE ROMAN EMPIRE, (History), Houghton-Mifflin, 1967

TO THE ENDS OF THE UNIVERSE, (Astronomy), Walker, 1967

MARS, (Astronomy), Follett, 1967

THE EGYPTIANS, (History), Houghton-Mifflin, 1967

STARS, (Astronomy), Follett, 1968

GALAXIES, (Astronomy), Follett, 1968

THE NEAR EAST, (History), Houghton-Mifflin, 1968

THE DARK AGES, (History), Houghton-Mifflin, 1968

ASIMOV'S GUIDE TO THE BIBLE, (Literature), Doubleday, 1968

WORDS FROM HISTORY, (History), Houghton-Mifflin, 1968

PHOTOSYNTHESIS, (Biochemistry), Basic Books, 1969

THE SHAPING OF ENGLAND, (History), Houghton-Mifflin, 1969

TWENTIETH CENTURY DISCOVERY, (General Science), Doubleday, 1969

ASIMOV'S GUIDE TO THE BIBLE, Volume 2, (Literature), Doubleday, 1969

OPUS 100, (Autobiography), Houghton-Mifflin, 1969

ABCS OF SPACE, (Astronomy), Walker, 1969

GREAT IDEAS OF SCIENCE, (General Science), Houghton-Mifflin, 1969

ASIMOV'S GUIDE TO SHAKESPEARE, VOLUME I, (Literature), Doubleday, 1970

ASIMOV'S GUIDE TO SHAKESPEARE, VOLUME II, (Literature), Doubleday, 1970

CONSTANTINOPLE, (History), Houghton-Mifflin, 1970

ABCS OF THE OCEAN, (Earth Science), Walker, 1970

LIGHT, (Physics), Follett, 1970

WHAT MAKES THE SUN SHINE?, (Astronomy), Little, Brown, 1971

THE SENSUOUS DIRTY OLD MAN, (Satire), Walker, 1971

ISAAC ASIMOV'S TREASURY OF HUMOR, (Humor), Houghton-Mifflin, 1971

THE LAND OF CANAAN, (History), Houghton-Mifflin, 1971

ABCS OF THE EARTH, (Earth Sciences), Walker, 1971

ASIMOV'S BIOGRAPHICAL ENCYCLOPEDIA OF SCIENCE AND TECHNOLOGY, revised ed., (History of Science), Doubleday, 1972

ASIMOV'S GUIDE TO SCIENCE, (General Science), Basic Books, 1972

MORE WORDS OF SCIENCE, (General Science), Houghton-Mifflin, 1972

ELECTRICITY AND MAN, (Physics), Atomic Energy Commission, 1972

ABCS OF ECOLOGY, (General Science), Walker, 1972

THE SHAPING OF FRANCE, (History), Houghton-Mifflin, 1972

THE STORY OF RUTH, (Bible), Doubleday, 1972

GINN SCIENCE PROGRAM-INTERMEDIATE LEVEL A, (Textbook), Ginn, 1972

GINN SCIENCE PROGRAM-INTERMEDIATE LEVEL B, (Textbook), Ginn, 1972

GINN SCIENCE PROGRAM-INTERMEDIATE LEVEL C, (Textbook), Ginn, 1972

GINN SCIENCE PROGRAM-ADVANCED LEVEL A, (Textbook), Ginn, 1972

GINN SCIENCE PROGRAM-ADVANCED LEVEL B, (Textbook), Ginn, 1972

ASIMOV'S ANNOTATED DON JUAN, (Literature), Doubleday, 1972

WORLDS WITHIN WORLDS, (Physics), Atomic Energy Commission, 1972

HOW DID WE FIND OUT THE EARTH WAS ROUND, (History of Science), Walker, 1973

COMETS AND METEORS, (Astronomy), Follett, 1973

THE SUN, (Astronomy), Follett, 1973

HOW DID WE FIND OUT ABOUT ELECTRICITY, (History of Science), Walker, 1973

THE SHAPING OF NORTH AMERICA, (History), Houghton-Mifflin, 1973

JUPITER, THE LARGEST PLANET, (Astronomy), Lothrop, Lee & Shepard, 1973

HOW DID WE FIND OUT ABOUT NUMBERS, (History of Science), Walker, 1973

PLEASE EXPLAIN, (General Science), Houghton-Mifflin, 1973

HOW DID WE FIND OUT ABOUT DINOSAURS, (History of Science), Walker, 1973

Science Essays

IS ANYONE THERE?, Doubleday, 1967

SCIENCE, NUMBERS AND I, Doubleday, 1968

THE SOLAR SYSTEM AND BACK, Doubleday, 1970

THE STARS IN THEIR COURSES, Doubleday, 1971

THE LEFT HAND OF THE ELECTRON, Doubleday, 1972

TODAY AND TOMORROW AND—, Doubleday, 1973

THE TRAGEDY OF THE MOON, Doubleday, 1973

Fritz Leiber

Ship of Shadows

by FRITZ LEIBER

"Issiot! Fffool! Lushshsh!" hissed the cat and bit Spar somewhere.

The fourfold sting balanced the gut-wretchedness of his looming hangover, so that Spar's mind floated as free as his body in the blackness of Windrush, in which shone only a couple of running lights dim as churning dream-glow and infinitely distant as the Bridge or the Stern.

The vision came of a ship with all sails set creaming through blue, wind-ruffled sea against a blue sky. The last two nouns were not obscene now. He could hear the whistle of the salty wind through shrouds and stays, its drumming against the taut sails, and the creak of the three masts and all the rest of the ship's wood.

What was wood? From somewhere came the answer: plastic alive-o.

And what force flattened the water and kept it from breaking up into great globules and the ship from spinning away, keel over masts, in the wind?

Instead of being blurred and rounded like reality, the vision was sharp-edged and bright—the sort Spar never told, for fear of Ssee ffar! Ssee fforever! Fforessee! Afftssee!"

Spar felt a surge of irritation at this constant talk of seeing—bad manners in the cat!—followed by an irrational surge of hope about his eyes. He decided that this was no witch cat left over from his dream, but a stray which had wormed its way through a wind tube into the Bat Rack, setting off his dream. There were quite a few animal strays in these days of the witch panic and the depopulation of the Ship, or at least of Hold Three.

Dawn struck the Bow then, for the violet fore-corner of the Bat

Rack began to glow. The running lights were drowned in a growing white blaze. Within twenty heartbeats Windrush was bright as it ever would be on Workday or any other morning.

Out along Spar's arm moved the cat, a black blur to his squinting eyes. In teeth Spar could not see, it held a smaller gray blur. Spar touched the latter. It was even shorter furred, but cold.

As if irked, the cat took off from his bare forearm with a strong push of hind legs. It landed expertly on the next shroud, a wavery line of gray that vanished in either direction before reaching a wall.

Spar unclipped himself, curled his toes round his own pencil-thin shroud, and squinted at the cat.

The cat stared back with eyes that were green blurs which almost coalesced in the black blur of its outsize head.

Spar asked, "Your child? Dead?"

The cat loosed its gray burden, which floated beside its head.

"Chchchchild!" All the former scorn and more were back in the sibilant voice. "It izzzz a rat I sssslew her, issssiot!"

Spar's lips puckered in a smile. "I like you, cat. I will call you Kim."

"Kim-shlim!" the cat spat. "I'll call you Lushshsh! Or Sssot!"

The creaking increased, as it always did after dayspring and noon. Shrouds twanged. Walls crackled.

Spar swiftly swiveled his head. Though reality was by its nature a blur, he could unerringly spot movement.

Keeper was slowly floating straight at him. On the round of his russet body was mounted the great, pale round of his face, its bright pink target-center drawing attention from the tiny, wide-set, brown blurs of his eyes. One of his fat arms ended in the bright gleam of pliofilm, the other in the dark gleam of steel. Far beyond him was the dark red aft corner of the Bat Rack, with the great gleaming torus, or doughnut, of the bar midway between.

"Lazy, pampered he-slut," Keeper greeted. "All Sleepday you snored while I stood guard, and now I bring your morning pouch of moonmist to your sleeping shroud.

"A bad night, Spar," he went on, his voice growing sententious. "Werewolves, vampires, and witches loose in the corridors. But I stood them off, not to mention rats and mice. I heard through the tubes that the vamps got Girlie and Sweetheart, the silly sluts! Vigilance, Spar! Now suck your moonmist and start sweeping. The place stinks."

He stretched out the pliofilm-gleaming hand.

His mind hissing with Kim's contemptuous words, Spar said, "I don't think I'll drink this morning, Keeper. Corn gruel and moon-brew only. No, water."

"What, Spar?" Keeper demanded. "I don't believe I can allow that. We don't want you having convulsions in front of the customers. Earth strangle me!—what's that?"

Spar instantly launched himself at Keeper's steel-gleaming hand. Behind him his shroud twanged. With one hand he twisted a cold, thick barrel. With the other he pried a plump finger from a trigger.

"He's not a witch cat, only a stray," he said as they tumbled over and kept slowly rotating.

"Unhand me, underling!" Keeper blustered. "I'll have you in irons. I'll tell Crown."

"Shooting weapons are as much against the law as knives or needles," Spar countered boldly, though he already was feeling dizzy and sick. "It's you should fear the brig." He recognized beneath the bullying voice the awe Keeper always had of his ability to move swiftly and surely, though half-blind.

They bounced to rest against a swarm of shrouds. "Loose me, I say," Keeper demanded, struggling weakly. "Crown gave me this pistol. And I have a permit for it from the Bridge." The last at least, Spar guessed, was a lie. Keeper continued, "Besides, it's only a line-shooting gun reworked for heavy, elastic ball. Not enough to rupture a wall, yet sufficient to knock out drunks—or knock in the head of a witch cat!"

"Not a witch cat, Keeper," Spar repeated, although he was having to swallow hard to keep from spewing. "Only a well-behaved stray, who has already proved his use to us by killing one of the rats that have been stealing our food. His name is Kim. He'll be a good worker."

The distant blur of Kim lengthened and showed thin blurs of legs and tail, as if he were standing out rampant from his line. "Assset izz I," he boasted. "Ssanitary. Uzze wasste tubes. Sslay ratss, micece! Sspy out witchchess, vampss ffor you!"

"He speaks!" Keeper gasped. "Witchcraft!"

"Crown has a dog who talks," Spar answered with finality. "A talking animal's no proof of anything."

All this while he had kept firm hold of barrel and finger. Now he

felt through their grappled bodies a change in Keeper, as though inside his blubber the master of the Bat Rack were transforming from
stocky muscle and bone into a very thick, sweet syrup that could
conform to and flow around anything.

"Sorry, Spar," he whispered unctuously. "It was a bad night and
Kim startled me. He's black like a witch cat. An easy mistake on my
part. We'll try him out at catcher. He must earn his keep! Now take
your drink."

The pliant double pouch filling Spar's palm felt like the philoso-
pher's stone. He lifted it toward his lips, but at the same time his toes
unwittingly found a shroud, and he dove swiftly toward the shining
torus, which had a hole big enough to accommodate four barmen at
a pinch.

Spar collapsed against the opposite inside of the hole. With a strain-
ing of its shrouds, the torus absorbed his impact. He had the pouch
to his lips, its cap unscrewed, but had not squeezed. He shut his eyes
and with a tiny sob blindly thrust the pouch back into the moonmist
cage.

Working chiefly by touch, he took a pouch of corn gruel from the
hot closet, snitching at the same time a pouch of coffee and thrusting
it into an inside pocket. Then he took a pouch of water, opened it,
shoved in five salt tablets, closed it, and shook and squeezed it
vigorously.

Keeper, having drifted behind him, said into his ear, "So you drink
anyhow. Moonmist not good enough, you make yourself a cocktail.
I should dock it from your scrip. But all drunks are liars, or become
so."

Unable to ignore the taunt, Spar explained, "No, only salt water
to harden my gums."

"Poor Spar, what'll you ever need hard gums for? Planning to
share rats with your new friend? Don't let me catch you roasting them
in my grill! I should dock you for the salt. To sweeping, Spar!" Then
turning his head toward the violet fore-corner and speaking loudly,
"And you! Catch mice!"

Kim had already found the small chewer tube and thrust the dead
rat into it, gripping tube with foreclaws and pushing rat with aft. At
the touch of the rat's cadaver against the solid wrist of the tube, a
grinding began there which would continue until the rat was macer-

ated and slowly swallowed away toward the great cloaca which fed the Gardens of Diana.

Three times Spar manfully swished salt water against his gums and spat into a waste tube, vomiting a little after the first gargle. Then facing away from Keeper as he gently squeezed the pouches, he forced into his throat the coffee—dearer than moonmist, the drink distilled from moonbrew—and some of the corn gruel.

He apologetically offered the rest to Kim, who shook his head. "Jusst had a mousse."

Hastily Spar made his way to the green starboard corner. Outside the hatch he heard some drunks calling with weary and mournful anger, "Unzip!"

Grasping the heads of two long waste tubes, Spar began to sweep the air, working out from the green corner in a spiral, quite like an orb spider building her web.

From the torus, where he was idly polishing its thin titanium, Keeper upped the suction on the two tubes, so that reaction sped Spar in his spiral. He need use his body only to steer course and to avoid shrouds in such a way that his tubes didn't tangle.

Soon Keeper glanced at his wrist and called, "Spar, can't you keep track of the time? Open up!" He threw a ring of keys which Spar caught, though he could see only the last half of their flight. As soon as he was well headed toward the green door, Keeper called again and pointed aft and aloft. Spar obediently unlocked and unzipped the dark and also the blue hatch, though there was no one at either, before opening the green. In each case he avoided the hatch's gummy margin and the sticky emergency hatch hinged close beside.

In tumbled three brewos, old customers, snatching at shrouds and pushing off from each other's bodies in their haste to reach the torus, and meanwhile cursing Spar.

"Sky strangle you!"

"Earth bury you!"

"Seas sear you!"

"Language, boys!" Keeper reproved. "Though I'll agree my helper's stupidity and sloth tempt a man to talk foul."

Spar threw the keys back. The brewos lined up elbow to elbow around the torus, three grayish blobs with heads pointing toward the blue corner.

Keeper faced them. "Below, below!" he ordered indignantly. "You think you're gents?"

"But you're serving no one aloft yet."

"There's only us three."

"No matter," Keeper replied. "Propriety, suckers! Unless you mean to buy by the pouch, invert."

With low grumbles the brewos reversed their bodies so that their heads pointed toward the black corner.

Himself not bothering to invert, Keeper tossed them a slim and twisty faint red blur with three branches. Each grabbed a branch and stuck it in his face.

The pudge of his fat hand on glint of valve, Keeper said, "Let's see your scrip first."

With angry mumbles each unwadded something too small for Spar to see clearly, and handed it over. Keeper studied each item before feeding it to the cashbox. Then he decreed, "Six seconds of moonbrew. Suck fast," and looked at his wrist and moved the other hand.

One of the brewos seemed to be strangling, but he blew out through his nose and kept sucking bravely.

Keeper closed the valve.

Instantly one brewo splutteringly accused, "You cut us off too soon. That wasn't six."

The treacle back in his voice, Keeper explained, "I'm squirting it to you four and two. Don't want you to drown. Ready again?"

The brewos greedily took their second squirt and then, at times wistfully sucking their tubes for remnant drops, began to shoot the breeze. In his distant circling, Spar's keen ears heard most of it.

"A dirty Sleepday, Keeper."

"No, a good one, brewo—for a drunken sucker to get his blood sucked by a lust-tickling vamp."

"I was dossed safe at Pete's, you fat ghoul."

"Pete's safe? That's news!"

"Dirty Atoms to you! But vamps did get Girlie and Sweetheart. Right in the starboard main drag, if you can believe it. By Cobalt Ninety, Windrush is getting lonely! Third Hold, anyhow. You can swim a whole passageway by day without meeting a soul."

"How do you know that about the girls?" the second brewo demanded. "Maybe they've gone to another hold to change their luck."

"Their luck's run out. Suzy saw them snatched."

"Not Suzy," Keeper corrected, now playing umpire. "But Mable did. A proper fate for drunken sluts."

"You've got no heart, Keeper."

"True enough. That's why the vamps pass me by. But speaking serious, boys, the werethings and witches are running too free in Three. I was awake all Sleepday guarding. I'm sending a complaint to the Bridge."

"You're kidding."

"You wouldn't."

Keeper solemnly nodded his head and crossed his left chest. The brewos were impressed.

Spar spiraled back toward the green corner, sweeping farther from the wall. On his way he overtook the black blob of Kim, who was circling the periphery himself, industriously leaping from shroud to shroud and occasionally making dashes along them.

A fair-skinned, plump shape twice circled by blue—bra and culottes —swam in through the green hatch.

"Morning, Spar," a soft voice greeted. "How's it going?"

"Fair and foul," Spar replied. The golden cloud of blonde hair floating loose touched his face. "I'm quitting moonmist, Suzy."

"Don't be too hard on yourself, Spar. Work a day, loaf a day, play a day, sleep a day—that way it's best."

"I know. Workday, Loafday, Playday, Sleepday. Ten days make a terranth, twelve terranths make a sunth, twelve sunths make a starth, and so on, to the end of time. With corrections, some tell me. I wish I knew what all those names mean."

"You're too serious. You should—Oh, a kitten! How darling!"

"Kitten-shmitten!" the big-headed black blur hissed as it leapt past them. "Izzz cat. IZZZ Kim."

"Kim's our new catcher," Spar explained. "He's serious too."

"Quit wasting time on old Toothless Eyeless, Suzy," Keeper called, "and come all the way in."

As Suzy complied with a sigh, taking the easy route of the ratlines, her soft taper fingers brushed Spar's crumpled cheek. "Dear Spar . . ." she murmured. As her feet passed his face, there was a jingle of her charm-anklet—all gold-washed hearts, Spar knew.

"Hear about Girlie and Sweetheart?" a brewo greeted ghoulishly. "How'd you like your carotid or outside iliac sliced, your—?"

"Shut up, sucker!" Suzy wearily cut him off. "Gimme a drink, Keeper."

"Your tab's long, Suzy. How you going to pay?"

"Don't play games, Keeper, please. Not in the morning, anyhow. You know all the answers, especially to that one. For now, a pouch of moonbrew, dark. And a little quiet."

"Pouches are for ladies, Suzy. I'll serve you aloft, you got to meet your marks, but—"

There was a shrill snarl which swiftly mounted to a scream of rage. Just inside the aft hatch, a pale figure in vermilion culottes and bra—no, wider than that, jacket or short coat—was struggling madly, somersaulting and kicking.

Entering carelessly, likely too swiftly, the slim girl had got parts of herself and her clothes stuck to the hatch's inside margin and the emergency hatch.

Breaking loose by frantic main force while Spar dove toward her and the brewos shouted advice, she streaked toward the torus, jerking at the ratlines, black hair streaming behind her.

Coming up with a *bong* of hip against titanium, she grabbed together her vermilion—yes, clutch coat with one hand and thrust the other across the rocking bar.

Drifting in close behind, Spar heard her say, "Double pouch of moonmist, Keeper. Make it fast."

"The best of mornings to you, Rixende," Keeper greeted. "I would gladly serve you goldwater, except, well—" The fat arms spread "—Crown doesn't like his girls coming to the Bat Rack by themselves. Last time he gave me strict orders to—"

"What the smoke! It's on Crown's account I came here, to find something he lost. Meanwhile, moonmist. Double!" She pounded on the bar until reaction started her aloft, and she pulled back into place with Spar's unthanked help.

"Softly, softly, lady," Keeper gentled, the tiny brown blurs of his eyes vanishing with his grinning. "What if Crown comes in while you're squeezing?"

"He won't!" Rixende denied vehemently, though glancing past Spar quickly—black blur, blur of pale face, black blur again. "He's got a new girl. I don't mean Phanette or Doucette, but a girl you've never seen. Name of Almodie. He'll be busy with the skinny bitch all morning. And now uncage that double moonmist, you dirty devil!"

"Softly, Rixie. All in good time. What is it Crown lost?"

"A little black bag. About so big." She extended her slender hand, fingers merged. "He lost it here last Playday night, or had it lifted."

"Hear that, Spar?" Keeper said.

"No little black bags," Spar said very quickly. "But you did leave your big orange one here last night, Rixende. I'll get it." He swung inside the torus.

"Oh, damn both bags. Gimme that double!" the black-haired girl demanded frantically. "Earth Mother!"

Even the brewos gasped. Touching hands to the sides of his head, Keeper begged. "No big obscenities, please. They sound worse from a dainty girl, gentle Rixende."

"Earth Mother, I said! Now cut the fancy, Keeper, and give, before I scratch your face off and rummage your cages!"

"Very well, very well. At once, at once. But how will you pay? Crown told me he'd get my license revoked if I ever put you on his tab again. Have you scrip? Or . . . coins?"

"Use your eyes! Or you think this coat's got inside pockets?" She spread it wide, flashing her upper body, then clutched it tight again. "Earth Mother! Earth Mother! Earth Mother!" The brewos babbled scandalized. Suzy snorted mildly in boredom.

With one fat hand-blob Keeper touched Rixende's wrist where a yellow blur circled it closely. "You've got gold," he said in hushed tones, his eyes vanishing again, this time in greed.

"You know damn well they're welded on. My anklets too."

"But these?" His hand went to a golden blur close beside her head.

"Welded too. Crown had my ears pierced."

"But . . ."

"Oh, you atom-dirty devil! I get you, all right. Well, then, *all right!*" The last words ended in a scream more of anger than pain as she grabbed a gold blur and jerked. Blood swiftly blobbed out. She thrust forward her fisted hand. "Now *give!* Gold for a double moonmist."

Keeper breathed hard but said nothing as he scrabbled in the moonmist cage, as if knowing he had gone too far. The brewos were silent too. Suzy sounded completely unimpressed as she said, "*And* my dark." Spar found a fresh dry sponge and expertly caught up the floating scarlet blobs with it before pressing it to Rixende's torn ear.

Keeper studied the heavy gold pendant, which he held close to his face. Rixende milked the double pouch pressed to her lips and her eyes vanished as she sucked blissfully. Spar guided Rixende's free hand to the sponge, and she automatically took over the task of holding it to her ear. Suzy gave a hopeless sigh, then reached her whole plump body across the bar, dipped her hand into a cool cage, and helped herself to a double of dark.

A long, wiry, very dark brown figure in skintight dark violet jumpers mottled with silver arrowed in from the dark red hatch at a speed half again as great as Spar ever dared and without brushing a single shroud by accident or intent. Midway the newcomer did a half somersault as he passed Spar, his long, narrow bare feet hit the titanium next to Rixende. He accordioned up so expertly that the torus hardly swayed.

One very dark brown arm snaked around her. The other plucked the pouch from her mouth, and there was a snap as he spun the cap shut.

A lazy musical voice inquired, "What'd we tell you would happen, baby, if you ever again took a drink on your own?"

The Bat Rack held very still. Keeper was backed against the opposite side of the hole, one hand behind him. Spar had his arm in his lost-and-found nook behind the moonbrew and moonmist cages and kept it there. He felt fear-sweat beading on him. Suzy kept her dark close to her face.

A brewo burst into violent coughing, choked it to a wheezing end, and gasped subserviently, "Excuse me, coroner. Salutations."

Keeper chimed dully, "Morning . . . Crown."

Crown gently pulled the clutch coat off Rixende's far shoulder and began to stroke her. "Why, you're all gooseflesh, honey, and rigid as a corpse. What frightened you? Smooth down, skin. Ease up, muscles. Relax, Rix, and we'll give you a squirt."

His hand found the sponge, stopped, investigated, found the wet part, then went toward the middle of his face. He sniffed.

"Well, boys, at least we know none of you are vamps," he observed softly. "Else we'd found you sucking at her ear."

Rixende said very rapidly in a monotone, "I didn't come for a drink, I swear to you. I came to get that little bag you lost. Then I was tempted. I didn't know I would be. I tried to resist, but Keeper led me on. I—"

"Shut up," Crown said quietly. "We were just wondering how you paid him. Now we know. How were you planning to buy your third

double? Cut off a hand or a foot? Keeper . . . show me your other
hand. We said show it. That's right. Now unfist."

Crown plucked the pendant from Keeper's opened hand-blob. His
yellow-brown eye-blurs on Keeper all the while, he wagged the precious bauble back and forth, then tossed it slowly aloft.

As the golden blur moved toward the open blue hatch at unchang-
ing pace, Keeper opened and shut his mouth twice, then babbled,
"I didn't tempt her, Crown, honest I didn't. I didn't know she was
going to hurt her ear. I tried to stop her, but—"

"We're not interested," Crown said. "Put the double on our tab."
His face never leaving Keeper's, he extended his arm aloft and
pinched the pendant just before it straight-lined out of reach.

"Why's this home of jollity so dead?" Snaking a long leg across
the bar as easily as an arm, Crown pinched Spar's ear between his big
and smaller toes, pulled him close and turned him round. "How're
you coming along with the saline, baby? Gums hardening? Only one
way to test it." Gripping Spar's jaw and lip with his other toes, he
thrust the big one into Spar's mouth. "Come on, bite me, baby."

Spar bit. It was the only way not to vomit. Crown chuckled. Spar bit
hard. Energy flooded his shaking frame. His face grew hot and his
forehead throbbed under its drenching of fear-sweat. He was sure
he was hurting Crown, but the Coroner of Hold Three only kept up
his low, delighted chuckle and when Spar gasped, withdrew his foot.

"My, my, you're getting strong, baby. We almost felt that. Have a
drink on us."

Spar ducked his stupidly wide-open mouth away from the thin jet
of moonmist. The jet struck him in his eye and stung so that he had
to knot his fists and clamp his aching gums together to keep from
crying out.

"Why's this place so dead, I ask again? No applause for baby and
now baby's gone temperance on us. Can't you give us just one tiny
laugh?" Crown faced each in turn. "What's the matter? Cat got your
tongues?"

"Cat? We have a cat, a new cat, came just last night, working as
catcher," Keeper suddenly babbled. "It can talk a little. Not as well
as Hellhound, but it talks. It's very funny. It caught a rat."

"What'd you do with the rat's body, Keeper?"

"Fed it to the chewer. That is, Spar did. Or the cat."

"You mean to tell us that you disposed of a corpse without notifying us? Oh, don't go pale on us, Keeper. That's nothing. Why, we could accuse you of harboring a witch cat. You say he came last night, and that was a wicked night for witches. Now don't go green on us too. We were only putting you on. We were only looking for a small laugh."

"Spar! Call your cat! Make him say something funny."

Before Spar could call, or even decide whether he'd call Kim or not, the black blur appeared on a shroud near Crown, green eye-blurs fixed on the yellow-brown ones.

"So you're the joker, eh? Well . . . joke."

Kim increased in size. Spar realized it was his fur standing on end.

"Go ahead, joke . . . like they tell us you can. Keeper, you wouldn't be kidding us about this cat being able to talk?"

"Spar! Make your cat joke!"

"Don't bother. We believe he's got his own tongue too. That the matter, Blackie?" He reached out his hand. Kim lashed at it and sprang away. Crown only gave another of his low chuckles.

Rixende began to shake uncontrollably. Crown examined her solicitously yet leisurely, using his outstretched hand to turn her head toward him, so that any blood that might have been coming from it from the cat's slash would have gone into the sponge.

"Spar swore the cat could talk," Keeper babbled. "I'll—"

"Quiet," Crown said. He put the pouch to Rixende's lips, squeezed until her shaking subsided and it was empty, then flicked the crumpled pliofilm toward Spar.

"And now about that little black bag, Keeper," Crown said flatly.

"Spar!"

The latter dipped into his lost-and-found nook, saying quickly, "No little black bags, coroner, but we did find this one the lady Rixende forgot last Playday night," and he turned back holding out something big, round, gleamingly orange, and closed with draw strings.

Crown took and swung it slowly in a circle. For Spar, who couldn't see the strings, it was like magic. "Bit too big, and a mite the wrong shade. We're certain we lost the little black bag here, or had it lifted. You making the Bat Rack a tent for dips, Keeper?"

"Spar—?"

"We're asking *you*, Keeper."

Shoving Spar aside, Keeper groped frantically in the nook, pulling aside the cages of moonmist and moonbrew pouches. He produced many small objects. Spar could distinguish the largest—an electric hand-fan and a bright red footglove. They hung around Keeper in a jumble.

Keeper was panting and had scrabbled his hands for a full minute in the nook without bringing out anything more, when Crown said, his voice lazy again, "That's enough. The little black bag was of no importance to us in any case."

Keeper emerged with a face doubly blurred. It must be surrounded by a haze of sweat. He pointed an arm at the orange bag.

"It might be inside that one!"

Crown opened the bag, began to search through it, changed his mind, and gave the whole bag a flick. Its remarkably numerous contents came out and moved slowly aloft at equal speeds, like an army on the march in irregular order. Crown scanned them as they went past.

"No, not there." He pushed the bag toward Keeper. "Return Rix's stuff to it and have it ready for us the next time we dive in—"

Putting his arm around Rixende, so that it was his hand that held the sponge to her ear, he turned and kicked off powerfully for the aft hatch. After he had been out of sight for several seconds, there was a general sigh, the three brewos put out new scrip-wads to pay for another squirt. Suzy asked for a second double dark, which Spar handed her quickly, while Keeper shook off his daze and ordered Spar, "Gather up all the floating trash, especially Rixie's, and get that back in her purse. On the jump, lubber!" Then he used the electric hand-fan to cool and dry himself.

It was a mean task Keeper had set Spar, but Kim came to help, darting after objects too small for Spar to see. Once he had them in his hands, Spar could readily finger or sniff which was which.

When his impotent rage at Crown had faded, Spar's thoughts went back to Sleepday night. Had his vision of vamps and werewolves been dream only?—now that he knew the werethings had been abroad in force. If only he had better eyes to distinguish illusion from reality! Kim's "Sssee! Sssee shshsharply!" hissed in his memory. What would it be like to see sharply? Everything brighter? Or closer?

After a weary time the scattered objects were gathered and he went back to sweeping and Kim to his mouse hunt. As Workday morning progressed, the Bat Rack gradually grew less bright, though so gradually it was hard to tell.

A few more customers came in, but all for quick drinks, which Keeper served them glumly; Suzy judged none of them worth cottoning up to.

As time slowly passed, Keeper grew steadily more fretfully angry, as Spar had known he would after groveling before Crown. He tried to throw out the three brewos, but they produced more crumpled scrip, which closest scrutiny couldn't prove counterfeit. In revenge he short-squirted them and there were arguments. He called Spar off his sweeping to ask him nervously, "That cat of yours—he scratched Crown, didn't he? We'll have to get rid of him; Crown said he might be a witch cat, remember?" Spar made no answer. Keeper set him renewing the glue of the emergency hatches, claiming that Rixende's tearing free from the aft one had shown it must be drying out. He gobbled appetizers and drank moonmist with tomato juice. He sprayed the Bat Rack with some abominable synthetic scent. He started counting the boxed scrip and coins but gave up the job with a slam of self-locking drawer almost before he'd begun. His grimace fixed on Suzy.

"Spar!" he called. "Take over! And over-squirt the brewos on your peril!"

Then he locked the cash box, and giving Suzy a meaningful jerk of his head toward the scarlet starboard hatch, he pulled himself toward it. With an unhappy shrug toward Spar, she wearily followed.

As soon as the pair were gone, Spar gave the brewos an eight-second squirt, waving back their scrip, and placed two small serving cages—of fritos and yeast balls—before them. They grunted their thanks and fell to. The light changed from healthy bright to corpse white. There was a faint, distant roar, followed some seconds later by a brief crescendo of creakings. The new light made Spar uneasy. He served two more suck-and-dives and sold a pouch of moonmist at double purser's prices. He started to eat an appetizer, but just then Kim swam in to show him proudly a mouse. He conquered his nausea, but began to dread the onset of real withdrawal symptoms.

A pot-bellied figure clad in sober black dragged itself along the ratlines from the green hatch. On the aloft side of the bar there appeared a visage in which the blur of white hair and beard almost hid leather-brown flesh, though accentuating the blurs of gray eyes.

"Doc!" Spar greeted, his misery and unease gone, and instantly handed out a chill pouch of three-star moonbrew. Yet all he could think to say in his excitement was the banal, "A bad Sleepday night, eh, Doc? Vamps and—"

"—And other doltish superstitions, which wax every sunth, but never wane," an amiable, cynical old voice cut in. "Yet, I suppose I shouldn't rob you of your illusions, Spar, even the terrifying ones. You've little enough to live by, as it is. And there *is* viciousness astir in Windrush. Ah, that smacks good against my tonsils."

Then Spar remembered the important thing. Reaching deep inside his slopsuit, he brought out, in such a way as to hide it from the brewos below, a small flat narrow black bag.

"Here, Doc," he whispered, "you lost it last Playday. I kept it safe for you."

"Dammit, I'd lose my jumpers, if I ever took them off," Doc commented, hushing his voice when Spar put finger to lips. "I suppose I started mixing moonmist with my moonbrew—again?"

"You did, Doc. But you didn't lose your bag. Crown or one of his girls lifted it, or snagged it when it sat loose beside you. And then I . . . I, Doc, lifted it from Crown's hip pocket. Yes, and kept that secret when Rixende and Crown came in demanding it this morning."

"Spar, my boy, I am deeply in your debt," Doc said. "More than you can know. Another three-star, please. Ah, nectar. Spar, ask any reward of me, and if it lies merely within the realm of the first transfinite infinity, I will grant it."

To his own surprise, Spar began to shake—with excitement. Pulling himself forward halfway across the bar, he whispered hoarsely, "Give me good eyes, Doc!" adding impulsively, "and teeth!"

After what seemed a long while, Doc said in a dreamy, sorrowful voice, "In the Old Days, that would have been easy. They'd perfected eye transplants. They could regenerate cranial nerves, and sometimes restore scanning power to an injured cerebrum. While transplanting tooth buds from a stillborn was intern's play. But now . . . Oh, I might be able to do what you ask in an uncomfortable, antique, inorganic fashion, but . . ." He broke off on a note that spoke of the misery of life and the uselessness of all effort.

"The Old Days," one brewo said from the corner of his mouth to the brewo next to him. "Witch talk!"

"Witch-smitch!" the second brewo replied in like fashion. "The flesh mechanic's only senile. He dreams all four days, not just Sleepday."

The third brewo whistled against the evil eye a tune like the wind.

Spar tugged at the long-armed sleeve of Doc's black jumper. "Doc, you promised. I want to see sharp, bite sharp!"

Doc laid his shrunken hand commiseratingly on Spar's forearm. "Spar," he said softly, "seeing sharply would only make you very unhappy. Believe me, I *know*. Life's easier to bear when things are blurred, just as it's best when thoughts are blurred by brew or mist. And while there are people in Windrush who yearn to bite sharply, you are not their kind. Another three-star, if you please."

"I quit moonmist this morning, Doc," Spar said somewhat proudly as he handed over the fresh pouch.

Doc answered with sad smile, "Many quit moonmist every Workday morning and change their minds when Playday comes around."

"Not me, Doc! Besides," Spar argued, "Keeper and Crown and his girls and even Suzy all see sharply, and they aren't unhappy."

"I'll tell you a secret, Spar," Doc replied. "Keeper and Crown and the girls are all zombies. Yes, even Crown with his cunning and power. To them Windrush is the universe."

"It isn't, Doc?"

Ignoring the interruption, Doc continued, "But you wouldn't be like that, Spar. You'd want to know more. And that would make you far unhappier than you are."

"I don't care, Doc," Spar said. He repeated accusingly, "You promised."

The gray blurs of Doc's eyes almost vanished as he frowned in thought. Then he said, "How would this be, Spar? I know moonmist brings pains and sufferings as well as easings and joys. But suppose that every Workday morning and Loafday noon I should bring you a tiny pill that would give you all the good effects of moonmist and none of the bad. I've one in this bag. Try it now and see. And every Playday night I would bring you without fail another sort of pill that would make you sleep soundly with never a nightmare. Much better than eyes and teeth. Think it over."

As Spar considered that, Kim drifted up. He eyed Doc with his close-set green blurs. "Resspectfful greetingss, ssir," he hissed. "Name izz Kim."

Doc answered, "The same to you, sir. May mice be ever abundant." He softly stroked the cat, beginning with Kim's chin and chest. The dreaminess returned to his voice. "In the Old Days, all cats talked, not just a few sports. The entire feline tribe. And many dogs, too—pardon me, Kim. While as for dolphins and whales and apes . . ."

Spar said eagerly, "Answer me one question, Doc. If your pills give happiness without hangover, why do you always drink moonbrew yourself and sometimes spike it with moonmist?"

"Because for me—" Doc began and then broke off with a grin. "You've trapped me, Spar. I never thought you used your mind. Very well, on your own mind be it. Come to my office this Loafday —you know the way? Good!—and we'll see what we can do about your eyes and teeth. And now a double pouch for the corridor."

He paid in bright coins, thrust the big squnchy three-star in a big pocket, said, "See you, Spar. So long, Kim," and tugged himself toward the green hatch, zigzagging.

"Ffarewell, ssir," Kim hissed after him.

Spar held out the small black bag. "You forgot it again, Doc."

As Doc returned with a weary curse and pocketed it, the scarlet hatch unzipped and Keeper swam out. He looked in a good humor now and whistled the tune of "I'll Marry the Man on the Bridge" as he began to study certain rounds on scrip-till and moonbrew valves, but when Doc was gone he asked Spar suspiciously, "What was that you handed the old geezer?"

"His purse," Spar replied easily. "He just forgot it now." He shook his loosely fisted hand and it chinked. "Doc paid in coins, Keeper." Keeper took them eagerly. "Back to sweeping, Spar."

As Spar dove toward the scarlet hatch to take up larboard tubes, Suzy emerged and passed him with face averted. She sidled up to the bar and unsmilingly snatched the pouch of moonmist Keeper offered her with mock courtliness.

Spar felt a brief rage on her behalf, but it was hard for him to keep his mind on anything but his coming appointment with Doc. When Workday night fell swiftly as a hurled knife, he was hardly aware of it and felt none of his customary unease. Keeper turned on full all of the lights in the Bat Rack. They shone brightly while beyond the translucent walls there was a milky churning.

Business picked up a little. Suzy made off with the first likely mark. Keeper called Spar to take over the torus, while he himself got a much-erased sheet of paper and holding it to a clipboard held against his bent knees, wrote on it laboriously, as if he were thinking out each word, perhaps each letter, often wetting his pencil in his mouth. He became so absorbed in his difficult task that without realizing he drifted off toward the black below hatch, rotating over and over. The paper got dirtier and dirtier with his scrawlings and smudgings, new erasures, saliva and sweat.

The short night passed more swiftly than Spar dared hope, so that the sudden glare of Loafday dawn startled him. Most of the customers made off to take their siestas.

Spar wondered what excuse to give Keeper for leaving the Bat Rack, but the problem was solved for him. Keeper folded the grimy sheet, and sealed it with hot tape. "Take this to the Bridge, loafer, to the Exec. Wait." He took the repacked, orange bag from its nook and pulled on the cords to make sure they were drawn tight. "On your way deliver this at Crown's Hole. With all courtesy and subservience, Spar! Now, on the jump!"

Spar slid the sealed message into his only pocket with working zipper and drew that tight. Then he dove slowly toward the aft hatch, where he almost collided with Kim. Recalling Keeper's talk of getting rid of the cat, he caught hold of him around the slim furry chest under the forelegs and gently thrust him inside his slopsuit, whispering, "You'll take a trip with me, little Kim." The cat set his claws in the thin material and steadied himself.

For Spar, the corridor was a narrow cylinder ending in mist either way and decorated by lengthwise blurs of green and red. He guided himself chiefly by touch and memory, this time remembering that he must pull himself against the light wind hand-over-hand along the centerline. After curving past the larger cylinders of the fore-and-aft gangways, the corridor straightened. Twice he worked his way around centrally slung fans whirring so softly that he recognized them chiefly by the increase in breeze before passing them and the slight suction after.

Soon he began to smell soil and green stuff growing. With a shiver he passed a black round that was the elastic-curtained door to Hold Three's big chewer. He met no one—odd even for Loafday. Finally he saw the green of the Gardens of Apollo and beyond it a huge black screen, in which hovered toward the aft side a small, smoky-orange circle that always filled Spar with inexplicable sadness and fear. He wondered in how many black screens that doleful circle was portrayed, especially in the starboard end of Windrush. He had seen it in several.

So close to the gardens that he could make out wavering green shoots and the silhouette of a floating farmer, the corridor right-angled below. Two dozen pulls along the line and he floated by an open hatch, which both memory for distance and the strong scent of musky, mixed perfumes told him was the entry to Crown's Hole. Peering in, he could see the intermelting black and silver spirals of the decor of the great globular room. Directly opposite the hatch was another large black screen with the red-mottled dun disk placed similarly off center.

From under Spar's chin, Kim hissed very softly, but urgently, "Sstop! Ssilencce, on your liffe!" The cat had poked his head out of the slopsuit's neck. His ears tickled Spar's throat. Spar was getting used to Kim's melodrama, and in any case the warning was hardly needed. He had just seen the half-dozen floating naked bodies and would have held still if only from embarrassment. Not that Spar could see genitals any more than ears at the distance. But he could see that save for hair, each body was of one texture: one very dark brown and the other five—or was it four? no, five—fair. He didn't recognize the two with platinum and golden hair, who also happened to be the two palest. He wondered which was Crown's new girl, name of Almodie. He was relieved that none of the bodies were touching.

There was the glint of metal by the golden-haired girl, and he could just discern the red blur of a slender, five-forked tube which went from the metal to the five other faces. It seemed strange that even with a girl to play bartender, Crown should have moonbrew served in such plebeian fashion in his palatial Hole. Of course the tube might carry moonwine, or even moonmist.

Or was Crown planning to open a rival bar to the Bat Rack? A poor time, these days, and a worse location, he mused as he tried to think of what to do with the orange bag.

"Sslink offf!" Kim urged still more softly.

Spar's fingers found a snap-ring by the hatch. With the faintest of clicks he secured it around the draw-cords of the pouch and then pulled back the way he had come.

But faint as the click had been, there was a response from Crown's Hole—a very deep, long growl.

Spar pulled faster at the centerline. As he rounded the corner lead-ing inboard, he looked back.

Jutting out from Crown's hatch was a big, prick-eared head nar-rower than a man's and darker even than Crown's.

The growl was repeated.

It was ridiculous he should be so frightened of Hellhound, Spar told himself as he jerked himself and his passenger along. Why, Crown sometimes even brought the big dog to the Bat Rack.

Perhaps it was that Hellhound never growled in the Bat Rack, only talked in a hundred or so monosyllables.

Besides, the dog couldn't pull himself along the centerline at any speed. He lacked sharp claws. Though he might be able to bound forward, caroming from one side of the corridor to another.

This time the center-slit black curtains of the big chewer made Spar veer violently. He was a fine one—going to get new eyes today and frightened as a child!

"Why did you try to scare me back there, Kim?" he asked angrily.

"I ssaw shsheer evil, isssiot!"

"You saw five folk sucking moonbrew. And a harmless dog. This time you're the fool, Kim, you're the idiot!"

Kim shut up, drawing in his head, and refused to say another word. Spar remembered about the vanity and touchiness of all cats. But by now he had other worries. What if the orange bag were stolen by a passerby before Crown noticed it? And if Crown did find it, wouldn't he know Spar, forever Keeper's errandboy, had been peep-ing? That all this should happen on the most important day of his life! His verbal victory over Kim was small consolation.

Also, although the platinum-haired girl had interested him most of the two strange ones, something began to bother him about the girl who'd been playing bartender, the one with golden hair like Suzy's, but much slimmer and paler—he had the feeling he'd seen her before. And something about her had frightened him.

When he reached the central gangways, he was tempted to go to Doc's office before the Bridge. But he wanted to be able to relax at Doc's and take as much time as needed, knowing all errands were done.

Reluctantly he entered the windy violet gangway and dove at a fore angle for the first empty space on the central gang-line, so that his palms were only burned a little before he had firm hold of it and was being sped fore at about the same speed as the wind. Keeper was a miser, not to buy him handgloves, let alone footgloves!—but he had to pay sharp attention to passing the shroud-slung roller bearings that kept the thick, moving line centered in the big corridor. It was an easy trick to catch hold of the line ahead of the bearing and then get one's other hand out of the way, but it demanded watchfulness.

There were few figures traveling on the line and fewer still being blown along the corridor. He overtook a doubled up one tumbling over and over and crying out in an old cracked voice, "Jacob's Ladder, Tree of Life, Marriage Lines . . ."

He passed the squeeze in the gangway marking the division between the Third and Second Holds without being stopped by the guard there and then he almost missed the big blue corridor leading aloft. Again he slightly burned his palms making the transfer from one moving gang-line to another. His fretfulness increased.

"Sspar, you isssiot—!" Kim began.

"Ssh!—we're in officers' territory," Spar cut him off, glad to have that excuse for once more putting down the impudent cat. And true enough, the blue spaces of Windrush always did fill him with awe and dread.

Almost too soon to suit him, he found himself swinging from the gang-line to a stationary monkey jungle of tubular metal just below the deck of the Bridge. He worked his way to the aloft-most bars and floated there, waiting to be spoken to.

Much metal, in many strange shapes, gleamed in the Bridge, and there were irregularly pulsing rainbow surfaces, the closest of which sometimes seemed ranks and files of tiny lights going on and off—red, green, all colors. Aloft of everything was an endless velvet-black expanse very faintly blotched by churning, milky glintings.

Among the metal objects and the rainbows floated figures all clad in the midnight blue of officers. They sometimes gestured to each other, but never spoke a word. To Spar, each of their movements was freighted with profound significance. These were the gods of Windrush, who guided everything, if there were gods at all. He felt reduced in importance to a mouse, which would be chased off chittering if it once broke silence.

After a particularly tense flurry of gestures, there came a brief distant roar and a familiar creaking and crackling. Spar was amazed, yet at the same time realized he should have known that the Captain, the Navigator, and the rest were responsible for the familiar diurnal phenomena.

It also marked Loafday noon. Spar began to fret. His errands were taking too long. He began to lift his hand tentatively toward each passing figure in midnight blue. None took the least note of him.

Finally he whispered, "Kim—?"

The cat did not reply. He could hear a purring that might be a snore. He gently shook the cat. "Kim, let's talk."

"Shshut offf! I ssleep! Ssh!" Kim resettled himself and his claws and recommenced his purring snore—whether natural or feigned, Spar could not tell. He felt very despondent.

The lunths crept by. He grew desperate and weary. He must not miss his appointment with Doc! He was nerving himself to move farther aloft and speak, when a pleasant, young voice said, "Hello, grandpa, what's on your mind?"

Spar realized that he had been raising his hand automatically and that a person as dark-skinned as Crown, but clad in midnight blue, had at last taken notice. He unzipped the note and handed it over. "For the Exec."

"That's my department." A trilled crackle—fingernail slitting the note? A larger crackle—note being opened. A brief wait. Then, "Who's Keeper?"

"Owner of the Bat Rack, sir. I work there."

"Bat Rack?"

"A moonbrew mansion. Once called the Happy Torus, I've been told. In the Old Days, Wine Mess Three, Doc told me."

"Hmm. Well, what's all this mean, gramps? And what's your name?"

Spar stared miserably at the dark-mottled gray square. "I can't read, sir. Name's Spar."

"Hmm. Seen any . . . er . . . supernatural beings in the Bat Rack?"

"Only in my dreams, sir."

"Mmm. Well, we'll have a look in. If you recognize me, don't let on. I'm Ensign Drake, by the way. Who's your passenger, grandpa?"

"Only my cat, Ensign," Spar breathed in alarm.

"Well, take the black shaft down." Spar began to move across the monkey jungle in the direction pointed out by the blue arm-blur.

"And next time remember animals aren't allowed on the Bridge."

As Spar traveled below, his warm relief that Ensign Drake had seemed quite human and compassionate was mixed with anxiety as to whether he still had time to visit Doc. He almost missed the shift to the gang-line grinding aft in the dark red main-drag. The corpse-light brightening into the false dawn of late afternoon bothered him. Once more he passed the tumbling bent figure, this time croaking, "Trinity, Trellis, Wheat Ear . . ."

He was fighting down the urge to give up his visit to Doc and pull home to the Bat Rack, when he noticed he had passed the second squeeze and was in Hold Four with the passageway to Doc's coming up. He dove off, checked himself on a shroud and began the hand-drag to Doc's office, as far larboard as Crown's Hole was starboard.

He passed two figures clumsy on the line, their breaths malty in anticipation of Playday. Spar worried that Doc might have closed his office. He smelled soil and greenery again, from the Gardens of Diana.

The hatch was shut, but when Spar pressed the bulb, it unzipped after three honks, and the white-haloed gray-eyed face peered out.

"I'd just about given up on you, Spar."

"I'm sorry, Doc. I had to—"

"No matter. Come in, come in. Hello, Kim—take a look around if you want."

Kim crawled out, pushed off from Spar's chest, and soon was engaged in a typical cat's tour of inspection.

And there was a great deal to inspect, as even Spar could see. Every shroud in Doc's office seemed to have objects clipped along its entire length. There were blobs large and small, gleaming and dull, light and dark, translucent and solid. They were silhouetted against a wall of the corpse-light Spar feared, but had no time to think of now. At one end was a band of even brighter light.

"Careful, Kim!" Spar called to the cat as he landed against a shroud and began to paw his way from blob to blob.

"He's all right," Doc said. "Let's have a look at you, Spar. Keep your eyes open."

Doc's hands held Spar's head. The gray eyes and leathery face came so close they were one blur.

"Keep them open, I said. Yes, I know you have to blink them, that's all right. Just as I thought. The lenses are dissolved. You've suffered the side-effect which one in ten do who are infected with the Lethean rickettsia."

"Styx ricks, Doc?"

"That's right, though the mob's got hold of the wrong river in the Underworld. But we've all had it. We've all drunk the water of Lethe. Though sometimes when we grow very old we begin to remember the beginning. Don't squirm."

"Hey, Doc, is it because I've had the Styx ricks I can't remember anything back before the Bat Rack?"

"It could be. How long have you been at the Rack?"

"I don't know, Doc. Forever."

"Before I found the place, anyhow. When the Rumdum closed here in Four. But that's only a starth ago."

"But I'm awful old, Doc. Why don't I start remembering?"

"You're not old, Spar. You're just bald and toothless and etched by moonmist and your muscles have shriveled. Yes, and your mind has shriveled too. Now open your mouth."

One of Doc's hands went to the back of Spar's neck. The other probed. "Your gums are tough, anyhow. That'll make it easier."

Spar wanted to tell about the salt water, but when Doc finally took his hand out of Spar's mouth, it was to say, "Now open wide as you can."

Doc pushed into his mouth something big as a handbag and hot. "Now bite down hard."

Spar felt as if he had bitten fire. He tried to open his mouth, but hands on his head and jaw held it closed. Involuntarily he kicked and clawed air. His eyes filled with tears.

"Stop writhing! Breathe through your nose. It's not that hot. Not hot enough to blister, anyhow."

Spar doubted that, but after a bit decided it wasn't quite hot enough to bake his brain through the roof of his mouth. Besides, he didn't want to show Doc his cowardice. He held still. He blinked several times and the general blur became the blurs of Doc's face and the cluttered room silhouetted by the corpse-glare. He tried to smile, but his lips were already stretched wider than their muscles could ever have done. That hurt too; he realized now that the heat was abating a little.

Doc was grinning for him. "Well, you would ask an old drunkard to use techniques he'd only read about. To make it up to you, I'll give you teeth sharp enough to sever shrouds. Kim, please get away from that bag."

The black blur of the cat was pushing off from a black blur twice his length. Spar mumbled disapprovingly at Kim through his nose and made motions. The larger blur was shaped like Doc's little bag, but bigger than a hundred of them. It must be massive too, for in reaction to Kim's push it had bent the shroud to which it was attached and—the point—the shroud was very slow in straightening.

"That bag contains my treasure, Spar," Doc explained, and when Spar lifted his eyebrows twice to signal another question, went on, "No, not coin and gold and jewels, but a second transfinite infinitude —sleep and dreams and nightmares for every soul in a thousand Windrushes." He glanced at his wrist. "Time enough now. Open your mouth." Spar obeyed, though it cost him new pain.

Doc withdrew what Spar had bitten on, wrapped it in gleam, and clipped it to the nearest shroud. Then he looked in Spar's mouth again.

"I guess I did make it a bit too hot," he said. He found a small pouch, set it to Spar's lips, and squeezed it. A mist filled Spar's mouth and all pain vanished.

Doc tucked the pouch in Spar's pocket. "If the pain returns, use it again."

But before Spar could thank Doc, the latter had pressed a tube to his eye. "Look, Spar, what do you see?"

Spar cried out, he couldn't help it, and jerked his eye away.

"What's wrong, Spar?"

"Doc, you gave me a dream," Spar said hoarsely. "You won't tell anyone, will you? And it tickled."

"What was the dream like?" Doc asked eagerly.

"Just a picture, Doc. The picture of a goat with the tail of a fish. Doc, I saw the fish's . . ." His mind groped, ". . . scales! Everything had . . . edges! Doc, is *that* what they mean when they talk about seeing sharply?"

"Of course, Spar. This is good. It means there's no cerebral or retinal damage. I'll have no trouble making up field glasses—that is, if there's nothing seriously wrong with my antique pair. So you still see things sharp-edged in dreams—that's natural enough. But why were you afraid of me telling?"

"Afraid of being accused of witchcraft, Doc. I thought seeing things like that was clairvoyance. The tube tickled my eye a little."

"Isotopes and insanity! It's supposed to tickle. Let's try the other eye."

Again Spar wanted to cry out, but he restrained himself, and this time he had no impulse to jerk his eye away, although there was again the faint tickling. The picture was that of a slim girl. He could tell she was female because of her general shape. But he could see her edges. He could see . . . details. For instances, her eyes weren't mist-bounded colored ovals. They had points at both ends, which were china-white . . . triangles. And the pale violet round between the triangles had a tiny black round at its center.

She had silvery hair, yet she looked young, he thought, though it was hard to judge such matters when you could see edges. She made him think of the platinum-haired girl he'd glimpsed in Crown's Hole.

She wore a long, gleaming white dress, which left her shoulders bare, but either art or some unknown force had drawn her hair and her dress toward her feet. In her dress it made . . . folds.

"What's her name, Doc? Almodie?"

"No. Virgo. The Virgin. You can see her edges?"

"Yes, Doc. Sharp. I get it!—like a knife. And the goat-fish?"

"Capricorn," Doc answered, removing the tube from Spar's eye.

"Doc, I know Capricorn and Virgo are the names of lunths, terranths, sunths, and starths, but I never knew they had pictures. I never knew they *were* anything."

"You— Of course, you've never seen watches, or stars, let alone the constellations of the zodiac."

Spar was about to ask what all *those* were, but then he saw that the corpse-light was all gone, although the ribbon of brighter light had grown very wide.

"At least in this stretch of your memory," Doc added. "I should have your new eyes and teeth ready next Loafday. Come earlier if you can manage. I may see you before that at the Bat Rack, Playday Night or earlier."

"Great, Doc, but now I've got to haul. Come on, Kim! Sometimes business heavies up Loafday night, Doc, like it was Playday night come at the wrong end. Jump in, Kim."

"Sure you can make it back to the Bat Rack all right, Spar? It'll be dark before you get there."

"Course I can, Doc."

But when night fell, like a heavy hood jerked down over his head, halfway down the first passageway, he would have gone back to ask Doc to guide him, except he feared Kim's contempt, even though the cat still wasn't talking. He pulled ahead rapidly, though the few running lights hardly let him see the centerline.

The fore gangway was even worse—completely empty and its lights dim and flickering. Seeing by blurs bothered him now that he knew what seeing sharp was like. He was beginning to sweat and shake and cramp from his withdrawal from alcohol and his thoughts were a tumult. He wondered if *any* of the weird things that had happened since meeting Kim were real or dream. Kim's refusal—or inability?—to talk any more was disquieting. He began seeing the misty rims of blurs that vanished when he looked straight toward them. He remembered Keeper and the brewos talking about vamps and witches.

Then instead of waiting for the Bat Rack's green hatch, he dove off into the passageway leading to the aft one. This passageway had no lights at all. Out of it he thought he could hear Hellhound growling, but couldn't be sure because the big chewer was grinding. He was scrabbling with panic when he entered the Bat Rack through the dark red hatch, remembering barely in time to avoid the new glue.

The place was jumping with light and excitement and dancing figures, and Keeper at once began to shout abuse at him. He dove into the torus and began taking orders and serving automatically, working entirely by touch and voice, because withdrawal now had his vision swimming—a spinning blur of blurs.

After a while that got better, but his nerves got worse. Only the unceasing work kept him going—and shut out Keeper's abuse—but he was getting too tired to work at all. As Playday dawned, with the crowd around the torus getting thicker all the while, he snatched a pouch of moonmist and set it to his lips.

Claws dug his chest. "Isssiot! Sssot! Ssslave of fffear!"

Spar almost went into convulsions, but put back the moonmist. Kim came out of the slopsuit and pushed off contemptuously, circled the bar and talked to various of the drinkers, soon became a conversation piece. Keeper started to boast about him and quit serving. Spar worked on and on and on through sobriety more nightmarish than any drunk he could recall. And far, far longer.

Suzy came in with a mark and touched Spar's hand when he served her dark to her. It helped.

He thought he recognized a voice from below. It came from a
kinky-haired, slopsuited brewo he didn't know. But then he heard
the man again and thought he was Ensign Drake. There were several
brewos he didn't recognize.

The place started really jumping. Keeper upped the music. Singly
or in pairs, somersaulting dancers bounded back and forth between
shrouds. Others toed a shroud and shimmied. A girl in black did
splits on one. A girl in white dove through the torus. Keeper put it
on her boyfriend's check. Brewos tried to sing.

Spar heard Kim recite:

> "Izz a cat.
> Killzz a rat.
> Greetss each guy,
> Thin or ffat.
> Saay dolls, hi!"

Playday night fell. The pace got hotter. Doc didn't come. But
Crown did. Dancers parted and a whole section of drinkers made way
aloft for him and his girls and Hellhound, so that they had a third of
the torus to themselves, with no one below in that third either. To
Spar's surprise they all took coffee except the dog, who when asked
by Crown, responded, "Bloody Mary," drawing out the words in such
deep tones that they were little more than a low "Bluh-Muh" growl.

"Iss that sspeech, I assk you?" Kim commented from the other
side of the torus. Drunks around him choked down chuckles.

Spar served the pouched coffee piping hot with felt holders and
mixed Hellhound's drink in a self-squeezing syringe with sipping tube.
He was very groggy and for the moment more afraid for Kim than
himself. The face blurs tended to swim, but he could distinguish Rixende by her black hair, Phanette and Doucette by their matching
red-blonde hair and oddly red-mottled fair skins, while Almodie *was*
the platinum-haired pale one, yet she looked horribly right between
the dark brown, purple-vested blur to one side of her and the blacked,
narrower, prick-eared silhouette to the other.

Spar heard Crown whisper to her, "Ask Keeper to show you the
talking cat." The whisper was very low and Spar wouldn't have heard
it except that Crown's voice had a strange excited vibrancy Spar had
never known in it before.

"But won't they fight then?—I mean Hellhound," she answered in a voice that sent silvery tendrils around Spar's heart. He yearned to see her face through Doc's tube. She would look like Virgo, only more beautiful. Yet, Crown's girl, she could be no virgin. It was a strange and horrible world. Her eyes *were* violet. But he was sick of blurs. Almodie sounded very frightened, yet she continued, "Please don't, Crown." Spar's heart was captured.

"But that's the whole idea, baby. And nobody dont's us. We thought we'd schooled you to that. We'd teach you another lesson here, except tonight we smell high fuzz—lots of it, Keeper!—our new lady wishes to hear your cat talk. Bring it over."

"I really don't . . ." Almodie began and went no further.

Kim came floating across the torus while Keeper was shouting in the opposite direction. The cat checked himself against a slender shroud and looked straight at Crown. "Yesss?"

"Keeper, shut that junk off." The music died abruptly. Voices rose, then died abruptly too. "Well, cat, talk."

"Shshall ssing insstead," Kim announced and began an eerie cater-wauling that had a pattern but was not Spar's idea of music.

"It's an abstraction," Almodie breathed delightedly. "Listen, Crown, that was a diminished seventh."

"A demented third, I'd say," Phanette commented from the other side.

Crown signed them to be quiet.

Kim finished with a high trill. He slowly looked around at his baffled audience and then began to groom his shoulder.

Crown gripped a ridge of the torus with his left hand and said evenly, "Since you will not talk to us, will you talk to our dog?"

Kim stared at Hellhound sucking his Bloody Mary. His eyes widened, their pupils slitted, his lips writhed back from needle-like fangs.

He hissed, "Schschweinhund!"

Hellhound launched himself, hind paws against the palm of Crown's left hand, which threw him forward toward the left, where Kim was dodging. But the cat switched directions, rebounding hindwards from the next shroud. The dog's white-jagged jaws snapped sideways a foot from their mark as his great-chested black body hurtled past.

Hellhound landed with four paws in the middle of a fat drunk, who puffed out his wind barely before his swallow, but the dog took off instantly on reverse course. Kim bounced back and forth between shrouds. This time hair flew when jaws snapped, but also a rigidly spread paw slashed.

Crown grabbed Hellhound by his studded collar, restraining him from another dive. He touched the dog below the eye and smelled his fingers. "That'll be enough, boy," he said. "Can't go around killing musical geniuses." His hand dropped from his nose to below the torus and came up loosely fisted. "Well, cat, you've talked with our dog. Have you a word for us?"

"Yesss!" Kim drifted to the shroud nearest Crown's face. Spar pushed off to grab him back, while Almodie gazed at Crown's fist and edged a hand toward it.

Kim loudly hissed, "Hellzzz ssspawn! Fffiend!"

Both Spar and Almodie were too late. From between two of Crown's fisted fingers a needle-stream jetted and struck Kim in the open mouth.

After what seemed to Spar a long time, his hand interrupted the stream. Its back burned acutely.

Kim seemed to collapse into himself, then launched himself away from Crown, toward the dark, open-jawed.

Crown said, "That's mace, an antique weapon like Greek fire, but well-known to our folk. The perfect answer to a witch cat."

Spar sprang at Crown, grappled his chest, tried to butt his jaw. They moved away from the torus at half the speed with which Spar had sprung.

Crown got his head aside. Spar closed his gums on Crown's throat. There was a *snick*. Spar felt wind on his bare back. Then a cold triangle pressed his flesh over his kidneys. Spar opened his jaws and floated limp. Crown chuckled.

A blue fuzz-glare, held by a brewo, made everyone in the Bat Rack look more corpse-like than larboard light. A voice commanded, "Okay, folks, break it up. Go home. We're closing the place."

Sleepday dawned, drowning the fuzz-glare. The cold triangle left Spar's back. There was another *snick*. Saying, "Bye-bye, baby," Crown pushed off through the white glare toward four women's faces and one dog's. Phanette's and Doucette's faintly red-mottled ones were close beside Hellhound's, as if they might be holding his collar.

Spar sobbed and began to hunt for Kim. After a while Suzy came to help him. The Bat Rack emptied. Spar and Suzy cornered Kim. Spar grasped the cat around the chest. Kim's forelegs embraced his wrist, claws pricking. Spar got out the pouch Doc had given him and shoved its mouth between Kim's jaws. The claws dug deep. Taking no note of that, Spar gently sprayed. Gradually the claws came out and Kim relaxed. Spar hugged him gently. Suzy bound up Spar's wounded wrist.

Keeper came up followed by two brewos, one of them Ensign Drake, who said, "My partner and I will watch today by the aft and starboard hatches." Beyond them the Bat Rack was empty.

Spar said, "Crown has a knife." Drake nodded.

Suzy touched Spar's hand and said, "Keeper, I want to stay here tonight. I'm scared."

Keeper said, "I can offer you a shroud."

Drake and his mate dove slowly toward their posts.

Suzy squeezed Spar's hand. He said, rather heavily, "I can offer you my shroud, Suzy."

Keeper laughed and after looking toward the Bridge men, whispered, "I can offer you mine, which, unlike Spar, I own. And moonmist. Otherwise, the passageways."

Suzy sighed, paused, then went off with him.

Spar miserably made his way to the fore corner. Had Suzy expected him to fight Keeper? The sad thing was that he no longer wanted her, except as a friend. He loved Crown's new girl. Which was sad too.

He was very tired. Even the thought of new eyes tomorrow didn't interest him. He clipped his ankle to a shroud and tied a rag over his eyes. He gently clasped Kim, who had not spoken. He was asleep at once.

He dreamed of Almodie. She looked like Virgo, even to the white dress. She held Kim, who looked sleek as polished black leather. She was coming toward him smiling. She kept coming without getting closer.

Much later—he thought—he woke in the grip of withdrawal. He sweat and shook, but those were minor. His nerves were jumping. Any moment, he was sure, they would twitch all his muscles into a stabbing spasm of sinew-snapping agony. His thoughts were moving so fast he could hardly begin to understand one in ten. It was like speeding through a curving, ill-lit passageway ten times faster than the main drag. If he touched a wall, he would forget even what little

Spar knew, forget he was Spar. All around him black shrouds whipped in perpetual sine curves.

Kim was no longer by him. He tore the rag from his eyes. It was dark as before. Sleepday night. But his body stopped speeding and his thoughts slowed. His nerves still crackled, and he still saw the black snakes whipping, but he knew them for illusion. He even made out the dim glows of three running lights.

Then he saw two figures floating toward him. He could barely make out their eye-blurs, green in the smaller, violet in the other, whose face was spreadingly haloed by silvery glints. She was pale and whiteness floated around her. And instead of a smile, he could see the white horizontal blur of bared teeth. Kim's teeth too were bared.

Suddenly he remembered the golden-haired girl who he'd thought was playing bartender in Crown's Hole. She was Suzy's one-time friend Sweetheart, snatched last Sleepday by vamps.

He screamed, which in Spar was a hoarse, retching bellow, and scrabbled at his clipped ankle.

The figures vanished. Below, he thought.

Lights came on. Someone dove and shook Spar's shoulder. "What happened, gramps?"

Spar gibbered while he thought what to tell Drake. He loved Almodie and Kim. He said, "Had a nightmare. Vamps attacked me."

"Description?"

"An old lady and a . . . a . . . little dog."

The other officer dove in. "The black hatch is open."

Drake said, "Keeper told us that was always locked. Follow through, Fenner." As the other dove below, "You're sure this was a nightmare, gramps? A *little* dog? And an *old* woman?"

Spar said, "Yes," and Drake dove after his comrade, out through the black hatch.

Workday dawned. Spar felt sick and confused, but he set about his usual routine. He tried to talk to Kim, but the cat was as silent as yesterday afternoon. Keeper bullied and found many tasks—the place was a mess from Playday. Suzy got away quickly. She didn't want to talk about Sweetheart or anything else. Drake and Fenner didn't come back.

Spar swept and Kim patrolled, out of touch. In the afternoon Crown came in and talked with Keeper while Spar and Kim were out of earshot. They mightn't have been there for all notice Crown took of them.

Spar wondered about what he had seen last night. It might really have been a dream, he decided. He was no longer impressed by his memory-identification of Sweetheart. Stupid of him to have thought that Almodie and Kim, dream or reality, were vamps. Doc had said vamps were superstitions. But he didn't think much. He still had withdrawal symptoms, only less violent.

When Loafday dawned, Keeper gave Spar permission to leave the Bat Rack without his usual prying questions. Spar looked around for Kim, but couldn't see his black blob. Besides, he didn't really want to take the cat.

He went straight to Doc's office. The passageways weren't as lonely as last Loafday. For a third time he passed the bent figure croaking, "Seagull, Kestrel, Cathedral . . ."

Doc's hatch was unzipped, but Doc wasn't there. Kim waited a long while, uneasy in the corpse-light. It wasn't like Doc to leave his office unzipped and unattended. And he hadn't turned up at the Bat Rack last night, as he'd half promised.

Finally Spar began to look around. One of the first things he noticed was that the big black bag, which Doc had said contained his treasure, was missing.

Then he noticed that the gleaming pliofilm bag in which Doc had put the mold of Spar's gums, now held something different. He unclipped it from its shroud. There were two items in it.

He cut a finger on the first, which was half circle, half pink and half gleaming. He felt out its shape more cautiously then, ignoring the tiny red blobs welling from his finger. It had irregular depressions in its pink top and bottom. He put it in his mouth. His gums mated with the depressions. He opened his mouth, then closed it, careful to keep his tongue back. There was a *snick* and a dull *click*. He had teeth!

His hands were shaking, not just from withdrawal, as he felt the second item.

It was too thick rounds joined by a short bar and with a thicker long bar ending in a semicircle going back from each.

He thrust a finger into one of the rounds. It tickled, just as the tube had tickled his eyes, only more intensely, almost painfully.

Hands shaking worse than ever, he fitted the contraption to his face. The semicircles went around his ears, the rounds circled his eyes, not closely enough to tickle.

He could see sharply! *Everything* had edges, even his spread-fingered hands and the . . . clot of blood on one finger. He cried out —a low, wondering wail—and scanned the office. At first the scores and dozens of sharp-edged objects, each as distinct as the pictures of Capricorn and Virgo had been, were too much for him. He closed his eyes.

When his breathing was a little evener and his shaking less, he opened them cautiously and began to inspect the objects clipped to the shrouds. Each one was a wonder. He didn't know the purpose of half of them. Some of them with which he was familiar by use or blurred sight startled him greatly in their appearance—a comb, a brush, a book with pages (that infinitude of ranked black marks), a wrist watch (the tiny pictures around the circular margin of Capricorn and Virgo, and of the Bull and the Fishes, and so on, and the narrow bars radiating from the center and swinging swiftly or slowly or not at all—and pointing to the signs of the zodiac).

Before he knew it, he was at the corpse-glow wall. He faced it with a new courage, though it forced from his lips another wondering wail.

The corpse-glow didn't come from everywhere, though it took up the central quarter of his field of vision. His fingers touched taut, transparent pliofilm. What he saw beyond—a great way beyond, he began to think—was utter blackness with a great many tiny . . . points of bright light in it. Points were even harder to believe in than edges, he had to believe what he saw.

But centrally, looking much bigger than all the blackness, was a vast corpse-white round pocked with faint circles and scored by bright lines and mottled with slightly darker areas.

It didn't look as if it were wired for electricity, and it certainly didn't look affire. After a while Spar got the weird idea that its light was reflected from something much brighter *behind* Windrush.

It was infinitely strange to think of so much *space* around Windrush. Like thinking of a reality containing reality.

And if Windrush were between the hypothetical brighter light and the pocked white round, its shadow ought to be on the latter. Unless Windrush were almost infinitely small. Really these speculations were utterly too fantastic to deal with.

Yet could anything be too fantastic? Werewolves, witches, points, edges, size and space beyond any but the most insane belief.

When he had first looked at the corpse-white object, it had been round. And he had heard and felt the creakings of Loafday noon, without being conscious of it at the time. But now the round had its fore edge evenly sliced off, so that it was lopsided. Spar wondered if the hypothetical incandescence behind Windrush were moving, or the white round rotating, or Windrush itself revolving around the white round. Such thoughts, especially the last, were dizzying almost beyond endurance.

He made for the open door, wondering if he should zip it behind him, decided not to. The passageway was another amazement, going off and off and off, and narrowing as it went. Its walls bore . . . arrows, the red pointing to larboard, the way from which he'd come, the green pointing starboard, the way he was going. The arrows were what he'd always seen as dash-shaped blurs. As he pulled himself along the strangely definite dragline, the passageway stayed the same diameter, all the way to the violet main drag.

He wanted to jerk himself as fast as the green arrows to the starboard end of Windrush to verify the hypothetical incandescence and see the details of the orange-dun round that always depressed him.

But he decided he ought first to report Doc's disappearance to the Bridge. He might find Drake there. And report the loss of Doc's treasure too, he reminded himself.

Passing faces fascinated him. Such a welter of noses and ears! He overtook the croaking, bent shape. It was that of an old woman whose nose almost met her chin. She was doing something twitchy with her fingers to two narrow sticks and a roll of slender, fuzzy line. He impulsively dove off the dragline and caught hold of her, whirling them around.

"What are you doing, grandma?" he asked.

She puffed with anger. "Knitting," she answered indignantly.

"What are the words you keep saying?"

"Names of knitting patterns," she replied, jerking loose from him and blowing on. "Sand Dunes, Lightning, Soldiers Marching . . ."

He started to swim for the dragline, then saw he was already at the blue shaft leading aloft. He grabbed hold of its speeding center-line, not minding the burn, and speeded to the Bridge.

When he got there, he saw there was a multitude of stars aloft. The oblong rainbows were all banks of multi-colored lights winking on and off. But the silent officers—they looked very old, their faces stared as if they were sleep-swimming, their gestured orders were mechanical, he wondered if they knew where Windrush was going— or anything at all, beyond the Bridge of Windrush.

A dark, young officer with tightly curly hair floated to him. It wasn't until he spoke that Spar knew he was Ensign Drake.

"Hello, gramps. Say, you look younger. What are those things around your eyes?"

"Field glasses. They help me see sharp."

"But field glasses have tubes. They're a sort of binocular telescope."

Spar shrugged and told about the disappearance of Doc and his big, black treasure bag.

"But you say he drank a lot and he told you his treasures were dreams? Sounds like he was wacky and wandered off to do his drinking somewhere else."

"But Doc was a regular drinker. He always came to the Bat Rack."

"Well, I'll do what I can. Say, I've been pulled off the Bat Rack investigation. I think that character Crown got at someone higher up. The old ones are easy to get at—not so much greed as going by custom, taking the easiest course. Fenner and I never did find the old woman and the little dog, or any female and animal . . . or anything."

Spar told about Crown's earlier attempt to steal Doc's little black bag.

"So you think the two cases might be connected. Well, as I say, I'll do what I can."

Spar went back to the Bat Rack. It was very strange to see Keeper's face in detail. It looked old and its pink target center was a big red nose criss-crossed by veins. His brown eyes were not so much curious as avid. He asked about the things around Spar's eyes. Spar decided it wouldn't be wise to tell Keeper about seeing sharply.

"They're a new kind of costume jewelry, Keeper. Blasted Earth, I don't have any hair on my head, ought to have something."

"Language, Spar! It's like a drunk to spend precious scrip on such a grotesque bauble."

Spar neither reminded Keeper that all the scrip he'd earned at the Bat Rack amounted to no more than a wad as big as his thumb-joint, nor that he'd quit drinking. Nor did he tell him about his teeth, but kept them hidden behind his lips.

Kim was nowhere in sight. Keeper shrugged. "Gone off somewhere. You know the way of strays, Spar."

Yes, thought Spar, this one's stayed put too long.

He kept being amazed that he could see *all* of the Bat Rack sharply. It was an hexagon criss-crossed by shrouds and made up of two pyramids put together square base to square base. The apexes of the pyramids were the violet fore and dark red aft corners. The four other corners were the starboard green, the black below, the larboard scarlet, and the blue aloft, if you named them from aft in the way the hands of a watch move.

Suzy drifted in early Playday. Spar was shocked by her blowzy appearance and bloodshot eyes. But he was touched by her signs of affection and he felt the strong friendship between them. Twice when Keeper wasn't looking he switched her nearly empty pouch of dark for a full one. She told him that, yes, she'd once known Sweetheart and that, yes, she'd heard people say Mable had seen Sweetheart snatched by vamps.

Business was slow for Playday. There were no strange brewos. Hoping against fearful, gut-level certainty, Spar kept waiting for Doc to come in zig-zagging along the ratlines and comment on the new gadgets he'd given Spar and spout about the Old Days and his strange philosophy.

Playday night Crown came in with his girls, all except Almodie. Doucette said she'd had a headache and stayed at the Hole. Once again, all of them ordered coffee, though to Spar all of them seemed high.

Spar covertly studied their faces. Though nervous and alive, they all had something in their stares akin to those he'd seen in most of the officers on the Bridge. Doc had said they were all zombies. It was interesting to find out that Phanette's and Doucette's red-mottled appearance was due to . . . freckles, tiny reddish star-clusters on their white skins.

"Where's that famous talking cat?" Crown asked Spar.

Spar shrugged. Keeper said, "Strayed. For which I'm glad. Don't want a little feline who makes fights like last night."

Keeping his yellow-brown irised eyes on Spar, Crown said, "We believe it was that fight last Playday gave Almodie her headache, so she didn't want to come back tonight. We'll tell her you got rid of the witch cat."

"I'd have got rid of the beast if Spar hadn't," Keeper put in. "So you think it was a witch cat, coroner?"

"We're certain. What's that stuff on Spar's face?"

"A new sort of cheap eye-jewelry, coroner, such as attracts drinks."

Spar got the feeling that this conversation had been prearranged, that there was a new agreement between Crown and Keeper. But he just shrugged again. Suzy was looking angry, but she said nothing.

Yet she stayed behind again after the Bat Rack closed. Keeper put no claim on her, though he leered knowingly before disappearing with a yawn and a stretch through the scarlet hatch. Spar checked that all six hatches were locked and shut off the lights, though that made no difference in the morning glare, before returning to Suzy, who had gone to his sleeping shroud.

Suzy asked, "You didn't get rid of Kim?"

Spar answered, "No, he just strayed, as Keeper said at first. I don't know where Kim is."

Suzy smiled and put her arms around him. "I think your new eye-things are beautiful," she said.

Spar said, "Suzy, did you know that Windrush isn't the Universe? That it's a ship going through space around a white round marked with circles, a round much bigger than all Windrush?"

Suzy replied, "I know Windrush is sometimes called the Ship. I've seen that round—in pictures. Forget all wild thoughts, Spar, and lose yourself in me."

Spar did so, chiefly from friendship. He forgot to clip his ankle to the shroud. Suzy's body didn't attract him. He was thinking of Almodie.

When it was over, Suzy slept. Spar put the rag around his eyes and tried to do the same. He was troubled by withdrawal symptoms only a little less bad than last Sleepday's. Because of that little, he didn't go to the torus for a pouch of moonmist. But then there was a sharp jab in his back, as if a muscle had spasmed there, and the symptoms got much worse. He convulsed, once, twice, then just as the agony became unbearable, blanked out.

Spar woke, his head throbbing, to discover that he was not only clipped, but lashed to his shroud, his wrists stretched in one direction, his ankles in the other, his hands and his feet both numb. His nose rubbed the shroud.

Light made his eyelids red. He opened them a little at a time and saw Hellhound poised with bent hind legs against the next shroud. He could see Hellhound's great stabbing teeth very clearly. If he had opened his eyes a little more swiftly, Hellhound would have dove at his throat.

He rubbed his sharp metal teeth together. At least he had more than gums to meet an attack on his face.

Beyond Hellhound he saw black and transparent spirals. He realized he was in Crown's Hole. Evidently the last jab in his back had been the injection of a drug.

But Crown had not taken away his eye jewelry, nor noted his teeth. He had thought of Spar as old Eyeless Toothless.

Between Hellhound and the spirals, he saw Doc lashed to a shroud and his big black bag clipped next to him. Doc was gagged. Evidently he had tried to cry out. Spar decided not to. Doc's gray eyes were open and Spar thought Doc was looking at him.

Very slowly Spar moved his numb fingers on top of the knot lashing his wrists to the shroud and slowly contracted all his muscles and pulled. The knot slid down the shroud a millimeter. So long as he did something slowly enough, Hellhound could not see it. He repeated this action at intervals.

Even more slowly he swung his face to the left. He saw nothing more than that the hatch to the corridor was zipped shut, and that beyond the dog and Doc, between the black spirals, was an empty and unfurnished cabin whose whole starboard side was stars. The hatch to that cabin was open, with its black-striped emergency hatch wavering beside it.

With equal slowness he swung his face to the right, past Doc and past Hellhound, who was eagerly watching him for signs of life or waking. He had pulled down the knot on his wrists two centimeters.

The first thing he saw was a transparent oblong. In it were more stars and, by its aft edge, the smoky orange round. At last he could see the latter more clearly. The smoke was on top, the orange underneath and irregularly placed. The whole was about as big as Spar's palm could have covered, if he had been able to stretch out his arm to full length. As he watched, he saw a bright flash in one of the orange areas. The flash was short, then it turned to a tiny black round pushing out through the smoke. More than ever, Spar felt sadness.

Below the transparency, Spar saw a horrible tableau. Suzy was strapped to a bright metal rack guyed by shrouds. She was very pale and her eyes were closed. From the side of her neck went a red sipping-tube which forked into five branches. Four of the branches went into the red mouths of Crown, Rixende, Phanette, and Doucette. The fifth was shut by a small metal clip, and beyond it Almodie floated cowering, hands over her eyes.

Crown said softly, "We want it all. Strip her, Rixie."

Rixende clipped shut the end of her tube and swam to Suzy. Spar expected her to remove the blue culottes and bra, but instead she simply began to massage one of Suzy's legs, pressing always from ankle toward waist, driving her remaining blood nearer her neck.

Crown removed his sipping tube from his lips long enough to say, "Ahhh, good to the last drop." Then he had mouthed the blood that had spurted out in the interval and had the tube in place again.

Phanette and Doucette convulsed with soundless giggles.

Almodie peered between her parted fingers, out of her mass of platinum hair, then scissored them shut again.

After a while Crown said, "That's all we'll get. Phan and Doucie, feed her to the big chewer. If you meet anyone in the passageway, pretend she's drunk. Afterwards we'll get Doc to dose us high, and give him a little brew if he behaves, then we'll drink Spar."

Spar had his wrist knot more than halfway to his teeth. Hellhound kept watching eagerly for movement, unable to see movement that slow. Slaver made tiny gray globes beside his fangs.

Phanette and Doucette opened the hatch and steered Suzy's dead body through it.

Embracing Rixende, Crown said expansively toward Doc, "Well, isn't it the right thing, old man? Nature bloody in tooth and claw, a wise one said. They've poisoned everything there." He pointed toward the smoky orange round sliding out of sight. "They're still fighting, but they'll soon all be dead. So death should be the rule too for this gimcrack, so-called survival ship. Remember they are aboard her. When we've drunk the blood of everyone aboard Windrush, including their blood, we'll drink our own, if our own isn't theirs."

Spar thought, Crown thinks too much in they's. The knot was close to his teeth. He heard the big chewer start to grind.

In the empty next cabin, Spar saw Drake and Fenner, clad once more as brewos, swimming toward the open hatch.

But Crown saw them too. "Get 'em, Hellhound," he directed, pointing. "It's our command."

The big black dog bulleted from his shroud through the open hatch. Drake pointed something at him. The dog went limp.

Chuckling softly, Crown took by one tip a swastika with curved, gleaming, razor-sharp blades and sent it off spinning. It curved past Spar and Doc, went through the open hatch, missed Drake and Fenner—and Hellhound—and struck the wall of stars.

There was a rush of wind, then the emergency hatch smacked shut. Spar saw Drake, Fenner, and Hellhound, wavery through the transparent pliofilm, spew blood, bloat, burst bloodily open. The empty cabin they had been in disappeared. Windrush had a new wall and Crown's Hole was distorted.

Far beyond, growing ever tinier, the swastika spun toward the stars.

Phanette and Doucette came back. "We fed in Suzy. Someone was coming, so we beat it." The big chewer stopped grinding.

Spar bit cleanly through his wrist lashings and immediately doubled over to bite his ankles loose.

Crown dove at him. Pausing to draw knives, the four girls did the same.

Phanette, Doucette, and Rixende went limp. Spar had the impression that small black balls had glanced from their skulls.

There wasn't time to bite his feet loose, so he straightened. Crown hit his chest as Almodie bit his feet.

Crown and Spar giant-swung around the shroud. Then Almodie had cut Spar's ankles loose. As they spun off along the tangent, Spar tried to knee Crown in the groin, but Crown twisted and evaded the blow as they moved toward the inboard wall.

There was the *snick* of Crown's knife unfolding. Spar saw the dark wrist and grabbed it. He butted at Crown's jaw. Crown evaded. Spar set his teeth in Crown's neck and bit.

Blood covered Spar's face, spurted over it. He spat out a hunk of flesh. Crown convulsed. Spar fought off the knife. Crown went limp. That the pressure in a man should work against him.

Spar shook the blood from his face. Through its beads, he saw

Keeper and Kim side by side. Almodie was clutching his ankles. Phanette, Doucette, Rixende floated.

Keeper said proudly, "I shot them with my gun for drunks. I knocked them out. Now I'll cut their throats, if you wish."

Spar said, "No more throat-cutting. No more blood." Shaking off Almodie's hands, he took off for Doc, picking up Doucette's floating knife by the way.

He slashed Doc's lashings and cut the gag from his face.

Meanwhile Kim hissed, "Sstole and ssecreted Keeper's sscrip from the boxx. Ashshured him you sstole it, Sspar. You and Ssuzzy. Sso he came. Keeper izz a shshlemiel."

Keeper said, "I saw Suzy's foot going into the big chewer. I knew it by its anklet of hearts. After that I had the courage to kill Crown or anyone. I loved Suzy."

Doc cleared his throat and croaked, "Moonmist." Spar found a triple pouch and Doc sucked it all. Doc said, "Crown spoke the truth. Windrush is a plastic survival ship from Earth. Earth—" He motioned toward the dull orange round disappearing aft in the window "—poisoned herself with smog pollution and with nuclear war. She spent gold for war, plastic for survival. Best forgotten. Windrush went mad. Understandably. Even without the Lethean rickettsia, or Styx ricks, as you call it. Thought Windrush was the cosmos. Crown kidnapped me to get my drugs, kept me alive to know the doses."

Spar looked at Keeper. "Clean up here," he ordered. "Feed Crown to the big chewer."

Almodie pulled herself from Spar's ankles to his waist. "There was a second survival ship. Circumluna. When Windrush went mad, my father and mother—and you—were sent here, to investigate and cure. But my father died and you got Styx ricks. My mother died just before I was given to Crown. She sent you Kim."

Kim hissed, "My fforebear came from Circumluna to Windrush, too. Great grandmother. Taught me the ffigures for Windrushsh . . . Radiuss from moon-ccenter, 2,500 miles. Period, ssixx hours—sso, the sshort dayss. A terranth izz the time it takess Earth to move through a consstellation, and sso on."

Doc said, "So, Spar, you're the only one who remembers without cynicism. You'll have to take over. It's all yours, Spar."

Spar had to agree.

Fritz Leiber

by JUDITH MERRIL

For more than thirty years, Fritz Leiber has been entertaining, inspiring, irritating, enlightening and delighting a growing audience for fantasy and speculative fiction. He has received every honor and award the field has to offer, as well as some distinctive personal tokens of esteem, from a following which includes the entire spectrum of the curious multigenre known as "science fiction": the weird-and-macabre, whimsical and "heroic" fantasy, hardware-sci-fi, sociological speculation and political satire, psychological symbolism and *avant-garde* surrealism. He is as highly regarded by the Newrock Generation as by the Old Guard collectors of 1926 *Amazings*—and perhaps most of all by his colleagues inside the field ("a writer's writer"). Yet his name is hardly known outside the genre.

This paradoxical state of affairs is in part due to his very range and variety. Leiber is equally the Romantic and the Realist: a Shakespearean, scholar, and surrealist; poet, prophet, pamphleteer, pacifist and profligate; occasional painter, sculptor, collagist, and pianist; sometime fencer, serious chess-player, novice canyon-climber. He has been a (Phi Beta Kappa) philosophy student, stage and screen actor, preacher, college teacher, factory worker, editor; has written (aside from s-f) encyclopaedia articles, Lovecraftian horror, popular science, political tracts, comic-strip continuity, plays, poetry, and critical and scholarly works; he is a frequent contributor to fan magazines and amateur publications, an inveterate letter writer and omniverous reader.

There are authors one admires, authors one agrees with, and authors one loves. The first two sorts are taught in schools, displayed on coffee tables and book shelves, discussed at cocktail parties, bought as gifts, and generously lent out. Leiber gets borrowed, tattered and read.

Fritz is my good friend, and has been for twenty years, but the fact is I fell in love with him half a decade before we met. This is not to say my passion is a purely literary one: simply that the man and his work are not separable.

Anyone in the author-meeting business (critic, editor, anthologist) quickly comes to know that the writer of the grisliest murders will turn out to be a tidy, milky little man; the author of a Noble Doctor story probably suffers from chronic acne complicated by gout; and the authoress of those innocent ladies' romances will undoubtedly be not just a tart, but a *tweedy* one. Not so Leiber. (Indeed if one were to invert his literary multiple-personality, he would be left with no character at all.) In appearance as well as manner, he could step into any one of dozens of characters he has written (and on one occasion at least did so with notable success): in fact the "noble barbarian" of the Fafhrd and Mouser stories is so nearly a self-caricature that he is known as "Faf" to his family. The rhythms of his prose are those of his speech; his letters and conversations seem to pick up where the last story stopped and run into the start of the next, if not in topic, then in theme and style. Writing about him, I find it difficult to remember whether this phrase or that image was from the public or private communications.

As critic and editor, I have had to learn to guard against underrating his work on just this account: the best of his stories are often the "transparent" ones that leave me feeling it was after all just a lovely letter from Fritz.

That this kind of *personal* response—although less accountable and much less self-conscious—is shared by thousands of other readers, has been made clear on several occasions. The November 1959 issue of *Fantastic,* for instance: Leiber had just come out of one of his recurrent dry spells, and editor Cele Lalli bought up all his new material until there was enough to fill an issue; the magazine came out with a big black headline across its cover—LEIBER IS BACK!

Or that "memorable occasion" mentioned above, when I saw—and heard—an ovation from hundreds of fans and fellow-writers when Leiber took an award at a convention hotel fancy-dress ball. The costume? A cardboard military collar slipped over turned-up jacket lapels, plus cardboard shoulder insignia, an armband, and a large spider black-pencilled on his forehead, to turn him into an officer of the "Spiders" in the Change-war of *The Big Time* and "No Great Magic." The only other component was the Leiber instinct for theatre.

Leiber was born on the day before Christmas in Chicago in 1910, and plunged immediately into the study of Shakespeare: until he was six, he toured the country with the repertory company in which his parents were actors ". . . memories redolent of grease paint, spirit gum, curling colored gelatins of flood- and spot-lights . . . I learned most of Hamlet at age 4 when my father was first learning it . . ." During his school years, he spent long winters in Chicago with two prim Germanic maiden aunts; summers, he was at home with his parents on the Jersey shore, learning more Shakespeare, stagecraft, and theatrical mores.

In 1932 he took a B.A. with honors in Philosophy from the University of Chicago, and went into the ministry: "Ran two Episcopalian 'missionary' churches in New Jersey as lay reader and minister while attending the General Theological Seminary in N.Y. (here a missionary church means one without a resident priest) . . . I had to get christened and confirmed quick for this odd junket which I tackled most sincerely with the feeling, which 'Beezie' Mandeville [the Rev. Ernest W., of Middletown, N.J.] approved, that I could view the job as one of rational social service rather than religious conviction and vocation. In about five months I found out this wasn't so and I worked out the 'season' and quit."

The next year he was back at Chicago doing graduate work in philosophy. Then a year touring with his father's Shakespearean company, and two years of (mostly male ingenue) bit parts in Hollywood, followed by a brief unsuccessful attempt at freelance writing —and back to Chicago again as a staff writer for the Standard American Encyclopedia (an extraordinary reference work, some of whose oddities are revealed in last year's *New Worlds* story, "The Square Root of Brain").

In the summer of 1937, the time of that first abortive try at "being a writer," two significant events occurred in the literary world: Howard Phillips Lovecraft died, and John W. Campbell, Jr., became editor of *Astounding,* and very shortly afterwards began gathering material for a new publication called *Unknown,* where Leiber's first story was published in 1939.

His interest in fiction had started at college, where most of the time left over from his education in Utopian Socialism, pacifism, fencing, and chess (the only subject in which he now has an official "expert" rating), was devoted to long literary correspondences. The most significant of these were with H. P. Lovecraft (and other members of the Lovecraft Circle) and with his friend Harry Fischer, of Louisville. It was in letters with Fischer that the characters and some of the background of Fafhrd and the Gray Mouser were first developed, and it was one of these that sold to *Unknown* and brought the author an immediate following among "heroic fantasy" fans. (Curiously, it was the second in the series, "Two Sought Adventure," that Campbell bought. The first, "Adept's Gambit," a far better story, did not see print until the publication of Leiber's first collection, *Night's Black Agents* by Arkham House in 1947.)

Between 1939–1943, there was a scattering of stories in *Unknown, Weird,* and *Future.* Meantime the Leibers (there was now a wife and infant son) left Chicago for Los Angeles again. A year teaching drama and speech at Occidental College was followed by another (very) brief try at free-lancing in 1942: just long enough to write the two novels that would place him firmly in the top rank of science-fantasy, and keep him there through his first long dry spell of five years. *Conjure Wife* (later filmed as *Burn, Witch, Burn!*) combined traditional witchcraft and a realistic contemporary setting derived largely from the year at Occidental; *Gather, Darkness!* went further in two directions, at least, using the apparatus and literature of witchcraft in juxtaposition with technological extrapolation and political prophecy to create one of the first truly modern science fiction novels.

If he had written nothing more, Leiber would still be a leading genre author. Few 30-year-old fond memories can stand intimate revisiting. These do. If I were coming across them for the first time today, I think I would respond with the same sense of discovery and astonishment I had in 1943.

The two novels were published almost simultaneously: *Conjure Wife,* complete, in the April *Unknown; Gather, Darkness!* as a serial starting in the May *Astounding.* By the time they appeared, however, Leiber had given up full-time writing again, and taken a war job as an inspector at Douglas Aircraft. (After a long struggle with his pacifist beliefs: "I very slowly came around to the view that the anti-fascist forces had been justified and 'right' in WW II.") In 1945, he joined the editorial staff of *Science Digest*—back in Chicago—where he stayed for twelve years. His literary productivity throughout this period was uneven both in quantity and quality. Only in the past fifteen years has Leiber finally settled down to full-time writing; and only now is he really coming into his own.

There are good reasons why this should be a time of recognition for him. In the television age, an audience of viewer-readers responds warmly to the specifically (and increasingly) theatric quality of his work: everything he writes has as much of the stage as the page in it. The best theatre, of course, is that in which the illusion is most complete, where the audience need not "suspend disbelief" but can just *believe*.

The current s-f audience is vastly more sophisticated literarily, as well as scientifically, than that of the forties. And of course television has accustomed the reader/viewer to the idea of the familiarly convincing character and sustained theme displayed in a constantly changing, and frequently fantastic, series of situations.

And then of course science fiction and short stories are both "in": and Leiber's short fiction, more than that of any other writer, reflects the development of the several sub-species presently subsumed under the (absurdly inappropriate) label, "science fiction," from the origins of the specialty field to its present acceptance as a contemporary literary form.

Indeed, there is an intriguing parallel between the role Leiber has played inside the field, and the situation of science fiction in the literary world generally. The rigid compartmentalizing of American literature in the first half of the twentieth century which produced, among other things, the specialized category of fantasy called science fiction, continued to function within the field as it grew; and it is those writers whose names attach directly to one or another phase of that growth who have become identified with it in the great outside literary world: Heinlein, Asimov, Sturgeon, Bradbury, Simak, Clarke, Wyndham, Bloch; each carved out for himself a distinct and separate niche clearly visible to publishers, critics, and scholars. Leiber has been ubiquitous, seminal, influential, widely read—and, critically, virtually ignored.

I first met Fritz at a science-fiction convention in 1949. It would have been a memorable night anyhow: I met a lot of people either already legendary in that tight little world, or—like myself—novice myth-makers who would be friends and colleagues later: Poul Anderson, Randall Garrett, Joe Winter. We all wound up at a uniquely bemuraled restaurant called The Purple Cow (such as could only happen, I think, in Paris or the American Midwest). But that was later. At the beginning it was just a very crowded hotel room, and I was the almost-unknown author of two published stories, and I could not seem to find a single face I remembered meeting earlier in the day.

I was quite certain I had not met the man sitting on the window ledge, darkly handsome, remote . . . brooding? a bit amused? Our eyes met, and he began to stand up. (It took a while. Fritz is 6'4".) We both smiled tentatively.

"I'm Fritz Leiber," he said.

I said nothing. (Remember: this was a man I had been in love with for six years.) When I got my breath back I said, "I'm Judy Merril." And he said, "Judith Merril? You mean *you wrote* . . . ?"

The next thing I remember clearly is that I was deep in conversation with Leiber (FRITZ LEIBER!—*who remembered my story!*) and that the room was even more crowded.

Nineteen years later, I sat talking to a bright young writer who was barely born on the Night of the Purple Cow. It was the first day of the Milford Science-Fiction Writers' Conference, and I mentioned that Fritz had just arrived. "Fritz *Leiber?*" he said, and I realized that glazed look must once have been my own. "FRITZ LEIBER?" Later, he came and told me, "Okay. I could even go home now, I mean, I met LEIBER."

Only one other name from the Great Old Days seems to evoke the same kind of response from the Bright Young People—Theodore Sturgeon—for much the same reasons.

Both men have been singularly uneven writers. Much of what they published was too hastily written, or too much limited by the narrowness of the specialty field they wrote for. But it is true of both of them that the *best* of what they wrote, at any time, remains as valid now as when it was written.

Leiber's writing began, remember, under the sepulchral Lovecraft spell: his first efforts were all directed at the "weird" market—stories of necromancy, midnight, murder and madness. But he had trouble selling to *Weird Tales* from the beginning: the reasons are apparent in "Smoke Ghost" (which eventually went to *Unknown*), and in one of the few titles that did appear in *Weird* (in 1942, as it began to move inward from its black pole), "The Hound". Here one of the characters speaks, apparently very much for the author:

" 'Meanwhile what's happening inside each one of us? I'll tell you. All sorts of inhibited emotions are accumulating. Fear is accumulating. Horror is accumulating. A new kind of awe of the mysteries of the universe is accumulating. A psychological environment is forming, along with the physical one. Wait, let me finish. Our culture becomes ripe for infection. From somewhere. It's just like a bacteriologist's culture—I didn't intend the pun—when it gets to the right temperature and consistency for supporting a colony of germs. Similarly, our culture suddenly spawns a horde of demons. And, like germs, they have a peculiar affinity for our culture. They're unique. They fit in. You wouldn't find the same kind any other time or place.

" '. . . our fears would be their fodder. A parasite-host relationship. Supernatural symbiosis. Some of us—the sensitive ones—would notice them sooner than others. . . . Frighten and terrorize you, yes. But surprise, no. It would fit into the environment. Look as if it belonged in a city and smell the same. Because of the twisted emotions that would be its food, your emotions and mine. A matter of diet.' "

His first active writing period came to a climax in 1943 with the publication of *Conjure Wife* and *Gather, Darkness!* Although he continued to make extensive use of the symbolism and melodrama of the supernatural afterwards, those two novels were the last major pieces in which conventional horror images dominated; *Conjure Wife* was the last in which they were used in what could be called a conventional way. His first "dry spell" began shortly afterwards, while he was working at Douglas in 1944.

In the next five years he wrote only a handful of stories, and sold only three. During this time, he was profoundly affected by events in the outside world: World War II and its holocaustic climax at Hiroshima; the ensuing atmosphere of anti-libertarian conformism, witch-hunts, and brainwashing in the heyday of Joe McCarthy; the not-yet-popular struggles of Negro-Americans for civil rights and full citizenship; the Mad Ave and PR explosion in the Wonderful Postwar World of television and "media"; the (sic) preverberations of the twin explosions of Western civilization into outer, and inner, space. Out of all these, in his own phoenix-like crucible he was "brewing his cultures," cultivating a knowledge of the new demons and modern horrors, learning new imageries, patterns, symbols.

Two of the three stories of this time of silence pointed to where he was going. "Mr. Bauer and the Atoms" was in *Weird* in 1946:

"Frank Bauer lived in a world where everything had been exploded. He scented confidence games, hoaxes, faddish self-deception, and especially (for it was his province) advertising-copy-exaggerations behind every faintly unusual event and every intimation of the unknown. He had the American's nose for leg-pulling, the German's contempt for the non-factual. Mention of such topics as telepathy, hypnotism or the occult—and his wife managed to mention them fairly often—sent him into a scoffing rage."

[Then he learned about atoms:]

". . . 'See, we always thought everything was so solid. Money, automobiles, mines, dirt. We thought they were so solid that we could handle them, hold on to them, do things with them. And now we find they're just a lot of little bits of deadly electricity, whirling around at God knows what speed, by some miracle frozen for a moment.' "

The next story to see print was three years later. This is in part how Marshall McLuhan described it in *The Mechanical Bride:*

"In a story called 'The Girl with the Hungry Eyes', by Fritz Leiber, an ad photographer gives a job to a not too promising model. Soon, however, she is 'plastered all over the country' because she has the hungriest eyes in the world. 'Nothing vulgar, but just the same they're looking at you with a hunger that's all sex and something more than sex.' Something similar may be said of the legs on a pedestal. Abstracted from the body that gives them their ordinary meaning, they become 'something more than sex', a metaphysical enticement, a cerebral itch, an abstract torment. Mr. Leiber's girl hypnotizes the country with her hungry eyes . . ."

I resist, with difficulty, the desire to quote in full here the final statement of the story (as written by Leiber, not McLuhan). When you have found it and read (or re-read) it, think back if you can—before Twiggy, Jane Fonda, Barbarella, before *Playboy,* Bardot, Monroe. "The Girl" was published in 1949, and McLuhan's book in 1951. They both had to wait for the audience to catch up.

When "The Girl" appeared, Leiber was in the middle of a new

spurt of activity which began with the publication of a mimeographed magazine called *New Purposes,* and grew into such bittersweet prophetic "Love Generation" stories as "The Moon is Green," "A Pail of Air," and "The Nice Girl with Five Husbands"; and (on the other side of a suddenly familiar coin) a strain of satire which emerged at its sharpest in the Spillane pastiche, "The Night He Cried," and at its most terrifyingly prophetic in "Coming Attraction," "Poor Superman," and finally the 1953 novel, *The Green Millennium.* These last three titles are part of a "future-history" satire system set in a world (circa 1990's) of "off-the-bosom" dresses and jewelled face masks, barbed auto-fenders and motorized sex/sadism, television brainwashing, automation redundancy, mystical cultism, violence-for-kicks, ocean-wide credibility gaps, and the sad dignity-in-defeat of the gentle "Dr. Opperly."

When they appeared, it was Joe McCarthy time. The science-fiction magazines were proud of being the last popular public arena for dissent and nonconformism—but one was not supposed to spell it out *too* clearly. It is not really surprising that editors began returning rueful notes about their readers' objections to certain stories—or that *The Green Millennium* had no magazine publication (at that time the main source of income from a genre novel)—*or* that "The Silence Game," a bitter story of the agonized-cool ultimate-dropout revolt, published at the time of the nationally televised Oppenheimer hearings (1954), was the prophetic last word from Leiber for another three years.

Once again there were stories left over. By 1957, the field seemed to be ready for them. "The Big Trek" and "Friends and Enemies," both first-drafted in *New Purposes* (eight years earlier) were published and, again, demand seemed to stimulate supply for a while—a short while, this time. The new stories of 1957–58 had two new themes, sometimes combined: time-travel and the hip (not-yet-hippy) beat scene. *The Big Time,* the first of the Change-war "Snakes" vs. "Spiders" stories, won the annual Hugo award for 1958—but stories like "Rump-Titty-Titty-Tum-TAH-Tee" and "A Deskful of Girls" once again upset and irritated more readers than they delighted. And "Little Old Miss MacBeth," by far the most advanced piece of symbolic writing Leiber had done, as well as his first really effective use of Shakespearean background, went almost unnoticed.

To what extent the financial and critical discouragement that accompanied each of his most fertile periods of literary growth were factors in the cyclical work stoppages is hard to determine: certainly, he never seemed to stop producing when his work was actively in demand; just as certainly, each time he would eventually outstrip the demand. And each time, there were other factors as well. Surveying the titles of 1957–1958, one thinks again of Poe, Fitzgerald, and the rest: "Damnation Morning," "Pipe Dream," "Tranquillity or Else," "Try and Change the Past." Leiber at this point was literally fighting for his life. His job at *Science Digest* had ended in 1956, when alcoholism and blood-poisoning incapacitated him in the hospital. For the next three years, his production was erratic: it was something of a victory headline when *Fantastic*'s cover shouted LEIBER IS BACK! in November, 1959, at the end of the last really silent spell he was to have. It marked the time of Leiber's highly specialized kind of "settling down."

The cycles of surge and discouragement did not stop there. But when the really new 1960 stories like "The Inner Circles" and "The Secret Songs" took too long to sell, he stopped writing—*that* kind of story—and did some continuity for the Buck Rogers comic strip. Or, when his 1964 novel, *The Wanderer,* took another Hugo but failed to pay for the time it took (again, no magazine sale), he accepted the novelization assignment for *Tarzan and the Valley of Gold* (the only *Tarzan* book ever authorized by the Burroughs family for publication under another byline). When *A Specter Is Haunting Texas* had trouble for some time finding book publication, Leiber went back to Fafhrd and the Mouser, finishing off a third volume for paperback publication. And when "Gonna Roll The Bones," a gamble-with-the-Devil modern horror story (a Dangerous Vision straight out of the *Unknown* period), won SFWA's Nebula Award for the best novelette of 1967, he was spending most of his time on critical writing.

One way and another, Leiber keeps sorting out the elements of his many "lives," using Shakespeare, sex, chess, science and the supernatural, politics and pacifism, alcohol, Hollywood, Academe, Church, Stage, and the publishing world, to cultivate his cunningly fashioned demons and daemons of the world of today, using them in new modes when he can, in old ones when he must. And in both veins, the young as well as the old continue to listen, with pleasure.

Bibliography of books by Fritz Leiber
Compiled by Al Lewis

NIGHT'S BLACK AGENTS, Arkham House, Sauk City, Wisconsin, 1947. 237pp. (story collection) Contains: Smoke Ghost, The Automatic Pistol, The Inheritance (The Phantom Slayer), The Hill and the Hole, The Dreams of Albert Moreland, The Hound, The Man Who Never Grew Young, [F] The Sunken Land, [F] Adept's Gambit.

GATHER, DARKNESS! Pellegrini and Cudahy, New York, 1950. 240pp. (novel)

CONJURE WIFE, Twayne Publishers, New York, 1953. 154pp. (novel)

THE GREEN MILLENNIUM, Abelard Press, New York, 1953. 256pp. (novel)

THE SINFUL ONES (novel) bound with BULLS, BLOOD, AND PASSION by David Williams. Universal, New York, 1953. A long version of You're All Alone.

DESTINY TIMES THREE, Galaxy Novels #28, 1956. 128pp. (novel)

TWO SOUGHT ADVENTURE, Gnome Press, Inc., New York, 1957. 186pp. (story collection) Contains: The Jewels in the Forest (Two Sought Adventure), Thieves' House, The Bleak Shore, The Howling Tower, The Sunken Land, The Seven Black Priests, Claws From the Night (Dark Vengeance). First collection of Fafhrd and Mouser stories.

THE BIG TIME (novel) dos-à-dos with THE MIND SPIDER (story collection) Ace Books, New York, 1961. #D-491. 129 and 127pp. Contains: [C] The Big Time, The Haunted Future (Tranquility or Else), [C] Damnation Morning, [C] The Oldest Soldier, [C] Try and Change the Past, The Number of the Beast, The Mind Spider.

THE SILVER EGGHEADS, Ballantine Books, New York, 1961. #F-561. 192pp. (novel)

SHADOWS WITH EYES, Ballantine Books, New York, 1962. #577. 128pp. (story collection) Contains: A Bit of the Dark World, The Dead Man, The Power of the Puppets, Schizo Jimmie, The Man Who Made Friends With Electricity, [C] A Deskful of Girls.

A PAIL OF AIR, Ballantine Books, New York, 1964. #U-2216. 192pp. (story collection) Contains: A Pail of Air, The Beat Cluster, The Foxholes of Mars, Pipe Dream, Time Fighter, The 64-Square Madhouse, Bread Overhead, The Last Letter, Rump-Titty-Titty-Tum-TAH-Tee, Coming Attraction, Nice Girl With Five Husbands.

THE WANDERER, Ballantine Books, New York, 1964. #U-6010. 318pp. Dennis Dobson, Ltd., London, 1967. 346pp. (novel) The Dobson edition is hard cover.

SHIPS TO THE STARS (story collection) bound dos-à-dos with THE MILLION YEAR HUNT by Kenneth Bulmer. Ace Books, New York, 1964. #F-285. 122pp. Contains: Dr. Kometevsky's Day, The Big Trek, The Enchanted Forest, Deadly Moon, The Snowbank Orbit, The Ship Sails at Midnight.

THE NIGHT OF THE WOLF, Ballantine Books, New York, 1966. #U-2254. 221pp. (story collection) Contains: The Lone Wolf (The Creature From Cleveland Depths), The Wolf Pair (The Night of the Long Knives), Crazy Wolf (Sanity), The Wolf Pack (Let Freedom Ring).

TARZAN AND THE VALLEY OF GOLD, Ballantine Books, New York, 1966. #U-6125. 317pp. Authorized novelization from the screenplay.

THE SECRET SONGS, Rupert Hart-Davis, Ltd., London, 1968. 229pp. (story collection) Contains: The Winter Flies (The Inner Circles), The Man Who Made Friends with Electricity, Rump-Titty-Titty-Tum-TAH-Tee, Mariana, Coming Attraction, The Moon is Green, A Pail of Air, Smoke Ghost, The Girl with the Hungry Eyes, [C] No Great Magic, The Secret Songs.

THE SWORDS OF LANKHMAR, Ace Books, New York, 1968. #H-38. 224pp. (novel) Expanded version of Scylla's Daughter. Second book of Fafhrd and Gray Mouser stories.

SWORDS AGAINST WIZARDRY, Ace Books, New York, 1968. #H-73. 188pp. (story collection) Contains: In the Witch's Tent, Stardock, The Two Best Thieves in Lankhmar, The Lords of Quarmall. Third book of Fafhrd and Gray Mouser stories.

SWORDS IN THE MIST, Ace Books, New York, 1968. #H-90. 190pp. (story collection) Contains: The Cloud of Hate, Lean Times in Lankhmar; Their Mistress, the Sea; When the Sea-King's Away, The Wrong Branch, Adept's Gambit. Fourth book of Fafhrd and Gray Mouser stories.

A SPECTER IS HAUNTING TEXAS, Walker & Co., New York, 1969. 224pp. (novel)

THE DEMONS OF THE UPPER AIR, Roy Squires, Glendale, California, 1969. 20pp. (poetry collection) Edition limited to 325 copies.

SWORDS AGAINST DEATH, Ace Books, New York, 1970. #79151. 256pp. (story collection) Contains all of the stories in TWO SOUGHT ADVENTURE plus: The Circle Curse, The Price of Pain-Ease, Bazaar of the Bizarre. A new edition of the first book of Fafhrd and Gray Mouser stories.

SWORDS AND DEVILTRY, Ace Books, New York, 1970. #79170. 256pp. (story collection) Contains: The Snow Women, The Unholy Grail, Ill Met in Lankhmar. Fifth collection of Fafhrd and Gray Mouser stories.

YOU'RE ALL ALONE, Ace Books, New York, 1973 (novel).

THE BOOK OF FRITZ LEIBER, DAW Books, New York, 1974. #87. 176pp. (story and article collection) Stories: The Spider, A Hitch in Space, Kindergarten, Crazy Annaoj, When the Last Gods Die, Yesterday House, [C] Knight to Move, To Arkham and the Stars, [F] Beauty and the Beasts, Cat's Cradle. Articles: Monsters and Monster Lovers, Hottest and Coldest Molecules, Those Wild Alien Words, Debunking the I Machine, King Lear, After Such Knowledge, Weird World of the Knight, The Whisperer Re-examined, Monsters of Mace and Magic.

NOTE: [F] in front of a title denotes a story of the Fafhrd and Gray Mouser series; [C] denotes a story of the Change War series.

Poul Anderson

The Queen of Air and Darkness

by POUL ANDERSON

The last glow of the last sunset would linger almost until midwinter. But there would be no more day, and the northlands rejoiced. Blossoms opened, flamboyance on firethorn trees, steel-flowers rising blue from the brok and rainplant that cloaked all hills, shy whiteness of kiss-me-never down in the dales. Flitteries darted among them on iridescent wings; a crownbuck shook his horns and bugled. Between horizons the sky deepened from purple to sable. Both moons were aloft, nearly full, shining frosty on leaves and molten on waters. The shadows they made were blurred by an aurora, a great blowing curtain of light across half heaven. Behind it the earliest stars had come out.

A boy and a girl sat on Wolund's Barrow just under the dolmen it upbore. Their hair, which streamed halfway down their backs, showed startlingly forth, bleached as it was by summer. Their bodies, still dark from that season, merged with earth and bush and rock, for they wore only garlands. He played on a bone flute and she sang. They had lately become lovers. Their age was about sixteen, but they did not know this, considering themselves Outlings and thus indifferent to time, remembering little or nothing of how they had once dwelt in the lands of men.

His notes piped cold around her voice:

> "Cast a spell,
> weave it well
> of dust and dew
> and night and you."

A brook by the grave mound, carrying moonlight down to a hill-hidden river, answered with its rapids. A flock of hellbats passed black beneath the aurora.

A shape came bounding over Cloudmoor. It had two arms and two legs, but the legs were long and claw-footed and feathers covered it to the end of a tail and broad wings. The face was half human, dominated by its eyes. Had Ayoch been able to stand wholly erect, he would have reached to the boy's shoulder.

The girl rose. "He carries a burden," she said. Her vision was not meant for twilight like that of a northland creature born, but she had learned how to use every sign her senses gave her. Besides the fact that ordinarily a pook would fly, there was a heaviness to his haste.

"And he comes from the south." Excitement jumped in the boy, sudden as a green flame that went across the constellation Lyrth. He sped down the mound. "Ohoi, Ayoch!" he called, "Me here, Mistherd!"

"And Shadow-of-a-Dream," the girl laughed, following.

The pook halted. He breathed louder than the soughing in the growth around him. A smell of bruised yerba lifted where he stood.

"Well met in winterbirth," he whistled. "You can help me bring this to Carheddin."

He held out what he bore. His eyes were yellow lanterns above. It moved and whimpered.

"Why, a child," Mistherd said.

"Even as you were, my son, even as you were. Ho, ho, what a snatch!" Ayoch boasted. "They were a score in yon camp by Fallowwood, armed, and besides watcher engines they had big ugly dogs aprowl while they slept. I came from above, however, having spied on them till I knew that a handful of dazedust—"

"The poor thing." Shadow-of-a-Dream took the boy and held him to her small breasts. "So full of sleep yet, aren't you?" Blindly, he sought a nipple. She smiled through the veil of her hair. "No, I am still too young, and you already too old. But come, when you wake in Carheddin under the mountain, you shall feast."

"Yo-ah," said Ayoch very softly. "She is abroad and has heard and seen. She comes." He crouched down, wings folded. After a moment Mistherd knelt, and then Shadow-of-a-Dream, though she did not let go the child.

The Queen's tall form blocked off the moons. For a while she regarded the three and their booty. Hill and moor sounds withdrew from their awareness until it seemed they could hear the north-lights hiss.

At last Ayoch whispered, "Have I done well, Starmother?"

"If you stole a babe from a camp full of engines," said the beautiful voice, "then they were folk out of the far south who may not endure it as meekly as yeomen."

"But what can they do, Snow-maker?" the pook asked. "How can they track us?"

Mistherd lifted his head and spoke in pride. "Also, now they too have felt the awe of us."

"And he is a cuddly dear," Shadow-of-a-Dream said. "And we need more like him, do we not, Lady Sky?"

"It had to happen in some twilight," agreed she who stood above. "Take him onward and care for him. By this sign," which she made, "is he claimed for the Dwellers."

Their joy was freed. Ayoch cartwheeled over the ground till he reached a shiverleaf. There he swarmed up the trunk and out on a limb, perched half hidden by unrestful pale foliage, and crowed. Boy and girl bore the child toward Carheddin at an easy distance-devouring lope which let him pipe and her sing:

"Wahaii, wahaii!
Wayala, laii!
Wing on the wind
high over heaven,
shrilly shrieking,
rush with the rainspears,
tumble through tumult,
drift to the moonhoar trees and the dream-heavy shadows beneath
    them,
and rock in, be one with the clinking wavelets of lakes where the star-
    beams drown."

As she entered, Barbro Cullen felt, through all grief and fury, stabbed by dismay. The room was unkempt. Journals, tapes, reels, codices, file boxes, bescribbled papers were piled on every table. Dust filmed most shelves and corners. Against one wall stood a laboratory setup, microscope and analytical equipment. She recognized it as compact and efficient, but it was not what you would expect in an office, and it gave the air a faint chemical reek. The rug was threadbare, the furniture shabby.

This was her final chance?

Then Eric Sherrinford approached. "Good day, Mrs. Cullen," he said. His tone was crisp, his handclasp firm. His faded grip-suit didn't bother her. She wasn't inclined to fuss about her own appearance except on special occasions. (And would she ever again have one, unless she got back Jimmy?) What she observed was a cat's personal neatness.

A smile radiated in crow's feet from his eyes. "Forgive my bachelor housekeeping. On Beowulf we have—we had, at any rate, machines for that, so I never acquired the habit myself, and I don't want a hireling disarranging my tools. More convenient to work out of my apartment than keep a separate office. Won't you be seated?"

"No, thanks. I couldn't," she mumbled.

"I understand. But if you'll excuse me, I function best in a relaxed position."

He jackknifed into a lounger. One long shank crossed the other knee. He drew forth a pipe and stuffed it from a pouch. Barbro wondered why he took tobacco in so ancient a way. Wasn't Beowulf supposed to have the up-to-date equipment that they still couldn't afford to build on Roland? Well, of course old customs might survive anyhow. They generally did in colonies, she remembered reading. People had moved starward in the hope of preserving such outmoded things as their mother tongues or constitutional government or rational-technological civilization. . . .

Sherrinford pulled her up from the confusion of her weariness: "You must give me the details of your case, Mrs. Cullen. You've simply told me your son was kidnaped and your local constabulary did nothing. Otherwise, I know just a few obvious facts, such as your being widowed rather than divorced; and you're the daughter of outwayers in Olga Ivanoff Land who, nevertheless, kept in close telecommunication with Christmas Landing; and you're trained in one of the biological professions; and you had several years' hiatus in field work until recently you started again."

She gaped at the high-cheeked, beak-nosed, black-haired and gray-eyed countenance. His lighter made a *scrit* and a flare which seemed to fill the room. Quietness dwelt on this height above the city, and winter dusk was seeping through the windows. "How in cosmos do you know that?" she heard herself exclaim.

He shrugged and fell into the lecturer's manner for which he was notorious. "My work depends on noticing details and fitting them together. In more than a hundred years on Roland, tending to cluster according to their origins and thought-habits, people have developed regional accents. You have a trace of the Olgan burr, but you nasalize your vowels in the style of this area, though you live in Portolondon. That suggests steady childhood exposure to metropolitan speech. You were part of Matsuyama's expedition, you told me, and took your boy along. They wouldn't have allowed any ordinary technician to do that; hence, you had to be valuable enough to get away with it. The team was conducting ecological research; therefore, you must be in the life sciences. For the same reason, you must have had previous field experience. But your skin is fair, showing none of the leatheriness one gets from prolonged exposure to this sun. Accordingly, you must have been mostly indoors for a good while before you went on your ill-fated trip. As for widowhood—you never mentioned a husband to me, but you have had a man whom you thought so highly of that you still wear both the wedding and the engagement ring he gave you."

Her sight blurred and stung. The last of those words had brought Tim back, huge, ruddy, laughterful and gentle. She must turn from this other person and stare outward. "Yes," she achieved saying, "you're right."

The apartment occupied a hilltop above Christmas Landing. Beneath it the city dropped away in walls, roofs, archaistic chimneys and lamplit streets, goblin lights of human-piloted vehicles, to the harbor, the sweep of Venture Bay, ships bound to and from the Sunward Islands and remoter regions of the Boreal Ocean, which glimmered like mercury in the afterglow of Charlemagne. Oliver was swinging rapidly higher, a mottled orange disc a full degree wide; closer to the zenith which it could never reach, it would shine the color of ice. Alde, half the seeming size, was a thin slow crescent near Sirius, which she remembered was near Sol, but you couldn't see Sol without a telescope—

"Yes," she said around the pain in her throat, "my husband is about four years dead. I was carrying our first child when he was killed by a stampeding monocerus. We'd been married three years before. Met while we were both at the University—'casts from School Central can only supply a basic education, you know— We founded our own team to do ecological studies under contract—you know, can a certain area be settled while maintaining a balance of nature, what crops will grow, what hazards, that sort of question— Well, afterward I did lab work for a fisher co-op in Portolondon. But the monotony, the . . . shut-in-ness . . . was eating me away. Professor Matsuyama offered me a position on the team he was organizing to examine Commissioner Hauch Land. I thought, God help me, I thought Jimmy—Tim wanted him named James, once the tests showed it'd be a boy, after his own father and because of 'Timmy and Jimmy' and—oh, I thought Jimmy could safely come along. I couldn't bear to leave him behind for months, not at his age. We could make sure he'd never wander out of camp. What could hurt him inside it? *I* had never believed those stories about the Outlings stealing human children. I supposed parents were trying to hide from themselves the fact they'd been careless, they'd let a kid get lost in the woods or attacked by a pack of satans or—well, I learned better, Mr. Sherrinford. The guard robots were evaded and the dogs were drugged and when I woke, Jimmy was gone."

He regarded her through the smoke from his pipe. Barbro Engdahl Cullen was a big woman of thirty or so (Rolandic years, he reminded himself, ninety-five percent of Terrestrial, not the same as Beowulfan years), broad-shouldered, long-legged, full-breasted, supple of stride; her face was wide, straight nose, straightforward hazel eyes, heavy but mobile mouth; her hair was reddish-brown, cropped below the ears, her voice husky, her garment a plain street robe. To still the writhing of her fingers, he asked skeptically, "Do you now believe in the Outlings?"

"No. I'm just not so sure as I was." She swung about with half a glare for him. "And we have found traces."

"Bits of fossils," he nodded. "A few artifacts of a neolithic sort. But apparently ancient, as if the makers died ages ago. Intensive search has failed to turn up any real evidence for their survival."

"How intensive can search be, in a summer-stormy, winter-gloomy wilderness around the North Pole?" she demanded. "When we are, how many, a million people on an entire planet, half of us crowded into this one city?"

"And the rest crowding this one habitable continent," he pointed out.

"Arctica covers five million square kilometers," she flung back. "The Arctic Zone proper covers a fourth of it. We haven't the in-dustrial base to establish satellite monitor stations, build aircraft we can trust in those parts, drive roads through the damned dark-lands and establish permanent bases and get to know them and tame them. Good Christ, generations of lonely outwaymen told stories about Graymantle, and the beast was never seen by a proper scientist till last year!"

"Still, you continue to doubt the reality of the Outlings?"

"Well, what about a secret cult among humans, born of isolation and ignorance, lairing in the wilderness, stealing children when they can for—" She swallowed. Her head drooped. "But you're supposed to be the expert."

"From what you told me over the visiphone, the Portolondon con-stabulary questions the accuracy of the report your group made, thinks the lot of you were hysterical, claims you must have omitted a due precaution, and the child toddled away and was lost beyond your finding."

His dry words pried the horror out of her. Flushing, she snapped, "Like any settler's kid? No. I didn't simply yell. I consulted Data Retrieval. A few too many such cases are recorded for accident to be a very plausible explanation. And shall we totally ignore the frightened stories about reappearances? But when I went back to the constabu-lary with my facts, they brushed me off. I suspect that was not entirely because they're undermanned. I think they're afraid too. They're re-cruited from country boys, and Portolondon lies near the edge of the unknown."

Her energy faded. "Roland hasn't got any central police force," she finished drably. "You're my last hope."

The man puffed smoke into twilight, with which it blent, before he said in a kindlier voice than hitherto: "Please don't make it a high hope, Mrs. Cullen. I'm the solitary private investigator on this world, having no resources beyond myself, and a newcomer to boot."

"How long have you been here?"

"Twelve years. Barely time to get a little familiarity with the rela-tively civilized coastlands. You settlers of a century or more—what do you, even, know about Arctica's interior?"

Sherrinford sighed. "I'll take the case, charging no more than I must, mainly for the sake of the experience," he said. "But only if you'll be my guide and assistant, however painful it will be for you."

"Of course! I dreaded waiting idle. Why me, though?"

"Hiring someone else as well qualified would be prohibitively ex-

194 POUL ANDERSON

pensive, on a pioneer planet where every hand has a thousand urgent
tasks to do. Besides, you have a motive. And I'll need that. I, who
was born on another world altogether strange to this one, itself altogether strange to Mother Earth, I am too dauntingly aware of how
handicapped we are."

Night gathered upon Christmas Landing. The air stayed mild, but
glimmer-lit tendrils of fog, sneaking through the streets, had a cold
look, and colder yet was the aurora where it shuddered between the
moons. The woman drew closer to the man in this darkening room,
surely not aware that she did, until he switched on a fluoropanel.
The same knowledge of Roland's aloneness was in both of them.

One light-year is not much as galactic distances go. You could walk
it in about 270 million years, beginning at the middle of the Permian
Era, when dinosaurs belonged to the remote future, and continuing
to the present day when spaceships cross even greater reaches. But
stars in our neighborhood average some nine light-years apart, and
barely one percent of them have planets which are man-habitable,
and speeds are limited to less than that of radiation. Scant help is
given by relativistic time contraction and suspended animation en
route. These make the journeys seem short, but history meanwhile
does not stop at home.

Thus voyages from sun to sun will always be few. Colonists will be
those who have extremely special reasons for going. They will take
along germ plasm for exogenetic cultivation of domestic plants and
animals—and of human infants, in order that population can grow
fast enough to escape death through genetic drift. After all, they
cannot rely on further immigration. Two or three times a century, a
ship may call from some other colony. (Not from Earth. Earth has
long ago sunk into alien concerns.) Its place of origin will be an old
settlement. The young ones are in no position to build and man interstellar vessels.

Their very survival, let alone their eventual modernization, is in
doubt. The founding fathers have had to take what they could get, in
a universe not especially designed for man.

Consider, for example, Roland. It is among the rare happy
finds, a world where humans can live, breathe, eat the food, drink
the water, walk unclad if they choose, sow their crops, pasture their
beasts, dig their mines, erect their homes, raise their children and

grandchildren. It is worth crossing three quarters of a light-century to preserve certain dear values and strike new roots into the soil of Roland.

But the star Charlemagne is of type F9, forty percent brighter than Sol, brighter still in the treacherous ultraviolet and wilder still in the wind of charged particles that seethes from it. The planet has an eccentric orbit. In the middle of the short but furious northern summer, which includes periastron, total insolation is more than double what Earth gets; in the depth of the long northern winter, it is barely less than Terrestrial average.

Native life is abundant everywhere. But lacking elaborate machinery, not yet economically possible to construct for more than a few specialists, man can only endure the high latitudes. A ten-degree axial tilt, together with the orbit, means that the northern part of the Arctican continent spends half its year in unbroken sunlessness. Around the South Pole lies an empty ocean.

Other differences from Earth might superficially seem more important. Roland has two moons, small but close, to evoke clashing tides. It rotates once in thirty-two hours, which is endlessly, subtly disturbing to organisms evolved through gigayears of a quicker rhythm. The weather patterns are altogether unterrestrial. The globe is a mere 9500 kilometers in diameter; its surface gravity is 0.42×980 cm/sec^2; the sea level air pressure is slightly above one Earth atmosphere. (For actually Earth is the freak, and man exists because a cosmic accident blew away most of the gas that a body its size ought to have kept, as Venus has done.)

However, Homo can truly be called sapiens when he practices his specialty of being unspecialized. His repeated attempts to freeze himself into an all-answering pattern or culture or ideology, or whatever he has named it, have repeatedly brought ruin. Give him the pragmatic business of making his living, and he will usually do rather well. He adapts, within broad limits.

These limits are set by such factors as his need for sunlight and his being, necessarily and forever, a part of the life that surrounds him and a creature of the spirit within.

Portolondon thrust docks, boats, machinery, warehouses into the Gulf of Polaris. Behind them huddled the dwellings of its 5000 permanent inhabitants: concrete walls, storm shutters, high-peaked tile roofs. The gaiety of their paint looked forlorn amidst lamps; this town lay past the Arctic Circle.

Nevertheless Sherrinford remarked, "Cheerful place, eh? The kind of thing I came to Roland looking for."

Barbro made no reply. The days in Christmas Landing, while he made his preparations, had drained her. Gazing out the dome of the taxi that was whirring them downtown from the hydrofoil that brought them, she supposed he meant the lushness of forest and meadows along the road, brilliant hues and phosphorescence of flowers in gardens, clamor of wings overhead. Unlike Terrestrial flora in cold climates, Arctican vegetation spends every daylit hour in frantic growth and energy storage. Not till summer's fever gives place to gentle winter does it bloom and fruit; and estivating animals rise from their dens and migratory birds come home.

The view was lovely, she had to admit: beyond the trees, a spaciousness climbing toward remote heights, silvery-gray under a moon, an aurora, the diffuse radiance from a sun just below the horizon.

Beautiful as a hunting satan, she thought, and as terrible. That wilderness had stolen Jimmy. She wondered if she would at least be given to find his little bones and take them to his father.

Abruptly she realized that she and Sherrinford were at their hotel and that he had been speaking of the town. Since it was next in size after the capital, he must have visited here often before. The streets were crowded and noisy; signs flickered, music blared from shops, taverns, restaurants, sports centers, dance halls; vehicles were jammed down to molasses speed; the several-stories-high office buildings stood aglow. Portolondon linked an enormous hinterland to the outside world. Down the Gloria River came timber rafts, ores, harvest of farms whose owners were slowly making Rolandic life serve them, meat and ivory and furs gathered by rangers in the mountains beyond Troll Scarp. In from the sea came coastwise freighters, the fishing fleet, produce of the Sunward Islands, plunder of whole continents further south where bold men adventured. It clanged in Portolondon, laughed, blustered, swaggered, connived, robbed, preached, guzzeled, swilled, toiled, dreamed, lusted, built, destroyed, died, was born, was happy, angry, sorrowful, greedy, vulgar, loving, ambitious, human. Neither the sun's blaze elsewhere nor the half year's twilight here—wholly night around midwinter—was going to stay man's hand.

Or so everybody said.

Everybody except those who had settled in the darklands. Barbro used to take for granted that they were evolving curious customs, legends, and superstitions, which would die when the outway had been completely mapped and controlled. Of late, she had wondered. Perhaps Sherrinford's hints, about a change in his own attitude brought about by his preliminary research, were responsible.

Or perhaps she just needed something to think about besides how Jimmy, the day before he went, when she asked him whether he wanted rye or French bread for a sandwich, answered in great solemnity—he was becoming interested in the alphabet—"I'll have a slice of what we people call the F bread."

She scarcely noticed getting out of the taxi, registering, being conducted to a primitively furnished room. But after she unpacked, she remembered Sherrinford had suggested a confidential conference. She went down the hall and knocked on his door. Her knuckles sounded less loud than her heart.

He opened the door, finger on lips, and gestured her toward a corner. Her temper bristled until she saw the image of Chief Constable Dawson in the visiphone. Sherrinford must have chimed him up and must have a reason to keep her out of scanner range. She found a chair and watched, nails digging into knees.

The detective's lean length refolded itself. "Pardon the interruption," he said. "A man mistook the number. Drunk, by the indications."

Dawson chuckled. "We get plenty of those." Barbro recalled his fondness for gabbing. He tugged the beard which he affected, as if he were an outwayer instead of a townsman. "No harm in them as a rule. They only have a lot of voltage to discharge, after weeks or months in the backlands."

"I've gathered that that environment—foreign in a million major and minor ways to the one that created man—I've gathered that it does do odd things to the personality." Sherrinford tamped his pipe. "Of course, you know my practice has been confined to urban and suburban areas. Isolated garths seldom need private investigators. Now that situation appears to have changed. I called to ask you for advice."

"Glad to help," Dawson said. "I've not forgotten what you did for us in the de Tahoe murder case." Cautiously: "Better explain your problem first."

Sherrinford struck fire. The smoke that followed cut through the green odors—even here, a paved pair of kilometers from the nearest woods—that drifted past traffic rumble through a crepuscular window. "This is more a scientific mission than a search for an absconding debtor or an industrial spy," he drawled. "I'm looking into two possibilities: that an organization, criminal or religious or whatever, has long been active and steals infants; or that the Outlings of folklore are real."

"Huh?" On Dawson's face Barbro read as much dismay as surprise. "You can't be serious!"

"Can't I?" Sherrinford smiled. "Several generations' worth of reports shouldn't be dismissed out of hand. Especially not when they become more frequent and consistent in the course of time, not less. Nor can we ignore the documented loss of babies and small children, amounting by now to over a hundred, and never a trace found afterward. Nor the finds which demonstrate that an intelligent species once inhabited Arctica and may still haunt the interior."

Dawson leaned forward as if to climb out of the screen. "Who engaged you?" he demanded. "That Cullen woman? We were sorry for her, naturally, but she wasn't making sense, and when she got downright abusive—"

"Didn't her companions, reputable scientists, confirm her story?"

"No story to confirm. Look, they had the place ringed with detectors and alarms, and they kept mastiffs. Standard procedure in country where a hungry sauroid or whatever might happen by. Nothing could've entered unbeknownst."

"On the ground. How about a flyer landing in the middle of camp?"

"A man in a copter rig would've roused everybody."

"A winged being might be quieter."

"A living flyer that could lift a three-year-old boy? Doesn't exist."

"Isn't in the scientific literature, you mean, Constable. Remember Graymantle; remember how little we know about Roland, a planet, an entire world. Such birds do exist on Beowulf—and on Rustum, I've read. I made a calculation from the local ratio of air density to gravity, and, yes, it's marginally possible here too. The child could have been carried off for a short distance before wing muscles were exhausted and the creature must descend."

Dawson snorted. "First it landed and walked into the tent where mother and boy were asleep. Then it walked away, toting him, after it couldn't fly further. Does that sound like a bird of prey? And the victim didn't cry out, the dogs didn't bark!"

"As a matter of fact," Sherrinford said, "those inconsistencies are the most interesting and convincing features of the whole account. You're right, it's hard to see how a human kidnaper could get in undetected, and an eagle type of creature wouldn't operate in that fashion. But none of this applies to a winged intelligent being. The boy could have been drugged. Certainly the dogs showed signs of having been."

"The dogs showed signs of having overslept. Nothing had disturbed them. The kid wandering by wouldn't do so. We don't need to assume one damn thing except, first, that he got restless and, second, that the alarms were a bit sloppily rigged—seeing as how no danger was expected from inside camp—and let him pass out. And, third, I hate to speak this way, but we must assume the poor tyke starved or was killed."

Dawson paused before adding: "If we had more staff, we could have given the affair more time. And would have, of course. We did make an aerial sweep, which risked the lives of the pilots, using instruments which would've spotted the kid anywhere in a fifty kilometer radius, unless he was dead. You know how sensitive thermal analyzers are. We drew a complete blank. We have more important jobs than to hunt for the scattered pieces of a corpse."

He finished brusquely. "If Mrs. Cullen's hired you, my advice is you find an excuse to quit. Better for her, too. She's got to come to terms with reality."

Barbro checked a shout by biting her tongue.

"Oh, this is merely the latest disappearance of the series," Sherrinford said. She didn't understand how he could maintain his easy tone when Jimmy was lost. "More thoroughly recorded than any before, thus more suggestive. Usually an outwayer family has given a tearful but undetailed account of their child who vanished and must have been stolen by the Old Folk. Sometimes, years later, they'd tell about glimpses of what they swore must have been the grown child, not really human any longer, flitting past in murk or peering through a window or working mischief upon them. As you say, neither the authorities nor the scientists have had personnel or resources to mount a proper investigation. But as I say, the matter appears to be worth investigating. Maybe a private party like myself can contribute."

"Listen, most of us constables grew up in the outway. We don't just ride patrol and answer emergency calls; we go back there for holidays and reunions. If any gang of . . . of human sacrificers was around, we'd know."

"I realize that. I also realize that the people you came from have a widespread and deep-seated belief in nonhuman beings with supernatural powers. Many actually go through rites and make offerings to propitiate them."

"I know what you're leading up to," Dawson fleered. "I've heard it before, from a hundred sensationalists. The aborigines are the Outlings. I thought better of you. Surely you've visited a museum or three, surely you've read literature from planets which do have natives—or damn and blast, haven't you ever applied that logic of yours?"

He wagged a finger. "Think," he said. "What have we in fact discovered? A few pieces of worked stone; a few megaliths that might be artificial; scratchings on rock that seem to show plants and animals, though not the way any human culture would ever have shown them; traces of fires and broken bones; other fragments of bone that seem as if they might've belonged to thinking creatures, as if they might've been inside fingers or around big brains. If so, however, the owners looked nothing like men. Or angels, for that matter. Nothing! The most anthropoid reconstruction I've seen shows a kind of two-legged crocagator.

"Wait, let me finish. The stories about the Outlings—oh, I've heard them too, plenty of them. I believed them when I was a kid—the stories tell how there're different kinds, some winged, some not, some half human, some completely human except maybe for being too handsome— It's fairyland from ancient Earth all over again. Isn't it? I got interested once and dug into the Heritage Library microfiles, and be damned if I didn't find almost the identical yarns, told by peasants centuries before spaceflight.

"None of it squares with the scanty relics we have, if they are relics, or with the fact that no area the size of Arctica could spawn a dozen different intelligent species, or . . . hellfire, man, with the way your common sense tells you aborigines would behave when humans arrived!"

Sherrinford nodded. "Yes, yes," he said. "I'm less sure than you that the common sense of nonhuman beings is precisely like our own. I've seen so much variation within mankind. But, granted, your arguments are strong. Roland's too few scientists have more pressing tasks than tracking down the origins of what is, as you put it, a revived medieval superstition."

He cradled his pipe bowl in both hands and peered into the tiny hearth of it. "Perhaps what interests me most," he said softly, "is why—across that gap of centuries, across a barrier of machine civilization and its utterly antagonistic world view—no continuity of tradition whatsoever—why have hard-headed, technologically organized, reasonably well-educated colonists here brought back from its grave a belief in the Old Folk?"

"I suppose eventually, if the University ever does develop the psychology department they keep talking about, I suppose eventually somebody will get a thesis out of your question." Dawson spoke in a jagged voice, and he gulped when Sherrinford replied:

"I propose to begin now. In Commissioner Hauch Land, since that's where the latest incident occurred. Where can I rent a vehicle?"

"Uh, might be hard to do—"

"Come, come. Tenderfoot or not, I know better. In an economy of scarcity, few people own heavy equipment. But since it's needed, it can always be rented. I want a camper bus with a ground-effect drive suitable for every kind of terrain. And I want certain equipment installed which I've brought along, and the top canopy section replaced by a gun turret controllable from the driver's seat. But I'll supply the weapons. Besides rifles and pistols of my own, I've arranged to borrow some artillery from Christmas Landing's police arsenal."

"Hoy? Are you genuinely intending to make ready for . . . a war . . . against a myth?"

"Let's say I'm taking out insurance, which isn't terribly expensive, against a remote possibility. Now, besides the bus, what about a light aircraft carried piggyback for use in surveys?"

"No." Dawson sounded more positive than hitherto. "That's asking for disaster. We can have you flown to a base camp in a large plane when the weather report's exactly right. But the pilot will have to fly back at once, before the weather turns wrong again. Meteorology's underdeveloped on Roland; the air's especially treacherous this time of year, and we're not tooled up to produce aircraft that can outlive every surprise." He drew breath. "Have you no idea of how fast a whirly-whirly can hit, or what size hailstones might strike from

a clear sky, or—? Once you're there, man, you stick to the ground."
He hesitated. "That's an important reason our information is so
scanty about the outway and its settlers are so isolated."

Sherrinford laughed ruefully. "Well, I suppose if details are what
I'm after, I must creep along anyway."

"You'll waste a lot of time," Dawson said. "Not to mention your
client's money. Listen, I can't forbid you to chase shadows, but—"

The discussion went on for almost an hour. When the screen
finally blanked, Sherrinford rose, stretched, and walked toward Barbro. She noticed anew his peculiar gait. He had come from a planet
with a fourth again of Earth's gravitational drag, to one where weight
was less than half Terrestrial. She wondered if he had flying dreams.

"I apologize for shuffling you off like that," he said. "I didn't expect to reach him at once. He was quite truthful about how busy he
is. But having made contact, I didn't want to remind him overmuch
of you. He can dismiss my project as a futile fantasy which I'll soon
give up. But he might have frozen completely, might even have put
up obstacles before us, if he'd realized through you how determined
we are."

"Why should he care?" she asked in her bitterness.

"Fear of consequences, the worse because it is unadmitted—fear
of consequences, the more terrifying because they are unguessable."
Sherrinford's gaze went to the screen, and thence out the window to
the aurora pulsing in glacial blue and white immensely far overhead.
"I suppose you saw I was talking to a frightened man. Down underneath his conventionality and scoffing, he believes in the Outlings—
oh, yes, he believes."

The feet of Mistherd flew over yerba and outpaced windblown
driftweed. Beside him, black and misshapen, hulked Nagrim the nicor, whose earthquake weight left a swath of crushed plants. Behind,
luminous blossoms of a firethorn shone through the twining, trailing
outlines of Morgarel the wraith.

Here Cloudmoor rose in a surf of hills and thickets. The air lay
quiet, now and then carrying the distance-muted howl of a beast. It
was darker than usual at winterbirth, the moons being down and
aurora a wan flicker above mountains on the northern worldedge. But
this made the stars keen, and their numbers crowded heaven, and

Ghost Road shone among them as if it, like the leafage beneath, were paved with dew.

"Yonder!" bawled Nagrim. All four of his arms pointed. The party had topped a ridge. Far off glimmered a spark. "Hoah, hoah! 'Ull we right off stamp dem flat, or pluck dem apart slow?"

We shall do nothing of the sort, bonebrain, Morgarel's answer slid through their heads. *Not unless they attack us, and they will not unless we make them aware of us, and her command is that we spy out their purposes.*

"Gr-r-rum-m-m. I know deir aim. Cut down trees, stick plows in land, sow deir cursed seed in de clods and in deir shes. 'Less we drive dem into de bitterwater, and soon, soon, dey'll wax too strong for us."

"Not too strong for the Queen!" Mistherd protested, shocked.

Yet they do have new powers, it seems, Morgarel reminded him. *Carefully must we probe them.*

"Den carefully can we step on dem?" asked Nagrim.

The question woke a grin out of Mistherd's own uneasiness. He slapped the scaly back. "Don't talk, you," he said. "It hurts my ears. Nor think; that hurts your head. Come, run!"

Ease yourself, Morgarel scolded. *You have too much life in you, human-born.*

Mistherd made a face at the wraith, but obeyed to the extent of slowing down and picking his way through what cover the country afforded. For he traveled on behalf of the Fairest, to learn what had brought a pair of mortals questing hither.

Did they seek that boy whom Ayoch stole? (He continued to weep for his mother, though less and less often as the marvels of Carheddin entered him.) Perhaps. A birdcraft had left them and their car at the now-abandoned campsite, from which they had followed an outward spiral. But when no trace of the cub had appeared inside a reasonable distance, they did not call to be flown home. And this wasn't because weather forbade the farspeaker waves to travel, as was frequently the case. No, instead the couple set off toward the mountains of Moonhorn. Their course would take them past a few outlying invader steadings and on into realms untrodden by their race.

So this was no ordinary survey. Then what was it?

Mistherd understood now why she who reigned had made her adopted mortal children learn, or retain, the clumsy language of their forebears. He had hated that drill, wholly foreign to Dweller ways. Of course, you obeyed her, and in time you saw how wise she had been. . . .

Presently he left Nagrim behind a rock—the nicor would only be useful in a fight—and crawled from bush to bush until he lay within man-lengths of the humans. A rainplant drooped over him, leaves soft on his bare skin, and clothed him in darkness. Morgarel floated to the crown of a shiverleaf, whose unrest would better conceal his flimsy shape. He'd not be much help either. And that was the most troublous, the almost appalling thing here. Wraiths were among those who could not just sense and send thoughts, but cast illusions. Morgarel had reported that this time his power seemed to rebound off an invisible cold wall around the car.

Otherwise the male and female had set up no guardian engines and kept no dogs. Belike they supposed none would be needed, since they slept in the long vehicle which bore them. But such contempt of the Queen's strength could not be tolerated, could it?

Metal sheened faintly by the light of their campfire. They sat on either side, wrapped in coats against a coolness that Mistherd, naked, found mild. The male drank smoke. The female stared past him into a dusk which her flame-dazzled eyes must see as thick gloom. The dancing glow brought her vividly forth. Yes, to judge from Ayoch's tale, she was the dam of the new cub.

Ayoch had wanted to come too, but the Wonderful One forbade. Pooks couldn't hold still long enough for such a mission.

The man sucked on his pipe. His cheeks thus pulled into shadow while the light flickered across nose and brow, he looked disquietingly like a shearbill about to stoop on prey.

"—No, I tell you again, Barbro, I have no theories," he was saying. "When facts are insufficient, theorizing is ridiculous at best, misleading at worst."

"Still, you must have some idea of what you're doing," she said. It was plain that they had threshed this out often before. No Dweller could be as persistent as she or as patient as he. "That gear you packed—that generator you keep running—"

"I have a working hypothesis or two, which suggested what equipment I ought to take."

"Why won't you tell me what the hypotheses are?"

"They themselves indicate that that might be inadvisable at the present time. I'm still feeling my way into the labyrinth. And I haven't had a chance yet to hook everything up. In fact, we're really only protected against so-called telepathic influence—"

"What?" She started. "Do you mean . . . those legends about how they can read minds too—" Her words trailed off and her gaze sought the darkness beyond his shoulders.

He leaned forward. His tone lost its clipped rapidity, grew earnest and soft. "Barbro, you're racking yourself to pieces. Which is no help to Jimmy if he's alive, the more so when you may well be badly needed later on. We've a long trek before us, and you'd better settle into it."

She nodded jerkily and caught her lip between her teeth for a moment before she answered, "I'm trying."

He smiled around his pipe. "I expect you'll succeed. You don't strike me as a quitter or a whiner or an enjoyer of misery."

She dropped a hand to the pistol at her belt. Her voice changed; it came out of her throat like knife from sheath. "When we find them, they'll know what I am. What humans are."

"Put anger aside also," the man urged. "We can't afford emotions. If the Outlings are real, as I told you I'm provisionally assuming, they're fighting for their homes." After a short stillness he added: "I like to think that if the first explorers had found live natives, men would not have colonized Roland. But too late now. We can't go back if we wanted to. It's a bitter-end struggle, against an enemy so crafty that he's even hidden from us the fact that he is waging war."

"Is he? I mean, skulking, kidnaping an occasional child—"

"That's part of my hypothesis. I suspect those aren't harassments, they're tactics employed in a chillingly subtle strategy."

The fire sputtered and sparked. The man smoked awhile, brooding, until he went on:

"I didn't want to raise your hopes or excite you unduly while you had to wait on me, first in Christmas Landing, then in Portolondon. Afterward we were busy satisfying ourselves that Jimmy had been taken further from camp than he could have wandered before collapsing. So I'm only now telling you how thoroughly I studied available material on the . . . Old Folk. Besides, at first I did it on the principle of eliminating every imaginable possibility, however absurd. I expected no result other than final disproof. But I went through everything, relics, analyses, histories, journalistic accounts, monographs; I talked to outwayers who happened to be in town and to what scientists we have who've taken any interest in the matter. I'm a quick study. I flatter myself I became as expert as anyone—though God knows there's little to be expert on. Furthermore, I, a comparative stranger to Roland, maybe looked on the problem with fresh eyes. And a pattern emerged for me.

"If the aborigines had become extinct, why hadn't they left more remnants? Arctica isn't enormous, and it's fertile for Rolandic life. It ought to have supported a population whose artifacts ought to have accumulated over millennia. I've read that on Earth, literally tens of thousands of paleolithic hand axes were found, more by chance than archeology.

"Very well. Suppose the relics and fossils were deliberately removed, between the time the last survey party left and the first colonizing ships arrived. I did find some support for that idea in the diaries of the original explorers. They were too preoccupied with checking the habitability of the planet to make catalogues of primitive monuments. However, the remarks they wrote down indicate they saw much more than later arrivals did. Suppose what we have found is just what the removers overlooked or didn't get around to.

"That argues a sophisticated mentality, thinking in long-range terms, doesn't it? Which in turn argues that the Old Folk were not mere hunters or neolithic farmers."

"But nobody ever saw buildings or machines or any such thing," Barbro objected.

"No. Most likely the natives didn't go through our kind of metallurgic-industrial evolution. I can conceive of other paths to take. Their full-fledged civilization might have begun, rather than ended, in biological science and technology. It might have developed potentialities of the nervous system, which might be greater in their species than in man. We have those abilities to some degree ourselves, you realize. A dowser, for instance, actually senses variations in the local magnetic field caused by a water table. However, in us, these talents are maddeningly rare and tricky. So we took our business elsewhere. Who needs to be a telepath, say, when he has a visiphone? The Old Folk may have seen it the other way around. The artifacts of their civilization may have been, may still be unrecognizable to men."

"They could have identified themselves to the men, though," Barbro said. "Why didn't they?"

"I can imagine any number of reasons. As, they could have had a bad experience with interstellar visitors earlier in their history. Ours is scarcely the sole race that has spaceships. However, I told you I don't theorize in advance of the facts. Let's say no more than that the Old Folk, if they exist, are alien to us."

"For a rigorous thinker, you're spinning a mighty thin thread."

"I've admitted this is entirely provisional." He squinted at her through a roil of campfire smoke. "You came to me, Barbro, insisting in the teeth of officialdom that your boy had been stolen, but your own talk about cultist kidnapers was ridiculous. Why are you reluctant to admit the reality of non-humans?"

"In spite of the fact that Jimmy's being alive probably depends on it," she sighed. "I know." A shudder. "Maybe I don't dare admit it."

"I've said nothing thus far that hasn't been speculated about in print," he told her. "A disreputable speculation, true. In a hundred years, nobody has found valid evidence for the Outlings being more than a superstition. Still, a few people have declared it's at least possible that intelligent natives are at large in the wilderness."

"I know," she repeated. "I'm not sure, though, what has made you, overnight, take those arguments seriously."

"Well, once you got me started thinking, it occurred to me that Roland's outwayers are not utterly isolated medieval crofters. They have books, telecommunications, power tools, motor vehicles; above all, they have a modern science-oriented education. Why *should* they turn superstitious? Something must be causing it." He stopped. "I'd better not continue. My ideas go further than this; but if they're correct, it's dangerous to speak them aloud."

Mistherd's belly muscles tensed. There was danger for fair, in that shearbill head. The Garland Bearer must be warned. For a minute he wondered about summoning Nagrim to kill these two. If the nicor jumped them fast, their firearms might avail them naught. But no. They might have left word at home, or— He came back to his ears. The talk had changed course. Barbro was murmuring, "—why you stayed on Roland."

The man smiled his gaunt smile. "Well, life on Beowulf held no challenge for me. Heorot is—or was; this was decades past, remember—Heorot was densely populated, smoothly organized, boringly uniform. That was partly due to the lowland frontier, a safety valve that bled off the dissatisfied. But I lack the carbon dioxide tolerance necessary to live healthily down there. An expedition was being readied to make a swing around a number of colony worlds, especially those which didn't have the equipment to keep in laser contact. You'll recall its announced purpose, to seek out new ideas in science, arts, sociology, philosophy, whenever might prove valuable. I'm afraid they found little on Roland relevant to Beowulf. But I, who had wangled a berth, I saw opportunities for myself and decided to make my home here."

"Were you a detective back there, too?"

"Yes, in the official police. We had a tradition of such work in our family. Some of that may have come from the Cherokee side of it, if the name means anything to you. However, we also claimed collateral descent from one of the first private inquiry agents on record, back on Earth before spaceflight. Regardless of how true that may be, I found him a useful model. You see, an archetype—"

The man broke off. Unease crossed his features. "Best we go to sleep," he said. "We've a long distance to cover in the morning."

She looked outward. "Here is no morning."

They retired. Mistherd rose and cautiously flexed limberness back into his muscles. Before returning to the Sister of Lyrth, he risked a glance through a pane in the car. Bunks were made up, side by side, and the humans lay in them. Yet the man had not touched her, though hers was a bonny body, and nothing that had passed between them suggested he meant to do so.

Eldritch, humans. Cold and clay-like. And they would overrun the beautiful wild world? Mistherd spat in disgust. It must not happen. It would not happen. She who reigned had vowed that.

The lands of William Irons were immense. But this was because a barony was required to support him, his kin and cattle, on native crops whose cultivation was still poorly understood. He raised some Terrestrial plants as well, by summerlight and in conservatories. However, these were a luxury. The true conquest of northern Arctica lay in yerba hay, in bathyrhiza wood, in pericoup and glycophyllon, and eventually, when the market had expanded with population and industry, in chalcanthemum for city florists and pelts of cage-bred rover for city furriers.

That was in a tomorrow Irons did not expect that he would live to see. Sherrinford wondered if the man really expected anyone ever would.

The room was warm and bright. Cheerfulness crackled in the fireplace. Light from fluoropanels gleamed off hand-carven chests and chairs and tables, off colorful draperies and shelved dishes. The outwayer sat solid in his high seat, stoutly clad, beard flowing down his chest. His wife and daughters brought coffee, whose fragrance joined the remnant odors of a hearty supper, to him, his guests, and his sons.

But outside, wind hooted, lightning flared, thunder bawled, rain crashed on roof and walls and roared down to swirl among the courtyard cobblestones. Sheds and barns crouched against hugeness beyond. Trees groaned, and did a wicked undertone of laughter run beneath the lowing of a frightened cow? A burst of hailstones hit the tiles like knocking knuckles.

You could feel how distant your neighbors were, Sherrinford thought. And nonetheless they were the people whom you saw oftenest, did daily business with by visiphone (when a solar storm didn't make gibberish of their voices and chaos of their faces) or in the flesh, partied with, gossiped and intrigued with, intermarried with; in the end, they were the people who would bury you. The lights of the coastal towns were monstrously further away.

William Irons was a strong man. Yet when now he spoke, fear was in his tone. "You'd truly go over Troll Scarp?"

"Do you mean Hanstein Palisades?" Sherrinford responded, more challenge than question.

"No outwayer calls it anything but Troll Scarp," Barbro said.

And how had a name like that been reborn, light-years and centuries from Earth's Dark Ages?

"Hunters, trappers, prospectors—rangers, you call them—travel in those mountains," Sherrinford declared.

"In certain parts," Irons said. "That's allowed, by a pact once made 'tween a man and the Queen after he'd done well by a jack-o'-the-hill that a satan had hurt. Wherever the plumablanca grows, men may fare, if they leave man-goods on the altar boulders in payment for what they take out of the land. Elsewhere—" one fist clenched on a chair arm and went slack again—" 's not wise to go."

"It's been done, hasn't it?"

"Oh, yes. And some came back all right, or so they claimed,

though I've heard they were never lucky afterward. And some didn't; they vanished. And some who returned babbled of wonders and horrors, and stayed witlings the rest of their lives. Not for a long time has anybody been rash enough to break the pact and overtread the bounds." Irons looked at Barbro almost entreatingly. His woman and children stared likewise, grown still. Wind hooted beyond the walls and rattled the storm shutters. "Don't you."

"I've reason to believe my son is there," she answered.

"Yes, yes, you've told and I'm sorry. Maybe something can be done. I don't know what, but I'd be glad to, oh, lay a double offering on Unvar's Barrow this midwinter, and a prayer drawn in the turf by a flint knife. Maybe they'll return him." Irons sighed. "They've not done such a thing in man's memory, though. And he could have a worse lot. I've glimpsed them myself, speeding madcap through twilight. They seem happier than we are. Might be no kindness, sending your boy home again."

"Like in the Arvid song," said his wife.

Irons nodded. "M-hm. Or others, come to think of it."

"What's this?" Sherrinford asked. More sharply than before, he felt himself a stranger. He was a child of cities and technics, above all a child of the skeptical intelligence. This family *believed*. It was disquieting to see more than a touch of their acceptance in Barbro's slow nod.

"We have the same ballad in Olga Ivanoff Land," she told him, her voice less calm than the words. "It's one of the traditional ones —nobody knows who composed them—that are sung to set the measure of a ring-dance in a meadow."

"I noticed a multilyre in your baggage, Mrs. Cullen," said the wife of Irons. She was obviously eager to get off the explosive topic of a venture in defiance of the Old Folk. A songfest could help. "Would you like to entertain us?"

Barbro shook her head, white around the nostrils. The oldest boy said quickly, rather importantly, "Well, sure, I can, if our guests would like to hear."

"I'd enjoy that, thank you." Sherrinford leaned back in his seat and stoked his pipe. If this had not happened spontaneously, he would have guided the conversation toward a similar outcome.

In the past he had had no incentive to study the folklore of the outway, and not much chance to read the scanty references on it since

Barbro brought him her trouble. Yet more and more he was becoming convinced that he must get an understanding—not an anthropological study, but a feel from the inside out—of the relationship between Roland's frontiersmen and those beings which haunted them.

A bustling followed, rearrangement, settling down to listen, coffee cups refilled and brandy offered on the side. The boy explained, "The last line is the chorus. Everybody join in, right?" Clearly he too hoped thus to bleed off some of the tension. Catharsis through music? Sherrinford wondered, and added to himself: No; exorcism.

A girl strummed a guitar. The boy sang, to a melody which beat across the storm noise:

> "It was the ranger Arvid
> rode homeward through the hills
> among the shadowy shiverleafs,
> along the chiming rills.
>> *The dance weaves under the firethorn.*

> "The night wind whispered around him
> with scent of brok and rue.
> Both moons rose high above him
> and hills aflash with dew.
>> *The dance weaves under the firethorn.*

> "And dreaming of that woman
> who waited in the sun,
> he stopped, amazed by starlight,
> and so he was undone.
>> *The dance weaves under the firethorn.*

> "For there beneath a barrow
> that bulked athwart a moon,
> the Outling folk were dancing
> in glass and golden shoon.
>> *The dance weaves under the firethorn.*

> "The Outling folk were dancing
> like water, wind, and fire
> to frosty-ringing harpstrings,
> and never did they tire.
>> *The dance weaves under the firethorn.*

"To Arvid came she striding
from where she watched the dance,
the Queen of Air and Darkness,
with starlight in her glance.
The dance weaves under the firethorn.

"With starlight, love, and terror
in her immortal eye,
the Queen of Air and Darkness—"

"No!" Barbro leaped from her chair. Her fists were clenched and tears flogged her cheekbones. "You can't—pretend that—about the things that stole Jimmy!"

She fled from the chamber, upstairs to her guest bedroom.

But she finished the song herself. That was about seventy hours later, camped in the steeps where rangers dared not fare.

She and Sherrinford had not said much to the Irons family, after refusing repeated pleas to leave the forbidden country alone. Nor had they exchanged many remarks at first as they drove north. Slowly, however, he began to draw her out about her own life. After a while she almost forgot to mourn, in her remembering of home and old neighbors. Somehow this led to discoveries—that he, beneath his professorial manner, was a gourmet and a lover of opera and appreciated her femaleness; that she could still laugh and find beauty in the wild land around her—and she realized, half guiltily, that life held more hopes than even the recovery of the son Tim gave her.

"I've convinced myself he's alive," the detective said. He scowled. "Frankly, it makes me regret having taken you along. I expected this would be only a fact-gathering trip, but it's turning out to be more. If we're dealing with real creatures who stole him, they can do real harm. I ought to turn back to the nearest garth and call for a plane to fetch you."

"Like bottommost hell you will, mister," she said. "You need somebody who knows outway conditions, and I'm a better shot than average."

"M-m-m . . . it would involve considerable delay too, wouldn't it? Besides the added distance, I can't put a signal through to any airport before this current burst of solar interference has calmed down."

Next "night" he broke out his remaining equipment and set it up. She recognized some of it, such as the thermal detector. Other items were strange to her, copied to his order from the advanced apparatus of his birth-world. He would tell her little about them. "I've explained my suspicion that the ones we're after have telepathic capabilities," he said in apology.

Her eyes widened. "You mean it could be true, the Queen and her people can read minds?"

"That's part of the dread which surrounds their legend, isn't it? Actually there's nothing spooky about the phenomenon. It was studied and fairly well defined centuries ago, on Earth. I daresay the facts are available in the scientific microfiles at Christmas Landing. You Rolanders have simply had no occasion to seek them out, any more than you've yet had occasion to look up how to build power beamcasters or spacecraft."

"Well, how does telepathy work, then?"

Sherrinford recognized that her query asked for comfort as much as it did for facts, and he spoke with deliberate dryness: "The organism generates extremely long-wave radiation which can, in principle, be modulated by the nervous system. In practice, the feebleness of the signals and their low rate of information transmission make them elusive, hard to detect and measure. Our prehuman ancestors went in for more reliable senses, like vision and hearing. What telepathic transceiving we do is marginal at best. But explorers have found extraterrestrial species that got an evolutionary advantage from developing the system further, in their particular environments. I imagine such species could include one which gets comparatively little direct sunlight—in fact, appears to hide from broad day. It could even become so able in this regard that, at short range, it can pick up man's weak emissions and make man's primitive sensitivities resonate to its own strong sendings."

"That would account for a lot, wouldn't it?" Barbro said faintly.

"I've now screened our car by a jamming field," Sherrinford told her, "but it reaches only a few meters past the chassis. Beyond, a scout of theirs might get a warning from your thoughts, if you knew precisely what I'm trying to do. I have a well-trained subconscious which sees to it that I think about this in French when I'm outside. Communication has to be structured to be intelligible, you see, and that's a different enough structure from English. But English is the only human language on Roland, and surely the Old Folk have learned it."

She nodded. He had told her his general plan, which was too obvious to conceal. The problem was to make contact with the aliens, if they existed. Hitherto, they had only revealed themselves, at rare intervals, to one or a few backwoodsmen at a time. An ability to generate hallucinations would help them in that. They would stay clear of any large, perhaps unmanageable expedition which might pass through their territory. But two people, braving all prohibitions, shouldn't look too formidable to approach. And . . . this would be the first human team which not only worked on the assumption that the Outlings were real but possessed the resources of modern, off-planet police technology.

Nothing happened at that camp. Sherrinford said he hadn't expected it would. The Old Folk seemed cautious this near to any settlement. In their own lands they must be bolder.

And by the following "night," the vehicle had gone well into yonder country. When Sherrinford stopped the engine in a meadow and the car settled down, silence rolled in like a wave.

They stepped out. She cooked a meal on the glower while he gathered wood, that they might later cheer themselves with a campfire. Frequently he glanced at his wrist. It bore no watch—instead, a radio-controlled dial, to tell what the instruments in the bus might register.

Who needed a watch here? Slow constellations wheeled beyond glimmering aurora. The moon Alde stood above a snowpeak, turning it argent, though this place lay at a goodly height. The rest of the mountains were hidden by the forest that crowded around. Its trees were mostly shiverleaf and feathery white plumablanca, ghostly amidst their shadows. A few firethorns glowed, clustered dim lanterns, and the underbrush was heavy and smelled sweet. You could see surprisingly far through the blue dusk. Somewhere nearby, a brook sang and a bird fluted.

"Lovely here," Sherrinford said. They had risen from their supper and not yet sat down again or kindled their fire.

"But strange," Barbro answered as low. "I wonder if it's really meant for us. If we can really hope to possess it."

His pipestem gestured at the stars. "Man's gone to stranger places than this."

"Has he? I . . . oh, I suppose it's just something left over from my outway childhood, but do you know, when I'm under them I can't think of the stars as balls of gas, whose energies have been measured, whose planets have been walked on by prosaic feet. No, they're small and cold and magical; our lives are bound to them; after we die, they whisper to us in our graves." Barbro glanced downward. "I realize that's nonsense."

She could see in the twilight how his face grew tight. "Not at all," he said. "Emotionally, physics may be a worse nonsense. And in the end, you know, after a sufficient number of generations, thought follows feeling. Man is not at heart rational. He could stop believing the stories of science if those no longer felt right."

He paused. "That ballad which didn't get finished in the house," he said, not looking at her. "Why did it affect you so?"

"I couldn't stand hearing *them*, well, praised. Or that's how it seemed. Sorry for the fuss."

"I gather the ballad is typical of a large class."

"Well, I never thought to add them up. Cultural anthropology is something we don't have time for on Roland, or more likely it hasn't occurred to us, with everything else there is to do. But—now you mention it, yes, I'm surprised at how many songs and stories have the Arvid motif in them."

"Could you bear to recite it?"

She mustered the will to laugh. "Why, I can do better than that if you want. Let me get my multilyre and I'll perform."

She omitted the hypnotic chorus line, though, when the notes rang out, except at the end. He watched her where she stood against moon and aurora.

"—the Queen of Air and Darkness
cried softly under sky:

" 'Light down, you ranger Arvid,
and join the Outling folk.
You need no more be human,
which is a heavy yoke.'

"He dared to give her answer:
'I may do naught but run.
A maiden waits me, dreaming
in lands beneath the sun.

" 'And likewise wait me comrades
and tasks I would not shirk,
for what is ranger Arvid
if he lays down his work?

" 'So wreak your spells, you Outling,
and cast your wrath on me.
Though maybe you can slay me,
you'll not make me unfree.'

"The Queen of Air and Darkness
stood wrapped about with fear
and northlight-flares and beauty
he dared not look too near.

"Until she laughed like harpsong
and said to him in scorn:
'I do not need a magic
to make you always mourn.

" 'I send you home with nothing
except your memory
of moonlight, Outling music,
night breezes, dew, and me.

" 'And that will run behind you,
a shadow on the sun,
and that will lie beside you
when every day is done.

" 'In work and play and friendship
your grief will strike you dumb
for thinking what you are—and—
what you might have become.

" 'Your dull and foolish woman
treat kindly as you can.
Go home now, ranger Arvid,
set free to be a man!'

"In flickering and laughter
the Outling folk were gone.

He stood alone by moonlight
and wept until the dawn.
The dance weaves under the firethorn."

She laid the lyre aside. A wind rustled leaves. After a long quietness Sherrinford said, "And tales of this kind are part of everyone's
life in the outway?"

"Well, you could put it thus," Barbro replied. "Though they're
not all full of supernatural doings. Some are about love or heroism.
Traditional themes."

"I don't think your particular tradition has arisen of itself." His
tone was bleak. "In fact, I think many of your songs and stories were
not composed by human beings."

He snapped his lips shut and would say no more on the subject.
They went early to bed.

Hours later, an alarm roused them.

The buzzing was soft, but it brought them instantly alert. They
slept in gripsuits, to be prepared for emergencies. Sky-glow lit them
through the canopy. Sherrinford swung out of his bunk, slipped
shoes on feet, and clipped gun holster to belt. "Stay inside," he
commanded.

"What's here?" Her pulse thuttered.

He squinted at the dials of his instruments and checked them
against the luminous telltale on his wrist. "Three animals," he
counted. "Not wild ones happening by. A large one, homeothermic,
to judge from the infrared, holding still a short ways off. Another
. . . hm, low temperature, diffuse and unstable emission, as if it
were more like a . . . a swarm of cells coordinated somehow . . .
pheromonally? . . . hovering, also at a distance. But the third's practically next to us, moving around in the brush; and that pattern looks
human."

She saw him quiver with eagerness, no longer seeming a professor.
"I'm going to try to make a capture," he said. "When we have a subject for interrogation—Stand ready to let me back in again fast. But
don't risk yourself, whatever happens. And keep this cocked." He
handed her a loaded big-game rifle.

His tall frame poised by the door, opened it a crack. Air blew in,
cool, damp, full of fragrances and murmurings. The moon Oliver

was now also aloft, the radiance of both unreally brilliant, and the aurora seethed in whiteness and ice-blue.

Sherrinford peered afresh at his telltale. It must indicate the directions of the watchers, among those dappled leaves. Abruptly he sprang out. He sprinted past the ashes of the campfire and vanished under trees. Barbro's hand strained on the butt of her weapon.

Racket exploded. Two in combat burst onto the meadow. Sherrinford had clapped a grip on a smaller human figure. She could make out by streaming silver and rainbow flicker that the other was nude, male, long haired, lithe, and young. He fought demoniacally, seeking to use teeth and feet and raking nails, and meanwhile he ululated like a satan.

The identification shot through her: A changeling, stolen in babyhood and raised by the Old Folk. This creature was what they would make Jimmy into.

"Ha!" Sherrinford forced his opponent around and drove stiffened fingers into the solar plexus. The boy gasped and sagged. Sherrinford manhandled him toward the car.

Out from the woods came a giant. It might itself have been a tree, black and rugose, bearing four great gnarly boughs; but earth quivered and boomed beneath its leg-roots, and its hoarse bellowing filled sky and skulls.

Barbro shrieked. Sherrinford whirled. He yanked out his pistol, fired and fired, flat whipcracks through the half-light. His free arm kept a lock on the youth. The troll shape lurched under those blows. It recovered and came on, more slowly, more carefully, circling around to cut him off from the bus. He couldn't move fast enough to evade it unless he released his prisoner—who was his sole possible guide to Jimmy—

Barbro leaped forth. "Don't!" Sherrinford shouted. "For God's sake, stay inside!" The monster rumbled and made snatching motions at her. She pulled the trigger. Recoil slammed her in the shoulder. The colossus rocked and fell. Somehow it got its feet back and lumbered toward her. She retreated. Again she shot, and again. The creature snarled. Blood began to drip from it and gleam oilily amidst dewdrops. It turned and went off, breaking branches, into the darkness that laired beneath the woods.

"Get to shelter!" Sherrinford yelled. "You're out of the jammer field!"

A mistiness drifted by overhead. She barely glimpsed it before she saw the new shape at the meadow edge. "Jimmy!" tore from her.

"Mother." He held out his arms. Moonlight coursed in his tears. She dropped her weapon and ran to him.

Sherrinford plunged in pursuit. Jimmy flitted away into the brush. Barbro crashed after, through clawing twigs. Then she was seized and borne away.

Standing over his captive, Sherrinford strengthened the fluoro output until vision of the wilderness was blocked off from within the bus. The boy squirmed beneath that colorless glare.

"You are going to talk," the man said. Despite the haggardness in his features, he spoke quietly.

The boy glared through tangled locks. A bruise was purpling on his jaw. He'd almost recovered ability to flee while Sherrinford chased and lost the woman. Returning, the detective had barely caught him. Time was lacking to be gentle, when Outling reinforcements might arrive at any moment. Sherrinford had knocked him out and dragged him inside. He sat lashed into a swivel seat.

He spat. "Talk to you, man-clod?" But sweat stood on his skin, and his eyes flickered unceasingly around the metal which caged him.

"Give me a name to call you by."

"And have you work a spell on me?"

"Mine's Eric. If you don't give me another choice, I'll have to call you . . . m-m-m . . . Wuddikins."

"What?" However eldritch, the bound one remained a human adolescent. "Mistherd, then." The lilting accent of his English somehow emphasized its sullenness. "That's not the sound, only what it means. Anyway, it's my spoken name, naught else."

"Ah, you keep a secret name you consider to be real?"

"She does. I don't know myself what it is. She knows the real names of everybody."

Sherrinford raised his brows. "She?"

"Who reigns. May she forgive me, I can't make the reverent sign when my arms are tied. Some invaders call her the Queen of Air and Darkness."

"So." Sherrinford got pipe and tobacco. He let silence wax while he started the fire. At length he said:

"I'll confess the Old Folk took me by surprise. I didn't expect so formidable a member of your gang. Everything I could learn had seemed to show they work on my race—and yours, lad—by stealth, trickery, and illusion."

Mistherd jerked a truculent nod. "She created the first nicors not long ago. Don't think she has naught but dazzlements at her beck."

"I don't. However, a steel-jacketed bullet works pretty well too, doesn't it?"

Sherrinford talked on, softly, mostly to himself: "I do still believe the, ah, nicors—all your half-humanlike breeds—are intended in the main to be seen, not used. The power of projecting mirages must surely be quite limited in range and scope as well as in the number of individuals who possess it. Otherwise she wouldn't have needed to work as slowly and craftily as she has. Even outside our mind-shield, Barbro—my companion—could have resisted, could have remained aware that whatever she saw was unreal . . . if she'd been less shaken, less frantic, less driven by need."

Sherrinford wreathed his head in smoke. "Never mind what I experienced," he said. "It couldn't have been the same as for her. I think the command was simply given us, 'You will see what you most desire in the world, running away from you into the forest.' Of course, she didn't travel many meters before the nicor waylaid her. I'd no hope of trailing them; I'm no Arctican woodsman, and besides, it'd have been too easy to ambush me. I came back to you." Grimly: "You're my link to your overlady."

"You think I'll guide you to Starhaven or Carheddin? Try making me, clod-man."

"I want to bargain."

"I s'pect you intend more'n that." Mistherd's answer held surprising shrewdness. "What'll you tell after you come home?"

"Yes, that does pose a problem, doesn't it? Barbro Cullen and I are not terrified outwayers. We're of the city. We brought recording instruments. We'd be the first of our kind to report an encounter with the Old Folk, and that report would be detailed and plausible. It would produce action."

"So you see I'm not afraid to die," Mistherd declared, though his lips trembled a bit. "If I let you come in and do your man-things to my people, I'd have naught left worth living for."

"Have no immediate fears," Sherrinford said. "You're merely bait." He sat down and regarded the boy through a visor of calm.

(Within, it wept in him: *Barbro, Barbro!*) "Consider. Your Queen can't very well let me go back, bringing my prisoner and telling about hers. She has to stop that somehow. I could try fighting my way through—this car is better armed than you know—but that wouldn't free anybody. Instead, I'm staying put. New forces of hers will get here as fast as they can. I assume they won't blindly throw themselves against a machine gun, a howitzer, a fulgurator. They'll parley first, whether their intentions are honest or not. Thus I make the contact I'm after."

"What d' you plan?" The mumble held anguish.

"First, this, as a sort of invitation." Sherrinford reached out to flick a switch. "There. I've lowered my shield against mind-reading and shape-casting. I daresay the leaders, at least, will be able to sense that it's gone. That should give them confidence."

"And next?"

"Next we wait. Would you like something to eat or drink?"

During the time which followed, Sherrinford tried to jolly Mistherd along, find out something of his life. What answers he got were curt. He dimmed the interior lights and settled down to peer outward. That was a long few hours.

They ended at a shout of gladness, half a sob, from the boy. Out of the woods came a band of the Old Folk.

Some of them stood forth more clearly than moons and stars and northlights should have caused. He in the van rode a white crown-buck whose horns were garlanded. His form was manlike but unearthly beautiful, silver-blond hair falling from beneath the antlered helmet, around the proud cold face. The cloak fluttered off his back like living wings. His frost-colored mail rang as he fared.

Behind him, to right and left, rode two who bore swords whereon small flames gleamed and flickered. Above, a flying flock laughed and trilled and tumbled in the breezes. Near them drifted a half-transparent mistiness. Those others who passed among trees after their chieftain were harder to make out. But they moved in quicksilver grace and as it were to a sound of harps and trumpets.

"Lord Luighaid." Glory overflowed in Mistherd's tone. "Her master Knower—himself."

Sherrinford had never done a harder thing than to sit at the main control panel, finger near the button of the shield generator, and not touch it. He rolled down a section of canopy to let voices travel. A gust of wind struck him in the face, bearing odors of the roses in his mother's garden. At his back, in the main body of the vehicle, Mistherd strained against his bonds till he could see the oncoming troop.

"Call to them," Sherrinford said. "Ask if they will talk with me."

Unknown, flutingly sweet words flew back and forth. "Yes," the boy interpreted. "He will, the Lord Luighaid. But I can tell you, you'll never be let go. Don't fight them. Yield. Come away. You don't know what 'tis to be alive till you've dwelt in Carheddin under the mountain."

The Outlings drew nigh.

Jimmy glimmered and was gone. Barbro lay in strong arms, against a broad breast, and felt the horse move beneath her. It had to be a horse, though only a few were kept any longer on the steadings and they only for special uses or love. She could feel the rippling beneath its hide, hear a rush of parted leafage and the thud when a hoof struck stone; warmth and living scent welled up around her through the darkness.

He who carried her said mildly, "Don't be afraid, darling. It was a vision. But he's waiting for us and we're bound for him."

She was aware in a vague way that she ought to feel terror or despair or something. But her memories lay behind her—she wasn't sure just how she had come to be here—she was borne along in a knowledge of being loved. At peace, at peace, rest in the calm expectation of joy . . .

After a while the forest opened. They crossed a lea where boulders stood gray-white under the moons, their shadows shifting in the dim hues which the aurora threw across them. Flitteries danced, tiny comets, above the flowers between. Ahead gleamed a peak whose top was crowned in clouds.

Barbro's eyes happened to be turned forward. She saw the horse's head and thought, with quiet surprise: Why, this is Sambo, who was mine when I was a girl. She looked upward at the man. He wore a black tunic and a cowled cape, which made his face hard to see. She could not cry aloud, here. "Tim," she whispered.

"Yes, Barbro."

"I buried you—"

His smile was endlessly tender. "Did you think we're no more than what's laid back into the ground? Poor torn sweetheart. She who's called us is the All Healer. Now rest and dream."

"Dream," she said, and for a space she struggled to rouse herself. But the effort was weak. Why should she believe ashen tales about . . . atoms and energies, nothing else to fill a gape of emptiness . . . tales she could not bring to mind . . . when Tim and the horse her father gave her carried her on to Jimmy? Had the other thing not been the evil dream, and this her first drowsy awakening from it?

As if he heard her thoughts, he murmured, "They have a song in Outling lands. The Song of the Men:

"The world sails
to an unseen wind.
Light swirls by the bows.
The wake is night.

But the Dwellers have no such sadness."

"I don't understand," she said.

He nodded. "There's much you'll have to understand, darling, and I can't see you again until you've learned those truths. But meanwhile you'll be with our son."

She tried to lift her head and kiss him. He held her down. "Not yet," he said. "You've not been received among the Queen's people. I shouldn't have come for you, except that she was too merciful to forbid. Lie back, lie back."

Time blew past. The horse galloped tireless, never stumbling, up the mountain. Once she glimpsed a troop riding down it and thought they were bound for a last weird battle in the west against . . . who? . . . one who lay cased in iron and sorrow—Later she would ask herself the name of him who had brought her into the land of the Old Truth.

Finally spires lifted splendid among the stars, which are small and magical and whose whisperings comfort us after we are dead. They rode into a courtyard where candles burned unwavering, fountains splashed and birds sang. The air bore fragrance of brok and pericoup, of rue and roses, for not everything that man brought was horrible. The Dwellers waited in beauty to welcome her. Beyond their stateliness, pooks cavorted through the gloaming; among the trees darted children; merriment caroled across music more solemn.

"We have come—" Tim's voice was suddenly, inexplicably a croak.

Barbro was not sure how he dismounted, bearing her. She stood before him and saw him sway on his feet.

Fear caught her. "Are you well?" She seized both his hands. They felt cold and rough. Where had Sambo gone? Her eyes searched beneath the cowl. In this brighter illumination, she ought to have seen her man's face clearly. But it was blurred, it kept changing. "What's wrong, oh, what's happened?"

He smiled. Was that the smile she had cherished? She couldn't completely remember. "I, I must go," he stammered, so low she could scarcely hear. "Our time is not ready." He drew free of her grasp and leaned on a robed form which had appeared at his side. A haziness swirled over both their heads. "Don't watch me go . . . back into the earth," he pleaded. "That's death for you. Till our time returns—There, our son!"

She had to fling her gaze around. Kneeling, she spread wide her arms. Jimmy struck her like a warm, solid cannonball. She rumpled his hair; she kissed the hollow of his neck; she laughed and wept and babbled foolishness; and this was no ghost, no memory that had stolen off when she wasn't looking. Now and again, as she turned her attention to yet another hurt which might have come upon him— hunger, sickness, fear—and found none, she would glimpse their surroundings. The gardens were gone. It didn't matter.

"I missed you so, Mother. Stay?"

"I'll take you home, dearest."

"Stay. Here's fun. I'll show. But you stay."

A sighing went through the twilight. Barbro rose. Jimmy clung to her hand. They confronted the Queen.

Very tall she was in her robes woven of northlights, and her starry crown and her garlands of kiss-me-never. Her countenance recalled Aphrodite of Milos, whose picture Barbro had often seen in the realms of men, save that the Queen's was more fair and more majesty dwelt upon it and in the night-blue eyes. Around her the gardens woke to new reality, the court of the Dwellers and the heaven-climbing spires.

"Be welcome," she spoke, her speaking a song, "forever."

Against the awe of her, Barbro said, "Moonmother, let us go home."

"That may not be."

"To our world, little and beloved," Barbro dreamed she begged, "which we build for ourselves and cherish for our children."

"To prison days, angry nights, works that crumble in the fingers, loves that turn to rot or stone or driftweed, loss, grief, and the only sureness that of the final nothingness. No. You too, Wanderfoot who is to be, will jubilate when the banners of the Outworld come flying into the last of the cities and man is made wholly alive. Now go with those who will teach you."

The Queen of Air and Darkness lifted an arm in summons. It halted, and none came to answer.

For over the fountains and melodies lifted a gruesome growling. Fires leaped, thunders crashed. Her hosts scattered screaming before the steel thing which boomed up the mountainside. The pooks were gone in a whirl of frightened wings. The nicors flung their bodies against the unalive invader and were consumed, until their Mother cried to them to retreat.

Barbro cast Jimmy down and herself over him. Towers wavered and smoked away. The mountain stood bare under icy moons, save for rocks, crags, and farther off a glacier in whose depths the auroral light pulsed blue. A cave mouth darkened a cliff. Thither folk streamed, seeking refuge underground. Some were human of blood, some grotesques like the pooks and nicors and wraiths; but most were lean, scaly, long-tailed, long-beaked, not remotely men or Outlings.

For an instant, even as Jimmy wailed at her breast—perhaps as much because the enchantment had been wrecked as because he was afraid—Barbro pitied the Queen who stood alone in her nakedness. Then that one also had fled, and Barbro's world shivered apart.

The guns fell silent; the vehicle whirred to a halt. From it sprang a boy who called wildly, "Shadow-of-a-Dream, where are you? It's me, Mistherd, oh, come, come!"—before he remembered that the language they had been raised in was not man's. He shouted in that until a girl crept out of a thicket where she had hidden. They stared at each other through dust, smoke, and moonglow. She ran to him.

A new voice barked from the car, "Barbro, hurry!"

Christmas Landing knew day: short at this time of year, but sunlight, blue skies, white clouds, glittering water, salt breezes in busy streets, and the sane disorder of Eric Sherrinford's living room.

He crossed and uncrossed his legs where he sat, puffed on his pipe as if to make a veil, and said, "Are you certain you're recovered? You mustn't risk overstrain."

"I'm fine," Barbro Cullen replied, though her tone was flat. "Still tired, yes, and showing it, no doubt. One doesn't go through such an experience and bounce back in a week. But I'm up and about. And to be frank, I must know what's happened, what's going on, before I can settle down to regain my full strength. Not a word of news anywhere."

"Have you spoken to others about the matter?"

"No. I've simply told visitors I was too exhausted to talk. Not much of a lie. I assumed there's a reason for censorship."

Sherrinford looked relieved. "Good girl. It's at my urging. You can imagine the sensation when this is made public. The authorities agreed they need time to study the facts, think and debate in a calm atmosphere, have a decent policy ready to offer voters who're bound to become rather hysterical at first." His mouth quirked slightly upward. "Furthermore, your nerves and Jimmy's get their chance to heal before the journalistic storm breaks over you. How is he?"

"Quite well. He continues pestering me for leave to go play with his friends in the Wonderful Place. But at his age, he'll recover—he'll forget."

"He may meet them later anyhow."

"What? We didn't—" Barbro shifted in her chair. "I've forgotten too. I hardly recall a thing from our last hours. Did you bring back any kidnaped humans?"

"No. The shock was savage as it was, without throwing them straight into an . . . an institution. Mistherd, who's basically a sensible young fellow, assured me they'd get along, at any rate as regards survival necessities, till arrangements can be made." Sherrinford hesitated. "I'm not sure what the arrangements will be. Nobody is, at our present stage. But obviously they include those people—or many of them, especially those who aren't full-grown—rejoining the human race. Though they may never feel at home in civilization. Perhaps in a way that's best, since we will need some kind of mutually acceptable liaison with the Dwellers."

His impersonality soothed them both. Barbro became able to say, "Was I too big a fool? I do remember how I yowled and beat my head on the floor."

"Why no." He considered the big woman and her pride for a few seconds before he rose, walked over and laid a hand on her shoulder. "You'd been lured and trapped by a skillful play on your deepest instincts, at a moment of sheer nightmare. Afterward, as that wounded monster carried you off, evidently another type of being came along, one that could saturate you with close-range neuropsychic forces. On top of this, my arrival, the sudden brutal abolishment of every hallucination, must have been shattering. No wonder if you cried out in pain. Before you did, you competently got Jimmy and yourself into the bus, and you never interfered with me."

"What did you do?"

"Why, I drove off as fast as possible. After several hours, the atmospherics let up sufficiently for me to call Portolondon and insist on an emergency airlift. Not that that was vital. What chance had the enemy to stop us? They didn't even try.—But quick transportation was certainly helpful."

"I figured that's what must have gone on." Barbro caught his glance. "No, what I meant was, how did you find us in the backlands?"

Sherrinford moved a little off from her. "My prisoner was my guide. I don't think I actually killed any of the Dwellers who'd come to deal with me. I hope not. The car simply broke through them, after a couple of warning shots, and afterward outpaced them. Steel and fuel against flesh wasn't really fair. At the cave entrance, I did have to shoot down a few of those troll creatures. I'm not proud of it."

He stood silent. Presently: "But you were a captive," he said. "I couldn't be sure what they might do to you, who had first claim on me." After another pause: "I don't look for any more violence."

"How did you make . . . the boy . . . co-operate?"

Sherrinford paced from her, to the window, where he stood staring out at the Boreal Ocean. "I turned off the mind-shield," he said. "I let their band get close, in full splendor of illusion. Then I turned the shield back on, and we both saw them in their true shapes. As we went northward, I explained to Mistherd how he and his kind had been hoodwinked, used, made to live in a world that was never really there. I asked him if he wanted himself and whomever he cared about to go on till they died as domestic animals—yes, running in limited freedom on solid hills, but always called back to the dream-kennel." His pipe fumed furiously. "May I never see such bitterness again. He had been taught to believe he was free."

Quiet returned, above the hectic traffic. Charlemagne drew nearer to setting; already the east darkened.

Finally Barbro asked, "Do you know why?"

"Why children were taken and raised like that? Partly because it was in the pattern the Dwellers were creating; partly in order to study and experiment on members of our species—minds, that is, not bodies; partly because humans have special strengths which are helpful, like being able to endure full daylight."

"But what was the final purpose of it all?"

Sherrinford paced the floor. "Well," he said, "of course the ultimate motives of the aborigines are obscure. We can't do more than guess at how they think, let alone how they feel. But our ideas do seem to fit the data.

"Why did they hide from man? I suspect they, or rather their ancestors—for they aren't glittering elves, you know; they're mortal and fallible too—I suspect the natives were only being cautious at first, more cautious than human primitives, though certain of those on Earth were also slow to reveal themselves to strangers. Spying, mentally eavesdropping, Roland's Dwellers must have picked up enough language to get some idea of how different man was from them, and how powerful; and they gathered that more ships would be arriving, bringing settlers. It didn't occur to them that they might be conceded the right to keep their lands. Perhaps they're still more fiercely territorial than we. They determined to fight, in their own way. I daresay, once we begin to get insight into that mentality, our psychological science will go through its Copernican revolution."

Enthusiasm kindled in him. "That's not the sole thing we'll learn, either," he went on. "They must have science of their own, a non-human science born on a planet that isn't Earth. Because they did observe us as profoundly as we've ever observed ourselves; they did mount a plan against us, one that would have taken another century or more to complete. Well, what else do they know? How do they support their civilization without visible agriculture or above-ground buildings or mines or anything? How can they breed whole new intelligent species to order? A million questions, ten million answers!"

"*Can* we learn from them?" Barbro asked softly. "Or can we only overrun them as you say they fear?"

Sherrinford halted, leaned elbow on mantel, hugged his pipe and replied, "I hope we'll show more charity than that to a defeated enemy. It's what they are. They tried to conquer us, and failed, and now in a sense we are bound to conquer them, since they'll have to make their peace with the civilization of the machine rather than see it rust away as they strove for. Still, they never did us any harm as atrocious as what we've inflicted on our fellow men in the past. And, I repeat, they could teach us marvelous things; and we could teach them, too, once they've learned to be less intolerant of a different way of life."

"I suppose we can give them a reservation," she said, and didn't know why he grimaced and answered so roughly:

"Let's leave them the honor they've earned! They fought to save the world they'd always known from that—" he made a chopping gesture at the city—"and just possibly we'd be better off ourselves with less of it."

He sagged a trifle and sighed, "However, I suppose if Elfland had won, man on Roland would at last—peacefully, even happily—have died away. We live with our archetypes, but can we live in them?"

Barbro shook her head. "Sorry, I don't understand."

"What?" He looked at her in a surprise that drove out melancholy. After a laugh: "Stupid of me. I've explained this to so many politicians and scientists and commissioners and Lord knows what, these past days, I forgot I'd never explained to you. It was a rather vague idea of mine, most of the time we were traveling, and I don't like to discuss ideas prematurely. Now that we've met the Outlings and watched how they work, I do feel sure."

He tamped down his tobacco. "In limited measure," he said, "I've used an archetype throughout my own working life. The rational detective. It hasn't been a conscious pose—much—it's simply been an image which fitted my personality and professional style. But it draws an appropriate response from most people, whether or not they've ever heard of the original. The phenomenon is not uncommon. We meet persons who, in varying degrees, suggest Christ or Buddha or the Earth Mother or, say, on a less exalted plane, Hamlet or d'Artagnan. Historical, fictional, and mythical, such figures crystallize basic aspects of the human psyche, and when we meet them in our real experience, our reaction goes deeper than consciousness."

He grew grave again: "Man also creates archetypes that are not individuals. The Anima, the Shadow—and, it seems, the Outworld. The world of magic, of glamour—which originally meant enchantment—of half-human beings, some like Ariel and some like Caliban, but each free of mortal frailties and sorrows—therefore, perhaps, a little carelessly cruel, more than a little tricksy; dwellers in dusk and moonlight, not truly gods but obedient to rulers who are enigmatic and powerful enough to be—Yes, our Queen of Air and Darkness knew well what sights to let lonely people see, what illusions to spin around them from time to time, what songs and legends to set going among them. I wonder how much she and her underlings gleaned from human fairy tales, how much they made up themselves, and how much men created all over again, all unwittingly, as the sense of living on the edge of the world entered them."

Shadows stole across the room. It grew cooler and the traffic noises dwindled. Barbro asked mutedly, "But what could this do?"

"In many ways," Sherrinford answered, "the outwayer *is* back in the Dark Ages. He has few neighbors, hears scanty news from beyond his horizon, toils to survive in a land he only partly understands, that may any night raise unforeseeable disasters against him and is bounded by enormous wildernesses. The machine civilization which brought his ancestors here is frail at best. He could lose it as the Dark Ages nations had lost Greece and Rome, as the whole of Earth seems to have lost it. Let him be worked on, long, strongly, cunningly, by the archetypical Outworld, until he has come to believe in his bones that the magic of the Queen of Air and Darkness is greater than the energy of engines; and first his faith, finally his deeds will follow her. Oh, it wouldn't happen fast. Ideally, it would happen too slowly to be noticed, especially by self-satisfied city people. But when in the end a hinterland gone back to the ancient way turned from them, how could they keep alive?"

Barbro breathed, "She said to me, when their banners flew in the last of our cities, we would rejoice."

"I think we would have, by then," Sherrinford admitted. "Nevertheless, I believe in choosing one's destiny."

He shook himself, as if casting off a burden. He knocked the dottle from his pipe and stretched, muscle by muscle. "Well," he said, "it isn't going to happen."

She looked straight at him. "Thanks to you."

A flush went up his thin cheeks. "In time, I'm sure, somebody else would have—What matters is what we do next, and that's too big a decision for one individual or one generation to make."

She rose. "Unless the decision is personal, Eric," she suggested, feeling heat in her own face.

It was curious to see him shy. "I was hoping we might meet again."

"We will."

Ayoch sat on Wolund's Barrow. Aurora shuddered so brilliant, in such vast sheafs of light, as almost to hide the waning moons. Firethorn blooms had fallen; a few still glowed around the tree roots, amidst dry brok which crackled underfoot and smelled like woodsmoke. The air remained warm but no gleam was left on the sunset horizon.

"Farewell, fare lucky," the pook called. Mistherd and Shadow-of-a-Dream never looked back. It was as if they didn't dare. They trudged on out of sight, toward the human camp whose lights made a harsh new star in the south.

Ayoch lingered. He felt he should also offer good-by to her who had lately joined him that slept in the dolmen. Likely none would meet here again for loving or magic. But he could only think of one old verse that might do. He stood and trilled:

> "Out of her breast
> a blossom ascended.
> The summer burned it.
> The song is ended."

Then he spread his wings for the long flight away.

Poul Anderson

by GORDON R. DICKSON

In the late nineteen forties through nineteen fifty-one, Poul Anderson and I were living in the same rooming house in North Minneapolis. Our rooms were side by side with a single wall between them, and I did most of my writing in the late morning and afternoon. Poul did a great deal of his in the late afternoon and evening. Just about the time when I was slowing down, I would hear his typewriter, like mine earlier, beginning to chatter by bursts and pauses. But then, more quickly than mine had, his would pick up speed; and I would soon hear it rattling along steadily just as I—by this time empty of energy and ingenuity alike—was drowsing off on the bed where I had lain down.

I would wake sometime later to find night dark beyond the unpulled shades of the windows of my room; and, if Poul's typewriter was still sounding, I would get up, eat something, and perhaps go out by myself for a drink. Or, if his typewriter was now silent, I would go and knock on his door; and perhaps we would both go out. That is how it was in those days.

Relating it like that now makes it sound like a very attractive and uncomplex sort of life. But if I stop to remember it in detail, I have to admit that the attractiveness and lack of complexity were only part of the story. The lives of authors, like authors themselves, are invariably a good deal more complicated than they, or even their writings, indicate. And there is a particular appropriateness in this. For when, as in Poul's case, you have an author whose work itself is a good deal more complex than its surface appearance indicates, the order of difference between work and man begins to extend itself out of reach of easy explanation. T. S. Eliot once noted in an introduction to an edition of the poems of Rudyard Kipling that most poets have to be protected from charges of obscurity in their work. But in the case of Kipling, he added, it was necessary to defend the man against the charge of writing jingles. Of course, poems of Rudyard Kipling are very definitely not jingles, although too much of their allegory and meaning is often hidden in the nineteenth century political situations upon which Kipling commented and criticized. Yet the very musicality of the rhymes and rhythms he used makes them read with a deceptive easiness as if they had been tossed off for the sound of their words alone. Similarly, the narrative art of Poul Anderson is not, and never was a simple one, although the sheer readability and entertainment of it can make it seem so.

Back when I lived in that same rooming house as Poul, we were both still students at the University of Minnesota, and Poul had no intention of being a full-time writer. He was after a degree in physics, which he in fact gained, with distinction, in June, 1948. However, by then he was already writing and selling well; and so, when he did graduate, he delayed going after a job in physics in favor of supporting himself for a while by writing. That "while" as Poul himself now says, seems to have stretched out to a lifetime, to the great pleasure of the rest of us, of course. Poul being Poul, he would undoubtedly have been writing some science fiction, fantasy, historical or detective fiction—and nonfiction as well—no matter how busy an ordinary job might keep him. But it would be too much to expect, even of him, that he would have produced so much so well in the years since 1948 as he has without other occupation to distract him. The tally of his published work stands now at thirty-four novels, plus fifteen collections of his shorter works, three books of nonfiction, and two books he has edited. All this, not counting the work he has in hand and under contract or the legion of his published short stories.

He has, as everyone knows, a talent for titles. To read these, where they have escaped changing by editor or publisher, is to pick up some of the intense note of poetry that runs through all his writing. Among the novels—*We Have Fed Our Sea* (from the line of the Kipling poem), *The High Crusade, Three Hearts and Three Lions, Tau Zero* . . . and among the shorter fiction, "Sam Hall," "Call Me Joe," "Starfog," "Kyrie," "No Truce With Kings" . . . titles like these, given half a chance, almost weave themselves into a ballad or a coronach. While at the same time there runs under their melody the strong control of the scientifically educated mind that gives Anderson's writing its point and purpose.

As A. J. Budrys has said—"The single man best qualified to analyze the classics—" he is speaking here of the classics of science fiction —"would be Poul Anderson. Thank a good Lord he spends his time doing so only for the purpose of constructing additional fiction . . ."

And indeed, someone should be thanked. Because the Anderson story is a unique and valuable production, and there is only one source for it in the known universe, the man himself, who has been unique and valuable from the beginning.

He was born in Pennsylvania, of Scandinavian parents, on November 25, 1926, hence the spelling of his first name. The proper pronunciation of that name falls somewhere between "pole" and "powl" for tongues accustomed to American English, but Poul, in fact, answers to all pronunciations of it. He was still a baby when his father was transferred to Port Arthur, Texas. There, the family spent the next eleven years, and Poul's brother John was born (the same John Anderson who later led the first expedition into the Heritage Mountains of Antarctica).

The death of his father at the end of that eleven years moved the family to Denmark for a while, where there were a great many maternal relatives and friends. The approach of World War II, however, caused the boys' mother to bring them back to the United States, where for a while she worked for the Danish Legation in Washington. The next move was to a farm in Minnesota, from which Poul came to Minneapolis and the University of Minnesota, in the nineteen forties.

There was a very loose organization at that time in the Twin Cities of Minneapolis and St. Paul, known as the MFS. Before the war it had been a science fiction fan organization called the Minneapolis Fantasy Society, with writers like Cliff Simak, Carl Jacobi, Donald Wandrei, Oliver Saari, and others on its membership lists. After the war, although it retained its connection with science fiction generally and all its original members still in the city remained part of it, it developed into an essentially unstructured social group with interests ranging from manuscript criticism to softball, with a great deal of drinking and talking along the way.

I, myself, had been a member of the original group before the war when the various armed services split us up and sent us all in different directions. Poul joined the MFS after the war. It was one of the criteria of the group then that you had to be able to do whatever was necessary in the ordinary way of your affairs and still be able to sit up until midnight or later, socializing. Poul was no exception. At the time that he and the MFS got together, he was majoring in physics, minoring in chemistry and mathematics—and I believe I mentioned that in 1948 he graduated with honors. That fact against the backdrop of the MFS in those days gives some idea of his capabilities.

It also gives some sort of index by which to judge the scientific part of his nature, and this is important because it is the strong blend of science and poetry in Poul's writing which marks its uniqueness in a field where neither science nor poetry separately have ever been in short supply. Both showed strongly in Poul in those days. One among the rather large number of MFS activities after the war was a great deal of singing, usually done late at night at one of our impromptu gatherings. What were sung were mostly ballads, but in a number of languages ranging from modern English through Swedish, Norwegian, German, French, Polish, Middle English, Old Danish, and others now forgotten. For many of the non-English ballads we were indebted to Poul. Not only that. There was also a good deal of setting of poems to music, and writing of lyrics, some writing of melodies, and—on Poul's part—a good deal of excellent translation of Scandinavian poets like Johannes V. Jensen.

This intermingled with another recreation, which was the verbal building of science fiction stories. Over the table an idea for a story would be produced and tossed from person to person, so to speak, being added to and shaped as it went until it developed into something that might or might not get written, but which was already a good way along the path to standing on its own narrative legs. Sitting in on one of these story-making moments, it was possible to see in Poul's contributions how saga and song, known science and hypothetical science complemented each other, working all together to come up as action clothed in the perfect armor of possibility. It is a rare talent, to mix such different materials so effectively; but Poul showed it invariably and successfully whenever he became involved in the story-building game.

Time, however, was shifting the scenery behind us all, even then. With the early fifties, the social group began to splinter and spread apart, just as the prewar MFS had been broken up and spread around by the services. In 1953, Poul married Karen, an author of fiction and poetry in her own right, and they moved to the Bay Area of San Francisco, ending up with their daughter Astrid in their present home in Orinda, California, over the mountains from the Bay, out of the fog and into the sunshine. But the move to the West Coast agreed with Poul. He became a more active producer of fiction than ever.

From *Brain Wave* on, most of his most memorable writing has been done in the Bay Area locations. His Hugo winners—"The Longest Voyage," "No Truce With Kings," and the latest, "The Sharing of Flesh"—all originated there. So did a host of his other well-remembered shorter stories—the classic "The Man Who Came Early," all the other stories I mentioned earlier when I was talking about the poetry of his titles, as well as "The Martian Crown Jewels," "The Sky People," "Kings Who Die," "Escape From Orbit" . . . and among the novels—his fine early fantasy *The Broken Sword,* recently rescued from out-of-printness and reissued in a revised version in paperback by Ballantine, and a number of favorites like *The Star Ways, War of the Wing-Men, We Claim These Stars, Shield, The Corridors of Time, The Star Fox* . . . The list goes on. Then, too, there are the Time Patrol stories; the stories about Van Rijn, Falkayn and the Polesotechnic League; and the Flandry series—as well as the F&SF fantasy series of which the last was "Operation Changeling." This last series, by the way, is due in novel form from Doubleday under the title *Operation Chaos.*

With all this, Poul still finds time to do a dozen other things. He travels, he builds houseboats, he sails, climbs mountains and finds time to belong to a host of organizations. He is a member of Mystery Writers of America, having been both vice-president and regional secretary in his time. He also belongs to the local chapter of the Baker Street Irregulars, where he has the investiture of The Dreadful Abernetty Business; to S.A.G.A. (Swordsmen and Sorcerers Guild of America, Ltd.); and of course to Science Fiction Writers of America, whose West Coast Regional Conference is Poul's invention.

And then there is The Society For Creative Anachronism, in which he has won a knighthood. He goes under the name Béla of Eastmarch, with coat of arms azure, two suns or in pale, a saltire argent, the devising of which owes its debt to Karen, who is a member of the College of Heralds of the Kingdom of the Mists.

Meanwhile, on the wider stages of the world, this tall, powerfully minded and gentle man remains deeply concerned in the struggle to improve the lot of his fellow writers, and in the ecology and conservation movement, where he was active long before these things caught public attention. In modern politics, he is that unusual figure, an eighteenth century liberal. In religion he stands self-accused as a devout scientist; and in pride, a centrist upon his family.

"The way things are shaping up," he says, "my chief claim to fame will probably be that I fathered Astrid."

This may be. But it is necessary to take him with more than a grain of salt when he goes on to say that he is, in writing, "an old-fashioned teller of tales."

He is that, indeed. But the inferable understatement involved is somewhat galloping. Just "a teller of tales" does not do him justice. We who read him know better.

Bibliography of books by Poul Anderson

I. NOVELS

VAULT OF THE AGES, Winston, 1952.

BRAIN WAVE, Ballantine 80, 1954. (The Escape)

THE BROKEN SWORD, Abelard, 1954. (Revised version, Ballantine, 1971)

NO WORLD OF THEIR OWN, Ace D-110, 1955. (The Long Way Home)

PLANET OF NO RETURN, Ace D-199, 1956. (Question and Answer)

THE STAR WAYS, Avalon, 1957.

WAR OF THE WING-MEN, Ace D-303, 1958. (The Man Who Counts)

VIRGIN PLANET, Avalon, 1959.

PERISH BY THE SWORD, Macmillan, 1959.

WE CLAIM THESE STARS!, Ace D-407, 1959. (A Handful of Stars)

THE ENEMY STARS, Lippincott, 1959. (We Have Fed Our Sea)

THE WAR OF TWO WORLDS, Ace D-335, 1959. (Silent Victory)

MURDER IN BLACK LETTER [The Book of Witches], Macmillan, 1960.

THE GOLDEN SLAVE [The Great Faring], Avon T-388, 1960.

THE HIGH CRUSADE, Doubleday, 1960.

ROGUE SWORD [The Grand Company], Avon T-472, 1960.

EARTHMAN, GO HOME!, Ace D-479, 1961. (A Plague of Masters)

THREE HEARTS AND THREE LIONS, Doubleday, 1961. (Full-length version)

MAYDAY ORBIT, Ace F-104, 1961. (A Message in Secret. Longer version)

MURDER BOUND, Macmillan, 1961.

AFTER DOOMSDAY, Ballantine 579, 1962.

THE MAKESHIFT ROCKET, Ace F-139, 1962. (A Bicycle Built for Brew. Bound with Un-Man and Other Novellas)

SHIELD, Berkley F-743, 1963. (Full-length version)

LET THE SPACEMAN BEWARE!, Ace F-209, 1963. (A Twelvemonth and a Day. Revised and expanded version)

THREE WORLDS TO CONQUER, Pyramid F-994, 1964. (Revised and expanded version)

THE CORRIDORS OF TIME, Doubleday, 1965. (Full-length version)

THE STAR FOX, Doubleday, 1965. (From the stories Marque and Reprisal, Arsenal Port, Admiralty)

THE FOX, THE DOG, AND THE GRIFFIN, Doubleday, 1966.

ENSIGN FLANDRY, Chilton, 1966.

WORLD WITHOUT STARS, Ace F-425, 1967. (The Ancient Gods)

SATAN'S WORLD, Doubleday, 1969.

THE REBEL WORLDS, New American Library T-4041, 1969.

TAU ZERO, Doubleday, 1970. (To Outlive Eternity. Full-length version)

A CIRCUS OF HELLS, New American Library T-4250, 1970. (Incorporates The White King's War)

THE BYWORLDER, New American Library (NAL) 1971.

OPERATION CHAOS, Doubleday, 1971.

THE DANCER FROM ATLANTIS, Science Fiction Book Club (SFBC) and NAL, 1971.

THE PEOPLE OF THE WIND, NAL, 1973.

THERE WILL BE TIME, SFBC 1972 and NAL, 1973.

HROLF KRAKI'S SAGA, Ballantine, 1973.

A MIDSUMMER TEMPEST, Doubleday, 1973.

THE DAY OF THEIR RETURN, SFBC and NAL, 1974.

STAR PRINCE CHARLIE (with Gordon R. Dickson), Putnam's, 1974.

II. COLLECTIONS (New material in these is italicized)

EARTHMAN'S BURDEN (with Gordon Dickson), Gnome Press, 1957. Contains: *Interludes,* The Sheriff of Canyon Gulch (Heroes Are Made), *Don Jones,* In Hoka Signo Vinces, The Adventure of the Misplaced Hound, Yo Ho Hoka!, The Tiddlywink Warriors. (The stories are related)

GUARDIANS OF TIME, Ballantine 422-K, 1960. Contains: Time Patrol, Brave To Be a King, The Only Game in Town, Delenda Est. (The stories are related)

TWILIGHT WORLD, Torquil, 1961. Contains: Tomorrow's Children, Logic, *The Children of Fortune.* (The stories are related)

STRANGERS FROM EARTH, Ballantine 483-K, 1961. Contains: Earthman, Beware!, Quixote and the Windmill, Gypsy, For the Duration, Duel on Syrtis, The Star Beast, The Disintegrating Sky, Among Thieves.

ORBIT UNLIMITED [A Place for Liberty]. Pyramid G-615, 1961. Contains: Robin Hood's Barn, The Burning Bridge, And Yet So Far, *The Mills of the Gods.* (The stories are related)

UN-MAN AND OTHER NOVELLAS, Ace F-139, 1962. Contains: Un-Man, Margin of Profit, The Live Coward. (Bound with The Makeshift Rocket)

TIME AND STARS, Doubleday, 1964. Contains: No Truce With Kings, Turning Point, Escape From Orbit, Epilogue, The Critique of Impure Reason, Eve Times Four.

TRADER TO THE STARS, Doubleday, 1964. Contains: Hiding Place, Territory, The Master Key. (The stories are related)

AGENT OF THE TERRAN EMPIRE, Chilton, 1965. Contains: Tiger by the Tail, Warriors from Nowhere, Honorable Enemies, Hunters of the Sky Cave [A Handful of Stars]. (The stories are related)

FLANDRY OF TERRA, Chilton, 1965. Contains: The Game of Glory, A Message in Secret, A Plague of Masters. (The stories are related)

THE TROUBLE TWISTERS, Doubleday, 1966. Contains: The Three-Cornered Wheel, A Sun Invisible, The Trouble Twisters. (The stories are related)

THE HORN OF TIME, New American Library P-3349, 1968. Contains: The Horn of Time the Hunter, A Man to My Wounding, The High Ones, The Man Who Came Early, Marius, Progress.

SEVEN CONQUESTS, Macmillan, 1969. Contains: *Foreword and commentaries,* Kings Who Die, Wildcat, Cold Victory, Inside Straight, Details, License, Strange Bedfellows.

BEYOND THE BEYOND, New American Library T-3947, 1969. Contains: Memory, Brake, Day of Burning, The Sensitive Man, The Moonrakers, Starfog.

TALES OF THE FLYING MOUNTAINS, Macmillan, 1970. Contains: *Prologue, epilogue, interludes, Nothing Succeeds Like Failure,* The Rogue, Say It with Flowers, *Ramble with a Gamblin' Man,* Que Donn'rez Vous?, Sunjammer, *Recruiting Nation.* (Published under author's own name. The stories are related)

III. NONFICTION BOOKS

THERMONUCLEAR WARFARE [A Choice of Tragedies], Monarch MS-15, 1963.
IS THERE LIFE ON OTHER WORLDS? [Life and the Start], Crowell-Collier, 1963. (Revised edition, Collier 06125, 1968)
THE INFINITE VOYAGE, Crowell-Collier, 1969.

IV. EDITED BOOKS (Both contain editorial introductions)

WEST BY ONE AND BY ONE, privately printed, 1965. (Includes the editor's In the Island of Uffa.)
NEBULA FOUR, Doubleday, 1969.

James Blish

Midsummer Century

by JAMES BLISH

1.

In all the ointment which the world had provided for the anointing of John Martels, D.Sc., F.R.A.S., etc., there was only one fly: there was something wrong with his telescope.

Martels, unmarried and 30, was both a statistic and a beneficiary of what his British compatriots were bitterly calling the brain-drain, the luring of the best English minds to the United States by higher pay, lower taxes, and the apparent absence of any class system whatsoever. And he had found no reason to regret it, let alone feel guilty about it. Both his parents were dead, and as far as he was concerned, he owed the United Kingdom nothing any more.

Of course, the advantages of living in the States were not quite so unclouded as they had been presented to him, but he had never expected anything else. Take the apparent absence of a class system, for instance: All the world knew that the blacks, the Spanish-Americans, and the poor in general were discriminated against ferociously in the States and that political opposition of any kind to the Establishment was becoming increasingly dangerous. But what counted as far as he was concerned was that it was not the same *sort* of class system.

Born of a working-class family in the indescribably ugly city of Doncaster, Martels had been cursed from the outset with a working-class Midlands dialect which excluded him from the "right" British circles as permanently and irrevocably as if he had been a smuggled Pakistani immigrant. No "public" school had been financially available to his parents to help him correct the horrible sound of his own voice, nor to give him the classical languages which in his youth had still been necessary for entry into Oxford or Cambridge.

Instead, he had ground, kicked, bitten and otherwise fought his way through one of the new redbrick polytechnics. Though he emerged at the end with the highest possible First in astrophysics, it was with an accent still so atrocious as to deny him admittance to any but the public side—never the lounge or saloon—of any bar in Britain.

In the States, on the other hand, accents were regarded as purely regional, and a man's education was judged not by his inflection but by his grammar, vocabulary, and the state of his knowledge. To be sure, Martels was disturbed by the condition of the Negro, the Spanish-Americans, and the poor; but since he was none of these things, he was not oppressed by it.

As for political activity, that was absolutely out for Martels; he was an alien here. Were he to so much as raise a placard, regardless of what was written on it, he could lose his passport.

The money situation had worked out in very much the same way. While there was a lot more of it available here than there was in England, in places like New York they took it away from you almost faster than you could make it; but Martels was not in New York. After a brief but moderately spectacular lectureship as a radio astronomer at Jodrell Bank, he had been hired as Director of Research in the field by a new but already sprawling university in the American midwest, where money went a good deal farther—and where, in addition, Negroes, Spanish-Americans, and the poor were in invisibly short supply. He could not quite put their plight out of his mind, but at least it was easier on the conscience to have it out of sight. The sailplaning here wasn't as good as it had been in the Childern Hills, but you can't have everything.

And there had been a final inducement: Sockette State had just completed construction of a radio telescope of a radically new design, a combination of mile-square dipole arrays and steerable dish with a peculiar, bowl-like glacial gouge in the landscape which made all its predecessors seem as primitive as the optical machine Galileo had filched from Hans Lippershey. The combination made it possible to mount a dish rather smaller than the one at Jodrell Bank and involved, instead, a wave-guide focal point almost as big, and as skeletal, as the tubular frame of a 65-inch optical reflecting telescope.

It took a startling amount of power to drive the thing—over and above the power necessary to steer it—but in theory at least, it ought to penetrate far enough around the universe to pick up the radio equivalent of the temperature at the back of Martel's own neck.

At first sight, he had been as pleased with it as a father who has just bought his son a new electric train. Just trying to imagine what great events might be recorded by such an instrument was splendid. It seemed to pose only one problem.

Thus far, it couldn't be made to pick up anything but the local rock-and-roll station.

There was nothing wrong with the theory, of that he was quite certain. The design was as sound as it could possibly be. So was the circuitry; he had tested that out repeatedly and intensively. The only other possibility was a flaw in the gross construction of the telescope, probably something so simple as a girder out of true in the wave guide which would distort either the field or the transmission.

Well, there was at least one thing to be said for a redbrick university: it did nothing for either your Greek or your English, but it insisted that its physical scientists also be passable engineers before it let you graduate. Warming up the amplifier, tuning it, and cranking the gain up all the way—a setting which should have effectively relocated the campus of Sockette State in the heart of Ursa Major No. 2, a cluster of galaxies half a billion light-years away—he crossed the parabolic aluminum basketwork of the steerable antenna and scrambled up the wave guide, field strength detector in hand; awkwardly, it was too big to be put into a pocket.

Gaining the lip of the wave guide, he sat down for a rest, feet dangling, peering down the inside of the tube. The program now was to climb down into there slowly in a tight spiral, calling out the field intensity readings at intervals to the technicians on the floor.

Redbrick polytechnics insist that their physical scientists also be engineers, but they neglect to turn them into steeplejacks as well. Martels was not even wearing a hard hat. Settling one sneakered foot into what appeared to be a perfectly secure angle between one girder and another, he slipped and fell headlong down the inside of the tube.

He did not even have time to scream, let alone to hear the shouts of alarm from the technicians, for he lost consciousness long before he hit bottom.

In fact, he never hit bottom at all.

It would be possible to explain exactly and comprehensively what happened to John Martels instead, but to do so would require several pages of expressions in the metalanguage invented by Dr. Thor Wald, a Swedish theoretical physicist, who unfortunately was not scheduled to be born until the year 2060. Suffice it to say that, thanks to the shoddy workmanship of an unknown welder, Sockette State's radical new radio telescope did indeed have an unprecedented reach —but not in any direction that its designers had intended, or could even have conceived.

2.

"Ennoble me with the honor of your attention, immortal Qvant."

Swimming upward from blackness, Martels tried to open his eyes and found that he could not. Nevertheless, in a moment he realized that he could see. What he saw was so totally strange to him that he tried to close them again, and found he could not do that, either. He seemed, in fact, completely paralyzed; he could not even change his field of view.

He wondered briefly if the fall had broken his neck. But that shouldn't affect his control of his eye muscles, should it? Or of his eyelids?

Besides, he was not in a hospital; of that much, at least, he could be sure. What was visible to him was a vast, dim hall in bad repair. There seemed to be sunlight coming from overhead, but whatever there was up there that was admitting it was not letting much through.

He had a feeling that the place ought to be musty, but he seemed to have no sense of smell left. The voice he had heard, plus a number of small, unidentifiable echoes, told him that he could still hear, at least. He tried to open his mouth, again without result.

There seemed to be nothing for it but to take in what little was visible and audible, and try to make as much sense as possible of whatever facts that brought him. What was he sitting or lying upon? Was it warm or cool? No, those senses were gone too. But at least he did not seem to be in any pain—though whether that meant that that sense was gone too, or that he was either drugged or repaired, couldn't be guessed. Nor was he hungry or thirsty—again an ambiguous finding.

About the floor of the hall within his cone of vision was a scatter of surpassingly strange artifacts. The fact that they were at various distances enabled him to establish that he could at least still change his depth of focus. Some of the objects seemed to be more decayed than the hall itself. In a number of instances the state, if any, of decay was impossible to judge, because the things seemed to be sculptures or some other kind of works of art, representing he knew not what—if anything, for representational art had been out of fashion all his life, anyhow. Others, however, were plainly machines; and though in no case could he even guess their intended functions, he knew corrosion when he saw it. This stuff had been out of use a long, long time.

Something was still functioning, though. He could hear the faintest of continuous hums, like a 50-cycle line noise. It seemed to come from somewhere behind him, intimately close, as though some spectral barber were applying to the back of his skull or neck a massaging device intended for the head of a gnat.

He did not think that the place, or at least the chamber of it that he seemed to be in, was exceptionally large. If the wall that was visible to him was a side rather than an end—which of course he had no way of determining—and the remembered echoes of the voice were not misleading, then it could not be much bigger than one of the central galleries in the Alte Pinakothek, say the Rubens room—

The comparison clicked neatly into place. He was in a museum of some sort. And one both without maintenance and completely unpopular, too, for the floor was thick with dust, and there were only a few footprints in that, and in some cases none at all, near the exhibits (if that was what they were). The footprints, he registered without understanding, were all those of bare feet.

Then, there came that voice again, this time with rather a whining edge to it. It said:

"Immortal Qvant, advise me, I humbly pray."

And with a triple shock, he heard himself replying:

"You may obtrude yourself upon my attention, tribesman."

The shock was triple because, first of all, he had had no intention or sensation of either formulating the reply or of uttering it. Second, the voice in which it came out was most certainly not his own; it was deeper, and unnaturally loud, yet seemed to be almost without resonance. Third, the language was one he had never heard before in his life, yet he seemed to understand it perfectly.

*Besides, my name is not and has never been Qvant. I don't even
have a middle initial.*

But he was given no time to speculate, for there now sidled into
sight, in a sort of cringing crouch which Martels found somehow
offensive, something vaguely definable as a human being. He was
naked and dark brown, with what Martels judged to be a mixture of
heredity and a deep tan. The nakedness also showed him to be
scrupulously clean, his arms short, his legs long, his pelvis narrow.
His hair was black and crinkled like a Negro's, but his features were
Caucasoid, except for an Asian eyelid-fold, rather reminding Martels
of an African bushman—an impression strengthened by his small
stature. His expression, unlike his posture, was respectful, almost
reverent, but not at all frightened.

"What would you have of me now, tribesman?" Martels' new
voice said.

"Immortal Qvant, I seek a ritual for the protection of our maturity
ceremonies from the Birds. They have penetrated the old one, for this
year many of our new young men lost their eyes to them, and some
even their lives. My ancestors tell me that such a ritual was known in
rebirth three, and is better than ours, but they cannot give me the
details."

"Yes, it exists," Martels' other voice said. "And it will serve you
perhaps two to five years. But in the end, the Birds will penetrate
this too. In the end, you will be forced to abandon the ceremonies."

"To do this would also be to surrender the afterlife!"

"That is doubtless true, but would this necessarily be a great surrender? You need your young men here and now, to hunt, procreate,
and fight the Birds. I am barred from any knowledge of the afterlife,
but what gives you any assurance that it is pleasant? What satisfac-
tions can remain for all those crowded souls?"

In some indefinable way, Martels could tell from Qvant's usage
that "Birds" was capitalized; he had caught no hint of this in the
speech of the petitioner, whose expression had now changed to one
of subdued horror. He noticed also that Qvant spoke to the pre-
sumable savage as anyone would address an educational equal and
that the naked man spoke in the same way. But of what use was the
information? For that matter, what was Martels, presumably a man
miraculously recovering from a major accident, doing in a moldering
museum, helplessly eavesdropping upon an insane conversation with

a naked "tribesman" who asked *queastiones* like a medieval student addressing St. Thomas Aquinas?

"I do not know, immortal Qvant," the petitioner was saying. "But without the ceremonies, we shall have no new generations of ancestors, and memory in the afterlife fades rapidly. Who in the end should we have left to advise us but yourself?"

"Who indeed?"

From the faint tone of irony in his voice, Qvant had probably intended the question to be rhetorical, but in any case Martels had had enough. Mustering every dyne of will power he could manage to summon, he strove to say:

"Will somebody kindly tell me what the hell is going on here?"

It came out, and in his own voice, though without any physical sensation of speaking. And in that same unknown language, too.

There was a moment of complete silence after the echoes died, during which Martels felt a sensation of shock which he was sure was not his own. Then the petitioner gasped and ran.

This time, Martels' eyes tracked, though not of his own volition, following the fleeing man until he had vanished through a low, groined, sunlit doorway beyond which was what appeared to be a dense green forest or jungle. His guess at the size and shape of the hall was thus confirmed, and he now knew also that it was at ground level. Then his eyes returned to their stony and boring regard of the facing wall and the neglected, meaningless artifacts.

"Who are you?" the Qvant-voice said. "And how have you invaded my brain?"

"*Your* brain?"

"This is my brain, and I am its rightful occupant—the precious personality of a master spirit, embalmed and treasured up on purpose to a life beyond life. I have been thus encased and maintained since the end of Rebirth Three, of which era what you see is the museum. The men of Rebirth Four regard me as a quasi-god, and they do well to do so." The menace in that last sentence was unmistakable. "I repeat, who are you, and how have you come here?"

"My name is John Martels, and I haven't the faintest idea how I got here. And nothing I've seen or heard makes the faintest sense to me. I was within a couple of seconds of certain death, and then suddenly, here I was. That's all I know."

"I caution you to tell the truth," Qvant said heavily. "Else I shall dispossess you, and then you will die within two or three seconds—or go on to the afterlife, which amounts to the same thing."

Martels felt an instant flash of caution. Despite the fact that the two of them seemed to share the same brain, this creature evidently could not read Martels' mind, and there might well be some advantage to be gained in withholding some of what little information he had. He had, after all, no guarantee that Qvant would not "dispossess" him anyhow, once the "quasi-god's" curiosity was satisfied. Martels said, with a desperation more than half real:

"I don't know what it is you want to know."

"How long have you been lurking here?"

"I don't know."

"What is your earliest memory?"

"Of staring at that wall."

"For how long?" Qvant said implacably.

"I don't know. I didn't think to count the days. Nothing ever seemed to happen, until your petitioner spoke."

"And what did you hear of my thoughts during that time?"

"Nothing I could understand," Martels said, being extremely careful not to hesitate after "nothing." Strange as it was to find himself apparently talking to himself like a split personality, it was stranger still to realize that neither psyche could read the mind of the other —and, somehow, immensely important that Qvant's opposite assumption should not be brought into question.

"That is not surprising. Yet I sense an anomaly in yours. You have the mind of a young man, but there is an aura about it which paradoxically suggests that it is even older than mine. To which Rebirth do you belong?"

"I'm sorry, but the question is completely meaningless to me."

"In what year were you born, then?" Qvant said, with obvious surprise.

"Nineteen fifty-five."

"By what style of dating?"

"Style? I don't understand that either. We called it A.D., *anno Domini,* after the birth of Christ. Insofar as anybody could be sure, He was born about seventeen thousand years after the human race invented written records."

There was quite a long silence after this. Martels wondered what Qvant was thinking. For that matter, he wondered what he himself was thinking; whatever it was, it was nothing useful. He was an alien personality in someone else's brain, and that someone else was talking nonsense to him—someone whose prisoner he was, and who also seemed to be a prisoner, though at the same time he claimed to be a sort of god, and Martels had seen him being consulted as one—

"I see," Qvant said suddenly. "Without the central computer I cannot be accurate, but precision seems hardly necessary here. By your system, the present year is roughly Twenty-Five Thousand A.D."

This last shock Martels could not take. His insecurely re-embodied mind, still aquiver with the sick edginess of its escape from death, bombarded with meaningless facts, now under a new threat of death whose very nature he could not begin to comprehend, went reeling back toward the pit.

And at the same instant, it was assaulted with cold, wordless ferocity. Qvant *was* going to throw him out.

Never before had he even dreamed it possible that a man could be thrown out of his own mind by someone else—and this was not even his own mind; here, he was the interloper. There seemed to be no way to resist, nothing that he could even grab hold of—even had he been inhabiting his own brain, he would have known no better than any other man of his time in what part of it his psyche resided. Qvant knew, that was evident, and was homing upon it with the mercilessness of a guided missile; and the terrible, ousting pressure was entirely emotional, without the faintest semantic cue which might have helped Martels to fight back.

The rotting hall wavered and vanished. Once more, Martels was without sight, and without hearing. By instinct alone, he dug into . . . something . . . and held hard, like a crab-louse resisting being shaken off the hide of a jackal.

The terrible battering went on and on. There was in the end nothing to cling to at all but a thought, one single thought:

I am I. I am I. I am I.

And then, slowly, miraculously, the attack began to subside. As before, sound returned first, the faint ambiguous echoes of the museum; and then, sight, the sight of that same stretch of wall and floor, and those same lumpy monuments to and momentos of some far past in Martels' even farther future.

"It appears that I cannot be rid of you yet," Qvant said. The tone of his amplified voice seemed to hover somewhere between icy fury and equally icy amusement. "Very well, we shall hold converse, you and I. It will be a change from being an oracle to tribesmen. But sooner or later, Martels-from-the-past, sooner or later I shall catch you out—and then you will come to know the greatest thing that I do not know: What the afterlife is like. Sooner or later, Martels . . . sooner or later . . ."

Just in time, Martels realized that the repetitions were the hypnotic prelude to a new attack. Digging into whatever it had been that he had saved himself with before, that unknown substrate of the part of this joint mind that belonged to him alone, he said with equal iciness:

"Perhaps. You have a lot to teach me, if you will, and I'll listen. And maybe I can teach you something, too. But I think I can also make you extremely uncomfortable, Qvant; you've just shown me two different ways to go about that. So perhaps you had better mind your manners, and bear in mind that however the tribesmen see you, you're a long way from being a god to me."

For answer, Qvant simply prevented Martels from saying another word. Slowly, the sun set, and the shapes in the hall squatted down into a darkness against which Martels was not even allowed to close his unowned eyes.

3.

Martels was alive, still, which was something to be grateful for, but it was hardly a famous victory. Qvant could not throw him out—as yet—but Martels still had no control over his eyes, or their eyes, except the minimum one of changing depth of focus; and it seemed either that Qvant himself could not close the eyes, or never bothered to. Always, except when the rare petitioner came into the museum, they stared at that same damn wall and the blobby things in front of it.

Furthermore, Qvant never slept, and therefore, neither did Martels. Whatever mechanism kept the brain going in its unviewable case, it seemed to make sleep unnecessary, which was perhaps fortunate, since Martels had no confidence in his ability to resist another of Qvant's attacks were he unconscious at the time.

This was just one of many aspects of their joint existence which

Martels did not understand. Obviously, some sort of perfusion pump —that persistent tiny hum at the back of his head, like a sort of tinnitus—could continuously supply oxygen and blood sugar, carry away lactic acid, abolish fatigue. But it was Martels' cloudy memory that there was more to sleep than that: dreams, for instance, were essential to clear the computer-analog that was the brain of the previous day's programs. Perhaps mere evolution had bred that need out of the race, although 25,000 years seemed like a prohibitively short time for so major a change.

Whatever the answer, it could not prevent boredom, to which Qvant seemed to be entirely immune. Evidently he had vast inner resources, accumulated over centuries, with which to amuse himself through the endless days and nights; but to these, Martels had no access whatsoever. Martels concealed this fact as best he could, for it seemed increasingly important to him that Qvant's impression that Martels could overhear some of his thoughts should be encouraged; for all his obvious power and accumulated knowledge, Qvant did not seem to suspect the totality of the mind-brain barrier between them.

Nor would Qvant allow Martels to talk except when the two of them were alone, and mostly not even then. He seemed essentially incurious, or preoccupied, or both; and months went by between petitioners. Between the rare apparitions of the brown savages, the few new things Martels was able to learn were mostly negative and useless.

He was helpless, and that was most thoroughly that. Every so often, he found himself almost wishing that this mad nightmare should end with the shattering impact of his own unprotected head upon the center of the radio telescope dish, like that merciless story that Ambrose Bierce had written about an incident at Owl Creek Bridge.

But occasionally there were the petitioners, and during their visits Martels listened and learned, a little. Even more rarely, Qvant had sudden, abortive bursts of loquaciousness, which were rather more productive of information, though always frustrating in the end. During one of these, Martels found himself allowed to ask:

"What was that business with the first tribesman that I saw—the one who wanted a protective ritual? Were you really about to give him some kind of rigmarole?"

"I was, and it would not have been a rigmarole," Qvant said. "It would have been an entirely functional complex of diagrams and dances. He will come back for it in due course."

"But how could it possibly work?"

"Between any two events in the universe which are topologically identical there is a natural affinity or repulsion, which can be expressed in diagrammatic form. The relationship is dynamic, and therefore must be acted out; whether attraction or repulsion occurs depends entirely upon the actions. That is the function of the dances."

"But that's magic—sheer superstition!"

"On the contrary," Qvant said. "It is natural law, and was practiced successfully for many centuries before the principles behind it were formulated. The tribesmen understand this very well, although they would not describe it in the same terms I have. It is simply a working part of their lives. Do you think they would continue to consult me if they found that the advice that I gave them did not work? They are uncivilized, but they are not insane."

And, upon another such occasion:

"You seem to accept the tribesmen's belief that there is really a life after death. Why?"

"I accept it on the evidence; the tribesmen communicate regularly and reliably with their recent ancestors. I have no personal experience in this field whatsoever, but there is also a sound theoretical basis for it."

"And what's that?" Martels said.

"The same principle which allows both of us to inhabit the same brain. The personality is a semistable electromagnetic field; to remain integrated, it requires the supplementary computing apparatus of a brain, as well as an energy source such as a body, or this case we live in, to keep it in its characteristic state of negative entropy. Once the field is set free by death, it loses all ability to compute and becomes subject to normal entropy losses. Hence, slowly but inevitably, it fades."

"Still, why have you had no personal experience of it? I should have thought that originally—"

"The discovery," Qvant said, in a voice suddenly remote, "is relatively recent. No such communication is possible except along the direct ancestral line, and my donors—whoever they were—had dissipated centuries before the mere possibility was known."

"Just exactly how old are you, anyhow?" Martels said. But Qvant would say no more.

That conversation, however, did give Martels a little further insight into the characters of the tribesmen, and together with some other bits and scraps of evidence, a vague picture of history as well. Various references to "Rebirths" had enabled him to guess that civilization had been destroyed and rebuilt four times since his own period, but had emerged each time much changed, and each time less viable. Rebirth II had apparently been snuffed out by a worldwide glaciation; inevitably, Rebirth III had taken the form of a tightly organized, high-energy culture upon a small population base.

Now, however, the whole Earth, except for the Poles, was at the height of a tropical phase. Some of the technological knowledge of Rebirth III was still here in the museum in which Martels was doubly imprisoned, a fraction of it still intact and a rather larger fraction not too far decayed to be unrecoverable by close study. But the tribesmen of Rebirth IV had no use for it. Not only did they no longer understand it, but they thought it not worth understanding or salvaging. The fact that food was to be had for the picking or hunting with relative ease made machinery unnecessary to them—and their legends of what Rebirth III had been like made machinery repugnant to them as well. Their placid, deep-jungle kind of economy suited them very well.

But there was more to it than that. Their outlook had undergone a racial change which could only be attributed to the discovery of the real existence of the ghosts of their ancestors. It had become mystical, ritualistic, and, in a deep sense, ascetic—that is, they were death-oriented, or afterlife-oriented. This explained, too, the ambiguity of their attitude toward Qvant. They respected, indeed were awed by, the depth of his knowledge, and called upon it occasionally for solutions to problems which were beyond their understanding—so far beyond as to override their fierce sense of individuality; yet worshiping him was out of the question. Toward an entity which had no rapport with its ancestors, had never ever once experienced such a rapport, and seemed destined never to have an afterlife of its own, they could feel only pity.

Doubtless it occasionally occurred to a few of them that even the apparently indestructible brain-case could not be immune to something really major in the way of disasters, such as the birth of a volcano immediately under the museum itself; but Qvant had been there, insofar as their own legends could attest, forever already; and their own lives were short. The death of Qvant was not in the short-term future of which they were accustomed to think.

Most of Qvant's conversation, however, was far less revealing. He seemed to be almost permanently in a kind of Zen state, conscious of mastery and at the same time contemptuous of it. Many of his answers to petitioners consisted only of abrupt single sentences which seemed to have no connection whatsoever with the question that had been asked. Occasionally, too, he would respond with a sort of parable which was not one whit more comprehensible for being longer. For example:

"Immortal Qvant, some of our ancestors now tell us that we should clear some of the jungle and begin to sow. Others tell us to remain content with reaping. How should we resolve this conflict?"

"When Qvant was a man, twelve students gathered upon a cliffside to hear him speak. He asked of them what they would have him say that they could not hear from their own mouths. All replied at once, so that no single reply could be heard. Qvant said: 'You have too many heads for one body,' and pushed eleven of them over the cliff."

Humiliatingly for Martels, in such situations the tribesmen always seemed to understand at once whatever it was Qvant was conveying, and to go away satisfied with it. On that particular occasion, though, Martels had managed to come up with an inspired guess:

"Obviously, agriculture can't be revived under these conditions."

"No," Qvant said. "But to what particular conditions do you refer?"

"None. I don't know anything about them. In fact, agriculture amidst jungle ecologies was quite common in my time. I could just somehow sense that that was what you meant."

Qvant said nothing further, but Martels could indeed feel, although dimly, his disturbance. Another phantom brick had been laid upon the edifice of Qvant's belief that he had less than total privacy from Martels.

Of course Qvant had deduced almost immediately from the nature and phraseology of most of Martels' questions that Martels had been some infinitely primitive equivalent of a scientist, and furthermore that Martels' eavesdropping did not go deep enough to penetrate to

Qvant's own store of scientific knowledge. Sometimes, Qvant seemed to take a perverse pleasure in answering Martels' questions in this area with apparent candor and at the same time in the most useless possible terms:

"Qvant, you keep saying you will never die. Barring accidents, of course. But surely the energy source for this brain-case apparatus must have a half-life, no matter how long it is, and the output will fall below the minimum necessary level *some* day."

"The source is not radioactive and has no half-life. It comes from the Void, the origin—in terms of spherical trigonometry—of inner space."

"I don't understand the terms. Or do you mean that it taps continuous creation? Has that been proven to go on?"

This term was in turn unfamiliar to Qvant, and for once he was curious enough to listen to Martels' explanation of the "steady state" theory of Fred Hoyle.

"No, that is nonsense," Qvant said at the end. "Creation is both unique and cyclical. The origin of inner space is elsewhere, and not explicable except in terms of general juganity—the psychology of the wavicle."

"*The* wavicle? There's only one?"

"Only one, though it has a thousand aspects."

"And it thinks?" Martels said in astonishment.

"No, it does not think. But it has will, and behaves accordingly. Understand its will, and you are the master of its behavior."

"But how does one tap this power, then?"

"By meditation, initially. Thereafter, it cannot be lost."

"No, I mean how does the machine—"

Silence.

Martels was learning, but nothing he learned seemed to get him anywhere. Then, one year, a petitioner asked another question about the Birds; and when in all innocence Martels asked afterwards, "What are these Birds, anyhow?" the levin-stroke of hatred and despair which stabbed out of Qvant's mind into his own told him in an instant that he had at long last happened upon something absolutely crucial—

If only he could figure out how to use it.

4.

So obvious was the depth of Qvant's emotions, into which were mixed still others to which Martels could put no name, that Martels expected no reply at all. But after a pause not much more than twice as long as usual, Qvant said:

"The Birds are humanity's doom—and mine and yours too, eventually, my uninvited and unwelcome guest. Did you think evolution had stood still during more than twenty-three thousand years—even without considering the peak in world-wide circumambient radio-activity which preceded Rebirth One?"

"No, of course not, Qvant. The tribesmen are obviously a genetic mixture that was unknown in my time, and naturally I assumed that there have been mutations, as well."

"You see nothing but surfaces," Qvant said with steely contempt. "They show many marks of evolutionary advance and change which are beyond your observation. For a single, simple-minded example, at the beginning of Rebirth Four, when the jungle became nearly world-wide, man was still an animal who had to practice the principles of nutrition consciously, and the tribesmen of that time did not have the knowledge. As a result, no matter how much they ate—and there was never any shortage even then, not even of protein—they died in droves of a typical disease of jungle populations whose name would mean nothing to you, but which might be described as 'malignant malnutrition'."

"That was well known in my time, and not only in jungle populations. We called it marasmus, but there were lots of local names: kwashiorkor, sukha—"

"None of these words, of course, have survived. In any event, shortly thereafter there occurred a major mutation which made proper nutrition a hereditary instinct—as it has always been with wild animals, and presumably was when man was a wild animal. Probably it was domesticated out.

"Another change, equally radical and perhaps not dissimilar in origin, occurred after the formulation of general juganity toward the very end of Rebirth Three. It was then found that the human brain had considerable hypnotic and projective power usable without the intervention of any prehypnotic ritual whatsoever. The theory showed how this could be done reliably, but the power had been perhaps always latent, or it may have been the result of a mutation—nobody is sure, nor does the question seem to be of any interest now.

"In me, these powers are massive—because I was specially bred to heighten them, among many others—but their action among the tribesmen is quite the opposite, in that their rapport with their ancestors makes them peculiarly *susceptible* to such hypnosis rather than good practitioners of it. They have become patients rather than agents.

"The animals, too, have changed—and in particular, the birds. Birds were always elaborate ritualists, and in the aura of pervasive ceremony and juganity characteristic of Rebirth Four, they have evolved dangerously. They are now sophonts—sentient, intelligent, self-conscious—and have an elaborate postprimitive culture. They properly regard man as their principal rival, and their chief aim is to exterminate him.

"In this they will succeed. Their chief drive is toward survival in the here-and-now; the tribesmen, on the other hand, are increasingly too interested in death itself as a goal to make effective antagonists for them, regardless of the fact that they are still man's intellectual inferiors by at least one order of magnitude."

"I find that hard to believe," Martels said. "We had humans in that stage in my time, operating that kind of culture—the Eskimos, the Australian aborigines, the South African bushmen. None of them were as aggressive as you imply that the Birds are, but even had they been, they never would have had a chance against the pragmatic intellectuals of the period. In fact, when I left, they were on the verge of extinction."

"The modern tribesman is neither intellectual or pragmatic," Qvant said scornfully. "He will not use machines, except for simple hunting weapons; his only major defenses are ritual and juganity, at which the Birds are instinctively expert, and becoming more so all the time. When they become also intellectually expert, the end will be at hand.

"And so will ours. I have detailed reasons, both theoretical and technical, to believe that once the human population falls below a certain level, the power which supports this brain-case of ours will begin to fail, and thereafter, the case itself will fall apart. Even if it does not, the Birds, if they win—as they are certain to—will have millennia to wait for it to fall apart by itself, which is not impossible.

Then they will pick the brain to pieces, and good-by to both of us."

In Qvant's voice there seemed to be a certain gloomy but savage satisfaction in the thought. Martels said cautiously:

"But why? You represent no threat to them whatsoever that I can see. Even the tribesmen consult you very seldom, and never about effective weapons. Why should the Birds not ignore you altogether?"

"Because," Qvant said slowly, "they are symbolists . . . and they hate and dread me above all other entities in the universe as a prime symbol of past human power."

"How can that be?"

"How have you failed to guess that? I was the reigning Supreme Autarch at the end of Rebirth Three, bred to the task and charged with the preservation of everything that Rebirth Three had learned, whatever happened. Without access to the computer, I am incapable of discharging that entire duty . . . but it is nevertheless to that charge that I owe my present immortal imprisonment. And my doom—and yours—beneath the beaks of the Birds."

"Can't you prevent this? For instance, by hypnotizing the tribesmen into some sort of positive action against the Birds? Or is your control too limited?"

"I could exercise absolute control of a tribesman if I so desired," Qvant said. "I shall put the next one through some paces to dispel your doubts about this. But the tribesmen who come to consult me are far from being the major figures in the culture of Rebirth Four, and even were they great heroes and leaders—which do not even exist in this culture—I could not change the cultural set, no matter what changes I made in the ways individual men think. The times are what they are; and the end is nigh."

"How long before the end?"

"Five years, perhaps; certainly no more."

Suddenly, Martels felt a fury of his own. "You make me ashamed to be a human being at all," he snarled, perforce in Qvant's voice. "Back in my time, people fought back! Now, here are your tribesmen, presumably intelligent and yet refusing to use the most obvious measures to protect themselves! And here are you, obviously the most intelligent and resourceful human mind in all of human history, able to take command of and help all the others, passively awaiting being picked to pieces by nothing but a flock of birds!"

As Martels' passion mounted, he was abruptly possessed by an image from his early youth. He had found a fallen robin chick in the scrawny back garden of the Doncaster house, thrown out of the nest before it was quite able to fly, and obviously injured—probably by one of the many starving cats of the neighborhood. Hoping to help it, he had picked it up, but it had died in his hands—and when he had put it down again, his hands were crawling with tiny black mites, like thousands of moving specks of black pepper. And it was to be *birds* that would supplant man? Bloody never, by God!

"You have no knowledge whatever of what it is you are talking about," Qvant said in his remotest voice. "Be silent now."

Thanks to the deception, Martels knew the depths of his own ignorance better even than Qvant did. But unlike Qvant, passivity was not in his nature; he had been fighting against circumstances all his life long, and was not about to stop now. Qvant was immensely his superior, in every imaginable way, but he would no more accede to Qvant's doom than he had to any past one.

Not that he said so, even had Qvant let him speak any further. What he wanted, chiefly, was not only to get the hell out of Qvant's brain—which Qvant obviously also would welcome—but back to his home century; and only in human techniques were there any hints of possible help in this direction. That malfunctioning perisher of a radio telescope had sent him up here, and that had been a human artifact; surely, by now, there must be some simpler way of reversing the effect.

Qvant had proven himself incapable of ridding himself of Martels simply as a nuisance in the present era, let alone of sending Martels back; and even did he know of such a way, it was bound to be more complicated than the simple exercise of throwing Martels out into the sad, dimming domain of the afterlife—an exercise which Qvant had tried, and failed to manage.

No, more human help was urgently necessary, and it would have to be sought from the tribesmen. They were, it was clear, scientifically innocent, but they were certainly preferable to the Birds, and besides, they had resources that Qvant did not. Most of these resources—such as their contact with their ancestors—were mysterious and problematical, but by the same token, they were outside Qvant's vast field of knowledge, and just *might* be applicable to the main problem.

And they were not savages. Martels had already realized that much

from the few petitioners that he had seen. If these tribesmen were not
the best samples of the men of Rebirth IV, what might the best
be like? It was essential to find out, regardless of Qvant's opinion in
the matter. Qvant had never seen them in their own environment;
all his knowledge of their customs, behavior and capabilities had
come from testimony, which is notoriously unreliable at its best, from
a sampling which he himself thought unrepresentative, and from
deduction. Nor did Qvant belong to this Rebirth himself; he might
well be inherently incapable of understanding it.

Moreover, from his perspective, which was based upon the dim
past, Martels thought he saw things in the petitioners which Qvant
was incapable of seeing. Their intellects were still operative, upon a
level which was beneath Qvant's notice; but to Martels, it could be
highly significant for himself. Even a brown man who struck him
initially as the veriest savage at one instant sometimes showed in the
next some almost supernatural talent, or at the very least some frag-
ment of knowledge which seemed to represent command of some
entire field of science Martels' contemporaries had not even known
existed. These things might be used. They *had* to be used.

But how? Suppose Martels were wholly in charge of the brain
which went under the name of Qvant; how could he ask enough questions of the petitioners to find out anything he needed to know without arousing instant suspicion? After all, the petitioners were used to
having the questions flow the other way. And even if he managed to
do that, to in fact even masquerade successfully as Qvant himself,
what could he tell the tribesmen that might provoke some action
against the Birds, let alone advising them how to go about it?

At the best, he would only provoke bafflement and withdrawal.
What he really needed to do was to get out of here and into the
world, in some sort of a body, but that was plainly out of the question.
His only option was to try to figure out some way of changing an age,
and then hope that the age would find some way to rescue him.

Put that way, the whole project looked impossibly stupid. But what
other way was there to put it?

Necessarily, he went on as before, biding his time, listening, asking
questions of Qvant when permitted, and occasionally getting answers.
Sometimes, he got a new fact which made sense to him; mostly, not.
And he began to feel, too, that the sleeplessness and the deprivation
of all his senses but sight and hearing were more and more eroding

his reason, despite the dubious and precarious access of his personality to the massive reasoning facilities of the Qvant brain. Even those facilities were somehow limited in a way he could not understand: Qvant had now several times mentioned having been deprived of a connection with a computer which would have enabled him to have performed even better. Was the computer in the museum, and Qvant's divorce from it simply a matter of a snapped input line which Qvant was unable to repair? Or did it lie far in the past, at the end of Rebirth III? Martels asked; but Qvant would not answer.

And in the meantime, for most of the time, Martels had to stare at the same spot on the far wall and listen to the same meaningless echoes.

The midsummer century wore on. A year went by. The petitioners became fewer and fewer. Even Qvant seemed to be suffering some kind of erosion, despite his interior resources: Into, indeed, some sort of somnambulistic reverie which was quite different from his previous state of constant interior speculation. Martels could no more overhear Qvant's thoughts than before, but their *tone* had changed; at the beginning, there had been an impression of leisurely, indeed almost sybaritic, but constant meditation and speculation, but now all that came through was a sort of drone, like a dull and repetitive dream which could not be gotten beyond a certain point, and from which it was impossible to awaken.

Martels had had such dreams himself; he had come to recognize them as a signal that he was on the verge of waking up, probably later in the day than he had wanted to; they were the mental equivalent of an almost self-awakening snore. Qvant, instead, seemed to be sinking deeper and deeper into them, which deprived the always-awake Martels even of Qvant's enigmatic conversation.

It had been a dull life to begin with, up here in 25,000 A.D. The boredom which had now set in with it was reaching depths which Martels had never imagined possible, and it looked like there was worse to come. He did not realize how much worse it was going to be until the day came when a tribesman came to petition Qvant—and Qvant did not answer, or even seem to notice.

Martels failed to seize the opportunity. He was entirely out of the habit of thinking fast. But when, perhaps six months later, the next petitioner appeared—halfway through the five years Qvant had predicted would end with the triumph of the Birds—Martels was ready:

"Immortal Qvant, I pray the benison of your attention."

There was no answer from Qvant. The background drone of his repetitive daydream went on. Martels said softly: "You may obtrude yourself upon my attention."

Qvant still failed to interfere. The tribesman sidled into view.

"Immortal Qvant, I am Amra, of the tribe of Owlshield. After many generations, the volcano to the west of our territory is again showing signs of stirring in its sleep. Will it awaken to full anger? And if it does, what shall we do?"

Whatever Qvant might know about the geology of the area from which Amra had come, it was, as usual, inaccessible to Martels. All the same, it seemed only the simplest common sense not to hang around any long-quiescent volcano that was showing new signs of activity, whatever the specifics. He said:

"It will erupt in due course. I cannot predict how violent the first outbreak will be, but it would be well to change territories with all possible speed."

"Immortal Qvant perhaps has not heard recently of the situation of our poor tribe. We cannot migrate. Can you not give us some rite of propitiation?"

"It is impossible to propitiate a volcano," Martels said, though with rather less inner conviction than he would once have felt. "It is also true that I have received little news from your area for long and long. Explain why you cannot move."

He thought that he was beginning to capture Qvant's style of speech pretty well, and indeed the tribesman showed no sign of suspicion as yet. Amra said patiently:

"To the north is the territory of the tribe of Zhar-Pitzha, through which I passed on my way to your temple. Naturally, we cannot obtrude ourselves upon that. To the south is the eternal ice, and the devils of Terminus. And to the east, of course, there are always and always the Birds."

This, suddenly, was the very opportunity Martels had been waiting for. "Then, tribesman Amra, you must make alliance with the tribe of Zhar-Pitzha, and with weapons which I shall give you, make war upon the Birds!"

Amra's face was a study in consternation, but gradually his expression hardened into unreadability. He said:

"It pleases immortal Qvant to mock us in our desperation. We shall not return."

Amra bowed stiffly, and vanished from the unvarying field of view. When the echoes of his going had died completely in the hall, Martels found that Qvant—how long had he been listening?—had taken over control of the voice box, with a distant, cold and deadly laugh.

But all that the once-Supreme Autarch of Rebirth III actually said was:

"You see?"

Martels was grimly afraid that he did.

5.

Nevertheless, Martels had picked up something else that was new, and now that Qvant was paying attention again—for however long that would last—Martels might as well try to pump him about it. He said:

"I thought it was worth trying. I was trained never to take any statement as a fact until I had tested it myself."

"And so was I. But that exacts no sympathy from me. These petitioners are my last contact with the human race—except for you, and you are worse than an anachronism, you are a living fossil—and I shall not allow you to frighten one of them away from me again."

"Compliments received, and I didn't think you would," Martels said. "I'm sorry myself that I scared him off. But I'm curious about some of the questions. From his references to the volcano and to 'the eternal ice,' I gather that his tribe is on the edge of Antarctica, in an area we used to call the Land of Fire."

"Quite correct."

"But what did he mean by 'the devils of Terminus'?"

"There is a small colony of men living in the south Polar mountains," Qvant said, with something very like hatred in his voice. "They are, or should still be, survivors of Rebirth Three, who were supposed to maintain a small, closed high-energy economy to power, tend and guard the computer which was designed to supplement my function. The tribesmen in the area call them devils because they rigidly bar entry from all the rest of the world, as they were instructed to do. But as I have told you, I no longer have access to that computer; and whether it is because the men of Terminus have degenerated and allowed it to break down, or whether they have deliberately cut me off from it, I have no way of telling."

So the jungle culture and the crumbling museum were not the end of the story after all! "Why don't you find out?" Martels demanded.

"How would you propose that I do that?"

"By taking control of the next petitioner, and marching him down there to take a look."

"One, because the route would take me through the country of the Birds. Two, because I cannot allow the brain to fall silent over the long period such a journey would take; by the time I returned—if I did—the petitioners would have abandoned me permanently."

"Rubbish," Martels said, giving the word a calculatedly sneering edge. "The loss of contact with that computer cripples you considerably, as you've told me over and over again. Getting back into contact with it had to be your first order of business, if it was at all possible. And if you could have done it, you would have. The present impasse suggests instead that you haven't got the hypnotic or projective powers to change the course of crawl of an insect, let alone a human being!"

Astonishingly, Qvant did not seem to lose his temper, rather to Martel's disappointment.

"In fact I do not," he said, even more astonishingly, "if by 'me' you mean the rather fragile jugomagnetic field which is my personality, ego, psyche, call it what you will. If that were not the case, instances of newly dead souls instantly seizing possession of another living body would be commonplace. Instead, there are only scattered, unconfirmable rumors of a few such possessions. These powers are a function of the brain, of the organ itself—and pre-eminently, of this brain. A physical substrate and an energy source are both required to use them.

"As I promised, I shall demonstrate them at the next opportunity, not because allaying your doubts interests me in the slightest, but only to abate the nuisance of your clumsy attempts at experiment. *How* to use them I certainly shall not show you. Now, silence."

Silence perforce descended; but Qvant had already been loquacious enough, and that had not been the first occasion when Martels had been grateful for it. Perhaps Qvant, too, did occasionally feel the pressure of loneliness or boredom, after all. Or perhaps it was just that, not being limited by the necessity to breathe, nothing prevented him from spinning out a sentence as long as he wished, and these immense periods went on to becoming speeches, without Qvant's really being aware of it.

And now Martels had a new program—to get through to Terminus, somehow. Surely even a remnant of Rebirth III, with energy and technology at its disposal, offered more help for his peculiar problem than could all the tribesmen of Rebirth IV.

Qvant's last remark had to be interpreted as meaning that Qvant already suspected Martels of having formulated exactly such a program, just to be on the safe side. No doubt Qvant would have refused to teach Martels how to use the hypnotic and projective powers anyhow, simply to prevent him from undertaking any further agitation among the tribesmen toward a campaign against the Birds; but Martels had also just finished announcing in the plainest possible terms that had he been Qvant, he would have tried to reach Terminus, an announcement an intellect far feebler than Qvant's could not fail to have registered as something to guard against. And as a one-time Autarch, he would know a great deal better than Martels that it never paid to underestimate one's opponent. Even back in Martels' own time, it was a fundamental assumption of games theory that the enemy's most probable next move was also likely to be the best one.

Against this Martels had no recourse but his ability to mask his own thoughts from his brain-mate, and lay his plans as best he could; to reshuffle his cards, rethink his position, plot alternate courses, and hope for still more new data. Seen in this light, for example, the positioning of the museum exhibits within his cone of vision took on new meaning: suddenly it had become important to assess their sizes and shapes, whether they were still mounted or had fallen over, whether they were intact or disjunct, and their exact distances from each other. The ones outside the cone didn't matter, except for the larger ones between the brain-case and the entrance to the hall, and these he mapped as precisely as possible from memory.

Beyond that, as always, he could only wait for the next petitioner, but this time he did not care how long that was delayed. The longer the interval, the more time he would have to consider every way in which his scheme might go wrong, how to deal with each possible failure-point, what other options he had if it failed completely all up and down the line, and finally, what his next moves were to be and his future might be like were it to succeed completely by first intention. Strategy and tactics had never been among his interests, but if there lay within him any latent talent for generalship at all, now was the time to develop it, with all deliberate speed.

As it happened, the next petitioner turned up only six months later —insofar as he could tell, for keeping a mental calendar of the invariable days was impossible, and in the seasonlessness of this midsummer century he was sure that he lost months as well. That, too, was just as well, for Martels had already reached the point where he had run out of alternatives and refinements, and was beginning to suspect that his major plot was starting to change from a plan of action into a wish-fulfillment daydream.

Qvant was instantly alert, not at all to Martels' surprise. There was the usual ritual salutation and response. Then, after the visitor had come into sight and identified himself as Tlam of the tribe of Hawk-burrow, the tribesman's eyes went glassy, he seemed to freeze solid, and not another word came from him. At the same time, Martels felt a curious lightness, a loss of pressure, almost a vacancy, as if Qvant were no longer present at all. Martels tried to speak, and found that he could.

"Qvant, are you doing that?"

"Yes," said the tribesman, in an eerie burlesque of Qvant's voice colored by his own. What was oddest about it, Martels found, was hearing Qvant speak without the usual blare of amplification. "Watch further."

The tribesman turned away and began to walk aimlessly among the monuments, occasionally making meaningless gestures before one or another of them. Martels found that he could also make his eyes track to follow. He said:

"Is he aware of what's going on?"

"No," the tribesman said, performing an absurdly solemn pirhouette. "I could make him aware, but I prefer not to alarm him. I shall return him to the same position from which he started, and when the episode is over, for him no time will have passed."

"I gather, then, that this is projection rather than hypnosis."

"Quite correct. Draw no hasty conclusions, however. You are powerless in any case, but should you make even the slightest attempt to take advantage of your present position, I should be back with you in the brain upon the instant—and thereafter will devote a sizable fraction of my attention to making you more miserable than you have ever been in your life."

Martels rather doubted that Qvant could much improve on the miseries of a Doncaster childhood, but he was more interested in noting that the statement and the threat contradicted each other. However, he made no comment. The wanderings of the possessed tribesman had already produced more footprints in the dust than had uncalculable decades of preceding visitors, and Martels was busily fitting them together with the tribesman's height and length of pace into the metrical frame of his map. It now seemed wholly unlikely that Qvant had any idea just how much new information he was providing by his somewhat vainglorious demonstration.

"Well," Martels said, "it doesn't look too different from effects of hypnosis well known in my time, except that there wasn't any preliminary routine. I would have thought that you were still in residence here, so to speak, and that the 'projection' consisted only of the use of some kind of line-of-sight microwave broadcast to override the poor fellow's own brain-waves."

"Quite possible, of course, but primitive and damaging," the tribesman said. "In a moment I shall show you the difference."

Qvant brought the tribesman back to exactly his original position. Without an instant's preparation or transition, Martels found himself looking at the brain-case from the outside.

As he had long suspected, it was transparent, and the brain inside it was as big as that of a dolphin; but he had spent many months preparing himself not to waste so much as a second in studying whatever it turned out to look like. Keeping his new body rigid and expressionless as if in shock, he changed the focus of his new eyes to seek out the tube, or tangle of tubes, which had to lead to the perfusion pump. It was there: One tube, and it looked heavily armored. Well, he had expected that, too.

Leaping one step back and three to the right, he swung up from the floor the club-like metal object he had long ago selected, and hurled it straight at the juncture of pipe and case.

The tribesman's jungle muscles, hunting aim, and speed of reflexes proved both true and far faster than anything Qvant could have anticipated. The heavy missile broke nothing, but a ghost of pain cried out in Martels' own mind at the impact.

Two leaps toward the entrance, another swooping grab at the floor, one leap back toward the case. As Martels swung the new and still heavier object high over his head, he felt Qvant's mind frantically trying to snatch his own back, but the new club—once probably a bus bar, rocker arm, limb of statuary, who knew what?—was already coming down with every dyne of force that Martels could demand from Tlam's arms and back. It hit the top edge of the brain-case with a noise like a pistol shot.

The case did not even scar, but all traces of Qvant's groping, powerful psyche blanked out. Tlam/Martels was already at a dead run toward the entrance—and Tlam proved to be able to run like a deer. Together they burst out into the glorious sunlight, and at once Martels relaxed all control. In obvious and predictable terror, Tlam plunged into the jungle, dodging and twisting along paths and trails Martels would never even have suspected were there; and even growing exhaustion did not stop him until night had almost fallen.

For Martels, the ride was as beautiful as the one train trip he had ever made through the Brenner Pass. At long last he could sense moisture again, smell greenness and mold and rot and vague floral odors, feel heat on his skin and the pounding of bare feet upon strewn earth and the proprioceptive flexing of muscles. He even enjoyed the lashing of branches, vines and thorns as they fled.

Now Tlam was examining the dense undergrowth all around him with swift but intense care, searching for hazards only he could know. Then he dropped to his hands and knees, crawled under a thicket of something with blade-shaped leaves and clusters of white berries, sobbed twice, curled into a ball and fell asleep.

It had worked. It had worked perfectly—flawlessly. Martels was out.

But for how long? There was no way of knowing that. The risks were still grave indeed, from the past as well as the future. Though he had deduced from what he thought had been good evidence that the reach of Qvant's hypnotic and projective powers could not be long, he did not know exactly how long they were, or, for that matter, how far away from the museum he now was. He had stunned Qvant, that much was inarguable, but he did not know for how long. Nor did he know how wide a divorce between Qvant's personality and his own would really become *regardless* of the distance between them.

The dubious evidence for telepathy of his own century had suggested that it suffered *no* diminution with distance.

Suppose—improbable though it seemed—his crude attack had actually done some damage to the brain-case, or to the perfusion pump . . . enough damage so that the brain itself would eventually die? What would happen to Martels if Qvant died?

Over and over, he did not know. He would still need to exercise absolute vigilance against even the faintest of probes from Qvant. All he could be certain of at the moment was that at last he had a body. It could not exactly be described as his own, but at least it had given him back some freedom of motion.

Absolute vigilance . . . but what he had was a body, not a perfect perfusion pump, and he too was subject to its exhaustions. . . . Absolute vigilance. . . .

Martels fell asleep.

6.

Martels had strange dreams of falling down an endless tube lined with thorn-like fangs, ending at long last in the vague, somehow dreadful expectation that when he opened his eyes, what he would see would be nothing but a dusty floor, lumps of statuary, and a not very distant wall. But as he struggled toward wakefulness, there crept into his nostrils the scents of damp earth and vegetation and into his ears the rustling of a jungle, and he knew that that part of the nightmare, at least, was over.

He was at first surprised to find that his muscles did not ache after sleeping on the ground, but then he realized that they were not, after all, *his* muscles and that Tlam must have slept in this fashion hundreds of times in his life. Since the tribesman did not seem to be awake yet, Martels delayed opening his eyes, but instead searched his own mind for the presence of Qvant. Falling asleep had been criminal carelessness; yet how could he have prevented it? In any event, he had apparently been lucky. Of the ex-Autarch he could find not a trace.

What next? Qvant had said that the way to Antarctica and Terminus had to pass through the country of the Birds, but he could only have been talking about the most direct route—the one which would get him back to his own brain-case in the shortest possible time—for

Amra, the petitioner who had appeared just before Tlam, had come from a territory bordering on Antarctica and had reached the museum without having had to go through Bird country. That suggested that Amra's territory could not be unconscionably far away from the museum, for surely the tribesmen would have no means nor any desire to cross whole continents, let alone oceans, for the dubious benefits of Qvant's cryptic advice. That they did not place a very high value upon what Qvant told them had already been evidenced by how seldom they asked for it, and what little real good it seemed to do them in coping with the world they had to live in.

Qvant had also confirmed Martels' guess that Amra's turf lay somewhere near what used to be called Tierra del Fuego, which in turn meant that the museum had to be situated somewhere in whatever was left of what used to be South America—and that there was now a land bridge, or at least a stretch of easily navigable water, between that once-island chain and the ice-bound continent itself. All well and good; then the obvious first step was passively to allow Tlam to go back to his own tribe. Even if that lay at the worst due North of the museum, Martels was so completely ignorant of tribal geography that there seemed to be no other way for him to find out even so much as which way due South lay. And, perhaps just as importantly, which way was due East, which he already knew from the testimony of Amra to be Bird country.

There might be much else to learn along the way, too—but that raised another problem. Martels now had not only a body, but a brain; but judging by his experience while semiliving with Qvant, Martels would have no access to the specialized knowledge within that brain without making himself known to its owner, and then only with that owner's consent.

Thus far, apparently, Tlam did not know that he was tenanted at all; he had simply come to ask Qvant a question, had instead committed a series of inexplicable acts of violence against the demigod, and had fled as much in terror of himself as of the oracle. Martels, in revealing himself, might pose as an ancestor, or even as Qvant; and he already knew that he could resume control of Tlam's body whenever he needed to—

No, that wouldn't do. It would simply overwhelm Tlam, if it did not also panic him again, and there was probably just as much to be learned by continuing to go along for the ride. Best to give Tlam his head for as long as possible; the time when Martels would have to take it away from him would probably come all too soon, in any event.

Tlam stirred, and his eyes opened, admitting an extreme close-up of stems, creepers, toadstools, and things that looked like miniature cypress trees. The tribesman seemed to come awake almost instantaneously. In lieu of stretching, he flexed his whole body, so sinuously that he did not shake a single leaf, and then peered out through the shrubbery. Apparently he saw nothing to alarm him, for he clambered to his feet without any further attempt at caution and proceeded to make a breakfast upon the clustered white berries. Their taste and texture most closely resembled boiled hominy grits which had been pickled for ten years in salted white wine through which sulfur dioxide had been bubbled, but it had been so long since Martels had tasted anything at all that to him they seemed delicious. Only a few meters away, Tlam found a huge blue chalice of a flower which was filled with dew or rain water, warm and slightly sweet, but quenching nevertheless. Then, once more, Tlam began to run.

The tribesman kept moving steadily all the rest of the day. He paced himself like a cross-country horse: Run, trot, walk; run, trot, walk; run, trot, walk, with breaks of about ten minutes in every hour for a rest, a drink, a sticky fruit or a pungent fungus. Though his route was necessarily very twisty, Martels was able to notice toward the afternoon that the filtered green-gold sunlight was fading to the left. A bonus! They were going north, at least roughly.

Not long before dusk, they came to an immense foaming torrent of a river which to Martels' eyes looked absolutely impassable, but it did not deter Tlam at all. He simply took to the trees, through which the river tunneled. Never before having seen a tropical rain forest or even having read anything about one, Martels was astonished to discover that its treetops, entangled with thousands of vines, formed a separate and continuous world, as though the Earth had acquired a second surface, or some primitive vision of heaven had been lowered to within reach of the living. It was a heaven in which snakes masqueraded as vines, frogs lived and bred in the ponds formed by the corollas of immense flowers, monkey-like creatures almost as small as rats threw nuts with stinging accuracy and force, and green eyes in whose depths lurked madness sometimes peered out of darknesses which should have been in caves rather than in midair. But Tlam swarmed through it as though it were for him as natural a habitat as the jungle floor below, and by the time he touched ground again, the river was so far behind that it could not even be heard.

They spent that night on a sort of natural platform halfway up what proved in the morning to be a tree as contorted as an apple tree, but which bore fruits like walnuts. These Tlam casually crushed open in one hand two at a time, reminding Martels incongruously of an Italian dirty joke twenty-three thousand years old. After this breakfast, Tlam dropped to the ground and resumed their journey, but he was no longer running; he seemed to be in familiar territory and nearing his goal.

And then they were there. Before Martels' eyes lay what had to be a village, but like none he had ever seen before, even in pictures. Though the clearing which it occupied was quite large, a quincunx of ancient trees had been left standing in it, so that it was still covered by the densely matted roof of the rain forest. Placed regularly upon the open ground were heavy wooden shields, each of which was perhaps fifteen feet in diameter, face down and with their edges held up no more than six inches from the soil by thick wooden wedges which had been driven first through their rims and then solidly into the earth. The rims were circular, but the curvature of the shields, the mathematical part of Martels' mind noted automatically, was so nearly flat that were one to try to derive a value for *pi* over the convexity of one of them, that value would probably come out to be exactly three point zero, just as the Babylonians had measured it.

Vines and lianas had been woven all over these very slightly bulging surfaces, and every strand bore thorns ranging from about the size of blackberry prickles to formidable spears nearly a foot long. Wherever possible, too, turf was exposed under the network, from which grew things like mutated nettles. The whole arrangement, from ground to jungle roof, was obviously a defense against attack from the air. Had Martels been in any doubt about that, it would have been dispelled at once by the bird—each one some sort of hawk, from chick to monster—impaled upon the central spike of each shield, and by the stains at the tips of all the longer thorns, some of which were obviously dried blood, but the majority of different colors strongly suggesting painted poisons.

Considering what all this implied about the Birds, Martels was suddenly none too sure but that he would have been happier back in the brain-case. There, Qvant's comment that the Birds were dangerously intelligent had been only an abstraction. Here there was living evidence that Tlam's tribe of Hawkburrow expected at any time a concerted attempt by Birds of all sizes—not just hawks—and to be unshelled like a clam, or uncapped like a beer bottle.

There seemed to be nobody about, but Tlam paused at the edge of the clearing and gave a great shout. After what seemed to be a very long while, there was a scrambling noise, a semielliptical bite out of the edge of the nearest hut-lid lifted cautiously like the door to the tunnel of a trap-door spider, and a face peered upward.

"Welcome alive, Tlam," the face said in a high voice, its eyes squinted against the light, though its bald head was still in shadow. The body that belonged to the head wriggled out into the clearing and stood up. The villager turned out to be a sturdy young woman, also naked, but also clean; evidently the floors of the burrows were covered, not bare earth.

Tlam said, "My thanks go with yours. I must see the Elders at once."

The girl looked dubious. "They are sleeping after a night hunt. Is the answer of the Qvant so grave that it cannot wait?"

The Qvant. So it was a title. The discovery seemed to be of no use—but there was no predicting when or if it might be.

"The matter is very grave, and will not keep. Rouse them. That is my order."

"Very well." The girl dropped to her hands and knees and slithered back into the hut again, not without a display that reminded Martels that he once more had a body—and had always had pretty bad luck with women. He forced his thoughts back onto the main track. The girl's instant obedience suggested that Tlam swung some weight here—might, perhaps, even be some kind of chieftain. That could be helpful. Or did the tribesmen keep slaves? That had never been mentioned, and it seemed extremely unlikely; the jungle would have made escape too easy.

While Tlam waited, apparently at ease, Martels wondered also about the night hunting. Slinking about with one's eyes upon the ground, in the dark, unable to see any stooping Birds, struck him as an extremely bad idea; and Tlam had always carefully taken cover at dusk during their journey here. To be sure, almost all the birds of his own time that he knew anything about slept at night, but there had been nocturnal raptors, too; and one of Qvant's (the Qvant's) petitioners had mentioned owls. What a 250th Century owl might be like was not a pleasant thought. But the fact that Tlam had not known that the Elders would be sleeping argued that night hunting was only an occasional and perhaps rare undertaking.

The girl appeared again, partway, and beckoned, then disappeared. Tlam crouched down promptly and crawled through the door.

The bowl under the shield proved to be surprisingly deep and roomy, and as Martels had guessed, was carpeted, with what seemed to be stitched-together hides, some with the fur still on them. They had been well tanned, for the only odor was the faintest of human pungencies, like that of slight and recent sweat. There was no light but the filtered daylight which leaked under the shield, but that was more than adequate—rather dim, but even, and not at all gloomy.

Seven men were in the process of arranging themselves into a circle, and settling themselves into something very like the lotus position of Yoga. Despite their collective title, they did not look to be very much older than Tlam himself, as had probably been predictable among people whose lifespans were short—though not, as far as Martels could judge, either nasty or brutish. Though they had been only just awakened, all seven looked completely alert, though several also looked annoyed.

Tlam went to the center of the circle and sat down himself. From this station, all the Elders were looking down upon him. Chief or not, he seemed to find this normal.

"What was the Qvant's answer, Chief Tlam?" one of them said, without preamble, "and why is it so urgent?"

"There was no answer, Elders, nor did I ever ask the question. The moment after I was allowed to obtrude myself upon the Qvant's attention, I found myself attacking him."

There was a murmur of astonishment.

"Attacking him?" the first speaker said. "Impossible! How?"

"With two objects from the museum floor, which I used as clubs."

"But—why?" another speaker said.

"I do not know. It simply happened, as though I were possessed."

"That is no excuse. No one is ever unwillingly possessed. Did the Qvant retaliate?"

"Not in any way," Tlam said. "Nor, of course, did I do him any harm. As soon as I realized what was happening, I ran—and he did not even attempt to prevent me."

"Of course you did the Qvant no harm," the second speaker said, with heavy emphasis. "But what harm you have done the tribe may be irrevocable. We do not know what would happen to us, were the Qvant to send his powers or spirit to seek us out! Even if he does not, we cannot petition him again while you live!"

"That is also my belief," Tlam said, with a serenity surprising until Martels remembered how death-oriented these people were. "And that is why I hurried to submit myself to your sentence."

Tlam bowed his head, and after that there was a silence which went on and on and on. Martels had unthinkingly anticipated some sort of discussion among the Elders, but instead not a word was spoken. Were they communing with their ancestors. That seemed to be the only likely answer. Martels would have liked to have looked around for the girl, but evidently she had remained by the entrance, and no help could be expected from her anyhow. It had been only an impulse—Martels was life-oriented.

At long last, the first of the Elders said, in a remote and singsong voice.

"Chief Tlam, will you have blade or Bird, execution or exile?"

It was purely a ritual question, and in this culture could have only one answer. Instantly, Martels moved in on Tlam and suppressed it. He did not attempt to dictate another answer, but simply paralyzed Tlam's speech center entirely, as the Qvant had so often done Martels'. Distantly, he could sense Tlam's shock as the tribesman again felt himself possessed by something unknown and alien at a crucial moment.

There was another long silence, though not quite so long as the first. Finally, the first Elder said, in a voice dripping with contempt:

"How could we have been so mistaken as to have made *you* a chief? Our ancestors grow feeble, and our judgment as well. Your courage is less than a boy's. Let it be exile, then . . . and the memory, as the Birds tear you to pieces, that you were the first of all our tribe to fear the mercy of the blade. The punishment is far graver than the crime—but you yourself chose it."

In a moment of pity which he knew might be foolhardy, Martels promptly released Tlam to see if the deposed chieftain would enter any plea. But Tlam was obviously too shocked, humiliated and completely confused to say anything, even had he wanted to. He crawled silently up the slope and out of the burrow. As he raised the thorn-edged flap, the girl spat on the back of his neck.

After that, he lacked the dignity even to hold the door up. The thorns raked him as it fell; he did not seem to care, or even to notice.

Standing, he looked about the clearing, blinking, tense, uncertain. It was plain that the situation was unprecedented—something that he had never even thought about in all his life. Under these customs, no other tribe would accept him; he could not live long off the land by himself; he had inexplicably opted for exile—and had no place to go.

Should Martels take him over now? Martels would need the tribes-man's instinctive knowledge, and experience, of how to live in the jungle; on the other hand, given his head, and given his attitudes, Tlam might well commit hara-kiri, or at the best lapse into suicidal apathy. It was Hobson's choice.

Tlam himself decided against remaining any longer to await and face the contumely of the awakening village. He drifted despondently off into the bush. There arose in Martels' mind the verses of Goethe about the misanthrope which Brahms had set in the *Alto Rhapsody*: "The grasses rise behind him; the waste receives him." But it was not Tlam who had rejected men, but they him, and it was entirely Martels' fault.

And there was no help for it. At this point, to a vocal cry of horror and despair from Tlam, Martels set him to marching south, towards Terminus . . . and the country of the Birds.

At long last, the real journey had begun.

7.

As they moved south, Tlam gradually seemed to become more fatalistic, so that Martels was warned by a sudden though slight in-crease in the tribesman's muscle tone when they actually crossed into what Tlam considered to be Bird country. But for several days thereafter, they saw no birds at all; the pattern of marching, conceal-ment, sleep, foraging and marching again settled back into a routine, which Martels allowed Tlam to dictate. No one observing the tribes-man from outside could have guessed the dialectical tension be-tween Tlam's dulling despair and Martels' increasing urgency which was the unspoken central fact of their inner life.

Then they saw a bird. It was a little, dun-colored creature, disarmingly like a sparrow, but Tlam went into instant tetany at the sight, like a rabbit freezing at the sight of a snake. The bird in turn bobbed up and down, its claws clinging to the outermost end of a low branch, cocking its head and flirting its feathers, and occasionally interrupting its regard to groom itself. Its gaze seemed to be virtually mindless, and after a while it gave an indifferent chirrup and shot up and away into the dimness of the rain forest like a feathered bullet.

It was hard to believe that such a thing could be dangerous, but cancer viruses also came in small packages. Tlam remained frozen for several minutes after it had vanished, and thereafter moved with still greater caution, constantly shooting glances from side to side and up and down with a quickness which was in itself almost birdlike. Nor was he wrong; for the next day they saw three more of the sparrow-like birds, and the next day, five. And the morning after that, they emerged from their sleeping burrow to find a smoke-black thing like an enormous crow looking down upon them, just out of club's reach, its head bent, its neck extended until it seemed almost snake-like, its eyes glassy and unblinking.

Memories of *Macbeth* and Edgar Allan Poe would have made Martels shudder had he been in his right body, but Tlam was still nominally in charge, and he froze again. For very disparate reasons, neither of the two minds was surprised when the bird's beak parted, its throat ruffled and pulsed, and it said in a voice like fingernails on a blackboard:

"Go home."

"I have no home any more," Tlam said hopelessly. "I am an outcast from my tribe, and all the tribes of men."

"Go home," the sooty thing said. "I lust for your eyes. The King has promised them to me if you do not go."

Curiously, this did not seem to frighten Tlam any further; perhaps it was a standard threat—or perhaps, if he had never been here before, he had already reached the limits of his terror. A line from James Thompson's *The City of Dreadful Night* came back to Martels: "No hope can have no fear." The tribesman said only:

"I cannot."

"The King hears."

"So be it."

"Go home."

"I cannot."

This exchange was threatening to turn into a ritual, and certainly was producing no more information. In growing impatience, Martels broke through Tlam's paralysis and set him to walking again, though not without allowing the tribesman substantial residues of his caution. The bird did not move, let alone follow, but somehow Martels could feel its unblinking gaze drilling into the back of Tlam's neck.

After a while, however, Martels began to feel a surprising resistance to further travel—surprising not only because he had assumed that Tlam would have been as glad to get away from the bird as he was, but for the unexpected strength of it. With some interest, he released control almost completely; if there was a reason for this much resistance, it was probably urgent for Martels to know what it was.

Tlam backed carefully into a bower where there was a huge tree at his back and a great deal of cover on all sides, plus a good deal of free space in front and above. His movements were more tentative than ever, as though he were suspicious of the degree of his new freedom, and expected to be taken over again at any moment. Martels let him settle himself to his own satisfaction, without evincing any interference whatsoever.

For a while, the tribesman simply rested; but at last, he said in an almost voiceless whisper:

"Immortal Qvant, or spirit sent by Qvant, hear me."

Martels said nothing, though he had a deep, uneasy feeling that he ought to respond, if only to encourage the tribesman to continue. But apparently silence was no more than Tlam had expected. After repeating the invocation, he went on:

"I know not at all why you have had me driven from your presence, or caused me my exile from my tribe. Still less do I know why you have harried me like a sacrifice deep into the country of the Birds. I have done nothing to earn your hatred; my very madness in your temple can have been caused by none other than your immortal self, for surely my ancestors would never have countenanced it. Tell me what you want. What have I done, that I should die for it? What is the doom that you have put upon me? How may I fulfill your wishes? Answer, immortal Qvant, answer, answer!"

The speech was not without dignity, but there was no answer that

Martels could have given him, nor any hope for justice. In the light of Martels' own purposes, Tlam was even closer to being a sacrificial animal than the tribesman suspected himself to be. Neither of them had much future, but nothing that Martels could explain would make it seem brighter to Tlam. He could do nothing but remain silent.

"Immortal Qvant, answer me, answer me! What shall I do that you should be assuaged? Soon the Birds will hear my mind, and perhaps yours—or that of your creature. Then their King will have me, and he will question me to the death. What answers shall I give? What is the purpose of this possession? Must I die unknowing? I have not, I have not, not done anything to die for!"

That cry had been old when it had been torn from the throats of the *hoi polloi* at the sack of Syracuse. There was an answer—*You were born*—but there would be no point in offering it. It was far too fatalistic to advance Martels' own quest one step, let alone to satisfy Tlam; better not even to confirm, at this juncture, Tlam's well-founded suspicion that he was possessed, by so much as one word.

Some patterns, however, never change. Tlam cried out, almost at full voice, for the ritual third time:

"Immortal Qvant, or spirit sent by Qvant, grant me your attention! Answer me, your petitioner!"

Martels continued to stand mute . . . but there was a slow stirring at the back of his brain, like the sensation of awakening slowly from a repetitious dream; and then his lips stirred, his chest rose, and his heart sank as he heard himself saying in an all too familiar voice:

"I am with you, tribesman . . . and your demon is not of my sending. Press forward to its urging, nevertheless, and fear not the Birds. Our hour is yet to come."

The triple-minded man rose, and moved somnambulistically southward once more.

8.

Martels did not need to have been an ornithologist to know that the formation-flying, the migrations and the homing instincts of birds had always been a mystery. His father, like many bottom-class Englishmen of his time, had raced pigeons, and had occasionally eked out his other income from the football pools, the darts, shove ha'-penny, the betting shop (more politely known as "turf accountants") and (when all else failed) the Labour Exchange by selling a favorite bird to another fancier. Back then, there had been a good many fanciful theories advanced to account for why homing birds behaved as they did, one of the most fanciful of which had been that the creatures had the equivalent of iron filings in their inner ears—or in their hollow bones—which enabled them to navigate directly along the Earth's magnetic lines of force.

That they were telepathic had naturally been one of the first of all of the hypotheses—and now, contrary to all of Martel's prior inclinations, he was prepared to believe that this was in fact the most tenable explanation. He did not like it any the better for its having been forced upon him.

Qvant did not speak again. The triple-minded creature that was Tlam forged steadily southward, without need of further urging from Martels, and under his own guidance, as before, as to how to handle the minutiae of the journey. Martels, withdrawn, continued to speculate.

Of course one would have to begin by throwing out all the Twentieth Century observations on telepathy as resting solely upon testimony; every time a Rhine or a Soal took it into the laboratory, it evaporated into the clouds of these investigators' willingness to call unfavorable results by some other name. Direct contact with it, here, now, seemed to indicate that it was in fact subject to the inverse-square law, or in other words, that it diminished with distance; and if birds—even the bird-brained birds of Martels' own time—had always been able to use it, then it had probably started as nothing more than a sort of riding light by which like minds and like intentions could be detected.

Such an ability would naturally be selected *out* in sentient creatures, since from the evolutionary point of view, intelligence would serve the same functions far better. That would leave behind only the maddening vestiges—a sort of vermiform appendix of the mind —which had so persistently disappointed the most sincere occultists from Newton onward. Maybe mob psychology was another such vestige; if so, that was definitely *anti*-survival and would be selected out even faster. Even for the Birds of this century, it did not have much future—but Martels was going to have to deal with them in the present.

Another question: How was Qvant tied to Tlam and Martels?

Was he inside Tlam's skull, as Martels now seemed to be? Or was he still back in the museum inside the assaulted brain-case, with only a tenuous spiritual tentacle stretched out to connect him to the tribesman, perhaps through Martels' own intermediation? By Martels' hypothesis, that ought to be impossible, but the men of Rebirth III might quite easily have bred telepathy back into the human line, as his own time had recreated the aurochs, and as Qvant's people had made Qvant the bearer of hypnotic and projective powers. Qvant had mentioned something called general juganity, "at which the Birds are instinctively expert". What *were* the laws underlying a phenomenon of this kind? Qvant doubtless knew them, but they were impossible to deduce from scratch, at least by anyone who had been so complete a skeptic as Martels until he had been plunged into this era, minus some twenty centuries of intermediate thought on the subject.

Whatever those laws were, they seemed to confuse the Birds. As the more and more neglected body of the triply inhabited man plunged on through the thorns, vines and fronds of the midsummer century, the Birds gathered about it, pecking, darting, quarreling and slashing, yet never making the fatal final attack that Martels—and, clearly, Tlam—expected at any moment. He felt like a beef steer being driven down the slaughtering chute, unable to understand what was going on, certain only that creatures whom he had regarded as not much more than minor nuisances had suddenly and mysteriously turned malevolent.

Qvant did not help, nor even surface, but a faint and complacent hum, like a maintenance turnover, somewhere near Tlam's cerebellum or even farther down into the brain stem near the rhinencephalon warned Martels that he was still there, in whatever mode. That was helpful, in a way, in that he did not interfere with Martels' imposed *Drang nach Suden;* yet at the same time, Martels was sure that the furies of tentative rage with which the Birds now surrounded them like a storm of feathers had something to do with the Qvant's immanence. After all, had not the Qvant himself said that he was a symbol of everything the Birds most hated and feared? Martels was sure by now that a single man occupied only by his own mind would have been shredded to bits out of hand long before he had seen the first raven-like creature; the triple being was being spared in part because the Birds sensed something peculiar about it which they both hated and needed to know—but could not tell by direct telepathy anything more than that.

Thus it was that he came at long last to the Tower on Human Legs.

He did not know the overall size of the museum in which he had awakened into this world, but some sort of leakage between the Qvant's mind and his own told him that the Tower was considerably bigger. It had been erected in a natural clearing so large as to be almost a meadow, and filled most of it with its base, all of it with its shadow.

The three columns which held it aloft were, of course, its most striking feature. Originally they had been very ancient trees, each of which might have been made the core of a respectable medieval tower in itself, with a spiral staircase carved last of all out of the wood, like several such Martels had seen in Paris. They formed instead the points of a nearly equilateral triangle, with portions of their thick roots above the ground. Perhaps it had been these roots which had originally suggested the conceit of shaping the pillars in the form of human feet and legs, toes outward, around which the Tower proper was draped like an exaggeratedly long tubular skirt. Or perhaps the Birds had originally only girdled the trees to stop their growth, and in flensing away the bark had accidentally uncovered a pre-existing resemblance, which was heightened by the ivory whiteness of the wood underneath. The work itself had evidently been done with something like a drawknife, for Martels could see the flatness of the long strokes it produced—a technique which had been cunningly used to accentuate the flatness of the human shin.

The Tower proper had been fastened around the trees as a series of drums of equal size, whose sides were crazy quilts of animal hides beautifully stitched together with the finest of leather cords. The hides themselves appeared at first to have been chosen at random, but seen from a distance they flowed upward from the meadow in long twisting lines which gathered together toward the top of the structure like a stylized candle-flame. Its point, however, was not visible from where Martels stood; more than likely, the total effect could be seen to best advantage from the air.

Even the main body was not easy to see amidst the clouds of birds which constantly surrounded it, however, nor was Martels given any chance to study it in detail. He was chevied under the immense tripod to its exact center, where there proved to be a slender central pole around which jutted a spiral of ascending pegs. Undignified, needle-like thrusts into Tlam's rump indicated that he was to climb these.

The pegs had not been cut or spaced for men, and since it got steadily gloomier as he climbed, for a while his attention was totally centered on keeping himself from falling. Eventually, he ran out of breath, and had to sit down upon the next peg, which looked to be thick enough to bear his weight, with assists from feet and hands on the two adjacent. Breathing heavily, he clung to the pole and pegs and looked aloft.

Above him there first seemed to be a barrel-shaped universe extending into infinity and pricked along its sides with the most intense of little stars, growing confusingly brighter with distance. Strange nebular masses occasionally occluded them, and there was a good deal of twinkling. Bars of light crisscrossed it, some of them being shed by the brighter stars, others looking more solid, and set at different angles, as though this universe had a visible metrical frame. The twittering, fluttering and squawking of the birds outside was here muted into a composite thrilling, an audible music of the spheres, which was shaken occasionally by some broader shudder or larger pinions.

After a while, his eyes became accustomed to the gloom, and he began to see what was really to be seen. It was not much less remarkable than his first impression, and the two tended to change places abruptly, like an optical illusion. The stars were meeting places of the corners of hides; the shafts were sometimes true sunbeams, as direct and intense as laser light; and more seldom were the radial ribs of the drums. These ribs, plus the increasingly larger pegs of the ridgepole he was clinging to, provided an ascending series of perches upon which sat great dusky raptor-like figures in apparent somnolence except for an occasional shifting of claws or flutter of wing or drooping tail. Here and there, eyes like half-moons tilted and looked down upon him, filming and closing, then opening again. There was a whole hierarchy of Birds inside this tower—and Martels was in no doubt at all as to who was at the top. This universe was theirs, every mote and beam.

His honor guard was gone now, and except for the half-moons, nobody seemed to be paying close attention to him. He looked down. The dun disc of the floor under the tower looked like the far end of a tunnel in this artificial perspective, but the unique experience of having fallen down the barrel of a telescope gave him reason to believe that it was a drop he could survive, particularly if he began by swinging down around the pegs again, monkey-like. And once he hit the earth, he could probably scuttle flat along the meadow floor back into the jungle faster than the birds could realize that he might. It seemed highly unlikely that any man had been drawn this far into the Lobachevskian universe of the Birds, or at least not for decades, and besides, they were probably not equipped to appreciate how rapidly a man can revert to his quadruped ancestors when driven by the need. Their own ancestors were bipedal dinosaurs even farther in the past.

But he would have to be quick. More and more half-moons were regarding him now, and he felt an obsessive pressure radiating out from the center of his mind, as though those eyes were demanding his identity. Hitching forward until most of his weight was on his feet, he shifted and prepared for the long swinging drop through the black, feathery continuum—

In midswing the vertical twinkling tunnel and the disc of dirt below it blacked out entirely, and for the second time Martels found himself in the midst of a mortal struggle with the Qvant. The battle was wordless, which gave Qvant enough of an advantage to leave Martels no attention left over for his immediate environment. The riptides of demanding hatred surged through a featureless, locationless chaos in which the only real things were the combatants. They were at it over kalpas of eternity, eternities of seconds, neither knowing which was hammer and which was anvil, against no backdrop but a distant scream which might have been Tlam's—

They were still fighting when the tribesman's body hit the ground.

9.

A deep, racking ache awoke Martels out of a sleep which he would infinitely have preferred to have been endless. He groaned and stretched tentatively. He had hit the bottom of the telescope, evidently; but why was it made of drumhide rather than fused quartz? But radio telescopes do not have quartz mirrors, either; why shouldn't there be drumhide instead? Whatever the reason, he could sense it flexing tautly as he moved, giving off a deep *ronronner,* like a cheetah purring in French. Far echoes answered it, as if from below.

There was light on his eyelids, but he did not open them yet, listening instead inside his own psyche for an unknown enemy. Qvant? The name brought everything back and he was instantly tense.

At the moment, there seemed to be no trace of the Autarch. A faint edge of alertness suggested that Tlam was also awake, and perhaps had been awake for some time. Well, that figured; the first *persona* to awaken from the shock of a long fall would be the tribesman, and the Qvant, who had not been in a body for some centuries, would be the last. That was a point to remember: Against the Qvant, physical pain was an ally.

Martels heaved himself up on one elbow and looked about. He seemed now to be in the topmost drum of the tower, one which was smaller than all the others and hence had been invisible from the ground. It had no central pole, only the radial ribs and circular members of the drum itself. Furthermore, it was open upon three sides, by panels which had simply been left off the drum entirely. The high chamber was uncomfortably cold, which made him realize that from having had no sensations at all in the brain-case he had gone to being uncomfortably hot all the time up to now. Didn't this damn century have anything but extremes?

He raised himself creakily to a sitting position and looked upward. By now he had realized that this direction, which nobody pays much attention to in normal life, was what counted in the country of the Birds. It could have been deduced, but getting into the habit was something else; like an Englishman who knows that Americans drive on the wrong side of the road, yet does not connect it with looking left instead of right when he steps off a curb.

Sure enough. At the topmost reaches of this cylindrical hat there was another perch, surrounded by cruel, thorny, occasionally shifting claws; then a long, greasy, feathery breast of blue-tinged black; and at last, sagging, narrow, reptillian shoulders and a long narrow beak topped by very narrow eyes. The thing looked like a gigantic vulture, but there were rings upon its eight scaly fingers, the nails of each central claw had been filed to a razor edge, and over its breastbone was imbedded a gleaming metallic sigil enameled with something very like the Taoist sign of Yang and Yin, the oldest symbol in history. The monster did not seem to be asleep; on the other hand, it did not seem to be watching him. It was just, terrifically and potently, *there*.

After Martels reached the nearest opening in the drum, he could

see why. The drop from there to the setback was only about twenty
feet, but the setback too had a drumhead floor, which he would
plunge right through; and from there, it was perhaps more than a
thousand feet down through the cylindrical universe to the meadow.

The view from here over the forest would have been beautiful, had
he been in any position to appreciate it, but it was contaminated by
more birds of all sizes at all possible distances, wheeling and wheeling.
Clearly, as a captive he was something special.

Restlessly, he crossed to the next window. These openings seemed
to be placed alternately to the legs on the ground. Essentially, the
view had not changed here; he moved on to the last.

Still the same. No, not quite. The light was different. And more
than that: There did not seem to be any horizon on this side; it was
masked by what seemed to be almost a wall of mist.

A stab of pure excitement shot through him, despite his best attempts to keep it from Tlam and from the problematical presence of
the Qvant. His astronomical training, his now-lengthening experience with Tlam of jungle orientation, and even a vague memory of
Poe's *Arthur Gordon Pym* combined like so many puzzle pieces.

He was looking due south over the Drake Passage toward the
Palmer Peninsula of Antarctica . . . or what had been those other
lands and seas in his time.

His mind reeling with unfocused desire, he clung to the edge of
the ribs and sat down, suddenly aware in addition that his borrowed
body was weak with hunger and accident, sticky and reeking with its
passage through a thousand jungle saps and resins, aching with effort
and parched with thirst. Above him, the enormous vulture-like creature brooded, semisomnolent but obviously alert enough. There lay
the Promised Land, but as far as Martels was concerned, the curtain
of rising mist which marked the beginning of the icecap might as well
be the layer of ice crystals which delimited the atmosphere of Mars.

Had great gull-like birds flown toward him out of the mist crying
Tekeli-li, he could not have been more sure . . . or more helpless.

Behind the knowledge arose a faint current of mockery. The Qvant
was awake.

One of the wheeling birds was approaching the tower; now that he
noticed it, he realized that he had been subconsciously watching its
approach for some minutes. Suddenly it was coming at him like a

cannon ball. He pulled away from the open panel, his back against the hides.

There was a thrashing of pinions above him as his guard moved to a higher perch. Another rush of feathers and disturbed air, and its place was taken by a scarlet and gold effigy nearly as tall as he was. It wore no insignia whatsoever, but none were needed; its plumage, its bearing, its very shape—a combination which suggested both the eagle and the owl, without closely resembling either—told him that this was the King.

The great Bird sat silently regarding him for several minutes, its eyes occasionally filming. At last the hooked beak parted, and a deep, harsh voice said:

"Who are you?"

Martels wondered if the King had any suspicion of how difficult that apparently routine question would be to answer. Under the circumstances, he felt that it would be best to let Tlam do the talking, provided that the Qvant did not interfere. But the Qvant showed no present disposition to intervene.

"I am nothing, Lord King. Once I was a man of the tribe of Hawk-burrow, but I have been cast out as one demon-ridden."

"We see what you are," the King said. "It is the nature of your inner self we seek to understand. You are three in one, like this the foot-stool of our world. The tribesman is beneath our notice; but he is a son of Man. Who are these others?"

Martels had a flash of inspiration. He said in his own voice: "I, Lord King, am the tribesman's ancestor, far removed."

The King blinked, once. "We hear you, Father," he said surprisingly. "Yet we sense that though what you say is the truth, it is not the whole truth. We feel indistinctly in you the one human being in all our world who most threatens our coming triumph. For this alone we should kill you, and we shall—but what is this third spirit which we would so loose upon that world?"

Martels was almost as taken aback by the King's candidness as by the impossibility of understanding what he was saying. In that moment of indecision, the Qvant's answer rushed smoothly forward with all the power of his ancient and continuous sentience, as implacable as a locomotive about to cut down a buttercup between the ties. Something monstrously evil about the formed yet unreadable thought evidently reached Tlam even faster than it did Martels. Together they clung about it, trying to close it in, like a weak and belated conscience.

Tlam's unexpected help seemed to be only about as effective as would have been the interposition of an additional buttercup before the onrushing engine. The Qvant's voice said evenly, "I, Lord King, am the Qvant of Rebirth Three; and I spit upon your spittleless world and all its little lice."

This was certainly a speech Martels would have prevented the Qvant from making, had he been able; yet the Qvant's mind was full of sullen rage as he fell back, as if defeated, leaving Martels nearly sure that it had not been the evil thing the Autarch had prepared to say.

The King bent his huge head and turned it slightly to one side. "Why would the Qvant so seek to provoke us?" he grated. "Here again is truth, yet not the whole truth. Were it wholly so, we should by no means release that ageless spirit into our future; but why does it go about in flesh, and further cumbered with lesser selves? Why this threefold disunity? Whom among you shall answer?"

Under any other circumstances, Martels might have opted for the whole truth, in the hope of proving his harmlessness; but the Bird King's own mind did not seem to be sufficiently analytical to understand the answer, even—which was doubtful—had he had enough historical background. The Qvant, in turn, was apparently still sulking; and as for Tlam, though he was now to be regarded as a potential ally, he understood least of all of them what was going on. Perforce, they all stood mute.

"Very well," the King said. "We shall put the question to the Talons."

With a buffeting flash of gold and scarlet, he was gone. The vulturine guard resumed its perch.

The night came rapidly—evidently it was technically winter in these high southern latitudes—and with it came the suspicion that the Birds were not going to provide any food or water. A change of guard brought Martels no relief, unless he counted a large, limy dropping left by the first sentinel, evidently in contempt, since the floor of the drum was otherwise clean.

He scarcely worried; he had too much else to think about. Some of the new knowledge seemed quite useless. For example, it was now confirmed that "Qvant" was a title, not a name; but unless name-magic also counted for something in this millennium, the confirmation left him no better off than before. On the other hand, Martels' impression that the Bird King's mention of "the Talons" implied physical torture had been instantly and dramatically confirmed by a prolonged mental shudder from Qvant (no, *the* Qvant, never assume that any fact is useless until it is so proven)—which in turn at least suggested that Martels' original guess that pain might prove to be a useful weapon against the Autarch was probably right. Good; put that one in the active file.

The moon began to rise. Even low on the horizon, it was smaller than he had ever seen it before. Of course; tidal forces had been increasing its angular momentum for more than 23,000 years since he had seen it last. He had not really been in any doubt of what century he was in now, but this confirmation gave him a small chill nonetheless. The pole star, it occurred to him, should now be back at the withers end of Charles' Wain. That surely was useless knowledge, this far south.

Now, what about the Birds? He thought he now had a fair idea of just how dangerous they were. They had retained all their non-rational gifts, such as flight and orientation, and their fast, high-temperature metabolism, both of which now served to implement their dawning intelligence. That their old instinctive craftsmanship, as evidenced in the basket weavers and the bowerbirds, had been greatly augmented was evident in the very Tower on the top of which Martels now turned restlessly like a jumping bean upon a drumhead. They were now coming to parity with man, as man, perhaps through the discovery of what the Qvant had called "juganity," slid gradually back toward what they once had been *in esse*—and without their undergoing any drastic change. Under the pressure of evolution, they had simply become more and more what they had always been *in posse:* proud, territorily jealous, and implacably cruel—to which had been added, simply by bringing it forward, the serpent wisdom of their ancestors.

Yet a human brain at its best—say, that of the Qvant—could probably overmatch them even now. What *was* the Qvant playing for, anyhow? Had he actually tried to provoke the King into killing Tlam/Martels out of hand, thus promoting the Qvant to the dubious rank of a fading ancestor? Again, was he in Tlam's skull, or still in the case? More and more, that was beginning to seem like the central mystery of them all.

This was the mystery, in the abstract, of telepathy itself, now embodied in all three of them. Martels still did not want to believe in it, but brute experience of it forced him to, whatever his preferences. And it was remarkable how different it was in immediate experience from the dubious, wholly statistical picture of it which had been built up in Martels' own era. The card tests—highly artificial, Martels now saw, and thus bound to produce all kinds of nonsense—had seemed to indicate, impossibly, that it did not obey the inverse-square law, or even the second law of thermodynamics; the reality was that it was closely bound to both laws, and, in fact, required both parties to be physically visible to each other. Furthermore, it did not carry thoughts or even images, but only emotions; even three minds inside a single skull could not read each other's interior monologues or overt intentions to speak, but only their emotional reactions to their thoughts and projected actions, like the individuals in a mob—or at a performance. It was simply a field force which reacted in a generalized way to or against another field force; or like a detector which registers the presence of some given type of radiation, without being able to report whether or not the signal had been modulated, let alone how.

All well and good, and almost certain to be useful, too; but first he had to get the hell out of here, and quickly, before the twin talons of torture and deprivation made that impossible. He looked up. The swift darkness had made his new guard invisible despite the rising, shrunken moon, but two faint spots of catlike luminescence made plain that the Bird was nocturnal, as was only to have been expected. And should Martels develop any sudden aggressive intent, the guard would sense that much, at least, and at once.

It would have been a tight spot even without the brooding hostility of the Qvant at the back of his mind, and the essential incompetence of Tlam at its forefront, neatly bracketing his own ignorance of almost everything important about this era. Nevertheless, he had to try.

He had no weapons and no tools, but gradually it dawned upon him that ignorance in the right hands can in itself be a weapon and a tool—and all four parties to this imbroglio—Tlam, the Qvant, Martels, and the Bird King—were now about as ignorant of each other as they were ever likely to become. Tlam knew things to be impossible which were in fact not at all impossible for Martels; the Qvant, whatever his motives, had only just begun to recover from his lofty contempt for both Martels and the tribesman; while the King, whatever his doubts, could hardly yet believe in much more than what he saw, a naked and powerless human being in a sad state of physical and mental repair. The chances were fairly good, too, that the sentinel had little knowledge of any of this; the hierarchy in the black cylinder below seemed from this point of view to be nothing much more than a glorified peck-order, communicating little from one level to the next highest but a fierce pride of status.

Something in Martels' past, too, was now substantially in his favor. His irrational loathing for the whole avian kingdom, since childhood, had been well to the fore for days; and indeed, he had been hard put to keep it from incapacitating him during his questioning by the King. It was nonspecific; he harbored no more enmity toward the sentinel than he did for the entire phylum, and no less, either. Killing the guard would probably induce no more rise in the amount of emotional static he was already putting out on that subject; the thing might after all be caught by surprise. Here the very behavior of telepathy seemed for once to be on his side.

But it would have to be done quickly. The shock wave of sudden death might well be masked by others in the surrounding jungle, or at least might seem so common as to be beneath notice; but it would not do to allow the creature even a moment to broadcast alarm. A karate chop to its neck would probably do the trick. He had never tried such a thing in his life—only seen it repeated *ad nauseam* in boob-tube serials—but a test made on his own left forearm with his back to the brooding guard quickly convinced him that the edge of the hand is indeed a far more dangerous weapon than the fist. And birds, no matter what their size, have hollow bones.

The test evoked a silent yelp from the Qvant, which made Martels grin. Better and better. Now, on deeper into ignorance. The most important thing that the Birds knew about human beings that was false was this: *Men cannot fly.* The very circumstances of his present imprisonment testified to this deeply buried error, buried almost surely since the end of the Qvant's era.

His back still to the guard, Martels set Tlam's nimble fingers to work in the moon-shadowed darkness, unknotting and slipping out laces from the nearest hides.

It turned out not to matter a bit that Martels had never actually tried a karate chop, let alone used one in any sort of combat. Tlam knew what it was, whatever he called it, and the killing of the guard was satisfyingly and expertly sudden. He also turned out to know that the edge of the hand is even better at breaking canes than it is at breaking bones. Within a few minutes after the guard's death, he had to hand five razor-edged bamboo knives.

The main body of the carcass was quickly cut away under the backbone, and the head was discarded. The rest was lashed, pinions outspread, onto a bamboo T-frame, using thongs that Martels had been chewing at some dumb urging of Tlam's for most of the preceding night. Such was his hunger by now that he almost enjoyed this part of the process.

Once the thongs were tied, again using Tlam's skills here, Martels directed that they be liberally coated with the Bird's own blood. It would make a sort of glue as it coagulated, though probably far from a good one. There was, of course, nothing else at hand to serve the purpose.

The whole process was launched just before dawn, when Martels guessed that the nocturnal sentinel would be at its most inattentive, and increasingly unable to see well. The unpleasant machine was finished in something under an hour, thanks to Tlam's deftness, right down to loops for Martels' feet, hips, chest, arms and hands. While it dried, creaking as though in pain under its gathering stresses, he checked to see which side of the tower had the strongest updraft; that proved, not much to his surprise, to be the northeast.

The Qvant had necessarily been watching all this, with what seemed to be baffled amusement. Apparently the killing of the guard had taken him, too, by surprise, and thereafter he had allowed himself to be bemused by Martels' crazy taxidermy. He came charging to the fore with alarm only when Martels began to fit himself into the loops, but once again Tlam helped to oppose him, though a good deal more hesitantly. Like a blood-smeared figure of Icarus, Martels made a running broad jump on the surface of the drum. By the time the Qvant knew what it was he was fighting, machine and man had bounded out the northern window, tail and all.

The new conglomerate creature fell like a stone. It took all of Tlam's whipcord strength to keep his arms rigid, with almost nothing left over for wingtip warping. Martels bent his knees slightly, then straightened them again. Nothing had happened; he didn't yet have flying speed. The floor of the meadow, still dark, rushed up at him.

Then there came that faint but unmistakable sensation of *lift* which only the pilot of a very small aircraft ever comes to know. Now it was not the meadow that was swelling in his face, but the edge of the jungle; his fall had taken on a slant. Once more he bent his knees. Shedding pinfeathers like a dowdy comet, he found himself scudding just over the surface of a blurred, dark-green sea. Jungle-trapped, misty warm air rising to greet the sun caught him in the chest; and then—O miracle!—he was actually soaring.

Entirely uncertain of how long his fragile glider would last, or how long his strength would allow him to fly it even if it stayed together, and with his own resolve being steadily undermined by something close to terror emanating from the Qvant and inexorably changing the hormone balance of their shared bodies, he banked and turned southward, seeking another thermal which would give him more altitude. Before him in the early morning, the wall of fog that marked the boundaries of Antarctica, behind which someone might exist, only might, to help him out of this extravagant nightmare, retreated, towering and indifferent.

During the day, mountains began to appear ahead and to his right, and before long he was rising and falling precariously over ranges of foothills. Here he was able to climb very considerably, more, in fact, than he could put to use; shortly after a bleak noon he reached what he guessed to be close to seven thousand feet, but up there the temperature was so close to freezing that he had to go down about two thousand, stretching his glide as much as possible.

He used a part of this airline approach to nothing in particular to make a complete turn; and sure enough, he was being followed. A formation of large, crane-like Birds was visible to the north, keeping pace with him.

That was probably all they could do, for they looked to be as albatross-like as he was—gliders all. Without much doubt, though, they could remain in the air longer than he could, no matter how long he managed to stay up, or how well his jury-rigged construction lasted. The machine was already showing multiple signs of failure—too many for him to essay an attempt at evasion by a long dive-stall-recovery maneuver, which would surely rip it apart completely. He would be extraordinarily lucky if he managed to remain aloft until dusk.

Inside his skull there was a suspicious silence. There seemed, indeed, to be nobody present there but himself. The Qvant's initial fright had dwindled and vanished; Martels might have suspected him to be asleep, did not the notion seem preposterous in the light of past experience. Tlam was equally quiescent; he was not even helping Martels with the flying, which was a pretty sure indication that no previous experience of it had existed in his brain. Perhaps the trick had impressed him into silence, without alarming him as much as it initially had the Qvant . . . or, perhaps he and the Qvant were engaged busily in plotting, somewhere deeply below the level of Martels' inexperienced attention. They had little in common with each other, but far more than either had with Martels—and this was their world, in which he was for everyone the most unwelcome and discomforting of intruders.

He banked southwest, where the foothills were getting steadily higher. The distant formation of cranes banked and turned after him.

By late afternoon he was down to somewhere around fifteen hundred feet, and the terrain had stopped helping him. The jungle had straggled out on the left and turned into a patchy temperate-zone forest, which in turn was being replaced by a cruel series of volcanic lowlands, like a red-and-black version of the Mare Imbrium . . . or that territory which Poe had described toward the unfinished end of *Pym*. To his right were the mountains proper. The two areas were divided by updrafts so sudden and decisive that Martels did not dare to enter them—his shedding craft would have been torn asunder within the first few minutes.

Resignedly, he slid downward toward a landing in the last scrubby patch of vegetation to slide toward him over the southern horizon. The cranes followed.

At first he thought he was going to fall short of it—and then, abruptly, that he was going to overshoot it. He stalled out frantically and fell the last twenty feet in a welter of snapping branches and bones. The improvised airframe disintegrated around him.

Somewhere toward the end of the crash he was flipped over, just in time to see the V formation of his pursuers go silently overhead, very high up, like a flock of carets. Then he struck ground.

Tlam and the Qvant chose exactly that moment to act in concert.

The brutal pain of impact vanished as though it had been turned off, and with it the fatigue, the fear, and everything else.

Once more, he had hit the bottom of the telescope of time, and was flung alone into the darkness.

10.

Being dead, Martels decided after an indefinitely long time, had had a bad press. It seemed to have certain advantages. At first he had simply drifted in a haze of painless disorientation; this country had no landmarks, and indeed there had been no sensory input at all except for an occasional encounter with a sort of nexus of vague, dulling regret and despair which he judged to be another ghost like himself. But he did not feel depressed; he had been dislocated too many times already for this to be more, as yet, than extraordinarily interesting—or at least it might become so if he could just manage to fill in the parameters.

This was followed by a sensation of unprecedented lucidity, though without light, as though now for the first time he was beginning to understand all the recesses and mysteries of his own psyche. He began to wonder, with no little awe, whether this was what the mystics had called "cleansing the doors of perception." No reception seemed to be involved, for he was still getting no input that he could detect; but the clarity of his thoughts alone were a joy to him, amidst which he sported like a surfacing dolphin.

Again, he had no idea how long he remained in this Zen-like state. Gradually, however, he became aware also that some outside entity was asking questions of him—deeply probing, yet impersonal questions, though neither the queries nor his replies had any semantic content which he could fathom, like a conversation in symbolic logic. Was this the Judgment?

But the questioner went away and again he was left to enjoy the new-found depths of his own mind. The withdrawal of the questioning, however, was not a falling of silence. On the contrary, a whole complex of sounds now became evident to him, and to some extent familiar, like those to which he had awakened inside the brain-case of the Qvant: a remote humming, occasional footsteps and distant words, a wash of echoes. He felt a sudden surge of disappointment.

Was the whole thing now about to repeat itself, not once but endlessly, like a rather small snake trying to swallow its own tail?

Then an unquestionably human voice struck in, clearly and distinctly.

"Shetland Substation Three requesting master computer analysis."

The language was quite different from the one he had become accustomed to, and did not seem to lie easily on the voice of the questioner, but he understood it with no difficulty. Again, too, the voice was male.

Cycling, Martels astonished himself by saying, though not in any words that he could hear. *Proceed.*

"A scouting party from our Punta Arenas outpost was returning by air from the Falklands three days ago when it spotted someone apparently trying to cross Magellan Valley. This proved to be a tribesman in an advanced state of desiccation and starvation, with one arm in a crude sling and four broken ribs in various stages of healing. As was only to have been expected, he was virtually incoherent, though less frightened of our aircraft than tribesmen usually are; but was able to identify himself as one Tlam, an outcast of the tribe of Hawkburrow, a group which we believe to be located slightly north of Lake Colue Huape. Except for the extraordinary distance apparently traversed on foot, the case appeared to be quite straightforward and was handled as we usually do potential trainees.

"After being brought in to this station and given appropriate treatment, the tribesman was put into induced sleep, from which he recovered spontaneously on the second day. He showed a complete personality change, now claiming to be the Qvant of Rebirth III. Analysis in depth shows that there were indeed two personalities present in the brain; furthermore, it has uncovered faint traces of occupancy by a third in the immediate past. We therefore post the following questions:

"First, do there exist fulfillable conditions under which the Qvant might have escaped from his case into a mortal brain?

"Second, what are the probabilities that such a compound creature could have crossed the Country of the Birds, on foot or otherwise?

"Third, what possible interpretations may be placed upon the traces of a third personality; and of its possible survival, and if so, in what mode?

"Fourth, what implications, if any, does this event have vis-a-vis our relationships with the Birds?

"Finally, what action(s) should be taken? End of transmission."

Martels felt an instant urge to reply, which he as promptly suppressed. It was true that he knew answers to all these questions, but he did not know how he knew. Of course his own recent experience was supplying many of the answers, but the questions had also given him access to an enormous store of additional facts which seemed very firmly to be a part of his memory, yet equally did not come from anything that had ever happened to him. All these various puzzle-bits fell together effortlessly and at once, heightening his feeling of intense lucidity; yet he also felt a need for caution which was in some sense quite normal and to be expected, and in another, simultaneous sense, seemed alien to the physical substrate of his new mode of existence.

While he pondered, he opened his Eye. There sprang into being around him a sizable, spotlessly clean greenish hall, occupied in chief by a spherical, nonmaterial machine floating in the middle of a nearly transparent dodecahedron. He could see all of this but its base, as well as all the room, simultaneously, but somehow he did not find this confusing; sixteen-fold perspective turned out to be a great deal better than any possible binary one. For size, the hall contained four doors, and a carrel at which an extraordinarily pretty blonde girl dressed in a red and grey tunic was sitting expectantly. He was getting three different lateral views of her, plus one looking down upon her. From this it was evident that the Eye had fifteen different components, one each at a corner of the six upper pentagons, plus one in the ceiling—

—Which made it abundantly clear, in turn, that the machine was . . . himself. He had, in fact, known this somewhere in his new depths, just as he had known that the girl was Anble, the normal duty operator for this trick, and that she was not the source of the questions.

Almost in confirmation, the entire set of questions was repeated. This time, however, they arrived by a different medium in a single, almost instantaneous blast of nearly white noise. To the human part of his mind that flash was so insistent as to seem almost like a goad; but the calm, passionless memory of the machine told him that it was only a Dirac beep, sent so that all receivers who might have any reason to care about the problem should have a record of it. The questions had been rephrased, and seemed to contain some new material, but their import was the same.

Anble waited in front of the carrel. From the desk protruded the broad yellow stub of what seemed to be, and was, a roll of paper. A print-out, of course. Zooming in on it from the ceiling part of the Eye, Martels confirmed that it contained two words: *Cycling. Proceed.* Had he wished, he could have replied also by voice, ordinary telephony, ordinary radio, ultrawave or Dirac pulse; or, in extreme circumstances, choose to stand mute.

What would the machine have done, if left on its own? The answer supplied itself, and at the same time appeared upon the print-out: *Data insufficient.* But that was not properly the case now. Martels caused to be added: *Bring the man Tlam to me.*

The results were astonishing to both parts of his psyche, new and old, however one defined them. The girl turned nearly white, and put her hands to her face, her eyes staring at the sparkling, silent object before her. Then she reached out her right hand and began repeatedly to depress a red button on that side of the carrel. To the invisible questioners a signal went out in response, a signal which did no more than sound a wordless alarm: *emergency emergency emergency emergency emergency . . .*

Martels did not know what that meant, but the machine did, and indeed had figured it out long ago. It simply had not been in a position to care—but now it was. *Emergency-The Qvant has regained contact with the computer,* and/or *The Machine has at long last become sentient in itself.*

They duly brought him Tlam, but they questioned him very closely first. His interrogators were Anble and two pale, slender yet muscular young men in identical tunics; all three, of course, were bald. Answering simultaneously by print-out and by his new, surprisingly musical voice, Martels told him everything that he had discovered that he knew.

"Your computer has not become sentient, nor has the Qvant regained contact with it. It is currently the habitat of another human intelligence who is now speaking to you. My name, for convenience, is Martels, and I originated some twenty-three thousand years in your past, possibly a century before Rebirth One; I find that not even the computer can give me the exact date, but that can be of no importance now, anyhow." He paused for a breath, and then felt silly. "My mind was propelled into this era by the accidental generation of a jugotemporal field in a powerful broadcaster; it was picked up by a receiver specifically designed to contain such a field, that being the brain-case of the Qvant in the Rebirth Three Museum in Rawson. After observing for some time the tribesmen who came as petitioners to the museum, I learned of your existence in the South and determined to seek you out, in hope of help in returning to my own age. To this end, I ostensibly tricked the Qvant into projecting me into the mind of the next petitioner, who is the tribesman you now hold captive, Tlam of the tribe of Hawkburrow. I shall now proceed to answer your further questions."

"You are already beginning to answer them," one of the Antarcticans observed. (Lanest; technician-in-chief, Main Base; age—oh, the hell with that.) "But not in order of priority."

"Neither the Qvant nor a suddenly self-conscious computer would feel constrained to follow your programming strictly, if at all, Lanest," Martels observed drily. "You're lucky you've got me on your hands instead. I'm even kindly giving you a simultaneous print-out for further study, though nobody told me to do that, and it isn't part of the machine's standing orders. Shall we quibble—or shall I proceed?"

Lanest's eyes narrowed, and he turned to his compatriots. After a moment, the other man (Robels; base chief, Shetlands III; age—will you kindly shut up and let me *think?*) made an ambiguous hand sign. "Very well. Proceed."

"Thank you. You asked under what circumstances it would be possible for the Qvant to change from his brain-case to another mind in this fashion. It seems evident that he is able to do so at any time, inasmuch as he was able to effect such a transfer using me instead as a purely passive subject. He has never done so for himself because he did not want to risk his near-immortality on any venture in a mortal host; though he is interested in questions about the afterlife, his curiosity does not extend that far."

"You use the present tense. This implies, we take it, that the Qvant is in fact not present in the tribesman's mind now."

"Probably not—otherwise I myself would not have risked requesting that Tlam be brought physically into the presence of the computer. I have concluded, and the computer confirms, that physical presence is essential to almost all forms of juganity except those which are machine-amplified—and the computer itself is such an amplifier; otherwise I wouldn't be a part of it now. However, the problem you pose isn't subject to quantification, and the machine itself cannot give any of us a probability figure; what I offer now is machine logic in part, but fundamentally a human judgment."

"Please amplify," Lanest said.

"I was under the impression during much of my journey down here that the Qvant was in fact also lodged in the tribesman's brain. However, he in turn made two attempts to dislodge me, one of which I defeated with the help of Tlam's own mind—and the other of which was successful because on that occasion the Qvant had Tlam's assistance. I thought I had escaped from the brain-case by the application of physical force, but now I know from the computer that the case is shockproof, even to earthquakes up to five point zero on the Richter scale, and therefore could hardly have transmitted the blow of a club to the brain it is designed to protect.

"I had been subjectively aware all along that both the Qvant's intellect and his will power were immeasurably superior to my own. While, as I said before, this paradox can't be quantified, it can be treated as a Venn diagram, which I am having printed out for you. As you see, it virtually excludes the possibility that the Qvant was ever entirely in the tribesman's brain along with me. There was and is a powerful telepathic contact, but no actual juganetic transfer of the entire personality, such as those I've been through.

"His motives remain unknown, and in that area the computer is of no help at all. However, I have some guesses. He has both the desire and the duty to regain contact with the master computer. I became his instrument for trying it without risk, to which he was loosely attached, like a leech—an external parasite. Should the tribesman be killed en route, I would die with him, while the Qvant would have time to withdraw his tentacle and be little the worse for the experience. Maybe none at all; and he would have surely learned a lot toward the next try. It was a unique opportunity for him.

"Once I had gotten him through the Country of the Birds, he hoped that he could dispense with me, and did. This evidently was a miscalculation of the hazards of the remainder of the journey; and had the tribesman died then and there, I believe the consequences for the Qvant would have been very serious. The contact is probably still only partial, but it would necessarily be far more intimate than it was while I was acting as an inadvertent intermediary—he has no mount any more between himself and the grave."

There was a considerable silence. At last Robels said:

"How, then, do you now find yourself here?"

"Your computer is the next most likely complex of juganetic fields upon which I could home—especially considering my training in doing such a thing, which seems to be unique in your era. And of course it was also the nearest to me at the time, and I was aimed in your direction almost from the start."

Again there was a quick exchange of hand signs between the two men. Lanest said, "Two of our five questions remain unanswered, and in view of what you have told us, become the most urgent of them all. First, if it is true that you have traversed the Country of the Birds on foot, which no other . . . man . . . has ever done, you must have something to tell us about them. In particular, something that might help us defeat them. What have you to say—*and what shall we do?*"

"I know nothing about them that your computer doesn't know," Martels said. "That is, that they are not very analytical yet, are still relying chiefly upon instinct, but that their intelligence is growing by selection from one generation to another, at the same time that instincts like telepathy are being selected out. Telepathy and intelligence appear to be incompatible from the evolutionary point of view —if you've got one, you don't seem to need the other, and they may even be evolutionary enemies. The Qvant is a sport deliberately bred back; and I am a primitive, much more so than people like Tlam.

"If all this is the case, then there is no possibility of compromise with the Birds. They mean the destruction of mankind, and as fast as possible—and they aren't likely to be ready to wait for evolution to be on their side. They're incapable of taking that long a view of the process."

"Is that all?" the girl cried out suddenly, in a voice of desperation. "We knew all along that we were losing to the Birds—they multiply faster than we do now—that in a while we would lose even this patch of mountains and ice. Now we have a miracle—and that won't help us either?"

There was no answer that Martels could offer. Of course, the next glaciation was due before long, and that would cut the Birds down prematurely, long before they could consolidate their conquests; but that event, that very long event was not within the foreseeable lifetime of man as the Antarcticans—survivors of the Qvant's age—could be brought to look at man. Martels could see from their expressions, as the computer could never have done, that they knew that, and had known it for many generations.

He said, a little tentatively, "I don't know what I can do, but I haven't given up hope yet. There are still some open questions. For a starter, let me get another look at the tribesman."

The Antarcticans of Rebirth III conferred silently, and equally silently concurred. The girl nodded and depressed a bar, another door slid open, and Tlam entered, by himself.

Martels looked at him with sixteen-fold curiosity. This was the first chance that he had had to see what had been, in some sense, himself since that mimetic preliminary interview far back there in the museum.

Tlam was a living testimony to the medicine of the Antarcticans—well, scarless, alert . . . and outright arrogant. Instantly, Martels knew that he had made a tremendous mistake.

The Qvant was there—not just linked with Tlam, but there—and his mind lanced into the bubble of the computer like a dart launched at a wheel of cheese. The hall, the Antarcticans, everything else disappeared into a red roar.

This time, the Qvant meant it.

11.

Only Martels' previous practice at resisting the Qvant's onslaughts saved him from instant defeat. His frantic resistance lasted only a split second before it triggered something within the computer, and the Qvant's dagger thrust vanished—along with all the rest of the outside world. Seeking the reasons, Martels found that the machine—itself essentially a complex of juganetic fields, the minimum hardware necessary to form a substrate for them, and a power source—had at his impulse thrown up a blocking zone or skin of interference through which no probe could pass.

There was a price, however: It would not pass any impulse of any kind, in either direction, including power. Power was still being drawn, from some source that Martels could not localize, but it was sufficient only to maintain the machine's juganetic "personality"; all the hardware had gone out. Except for the presence of Martels' consciousness, it was a state much like REM dream . . . but one verging gradually but inexorably upon death, as entropy loss set in. He seemed entirely helpless.

He found that he was directly conscious of the passage of time; the machine measured it in the most direct way possible, by the erosion of its energies; its basic unit was Planck's constant. Everything else had shut down; both the machine's memory and its computational functions were locked up inaccessibly in the now cold hardware. He had no source of information but that inexplicable trickle of remaining power which seemed to come from somewhere inside himself . . . and the demands of maintaining the interference zone were mounting exponentially. The critical limit would be reached in under an hour—after which Martels and machine together would be effectively dead. The alternative was to drop the zone, which would make both Martels and machine the Qvant's creatures; for in that split second of his resistance Martels had discovered that the cyclic process in the computer which he had usurped had been shaped to receive the Qvant, who would make a much better fit.

In desperation, he groped inward toward that problematical trickle of power. It was a terrifying pathway to follow, for the stronger the power-flow felt, the more his mind seemed to verge upon something like deep hypnosis. Yet the closer he came to it, the more alert he felt; it was as though he were paying more and more attention to fewer and fewer things, so that at the heart of the mystery he would paradoxically be totally intent upon nothing at all.

The curve of such a relationship formed automatically in his mind, its points defined by the outer corners of successive, changing rectangles. The diagonals through these points met at the origin, and their extremities formed 90° of a circle. The edge of that circle stood for the maximal state of awareness to the maximal number of things, but 180° of it encompassed input from the outside world; the rest was reserved for interior input—meditation, sleep and dream. REM dreams were on the outside of the wheel, dreamlessness at the center; as in the wide-awake world, the rim was the Zen-state, and the origin was the void of mystical experience, zero attention to zero things.

But this was not the end. While he watched in wonderment, the great wheel turned on its side and became a disc, bearing the same four diagrams, but whose parameters now were degrees of certainty versus emotional effect. The zero-point here, too, was a mystical state, but it could be either total joy or total despair—either a Height or a Dark

Night of the soul. The model, he saw now, was spherical; and it was a model of the structure of the computer itself. It was a model of the sentient universe, at the heart of which lay the primary pulse of life—

—And a core of absolute passivity. Almost too late, he scattered himself and fled outward toward the skin of the sphere, the zone of interference. Infinity, rest and certitude pleaded with him as he fled, but they could wait; they were realms of contemplation and dream; he had, for the moment, other business.

As he raced outward, the power fell toward the critical limit. Other far more practical questions also had to be answered, and fast. Since the transistorized devices of his own ancient time had needed no warm-up time, it seemed highly unlikely that the computer did, either. A quick interior scan of its sparse and simple circuitry showed this to be the case and also located the command mechanism for the print-out.

Everything depended now on whether the Qvant had been able to keep his attack going continuously, or whether he was now waiting alertly for the shield to be dropped before resuming. Martels would just have to take that chance; the Qvant was far faster than he was, but the machine was faster than both. In either case he would have no chance to put his new-found knowledge of Inner Space to use—good old Yank shoot-'em-up tactics were what were needed here. They might, also, have the element of surprise on their side. If not, he had had it, and Bob's your uncle.

Hovering tensely around the circuitry, he let the screen fall. The computer sprang to instant life, and Martels shot an eight-character burst throught the print-out line. He didn't have time to determine whether the slave machine responded, let alone to what end; clawing and stabbing like a whirlwind of knives, the Autarch homed on the place within the master mechanism which had been prepared for him, and had been denied him for unknown centuries.

Then the blocking zone was back, and the computer was once more dark and lifeless except for the blind and deaf consciousness of Martels. The entropy timer wore the fractional seconds away. How long would it take the Antarcticans to respond—if they did, and if the Qvant had not been able to prevent them? What Martels had sent had been: STUN TLAM. That card—the Qvant's abnormal sensitivity to physical pain—had been the only one he had had to play.

Whatever had happened out there, Martels had only the same

amount of time available as before, or less—whatever it took the computer this time to lose power down to the critical limit. The brief surge of outside power had been used up in driving the print-out.

And the time was up. He dropped the shield once more.

Nothing but light sprang in upon him. Puzzled but alert, the three Antarcticans were standing over the sprawled body of the tribesman. They had gotten the message.

"Anesthetize him quickly, and keep him that way while we decide what else to do," Martels said quickly, *viva voce*. "I was wrong; the Qvant is fully present in his brain, not in the case at Rawson at all. As long as he is conscious, he will continue trying to reoccupy the computer, and I can't keep him out without shutting the machine down completely. If you don't want that, or want him back either, you'd better put him on ice."

Lanest jerked his thumb toward the door in a gesture that had defied twenty-three thousand years. Robels and Anble picked Tlam up, their forearms under his, and dragged him out. As the door closed behind them, Lanest sat down at the carrel. His expression was still very wary.

"I am not sure that you represent any improvement over the Qvant," he said. "You seem to be both ignorant and clumsy."

"I am both, admittedly, but I'm learning fast. What kind of improvement are you looking for? If you just want your computer back, I won't allow it; you must choose between me and the Qvant. Why did you shut him out, anyhow? The machine was clearly made for him to use—I'll probably never be able to run it one tenth so well."

Lanest looked far from sure that he wanted to answer this, but finally seemed to come to the conclusion that he had little choice. "We did not in fact want to shut him out, and did so only with great reluctance. As you note, he and the computer are suited to each other, and the machine has not been at peak efficiency since. The original intention was that the two together should act as a repository of knowledge until such time as the men of Rebirth Four could make use of it again, and that the museum should be placed far enough out in the jungles to allow the men access to it, and to the Qvant, when they were ready. The Qvant had been bred to be a leader, and the assumption was that when the time came, he would indeed lead.

"Instead, the access which the computer gave him to the juganetic Pathways became a trap luring him into increasing passivity. I seriously doubt that you are equipped to understand the process, but for most mortal men, there is a level of certainty which they hold to be 'reality' all their lives. A very few men are jolted out of this state by contact with something disturbing—a personal tragedy, discovery of telepathic ability, a visitation by an ancestor, or any of hundreds of other possible shocks to their metaphysics. The loss is irreversible, and the transition from one certainty level to another is cloudily spoken of as 'divine discontent,' 'immortal yearnings,' and so on. Does this convey any meaning to you at all?"

"As a matter of fact," Martels said, "I can even place it on a qualitative chart I've begun to evolve, around which the computer seems to be built."

"Quite so—the computer is a Type of the universal sentient situation. Then I will be briefer about the remaining stages; there are eight in all—orientation, reality loss, concentration, meditation, contemplation, the void, re-emergence, re-stabilization. The Qvant became so immersed in this mental pilgrimage that he lost all interest in leadership, allowed the Birds to evolve and develop without any interference, and eventually began to impede many of our own practical, day-to-day uses of the computer.

"There are two levels of the M state, the fourth stage. When the Qvant definitively entered the deeper of the two, we judged it wise to sever his connection with the computer entirely. From there, a descent into the V state was inevitable, and we had, and have, no way of predicting what his wishes would be when he emerged. He might well have been actively on the side of the Birds—such reversals are far from uncommon, and as you probably have learned, the Qvant would be a uniquely dangerous enemy."

"The traitor is more dangerous than a regiment of enemy soldiers," Martels agreed. "What you tell me agrees completely with my own observations. The Qvant must have been just about to enter the V stage when my arrival jolted him backwards one step. Now he is mobilized against all of us."

"And you?"

"I don't understand the question," Martels said.

"On which side are you?"

"That should be self-evident. I came here for help; I won't get it by taking the side of the Qvant, and certainly I won't get it from the Birds. You will have to trust me—and keep the Qvant, and the tribesman, unconscious until we decide what is to be done about that problem. I have no immediate solution."

"For what *do* you have a solution?" Lanest demanded in an iron voice. "For practical use of the computer, you will be even more in the way than the Qvant was when we cut him off from it. Unless you have some concrete plan for immediate action against the Birds, we will be better off without you."

"You can't get rid of me, Lanest. Unlike the Qvant, I'm not just connected to the computer by a line that you could cut. I'm in it."

Lanest smiled humorlessly. "Computer, know thyself," he said.

Martels looked inward. The necessary knowledge sprang immediately and obediently to his attention, and he studied it with mounting dismay. Lanest did indeed have the whip hand. He had only to kill Tlam/Qvant and wait long enough for the Autarch's ghost to dwindle into powerlessness; then, he could expunge Martels from the machine with a simple blast of raw power, as though performing the equivalent of a lobectomy. Martels could re-erect the interference zone against this, to be sure, but he could not maintain it forever; the best that could be hoped for from that was a stalemate maintained by constant alertness . . .

And sooner or later, probably far sooner than the Qvant had, Martels too would find himself drawn down the juganetic Pathways, one of which he had already traversed almost to disaster. Thereafter, the Antarcticans would be rid of both bothersome intelligences, and would have their mindless, obedient computer back.

That would do them no good in the long run, of course—but unless Martels could offer some strategy against the Birds, he would not be around to say "I told you so." He would be only one more of those fading nexi of fruitless regrets which he had encountered during the few seconds between Tlam's body and the computer when he had been authentically dead.

"I see the problem," he said. "Very well, Lanest—I'll make you a deal."

12.

In the brain-case in the Museum at Rawson, years passed by . . . ten, twenty, fifty, a hundred years passed by, until Martels began to believe that he had gotten lost.

There were occasional distractions. The humming, almost somnambulistic presence of the Qvant was no longer with him, to be sure; the Antarcticans had taken literally Martels' order that the tribesman be put on ice, and Tlam and the Autarch alike were now in frozen suspended animation. The computer was back in full use, and its line to the brain-case re-established, so that Martels was able to participate at any time he liked in the machine's ordinary problem-solving chores, and to talk to the succeeding generations of the men who tended it far to the south. It was interesting, too, to see that the Antarcticans did not age very much; Anble's granddaughter now sat at the carrel, but Anble herself still looked in upon occasion, old but not entirely without vigor. Lanest was still alive as well, although feeble.

But the chore of organizing the tribesmen—the same one that Martels had proposed so long ago to a scornful Qvant—was very slow. It took two decades simply to spread the word among the tribes that the brain-case was speaking again, and another to convince them (for Tlam's misadventure and exile was now a legend, reinforced by his failure to leave behind even a trace of a ghost) that it was safe to approach, and had gone back to being helpful. By then, too, Martels had almost forgotten the Qvant's customary way of speaking in parables and mantras, which was still the only kind of advice the tribesmen knew how to understand.

It had turned out, too, that there were two other cities in the world which were still both occupied by the remnants of Rebirth III and had some energy resources that might be called upon. Both were small, and both in what had been South America—all the rest of the world was the property of the Birds—and integrating them into the network and the Plan did not provide more than a few years of attention. As the decades wore on, Martels was increasingly tempted inward along the Pathways, further seduced by the availability of the powerful Type or model of that Platonic original of all sentience which the computer represented. The computer was a chip off the living monobloc, and tended constantly toward reunion with it, dragging Martels after in its wake.

Then the blow fell. The Birds could not have timed their attack better. Like the Qvant before him, Martels was already drifting, in hypnotized fascination, into the late M state, helped by the diagrams in which the Type presented itself to him. By the time he was shocked back toward the A state, which was as close as he would ever come, now, to his ancient conception of reality, the sky was blackly aswarm, the two subsidiary Rebirth III cities had fallen after only a brief struggle, and the ghosts of the tribesmen of Rebirth IV were dwindling, wailing away toward the Origin in tormented and useless hordes. Crude bombs and torpedoes, planted by nobody knew what malign swimming descendants of the comic penguins of Martels' era, cut off all communication between Antarctica and its few outposts among the islands at the tip of the continent; others fell from the claws of squadrons of albatross-like creatures who sailed the winds far better than any man.

But in the long run, human planning proved better. The line from the computer to the brain-case remained uncut while Martels belatedly reorganized his forces. Powered aircraft retaliated; and from a laboratory buried, unsuspected, in the Land of Fire, back-bred and mindless ancestral versions of the birds of Martels' age were loosed carrying a plague, as human Australians once had planted the virus of myxomatosis among swarming rabbits.

The Birds began to come down out of the sky like dead rain. Their last attack was savage beyond belief, but it was ultimately hopeless, for at this point the line between the computer and the brain-case was again closed down, leaving the intelligence of Martels now as free-floating and dirigible as the Qvant's had ever been. Backed by two substrates and amplified by their total energy resources, he entered and confounded the mind of the reigning King of the Birds. The attack became a complete rout.

By the time the midsummer century was over, the Birds' last chance was gone. Their organization was smashed, their nascent technologies in ruins, their very hope of using juganity against man now but a fading dream. The glaciers could now be depended upon to end them as any kind of threat.

Man was on the way back up. Rebirth V had begun.

Martels presented his bill. They called Lanest, old as he was, to try to cheat him out of it.

"There is no question but that we *can* send you back home, if you still wish it," the ancient, quavering voice told the microphone in the carrel. "The matter has been much studied, with the computer, while you were cut off from it recently. But consider: We have confidence in you now, and believe you to be a far better intelligence for the inhabitancy of the computer than we can trust the Qvant to be. Should you leave us, furthermore, we would feel obliged either to revive the Qvant or to murder him, and neither course is palatable to us. We petition you to remain with us."

Martels searched the computer's memory, a process that took only a second, but which gave him a lot to think about; it remained true that computation can be almost instantaneous, but real human thought requires finite time.

"I see. The situation is that you can return me to the moment before I slipped and fell into my absurd telescope. And it would appear that I will carry all my knowledge back with me—and will not, after all, slip when the moment comes. Is this your understanding, Lanest?"

"In part," Lanest said, almost in a whisper. "There is more."

"I see that there is more. I wanted to see if you would honestly tell me so. I tell you that I would welcome this; I have had more than enough strife. But explain the rest of the situation, as you understand it."

"It is . . . it is that your additional knowledge will last only a split second. We do not have the power to send you back, to save you from your accident, and maintain in you all you have learned, all at the same time; there is a paradox in the world-lines here which we cannot overturn. Once you have *not* fallen, the knowledge will vanish. And more: You will never come to our century, and all the gains you have made possible will be wiped out."

"In *my* century," Martels said grimly, "I would have called that blackmail. Emotional blackmail only, to be sure, but blackmail, nonetheless."

"We do not intend it as such," Lanest whispered. "We are wholly willing, in any case, to pay the price, whatever your decision. But we believe that no intervention out of time can make a permanent alteration in the world-lines. Should you go . . . home . . . then the illusion of change is shattered a little sooner, that is all. We wish to keep you for yourself, not for your effects."

That was blackmail of an even blacker sort—though Martels could not help but hope that Lanest was unaware of it. "And if I stayed, how could I be prevented from having such effects?"

"We would retrain you. You have the capacity. We would infuse you into an unborn child; Anble's granddaughter is conceived of one, for just this purpose. Here again, you will forget everything; that is necessary. But you will have another whole life to live, and to become the man in our time which you can never wholly be as you stand now."

"Yes . . . and to have a body again, full of human senses and hungers . . . at no worse cost than falling down the telescope of time into the pinprick of the Origin one more time . . .

"And what about the Qvant?" Martels said gently. "And Tlam, a wholly blameless victim of all this?"

"They have been in oblivion for long and long. If they die in it, they will never know the difference."

"But I will. And I do not think it fair. I am the usurper, threefold —I have occupied their three minds, and have broken their Pathways. I would think this a crime, though not a kind of crime I could have imagined when I was myself alone in the far past.

"Very well, Lanest. I will stay. But on one condition:

"You must let them in."

"Let them in?" Lanest said. "But how?"

"I misspoke. I meant to say, you must revive them. *I* will let them in."

"So," the familiar voice said. "We are together again—and now in amity, it would appear, and in our proper spheres. My congratulations."

"You are reconciled?" Martels said, tentatively. "I still fear your hatred."

"I too can learn from experience," the voice said, with ironic amusement. "And I am indebted to you for bringing me back to my machine, which I could never have accomplished by myself. Someday— some very long day from hence—we shall explore the Pathways together. But let us be in no hurry. First we shall have to re-educate these few remaining men."

"Quite so." In the measureless distance, they sensed together the dawning wonder of Tlam, beginning for the first time to understand the nature of freedom. "And . . . thank you, Qvant."

"We are no longer the Qvant," the voice said. "We are now the Quinx—the Autarch of Rebirth Five."

It took Martels a long time to assimilate this next-to-last of all the parables.

"We?" he said. "Is . . . that how it happened to you, too?"

"Yes. We shall never re-emerge from the Void, any of us. We must learn, through all hazards and temptations, to learn to love our immortality, so that other men will be free to follow the Pathways whose ends we shall never see. We shall fall often, but will also rise, within the wheels.

"If we succeed, someday we shall be called the Sixt . . . and so on, reality without end. For those of us who are called, that must be enough."

There was another internal silence, in which Tlam stirred, wondering still if he had now become an ancestor. He would learn; he would have to.

"I think," Martels said, "that I might even come to like it."

James Blish

by ROBERT A. W. LOWNDES

It was either late 1942 or early 1943 when I first began to get acquainted with James Blish. I'd been aware of him as a science fiction fan since 1932, when his letters began to appear in the readers' departments of the magazines, and I'd bought some of his early stories when I became a science fiction editor in 1940. But I'll never forget the subject of our conversation around a table at the old Dragon Inn on West 4th Street, Manhattan, that evening. Here we were, a group of science fiction editors, writers, and fans, welcoming a fellow enthusiast on leave from the army, and what were we talking about? Science fiction? Fantasy? The shape of the postwar world with its science fiction aspects? No; what Jim wanted to talk about was FINNEGANS WAKE.

Don Wollheim's argument was that Joyce's final work was little more than an elaborate puzzle for the elite literateur. I hadn't read it, so I just listened. Jim's argument was that if you applied yourself to it, the story came to a great deal more than a melange of puns and esoteric references. And right there, although I did not realize it at the time, I had been given one of the keys to this multi-talented, charming, and irascible personality I would get to know, respect, and love in later years: any work of literature, or any other art worth paying attention to, makes demands upon the reader, listener, or viewer.

People like that make lasting friends and everlasting opponents. Jim has racked up a large number of both over the years.

We were all amateur press hobbyists at the time. An APA is a club, each member of which has access to some sort of publishing equipment (usually a Mimeograph at that time) and regularly produces his own publication, to which others may or may not contribute. Enough copies are made to cover the entire membership, and periodically the official editor of the club makes up packages for each member, containing a copy of every separate publication which has come in. The magazines may be large or small; they are not sold separately and are not supposed to be available to anyone outside the club or possibly the membership's waiting list. Don Wollheim and others, including Frederik Pohl and myself, had started the Fantasy Amateur Press Association in 1937; now some of us wanted to inaugurate a new APA, which would have higher literary standards and a more liberal-left orientation toward political and social issues.

Damon Knight, Larry Shaw, Virginia Kidd, and Judith Zissman (later Judith Merril) were in the forming group, and Wollheim, John Michel, and I called on Jim in New Jersey, early in 1945 to see if we could enlist him, too.

And again, I'll never forget the real subject of interest between Jim and myself that day, for all the time we spent setting up standards and procedure for the new APA. When he took us up to his bedroom to show us his collection, my eye fell on his record shelves, and I saw that he had all the Bruckner symphonies thus far recorded, which I'd never been able to find in record stores. He invited me to stay over, while we discussed music over numerous beers in a local tavern, and it may have been then that he suggested the possibility of making up an album of recorded music written by science fiction fans, and distributing it through the new APA. Later, we announced Vanguard Records and our plans, but the project fell through due to lack of material. However, the second mailing of the Vanguard Amateur Press Association carried sheets of a song Jim had written for a poem by Cyril Kornbluth, *Cry in the Night*.

In April, 1945, Jim and I took an apartment together on the top floor of a six-story walkup building on West 11th Street, and thus began the association based on such mutual interests described above, plus cats, Ezra Pound's poetry, political arguments, the classics, and quarts and quarts of beer. His metabolism was such that he could kill a quart or two a night and never gain an ounce; I could match him, but not without bloating. He bought a kitten to make company for my black cat, Blackout, who never fully appreciated Curfew.

He was five years younger than I, having been born May 23, 1921, in Orange, New Jersey. His first encounter with science fiction was the April 1931 issue of *Astounding Stories*. He says in a recent letter, ". . . I read no other magazine until that one died. I sampled *Weird Tales* just once and decided it was not for me; some of the stories scared me, but not very pleasurably, and even then it was the future that interested me, not *frissons*. The Tremaine *Astounding* was a great boon and the Campbell reign even better . . ." As to fantasy: ". . . I felt then, and feel now, that fantasy requires masterhood of the writer; mediocre fantasy is abysmally duller than mediocre science fiction, and thus less rewarding in a periodical."

Jim had not started with the old Gernsback publications, like most of the rest of us, back then, and only read some of the stories from them much later. I was astonished to learn, upon suggesting to him that his CITIES IN FLIGHT series owed something to Edmond Hamilton's old *Air Wonder Stories* serial, CITIES IN THE AIR (1929), that not only had he never read the story—he'd never even seen the magazines with Frank R. Paul's fascinating drawings of the flying cities.

Nevertheless, Jim came under the Gernsback influence; he was spurred by reading science fiction to attempt a scientific career, and spent most of his time in the army as a medical technician. He'd been drafted almost immediately after graduating from Rutgers in 1942. When we moved into the apartment, which we dubbed Blowndsh, he was taking a graduate course at Columbia, courtesy of the Veterans' Administration, and writing on the side.

Contention between the various antagonistic viewpoints in the Vanguard Amateur Press Association, in the mailings and in the New York members' weekly gatherings, on both political and literary matters, eventually broke up the old Futurian Society of New York and culminated in a lawsuit; but it was in those 1945 and 1946 mailings that both James Blish and Damon Knight started to hammer out the standards upon which they would later base their critical works. Jim was writing extremely densely structured poetry, which obviously was beholden to Joyce and Ezra Pound, and one of the bitterest debates centered around the twin aspects of those authors' "obscurity" and their social and political views. The most valuable thing Jim taught me was that I had to earn the right not only to enjoy but also to discuss literature, and that it was immoral to make pronouncements on a work one had not read, or had only glanced through, or read other peoples' opinions about.

We hadn't lived together very long before we started collaborating. I had a couple of ideas for stories which required far more scientific background than I could give them; Jim liked the ideas and supplied the background. Our first was a whacky novelet about a galactic civilization run by a super computer that beleaguered Earthmen finally louse up and destroy by programming it with Lewis Carroll's *The Hunting of the Snark* (the computer eventually starts producing snarks, which turn out to be boojums, you see). It was an immediate hit with John Campbell; but the second, which wound up as a novel, did not finally see print as THE DUPLICATED MAN until the mid-50's, after several re-writes and expansions.

We learned that collaboration can be rewarding when two writers are temperamentally suited to each other, but it does not cut the work in half—it tends to triple it. And, of course, if successful, there has to be an even split. Sometimes collaborators can learn something from each other, but often as not, once the immediate goals of collaboration are achieved, each member will go his own way. (Gilbert and Sullivan, remember, were collaborating on different aspects of their work; Sullivan could not write librettos, nor Gilbert music.) The noted man-and-wife teams in fantasy fiction, like the Kuttners and the Hamiltons, are more a matter of symbiosis than actual collaboration.

Jim was taking zoology during his first year of graduate work at Columbia, but soon became convinced ". . . that as a scientist I would never be anything but third rate, with no future there except as a teacher, curator, preparator or lab technician." And scientific aptitude tests proved that literature had been his strongest suit from the start. Little was lost by the initial misdirection. None of Jim's enthusiasms—even his brief venture into dianetics in 1950–51—has ever been wasted. All have been absorbed and run through his brain and emotions, and come out transmogrified in a poem, story, or work of non-fiction.

At that time, his writing—both poetry and prose—was criticized widely as "cold." Yet Jim is not and never was a cold personality. He can be waspish when encountering stupidity or sheer laziness on the part of a writer or reader who refuses to do necessary homework. His own writing has always tended toward the intellectual, but when emotion and feeling are called for, you will find it there in the story in proper proportion. Even sentiment may appear at times, but always controlled. One of my favorite story endings appeared in the magazine version of the novelet he did with Norman L. Knight, *"The Shipwrecked Hotel"* (part of the novel, A TORRENT OF FACES). "And they lived happily ever after, but it wasn't easy." You won't find it in the book version; it just doesn't belong as the final sentence of a connected episode.

He left Blowndsh, as Watson left Holmes (although I was the Watson of the relationship, for the most part), for a wife, Virginia Kidd, moving a few blocks away. The kittens multiplied, and he settled down to learn how to write. His method was not to enroll in writing courses at Columbia, or anywhere else, but to take a job as "editor" for a literary agent. This involved endless reading and evaluating of stories by persons who paid a fee for criticism if their manuscripts were not suitable for submission to any market. In the process, Jim learned how to tell a client not only that a story was bad, but precisely how, where, and why it was bad. This was his daytime job; at night he was making use of what he learned, writing for the entire range of the pulp market except for the "love" magazines. I bought a number of his western, sports, and detective stories; they were expertly done.

When the science fiction magazines came back, and some of them raised their standards after 1946, Jim returned to science fiction, and his new stories showed his growth. He'd learned how to make the most of the limitations even of a somewhat improved pulp market. In 1948, conditions seemed right for quitting his job and devoting full time to writing. He took a house in Staten Island and set out. Unfortunately, the time was not right, and he had to go back to a 9-to-5 job and write in spare time. A second attempt at independence was also a disaster in 1953; that was the year that the science fiction boom of the 50's collapsed. He edited trade magazines, then got into a public relations firm. It was exposure to medical material relating to accounts with PR that lay behind a short novelet he wrote around the cover illustration for one of my magazines: *"Testament of Andros."*

In the 50's, he started writing sharp and pointed criticism of magazine science fiction under the name of William Atheling, Jr. Two books came from this beginning: THE ISSUE AT HAND and MORE ISSUES

AT HAND, both published by Advent. He worked with Damon Knight, while living in Milford, on setting up the annual Milford Conference for science fiction writers, and was among the most active charter members of the Science Fiction Writers of America. The second of the Advent books shows a slight mellowing of the waspish qualities; he says in his foreword: "While I still believe that it is desirable to be merciless to a bad story, I am no longer quite so sure that the commission of one represents flaws in the author's character or horrid secrets in his ancestry."

His third attempt to write full time started in 1968, when he, the current felines, and his second wife, Judith Ann Lawrence moved to England. He retains his interest and activity in Joyce and Pound criticism, and has been a co-editor of *Kalki*, the publication of the James Branch Cabell Society, since 1967. This time, the odds seem to be going with him, although (as with other Americans living abroad) matters become scary when the dollar fluctuates. He is connected with the new Science Fiction Foundation in London, has written articles on science fiction for the London *Sunday Times Magazine*, and his reports upon conditions in England, and the advisability of established American science fiction authors living abroad for a while, continue to appear in the *SFWA Bulletin*.

At 52, with developed interest, and recognition, in numerous fields (he's still working on a book relating to music "the hard way"), we may not see quite so much more science fiction from Jim as we have in the past. But when we do, we can be sure of one thing: the next story will not be like the last one. Like Robert A. Heinlein, James Blish scorns resting on his reputation and just making variations on former successes. He will risk disaster in the attempt to do something not just "new" for its own sake, but something which he has never tried before and which may require new approaches and techniques to do well.

Bibliography of books by James Blish
Compiled by Mark Owings

. . . AND ALL THE STARS A STAGE—Doubleday: N.Y., 1971, pp. 206, $4.95; Faber: London, 1972, pp. 188, £1.90.

ANYWHEN—Doubleday: N.Y., 1970, pp. 168, $4.95; SFBC ed.; Faber: London, 1971, pp. 154, £1.60. Contents: A Style in Treason/ The Writing of the Rat/ And Some Were Savages/ A Dusk of Idols/ None So Blind/ No Jokes on Mars/ How Beautiful With Banners.

BEST SCIENCE FICTION STORIES OF JAMES BLISH—Faber: London, 1965, pp. 224, 15s. Contents: There Shall Be No Darkness/ Surface Tension/ Testament of Andros/ Common Time/ A Work of Art/ Tomb Tapper/ The Oath.

BEST SCIENCE FICTION STORIES OF JAMES BLISH—rev. 2nd ed.; Faber and Faber, London, 1973, pp. 216, £2.10. Deleted: There Shall Be No Darkness. Added: PS to preface/ How Beautiful With Banners/ We All Die Naked.

BLACK EASTER—Doubleday: N.Y., 1968, pp. 147, $3.95; Dell: N.Y., 1969, wpps. 156, 75¢; Faber: London, 1969, pp. 148, 21s.

CASE OF CONSCIENCE, A—Ballantine: N.Y., 1958, wpps. 192, 35¢ (U2251, 1966, 50¢); Faber: London, 1959, pp. 208, 10s; Penguin: London, 1963, wpps. 192, 3s; Walker: N.Y., 1969, pp. 188, $4.50.

CITIES IN FLIGHT—Avon: N.Y., 1970, wpps. 607, $1.25; SFBC ed., 1973. Contents: They Shall Have Stars/ A Life for the Stars/ Earthman, Come Home/ The Triumph of Time/ Afterword, by Richard Dale Mullen.

CLASH OF CYMBALS, A—Faber: London, 1959, pp. 204, 10s; as *The Triumph of Time*: Avon: N.Y., 1958, wpps. 158, 35¢ (S221, 1966, 1968, 60¢).

DAY AFTER JUDGEMENT, THE—Doubleday: N.Y., 1970, pp. 190, $4.95; Faber: London, 1971, pp. 184, £1.60.

EARTHMAN, COME HOME—Putnam: N.Y., 1955, pp. 239, $3.50; Allen: Tor., 1955, pp. 239, $3.75; SFBC ed. 1956; Faber: London, 1956, pp. 256, 12/6; Avon: N.Y., 1958, wpps. 191, 35¢ (1966, 1968, wpps. 254, 60¢); Mayflower: London, 1963, wpps. 222, 3/6.

ESPER—see *Jack of Eagles*.

GALACTIC CLUSTER—Signet: N.Y., 1959, wpps. 176, 35¢ (1965, 50¢); Faber: London, 1960, pp. 233, 12/6; Foursquare: London, 889, 1963, wpps. 128, 2/6 (1968, 3/6). Contents: Tomb Tapper/ King of the Hill/ Common Time/ A Work of Art/ To Pay the Piper/ Nor Iron Bars/ Beep/ This Earth of Hours. British editions omit 1st, 2nd, and last stories and include: Beanstalk.

JACK OF EAGLES—Greenberg: N.Y., 1952, pp. 246, $2.75; Galaxy: N.Y., 19, 1954, wpps. 128, 35¢; Nova: London, 1955, wpps. 159, 2s; as ESPer: Avon: N.Y., 1958, wpps. 190, 35¢; Avon: N.Y., 1968, wpps. 176, 60¢; Faber: London, 1973, pp. 246, £2.10.

LIFE FOR THE STARS, A—Putnam: N.Y., 1962, pp. 224, $3.50; Avon: N.Y., 1963, wpps. 143, 45¢ (1966, 50¢); Faber: London, 1964, pp. 148, 15s.

MIDSUMMER CENTURY—Doubleday: N.Y., 1972, pp. 106, $4.95; SFBC ed.

MISSION TO THE HEART STARS—Faber: London, 1965, pp. 136, 13/6; Putnam: N.Y., 1968, pp. 158, $3.75.

NIGHT SHAPES, THE—Ballantine: N.Y., 1962, wpps. 125, 50¢; Foursquare: London, 1963, wpps. 125, 2/6 (1965, 3/6).

QUINCUNX OF TIME, THE—Dell: N.Y., 1973, wpps. 128, 95¢.

SEEDLING STARS, THE—Gnome Press: N.Y., 1957, pp. 185, $3.00; Signet: N.Y., 1959, wpps. 158, 35¢ (1964, 50¢); Faber: London, 1967, pp. 185, 18s.

SO CLOSE TO HOME—Ballantine: N.Y., 1961, wpps. 142, 35¢ (1962, 35¢). Contents: Struggle in the Womb/ Sponge Dive/ One-Shot/ The Box/ First Strike/ The Abbatoir Effect/ The Oath/ FYI/ The Masks/ Testament of Andros.

SPOCK MUST DIE!—Bantam: N.Y., 1970, wpps. 118, 60¢.

STAR DWELLERS, THE—Putnam: N.Y., 1961, pp. 224, $3.50; Faber: London, 1963, pp. 153, 13/6; Avon: N.Y., 1962, wpps. 128, 40¢ (1965, wpps. 128, 50¢); Berkley: N.Y., 1970, wpps. 118, 75¢.

STAR TREK—Bantam: N.Y., 1967, wpps. 136, 50¢. Contents: Charlie's Law/ Dagger of the Mind/ The Unreal McCoy/ Balance of Terror/ The Naked Time/ Miri/ The Conscience of the King.

STAR TREK 2—Bantam: N.Y., 1968, wpps. 122, 50¢. Contents: Arena/ A Taste of Armageddon/ Tomorrow Is Yesterday/ Errand of Mercy/ Court Martial/ Operation—Annihilate/ City on the Edge of Forever/ Space Seed.

STAR TREK 3—Bantam: N.Y., 1969, wpps. 122, 50¢. Contents: The Trouble With Tribbles/ The Last Gunfight/ The Doomsday Machine/ Assignment: Earth/ Mirror, Mirror/ Friday's Child/ Amok Time.

STAR TREK 4—Bantam: N.Y., 1971, wpps. 134, 75¢. Contents: All Our Yesterdays/ The Devil in the Dark/ Journey to Babel/ The Menagerie/ The Enterprise Incident/ A Piece of the Action.

STAR TREK 5—Bantam: N.Y., 1972, wpps. 136, 75¢. Contents: Preface/ Whom Gods Destroy/ The Tholian Web/ Let That Be Your Last Battlefield/ This Side of Paradise/ Turnabout Intruder/ Requiem for Methusalah/ The Way to Eden.

STAR TREK 6—Bantam: N.Y., 1972, wpps. 149, 75¢. Contents: Preface/ The Savage Curtain/ The Lights of Zetar/ The Apple/ By Any Other Name/ The Cloud Minders/ The Mark of Gideon.

STAR TREK 7—Bantam: N.Y., 1972, wpps. 155, 75¢. Contents: Who Mourns for Adonais?/ The Changeling/ The Paradise Syndrome/ Metamorphosis/ The Deadly Years/ Elaan of Troyius.

STAR TREK 8—Bantam: N.Y., 1972, wpps. 170, 75¢. Contents: Spock's Brain/ The Enemy Within/ Catspaw/ Where No Man Has Gone Before/ Wolf in the Fold/ For the World Is Hollow and I Have Touched the Sky.

STAR TREK 9—Bantam: N.Y., 1973, wpps. 183, 75¢. Contents: Return to Tomorrow/ The Ultimate Computer/ That Which Survives/ Obsession/ The Return of the Archons/ The Immunity Syndrome.

THEY SHALL HAVE STARS—Faber: London, 1966, pp. 131, 12/6; (as *Year 2018!*) Avon: N.Y., 1957, wpps. 159, 35¢; Foursquare: London, 1963, wpps. 158, 2/6 (1306, 1965, 3/6); Avon: N.Y., 1966, wpps. 159, 60¢ (1967, 60¢); New English Library: London, 1968, wpps. 159, 5s.

TITAN'S DAUGHTER—Berkley: N.Y., 1961, wpps. 142, 35¢ (1966, 50¢); Foursquare: London, 1963, wpps. 142, 2/6 (1965, 3/6).

TRIUMPH OF TIME, THE—see *A Clash of Cymbals.*

VANISHED JET, THE—Weybright & Talley: N.Y., 1968, pp. 117, $4.50.

VOR—Avon: N.Y., 1958, wpps. 159, 35¢ (1967, 60¢); Corgi: London, 1959, wpps. 156, 2/6.

WARRIORS OF DAY, THE—Galaxy: N.Y. 16, 1953, wpps. 125, 35¢; Lancer: N.Y., 1966, wpps. 159, 50¢.

YEAR 2018!—see *They Shall Have Stars.*

WELCOME TO MARS!—Putnam: N.Y., 1968, pp. 168, $3.75.

In collaboration with Norman L. Knight:
TORRENT OF FACES, A—Doubleday: N.Y., 1967, pp. 270, $4.95; SFBC ed.; Faber: London, 1968, pp. 279, 25s; Ace: N.Y., 1968, wpps. 286, 75¢.

In collaboration with Robert A. W. Lowndes:
DUPLICATED MAN, THE—Avalon: N.Y., 1959, pp. 222, $2.95; Airmont: N.Y., 1964, wpps. 128, 40¢.

James Blish has also edited two anthologies of science fiction:
NEBULA AWARD STORIES FIVE—Doubleday: N.Y., 1970, pp. 215, $4.95.
NEW DREAMS THIS MORNING—Ballantine: N.Y., 1966, wpps. 190, 50¢.

And has written two books of sf criticism (as William Atheling, Jr.):
THE ISSUE AT HAND—Advent: Chicago, 1964, pp. 136, $5.00; 1965, pb, $1.95.

MORE ISSUES AT HAND—Advent: Chicago, 1970, pp. 154, $5.00; 1971, pb, $1.95.

and a contemporary novel:
THE FROZEN YEAR—Ballantine: N.Y., 1957, pp./wpps. 155, 35¢; Faber: London, 1957, pp. 224, 15s; Foursquare: London, 1961, wpps. 156, 2/6. British editions are entitled *Fallen Star.*

and a historical novel:
DOCTOR MIRABILIS—Faber: London, 1964, pp. 287, 25s; Author: N.Y., 1966, wpps. 96, mimeo., $5.00; rev- Dodd, Mead: N.Y., 1971, pp. 335, $6.95.